# THE SHAPE OF POWER

# THE SHAPE OF POWER

BEING THE FIRST PART OF

**THE SPARKGAZER SAGA TRILOGY**

BY
**DAN F. SWINNEN**

COPYRIGHT © 2025 BY DAN F. SWINNEN
All rights reserved.

No part of this publication may be reproduced, distributed, or transmitted in any form or by any means, including photocopying, recording, or other electronic or mechanical methods, without the prior written permission of the publisher, except as permitted by U.S. copyright law.

For permission requests, contact dan.f.swinnen@gmail.com.

The story, all names, characters, and incidents portrayed in this production are fictitious. No identification with actual persons (living or deceased), places, buildings, and products is intended or should be inferred.

Editing by Sarah Grace Liu
Illustration by iobard @ Shutterstock

Book Cover/Layout by Benoit Vangeel

First edition 2025

For Janne,

the center of my universe.

\*\*\*

For Liliane,

who had more heart than anyone.

# CHAPTER 1

*10th day of the 10th cycle, 569th year of the Keeper's Reign*
**Barrow's Perch**

A fetid stench rose from the entrance of the mineshaft like rotted breath from a giant's throat. Brina hesitated.

They were here all right. Four-toed footprints littered the muddy underground. A crimson smear contrasted against the dark soil, extending into the tunnel. *Pus and plague, they've already hunted.* That would make things infinitely more annoying.

The dead hare she'd brought as bait swayed on her belt as she knelt to take a count. *Guess I'll end up eating that.* Brina traced the prints with her index finger. *At least a dozen.*

More concerning were a handful of deep prints, at least thrice as large as the others. They'd been trampled to the point of being barely legible, which could only mean that whatever had made these had gone in first, leading the pack of wampyr. Brina shuddered.

She turned around one last time. The first chariot sat high in the sky, radiating pale moonlight over the shrouded hills of Barrow's Perch. Wisps of mist curled around the dolmens in the vale below like the grasping fingers of their withered occupants. It would be a long night.

Brina sighed, withdrew a torch from her belt, and strode into the deep dark ahead. *The things I do for a hot meal.* She needed to get this right. The last few months had been rough, and her lithe body was slipping from leanly muscled into emaciated.

Like most of the abandoned mines in the area, this one had been dug out in squares. Every dozen yards, two new shafts branched out on either side of the main path. These side branches then split again and again to form a labyrinthine grid. It would be all too easy to take a single wrong turn and disappear forever.

Brina had heard the stories. She had found the bodies. On multiple occasions she'd found the barren bones of some unfortunate roamer, covered in gnaw marks.

Once, years ago, she'd even heard cries for help emanate from deep within the earth. Brina swallowed at the memory. The guilt had never quite faded. *There was nothing to be done,* she reminded herself. *Once lost here, they were already dead. I just caught the echo.*

When she reached the first crossing, she set her pack down onto the stone floor and retrieved a fist-sized lump of charcoal. With a flourish, she marked the exit on the white wall. As long as she had light, she'd be okay.

As Brina progressed further down the corridor, marking every crossing, the silence came alive around her. Tiny drops of water became hammers, slamming into the echoing iron of puddles below. The remnants of the outside breeze whistled around her like a demented whisper. Was that a footstep or the mere falling of a pebble?

*One wampyr, one shard.* She mouthed it like a mantra, as though it were a warding spell. If she could catch three, that would be enough to carry her through the week. Make it four, and she'd be able to add a shard to the backup plan under the floorboards at home.

Then again, she knew that any time she crossed the threshold into the deep of Mosul Anh, the elder mine, could very well be the last time she'd breathe fresh air. Wampyr and starvation were only two of the mine's threats, and neither ranked anywhere near the top.

A screech, halfway between a squawk and a bark, erupted from a point to the left. Brina's heart lurched. *Here we go.* She crept into the lefthand passage, withdrawing her silver lamp from her belt as she went. She'd loaded it with enough powder for two flashes, which ought to be enough. In theory.

She smelled the nest long before she turned the corner. An overpowering stench of excrement, sweat, and decayed flesh seeped from the crossing ahead. Wampyr left their prey to rot where it lay once they were done with it. According to Brina's nose, this pack had been successful recently. She lifted the torch and froze in her tracks.

Two dozen yellow eyes lit up among the shadows. Taking advantage of their momentary doubt, Brina strode forward. The silver lamp creaked and swayed in her sweaty palm. *Patience. Not yet.*

The eyes receded as she approached, staying just out of reach. Wampyr were clever that way. They were clever in general. They were always lurking and waiting for an advantage to exploit. Brina didn't like to dwell on that. It

## CHAPTER 1

only made it harder to capture and sell them. *Think of the D'Hooghe twins, the empty cribs, the wailing.* Everyone in Doorstep's Ditch remembered that night. Hare or human child, there was no difference to a hungry wampyr.

Three nests filled the passage. Circles of stacked bones and matted furs, held together with dirt and limestone rubble. The flickering torchlight lit up the floor, revealing the twitching form of a stag. The creature stared up at Brina with terrified eyes. Dripping puncture wounds lined its neck. It fought to get up, but the wampyr's venom had paralyzed its legs.

Brina held up the silver lamp and took one more step. As soon as they thought she was attempting to steal their prey, they would swarm. She took a deep breath and stepped up to the dying stag. The attack didn't come. Yellow eyes were now on all sides of her, yet they kept their distance. *Something's wrong.*

A slapping sound echoed through the crossing as two beaming red flares approached. The unnatural creature crept into the light's edge, its webbed feet pattering with every step. Brina had never seen a wampyr grow so large. Back to back, it would only be a head smaller than she was. Its pale, bald skin glistened in the torchlight. It seemed too small to envelop its overgrown frame, as though it could burst at any moment. The corners of its mouth were raw and torn where the skin had stretched. Its spindly limbs were wrought in unnatural angles, like a tangled puppet. It leered at Brina, a rivulet of drool running down its protruding chin.

*Alive, take them alive,* she reminded herself as the urge to reach for her mace intensified. Huygen, the apothecary, had no use for dead ones. Nor did anyone else. Still, once this monstrosity grew enraged, she'd have a terrible time subduing it.

The creature's eyes strayed to the glinting lamp in her hand. *That's right, silver.* Brina smirked to herself. The wampyr were funny, in their own twisted sort of way. They'd been devouring this live stag mere moments before she had interrupted them. Yet now, their leader stared up at the silver in her hand with a sort of polite interest, the kind you might conjure up when spotting a distant acquaintance at a market. Brina had often wondered what went on beyond those glassy, mean eyes.

She took another step toward it, holding her torch at the ready. To her surprise, the creature shambled forward to meet her. *Uh oh, that's not how that's supposed to work.*

The overgrown wampyr lunged. Brina flung herself aside just in time to miss the swipe of its claws. She tripped over one of the stag's legs, stumbled, and fell against the rough stone wall. An excited chittering erupted all around her as the other wampyr closed in.

Brina sprang to her feet, dizzy from the impact. She swung the torch around, desperate to keep all the bloodsuckers within view. Three of them advanced on her from the shadowy corridor behind her. In front of her, the crossing was overrun with what looked like three packs' worth of the little creeps. All pattering feet and razor teeth.

For a split second, Brina stood frozen. She had wanted to get all of them with the first flash, keeping the second charge purely as a safety measure. That was no longer an option.

*She who hides too long in a tree, waiting for the perfect opportunity, risks getting struck by lightning first.* Her father's voice drifted into her ear. He used to be full of such wisdoms. As a child, she had hated them, though somewhere along the way they had irreversibly lodged themselves in her brain.

She aimed the lamp at the crossing, held the torch to it, and closed her eyes. A crack echoed through the mine. Even through her closed eyelids, the flash burned bright, an all-encompassing storm of white, followed by a brief, but highly satisfactory, silence.

Before she could open her eyes again, a searing pain sliced across her lower belly. She screamed in surprise. Lightning had struck.

The overgrown leader was on her. Unbelievable. The silver flash had failed. This monstrosity had run straight through the brunt of it without so much as a stumble. In the crossing behind it, its compatriots lay paralyzed. *What in the Seven has this thing been feeding on?* Brina could hear the trio behind her creep closer, emboldened by their oversized leader. She had to act soon.

Blood seeped out of a long cut just above her waist. Her tunic, her very last one, was ruined. "You've just cost me a lot of money, you moron," she yelled at the beast. It looked up at her curiously. Brina could've sworn there was amusement in those yellow eyes.

She reached for her mace. The creature's sluggish dodge prevented the heavy steel from shattering its skull, causing the brunt of the attack to land on its shoulder, which dislocated with a sickening crack. The creature clawed at its limp arm and retreated toward the crossing.

Brina spun 'round, just in time to swap the mace for the lamp and blast the wampyr behind her at close range. Two went down instantly. The third leapt at her. She tried to sidestep, but the narrow corridor limited her movement. A row of sharp teeth sank into her calf. Brina instinctively

# CHAPTER 1

kicked at the wampyr's head, and it let go. It stared at her for a second, as though calculating the odds. Brina made a wild movement with her arms. "Shoo." The bloodsucker turned and ran, but the damage had been done.

A lurch of nausea swept over her. The surrounding mineshaft grew blurry around the edges. *Just what I needed, a wet bite.* She cursed, forcing herself to her feet. She had to keep moving. If she allowed the venom to take hold, she'd end up like the stag in the crossing, paralyzed and defenseless.

Wampyr venom was alcohol's conniving, evil twin. All the delirium and the hangover, none of the fun. While one bite wouldn't kill her, the mutated freak in the crossing surely would if she were to pass out. She could see the creature sitting atop the stag's carcass, fiddling with something in its right hand. *Wampyr don't use tools.* It looked up at her, and Brina was shocked to see its eyes glowing bright red. *What in the...*

Without looking away, she scooped up two immobilized wampyr at her feet into a jute sack. Two shards. If she ran down the corridor and took the first right, she *should* arrive at the same passage she'd come down when entering. With any luck, she'd be able to avoid another fight. Already, the venom circulated in her bloodstream, scalding her veins and slowing her thoughts. It was the sensible thing to do.

Yet, two shards wouldn't even cover medicine to treat the bite. She'd have to tough it out the natural way, which would mean at least two days of pounding headaches and debilitating nausea. On the other hand, if she could bring in all of those wampyr piled atop each other in the crossing, she'd make a king's ransom. She could already taste the rare delight of Versa's fried squid and homebrewed kelp rum. Not to mention what Huygen may offer for such a large and mutated specimen. Two days of certain misery, but safety, versus a life and death struggle for a shiny stack of shards.

The silver lamp clattered to the ground. The mace felt twice as heavy as Brina raised it with trembling hands. *Bring it on.*

The overgrown wampyr cocked its ugly head as she approached, leering at her. It reclined on the deer carcass as though it were a throne. The coppery stench of blood pricked in Brina's nose when she entered the crossing. It did nothing to stall the rapid onset of nausea from the venom. There was no more powder in the lamp. This one would have to be done the old-fashioned way.

"Alright, baldy," she told the creature, "try not to die." It didn't matter *what* you told a wampyr. Some of the older ones learned a few basic words, but most of them had too little exposure to humans to master even that. What mattered was chattering on until they grew confused and enraged.

"What have you got there, eh?" She gestured at the creature's fist. "Something shiny?" The corners of the wampyr's mouth twitched. It was working. She tightened her grip on the mace to keep the heavy weapon from slipping out of her numbing fingers. One blow, that was all she needed.

"How about a trade?" She pointed at the silver lamp on the floor behind her. "Shiny lamp for shiny whatever it is you got." The wampyr looked from the lamp to Brina and back as though contemplating the offer. Its mouth worked furiously as it tried to work out what she was saying.

"Hurry, you big dummy." Brina could feel her heartbeat slowing, gradually but certainly. She needed to get this over with.

Then, to her astonishment, the wampyr opened its hand and threw something onto the floor at her feet. Its eyes returned to their original yellow, tracing Brina's every movement. Brina took a reflexive step back. Surely not. It couldn't have *understood*, could it? She glanced down. It was a bronze trinket shaped like a pyramid. Deep grooves ran along all four of its sides, connecting in an intricate pattern of shapes and angles. Instinctively, her eyes began tracing the grooves as they curved and bent and intersected, flowing across the metal surface with the smooth grace of a river carved into a landscape over centuries. Every bump and twist was exactly where it should be. As she stared, a tiny spark of red sprouted in a dead end of the infinite pattern, no larger than a grain of sand. Brina's mouth fell open as it started spreading through the groove.

"Aargh." She snapped back to the present as her scalp exploded with pain. *It tricked me. The bastard actually tricked me.* The wampyr's nasty, spindly fingers were grasping and tugging at her short, black hair. It pulled harder as Brina started fighting, attempting to pull her neck closer to its rotten mouth. "No. You. Don't."

Adrenaline flooded her system with a jolt, momentarily dulling the venom's effects. She punched the wampyr in the stomach as hard as she could. It screeched, its grip slackening. With a surge of strength she didn't know she possessed, she grabbed its thin wrists and twisted until she felt the bones snap in her hands. For one moment, right before she let go, she saw herself reflected in the creature's eyes. Her swollen, bloody lips, her crooked nose, which she'd broken thrice so far, and two eyes burning a deep crimson.

# CHAPTER 1

She let go of the creature as though it were on fire. Without a second glance, it turned and ran, scurrying away down a corridor, irretrievably lost in the dark of Mosul Anh. Brina looked down at the bronze pyramid. The red grain was gone, leaving a simple lump of engraved metal behind. It was much heavier than she'd anticipated. A sudden disquiet overcame her.

Where had this thing come from? The wampyr must have picked it up somewhere in the deeper halls of the mine. Which might mean that this fist-sized chunk of metal hadn't seen the light of day in centuries. Who knew what it might be worth? Excitement was slowly building. If she played this right, she may have just found herself a significant addition to the floorboard fund. Brina pocketed the artifact with great care, wrapping it gently in her handkerchief.

The flashed wampyr around her stirred. *Plague, almost forgot. Best wrap these up for the journey.*

When she exited Mosul Anh an hour later, she was rewarded with the first tentative beams of sunlight. Morning air flooded her lungs, a welcome change after the moist and stuffy atmosphere of the mine. The light aggravated her venom-induced headache, but it hardly mattered now. She'd survived the night with seven wampyr in the bag. And a strange bronze cherry on top.

As she set out for the village, she could already smell the victorious aromas of squid and rum.

Brina's good mood lasted a good half hour into the march to the nearby village of Doorstep's Ditch before the effects of the bite took their toll. The trees beside the path split into divergent shadowy pillars, fading in and out of focus. With every step, the path over the King's Barrow seemed to grow steeper. Once she reached the top, it would be downhill the rest of the way, but that would count for precious little if she were to pass out between the brambles on her way up.

Brina squeezed one last sip of water from her deflated waterskin. She swished the cool liquid around twice before swallowing, desperate to make the feeling last. The captive wampyr squirmed and fought in their sacks, making it even harder to stay upright. Her shoulders ached and sagged under the weight.

If only she could sit down. Just for a moment. A flat boulder beside the path seemed to beckon, inviting her to take a well-deserved rest. *I can't.* Stopping now would make it ten times harder, if not impossible, to get back up. She was trying to outrun the venom, and as soon as she stopped, it would catch up. When it did, she'd better have an antidote ready.

Huygen would have it, of course. The old apothecary kept his shop stocked with all manner of remedies. Reedblossom tincture would be at the top of that list. The problem was money. Karoling Huygen wasn't the type of man to succumb to generosity.

Still, he had only put up the order for live wampyr yesterday morning, and here she was, ready to deliver seven of them within twenty-four hours. That made three orders in a row that Brina had been the first to deliver on. That kind of service had to count for something. *I hope.*

She crested King's Barrow Hill and was greeted by the familiar view of Mallion's Depth. The glittering white walls and gray tiled roofs of the city wrapped around the sapphire water of the Sundered Sea. Dozens of ships lay moored at the docks, tiny figures scuttling across their decks.

Even from up here, the lower quarters of the city were hidden entirely behind the monstrous stoneward, a hundred-foot-high bulwark of stone and steel. The ward circled the whole of the city. Countless pinpricks of light moved along the battlements on all sides.

The great wall. The great divider. You were in, or, like Brina, you were out.

# CHAPTER 2

*11th day of the 10th cycle, 569KR*
**Doorstep's Ditch**

Even in the faint gloom of first light Doorstep's Ditch was the filthiest place in the known universe. The place looked like something a leviathan had spat out onto a beach after devouring an entire merchant fleet. Rickety shanties lined the town's narrow alleyways, leaning against each other like drunks outside a pub.

If Mallion's Depth was the crown of the empire, Doorstep's Ditch was the pus-filled boil sprouting from its bottom. For centuries, the order of Heil had ruled the city according to the seven tenets of Heil. In theory, the tenets were the key to peace, civilization, and harmony. In practice, they were convenient excuses to get rid of anyone deemed undesirable.

The first tenet forbade death as punishment, save for the gravest of offenders. Ever creative with their own rules, the Reynziels had been exiling people from the city for centuries. *Stealing?* Outwalled. *Brawling?* Outwalled. *Troublesome political opinions?* Outwalled.

The result was a spider's web, a network of claustrophobic paths that clung to anyone shoved into it, ready to ensnare its unsuspecting victims in a never-ending cycle of empty stomachs, dice, and poorly distilled kelp rum. Execution with extra steps.

Brina held a dirty hand to her nose as she passed a rack of drying squid. Behind it, a girl no older than ten sat on a barrel clutching a windup bow that looked comically huge in her tiny hands. The weapon's string hadn't been wound properly. Most children didn't have the strength to crank the wooden lever on top of the bow's stock back far enough for a proper shot. But what the kid lacked in physical strength, she made up for in character. The girl gave Brina a fierce glare, as though daring her to steal one of the squid.

"Careful with that finger on the trigger, kid." Brinna grinned. "That thing'll take your foot right off."

Once, she had been that kid. A wisp of a girl traipsing around this jungle of driftwood and rotting netting with the innocent overconfidence of youth. She had learned to recognize the tense silence before a riot, which alleys to avoid, and how to spot an imbalanced scale. Life had been harsh, but good.

Then everything had changed.

At the end of the sandy lane, the south gate of the stoneward towered over straw and tarp roofs. A sandstone and steel giant dwarfing the uneven shacks of the Ditch.

Brina hobbled along Wicket Row, mud sucking at her feet with every step. The wriggling and squawking wampyr tied to her pack seemed to have tripled in weight over the last few hours. Brina winced as her headache spiked to new heights. The march had given the venom ample time to spread through every inch of her body, her heart dutifully pumping the substance around with every beat. She needed an antidote, fast.

As she passed The Wistful Chimera, the Ditch's best inn by a mile, the front door flew open. Bleary candlelight spilled out into the street, followed by a tangle of limbs and shouts. A black-haired man dressed in a torn gray tunic stumbled on the wooden steps and toppled face first into a puddle. Behind him, two others clung to each other to avoid the same. An older woman with a large potbelly and dirty, clotted hair held up her companion, a reedy man with cheekbones protruding from his face like a second pair of ears.

"Zot will hear about this," whined the thin man, turning to glower at someone inside the inn. "Can't kick us out like a pair of dogs, oh no…"

A booming laugh emanated from the doorway. "You tell him, Guste, that Versa sends their regards and that I won't allow so much as a wisp of cloud to be dealt in my *Chimera*. No matter how many of you he sends." The man named Guste spat before allowing the woman by his side to pull him away from the scene. Their muddy companion scrambled to get up, slipping and sliding as he scurried after them.

Brina laughed, shaking her head. The motion made her headache spike, but she couldn't help herself. Every floater and petty dealer in the Ditch claimed to be associated with the infamous Dimimzy Zot these days. At least once a week, some common coward would brandish that name as though it were a morning star.

## CHAPTER 2

She supposed the rumors were true then. Zot must indeed have vanished if he allowed these amateurs to soil his carefully built reputation. Only last winter that would have been enough to be found face up underneath the ice in the bay.

"By the Seven, if I don't recognize that laugh anywhere," the deep voice rang out again as the door swung open fully. "Brina Springtide, come to grace me with your company?" The innkeeper leaned against the doorframe, a towering seven-foot figure, thin as a blade of grass.

As always, Versa's face was hidden. They wore a gaudy noble woman's mask with exaggerated deep-red lips and blue circles around huge painted eyes, slits in which revealed Versa's own dark eyes. The rest of the innkeeper's head was shrouded in the hood of their cloak. It was clearly too early for wigs. No one knew what Versa's real face looked like. Rumor had it a childhood accident had savagely disfigured them, but few dared ask, and even fewer had gotten answers. As far as Brina was aware, she was the only one who knew the truth.

"Yes and no," Brina shouted back from across the road, "I've got some business with Huygen first." She tapped the side of her head gingerly. "Wampyr bite. Afterward, I'm coming straight here. I've got some shards struggling to vacate my purse." She turned her back to the innkeeper to show them the squirming jute sack full of wampyr.

"Want me to prepare the usual?"

Brina nodded, grinning. "Make it a big one. I haven't eaten since yesterday's breakfast."

\*\*\*

The Enclave's gilded gate was still locked when she arrived. A handful of darkhelms in clanking armor patrolled on the walkway on top of it, their namesake black helmets obscuring their faces. The golden microscope of the jeweler's guild gleamed on their black breastplates.

The Enclave was a channel, a neutral zone where wallborn merchants and artisans could trade with outwalled in a contained environment. Its wall attached to the stoneward like a barnacle to a ship's hull. From afar, it looked flimsy and crooked compared to the mighty ward, but up close, the gate towered over Brina with an air of resolute immovability.

The crumpled form of a woman lay in front of the solid golden double gates. Two quarrels protruded from her chest like slanted flags. A thick crimson stain covered the surrounding cobbles. *Another one who couldn't resist.* Brina sighed to herself. She took a few steps toward the woman to get a better look. She was dead. Had been for hours by the looks of it. *Nothing I can do.*

The woman's dark face was caved in from prolonged starvation, her muddy hair brittle and thin. Still clutched in her right hand was the thing that had gotten her killed. A rusty chisel.

"Stupid," Brina muttered under her breath, looking up at the watchers above. At least once a month, some desperate soul would get tempted to shave some gold off the gate. It invariably ended like this. Truth be told, you'd have to be quite the moron to even consider it at this point. Then again, Brina suspected the guilds had created the situation on purpose. Just one more "screw you" to the scum outside the wall, one more excuse to get rid of undesirables with the thinnest veneer of righteousness.

The gate opened at the fifth chime of the booming clock tower on the other side of the ward, and Brina stepped over the dead woman without a second glance. You couldn't afford to dwell on these things. It would drive anyone insane.

The storefronts inside the Enclave were as diverse as the guilds that had given rise to them. They ranged from bare brickwork with thin gray cement to marble columned atrocities slathered with a gilded trim. Karoling Huygen's apothecary leaned toward the latter but gave off the distinct impression that its owners had given up the pretense two generations ago. Huygen's store window was opaque with dust and cobwebs. The elaborate wooden carvings surrounding it looked weathered and cracked. Here and there, a crumbling inch of paint suggested that it had once been a colorful display. But like its owner, Huygen's Herbs and Tinctures had passed its prime before Brina was born.

Brina was about to step inside when a flash of crimson stopped her dead in her tracks. A scarlet sheet of parchment covered almost all of Huygen's front door. *Again? Already?*

She didn't need to read the notice to know what it would say, yet she couldn't help herself. It was like picking at a scab. She had to draw blood before she'd stop.

CHAPTER 2

## SCARLET NOCTURNE 569KR

*"On the twenty-fourth day of the tenth chariot cycle the work of justice for the death of our beloved Cardinal Estav II shall once more take a step toward its completion with the hanging of co-conspirator number eleven, the sorceress Azaria Oldenbreeze, also known as 'Sin Eater.'"*

A crude sketch of a woman with long matted hair, soulless black eyes, and a wicked grin of crooked, sharp teeth followed these words. More was written below the illustration, but Brina couldn't bring herself to read on.

*Conspirator number eleven.* There's was only one left after that.

Brina swallowed, her mouth suddenly dry. She'd always known the day would come, but there had been others first. Obstacles to hide behind. Every year, the weight of what was to come had grown heavier. One by one they had fallen until soon only one would remain. Abrasax, "The Viper." Occultist, leader of the Cardinal's assassins, and Brina's father. A selfish coward.

A guilty weight dropped in her stomach at the thought. She didn't mean that. Not really. After the fever had taken her mother, it had been just Brina and him. For years, it had been the two of them against the world. Or so Brina had thought, before "The Viper's" true nature had reared its ugly head.

A bell rang as the apothecary's door swung shut behind her. An overpowering scent like herbal tea pricked Brina's nostrils. *Yuck, ginger.* All around her, tall shelves teetered dangerously under the weight of countless vials, jars, and boxes, containing everything from dried oak root to glimmering onyx manticore eyes. The wampyr in the sack tied to Brina's pack screeched and put in a renewed effort to escape. Most creatures hated the smell of Huygen's shop, as though they could smell their impending doom on the air.

Brina set down the pack against the closed door and brushed past a bundle of dead tinheads on her way to the counter, their scaly serpentine bodies clinking together behind her.

"Master Huygen, are you here?" she called out.

A gasp emanated from the adjacent room, followed by the unmistakable crash of shattering glass. Huygen spat out a string of curses and something that sounded like "darn rascals" as he limped through the open door. He stared at Brina with beady blue eyes that almost disappeared in folds of pale gray skin. "Oh. It's *you*." He emphasized the last word with a mixture of surprise and distaste. "What do you want?"

"I came to deliver your wampyr order." Brina clenched her jaw, trying to force her face into a smile. Maybe if she could get him in a good enough mood, he'd throw in the reedblossom tincture as a bonus. She gestured over her shoulder at the sack near the door. "Seven specimens, alive. Freshly caught tonight. They fed just after midnight."

Huygen looked confused for a moment, his wrinkly face screwed up like crumpled parchment. Then his eyes lit up. "Ah. Yes. I see," he croaked. There was a newfound fervor to his limp as he made his way across the room. With a silver flash, he created an opening in the sack. His bony hand darted inside to pull out a four-fingered hand. The wampyr squawked, fighting to pull the limb free, but Huygen's frailty seemed to have left him entirely. There was a glint in his eye as he drew the point of a silver dagger across the creature's palm. A stench like burnt hair filled the room as a gash appeared in the gray flesh, smoke rising where the silver made contact. "The real thing," he wheezed. "On to the next."

Brina turned away as Huygen made to "test" the others. She couldn't bear to look. The creatures' piteous wails would haunt her that night, and possibly the next, but there was nothing she could do. She couldn't afford to lose this sale. Not if she wanted to eat this week.

Desperate for a distraction, she wandered over to a display of ground up claws and teeth from a variety of creatures. Though Brina knew little about alchemy, she had learned a few basics as a child. The properties of an ingredient were said to be determined by their original purpose. Which meant that a griffin's claw, made for slashing open the bellies of sheep and trihorns alike, was best used in powerful, violent concoctions. By contrast, a ground up archelon shell could infuse a brew with fortifying, hardening properties.

Brina tried to pick out the materials she herself had delivered to Huygen, curious to see just how bad the old man had ripped her off on the orders she'd filled for him. *"Sheikan tail - Two shards a hair,"* read a scribbled note stuck to a jar that looked like a bird had nested inside. *I crawled inside its lair to cut that,* Brina thought in disgust. Bastard had paid her five shards for the lot.

"You almost done with that?" she snapped at Huygen as another cry rang out from behind her.

"Almost, almost. What's got you all in a hurry?"

## CHAPTER 2

"I've been bit, if you hadn't noticed." She spun round to face him and swayed on the spot, dizzy from the sudden motion.

"Now that you mention it," Huygen agreed, "I just assumed you'd gone on the cloud, like all the other vermin in this dump." He grinned, baring a handful of rotten teeth. Black specks stained the floorboards at his feet. He kicked at the quivering sack in front of him. "Nasty little things, aren't they?"

"I've seen nastier." She smiled at Huygen with as much innocence as she could muster. The old man gave her a shrewd expression, one corner of his mouth twitching, as though he were chewing on what she had just said.

"I can imagine."

"So, do you think you could help me out?" Brina gestured at the wound on her calf. "Without some reedblossom, this'll haunt me for the rest of the week."

Huygen nodded and shambled over toward a blue glass vial stuffed to the brim with white flower petals. They floated up and down in a clear liquid, like stars suspended in outer space. "I have some right here, young lady." He grinned. Brina instantly realized he looked far too pleased with himself. "Since you've served me so well, you can have it for five shards." He righted his crooked back and leered at her, slavering for a reaction.

Brina's heart dropped through her midriff and into her guts. He couldn't be serious. Yet he was. She could see as much in those tiny watery eyes. There was malice there, the savage glee of a man who realizes exactly what kind of leverage he has. As her indignation boiled over into fury, her fingers absently closed around the bronze pyramid in her pocket.

"I got bit on the job for you," she said, delicately cradling each word as though they were bombs that could go off at any moment.

"I pay you for your wares, not for your own carelessness."

It cost her everything not to scream. Taking her silence for an opportunity, Huygen pressed on.

"Not to worry, I'm not a difficult man." The pleasure in the ancient face deepened. "I will accept payment in goods." He nodded at the wampyr. "That already covers most of it."

"Most?" Brina squeezed the pyramid in her pocket so hard she thought it might crumble. "One live wampyr, one shard. That's what the order said. I've brought you seven."

Huygen sighed. "Frankly, seven is too many. I've only got a handful of cages available in the lab, anyway. I'm likely to lose money on them if I have to feed so many, you know."

Brina's patience had run out. Her headache was reaching new heights. Soon she wouldn't even know where she was, and now this ancient wall-dweller was going to rip her off. *Again.*

"How dare you?" She took a step toward Huygen. "You put this order on the noticeboard yesterday." She whipped the scroll out of her pocket and flung it at him. "There's no mention of a limit."

Huygen shrugged. "Things change."

"Overnight?"

"What can I say? Alchemy is a dynamic business, young lady."

Brina couldn't think of a less dynamic business than alchemy. Huygen probably used the same diagrams Mallion himself had used five hundred years earlier. What really set her off, though, was the tone. *Young lady.* Her skin crawled. "You'll give me seven shards and throw in the reedblossom as a bonus, or I'd rather set these wampyr loose in here than sell anything to you ever again."

Huygen chuckled. "I suppose you could always choose to work for my competitors." He placed a gnarled finger to his chin, as though considering the situation. He didn't even need to say it. They both knew there were none.

Most herbalists in the city didn't bother trying to purchase ingredients directly from roamers. They sourced them from Huygen, the only one old and decrepit enough to be forced to spend his days forgoing the luxuries of life within the ward. Huygen chuckled again, a sound halfway between a laugh and a wheeze.

It was too much. The frustration and anger had sapped the last drop of Brina's strength. The venom had won. Around her, the apothecary's shelves contracted into a blur. The edges of her vision grew dark. Her knees gave way, and she stumbled backward into the counter, where she slid down onto the floor. *Too late.*

Huygen's face appeared in front of her, a dozen miles away like a distant tower seen through fog. "Looks like we're in trouble."

Brina tried to open her mouth to speak, but the effort was too great.

"Fine. You didn't have to be so melodramatic about it." Huygen disappeared. Whether it took seconds, minutes or hours, Brina couldn't tell. The next thing she knew, something icy cold touched her bottom lip. "Drink."

# CHAPTER 3

*11th day of the 10th cycle, 569KR*
**Doorstep's Ditch**

"Ceil almighty," Versa growled. "What happened to you?"

Brina winced at the sound. She slumped against the bar of The Wistful Chimera, a mercifully solid stool beneath her. How she had gotten here was a blur. She had been at Huygen's, hadn't she?

A wave of panic struck her as an image of the apothecary looming over her rippled across the surface of her mind. The pyramid. Her fingers plunged into her pocket, relief washing over her as they closed against the icy metal of the engraved artifact. Huygen must have missed it. She instinctively traced the pyramid's grooves with the tip of her finger, the smooth motion soothing her jangling nerves.

"Wampyr venom," Brina muttered. She took a deep breath. The reed-blossom was taking effect. Around her, the interior of the inn came into focus.

The place was deserted. Mismatched chairs stood in circles around crates or planks nailed to stumps. The street-side windows were boarded up, and those looking out over the shanties on the other side of the common room were filthy with a decade's worth of grime and condensed breath and sweat. Through them, the gloomy landscape of Doorstep's Ditch looked like a splotchy oil painting by a mediocre artist. One who may have been significantly drunk. It seemed fitting enough. It was about the same amount of artistry that had gone into building this entire disaster of a nation.

Versa dipped below the bar, retrieving a green bottle with a squid on the label. A slimy strand of seaweed twirled around inside as the innkeeper set it down in front of Brina.

"Nothing a good nip won't fix, I reckon," they said, a dark eye winking through the slits in their mask.

The noblewoman's mask from earlier was gone, replaced by a porcelain-skinned jester with reddened lips and eyes circled in blue. The hood of Versa's trademark cloak cast an eerie half-moon shadow over their face.

Brina eyed the bottle with a mixture of longing and bitterness.

"Would love to, Verse, but..." She pulled her empty purse out of her breast pocket and slapped it against the bar demonstratively. To her surprise, something inside clinked as it collided with the driftwood countertop.

She loosened the cord holding the thing together and held it upside down. A single, jagged emerald shard, the size of a child's pinky, rolled out into the light. Brina picked it up between thumb and forefinger, the sharp edges pricking into her skin. It seemed real enough. Being emerald, it was worth twice as much as a standard sapphire shard.

Was this just one last jab from Huygen, a pittance to add insult to injury? It seemed like something he'd take pleasure in. She could hardly bear to look at the gemstone. The memory of the encounter inside the apothecary welled up inside her like bile.

Brina slid the emerald shard across the bar, glad to be rid of it. "Make it a triple," she grumbled. "And use the rest to cover whatever is still open on my tab."

The innkeeper nodded, then filled two clay mugs to the brim. The silty scent of the sea filled the air. "So the contract didn't go as planned, I take it?"

"That bastard Huygen just ripped me off for the second time this month." As the reedblossom drove away the venom's aftereffects, nausea shifted to fury.

Versa listened dutifully, nodding and "mmh"-ing in the appropriate places as Brina recounted the morning's events.

"They can't keep getting away with this, Verse," Brina concluded. "They just can't. By the Seven, these days most of us are born outside the wall. We did nothing besides being born to the wrong parents, and still they treat us like vermin."

Versa leaned forward on the bar, shifting their gaze across the empty room as though scared the shadows were eavesdropping. Their long frame towered over Brina.

"That's dangerous language." It wasn't a rebuke, nor a warning. Just a simple fact of life as an outwalled. Versa aimed a thumb over their shoulder, pointing in the stoneward's direction. "We exist to scare everyone in there into toeing the line. That's all we are to them, walking examples.

## CHAPTER 3

So please, don't give them an excuse to turn you into one. I don't fancy losing my best customer."

Brina gritted her teeth. She knew what they were referring to. Her father hadn't been able to accept the status quo either, and everyone knew exactly where he and his eleven accomplices had ended up.

God's Maul, the island prison, built for those the scepter deemed too dangerous to release outside the wall.

On a clear day, the black spires of the fortress could be seen rising from the sea in the distance. In the past, Brina had often stared at the silhouette for hours at a time, wondering what remained of the man she had known. These days she avoided the sight altogether. It was better to forget.

"It's coming up again," Brina said, taking a deep gulp of green rum. Salt and fire raced each other down her throat. "The nocturne, I mean. I saw the posters in the Enclave."

Without a word, Versa refilled both of their mugs. Their gloved hands trembled slightly, causing the bottle to rattle against the wood. They sat in silence for a while, drinking, with their eyes glued to the glimmering liquid in front of them.

"And?" Versa didn't look up.

"It's not him," Brina said. A weight fell off her shoulder as she spoke the words out loud. Not her father, not yet. They had bought another year. Another year of waiting before the axe would finally drop.

It was hard to tell what Versa was thinking beneath that leering jester's mask. They both knew where this conversation would lead. Each year Brina asked, and each year Versa's response was the same.

"You were there, Verse," Brina began, her voice thick with drink. "I need to know what it's like in there."

"That wasn't me." The innkeeper turned their back on her, pretending to wipe down a stack of already clean bowls with a rag. "Whoever entered that godforsaken prison died there. I'm the shell that remained when they were done with them. Nothing more." They whipped 'round with a sudden motion and poured their entire mug into the slit in their mask, coughing and spluttering.

"I'm sorry, I shouldn't have brought it up," Brina said, watching her only friend shake uncontrollably as the memories of their time at God's Maul came flooding back.

Versa shook their head, still coughing.

"I get it, I do. It's not like there's anyone else you could ask. Not that I know of." The innkeeper took a deep breath, then straightened up. "Maybe one day. Part of me feels like I owe it to you. But for now, I'm just trying to forget." Brina nodded. Those black towers burned in her mind's eye.

Eager to change the subject, she placed the pyramid, which she had been clutching tight in her right fist, on the bar. It hit the wood with a surprisingly heavy thunk.

The rolling circles and curls on the metal surface shone brightly in the dim room, as though it amplified the thin rays of sunlight that fell on it through the nearby window.

"Ever seen anything like this?" Brina asked. She had considered the matter, and, aside from Huygen, Versa was the only person she could think of who might know more about the mysterious artifact. Roamers from all over the island had passed through the Chimera over the years, and Versa didn't miss a single word that was uttered in their inn.

The innkeeper bent down to inspect it, then lurched backward as though Brina had plopped a scorpion down in front of them.

"Where did you get that?" The question bordered on an accusation. Brina frowned, taken aback.

"I was tracking that pack of wampyr in—"

The inn's door swung wide open. A gale of raucous laughter swept away the peaceful atmosphere inside.

"—should have seen the beast," an unpleasantly familiar voice wheezed, "trying to claw its way up a tree with broken paws. It was pathetic."

Brina turned around to see Mattheus Fortuyn saunter up to the bar. His foot-long golden hair was tied in a tight bun atop his head, barely distinguishable from his unusually light skin. His black leather armor was decorated with sapphire studs along the seams, making him look like a walking gem purse. Trailing behind him were two men with dull expressions and oversized limbs, the remnants of their obedient giggles still lingering on their faces. One of them carried Mattheus's sword and windup bow, the other had a large sack with an ominous bloody stain on it slung over his shoulders.

"Put that thing away," Versa hissed at Brina, shoving the artifact toward her. It was already too late by the time Brina's hand disappeared into her pocket.

"If it isn't my esteemed colleague," Mattheus drawled, sitting down on the stool right next to Brina's. His goons seemed unsure whether they ought to laugh.

## CHAPTER 3

Brina raised an eyebrow. "We might both carry a bow, but that's where the similarities end, I'm afraid."

"Nice work, by the way." She poked at the bloody sack with her index finger. "What's in there, another starved hummingbear you surprised during its spring sleep? A baby archelon, straight from the nest?"

Mattheus's face fell for a split second before he hoisted his arrogant sneer back up. "It's a sheikan, if you must know." He puffed out his chest. "I spent an entire week tracking the beast."

Brina groaned. "Was it the one with the black mark under its left eye?"

Mattheus's disgruntled expression was answer enough. "Maybe. Why?"

"You idiot," Brina burst out, spurred on by the rum. "That one gave birth to a litter of six near Western Spire last month. You just ended their last active bloodline south of the mountains."

She shook her head, eying the bloody sack with a new level of disgust. Guys like Mattheus didn't bother looking at the bigger picture. They killed first and asked questions later. Odds were he didn't even have a buyer lined up for the creature's valuable eyes.

Mattheus's face flashed with anger. "Look who's acting all high and mighty." He leaned in, eyes glittering with malice. "How's daddy? Is it his turn—"

*Smack.*

Brina's fist collided with Mattheus's jaw before he could get the rest of the words out. She flew to her feet, ramming a shoulder into the man's armored torso.

He tilted backward off the stool, and the back of his head thudded onto the dirt floor of the common room.

Somewhere far away, Versa shouted, but the noise was drowned out in the onslaught of blood pumping in Brina's ears.

Mattheus's goons rushed forward to pull Brina off their master. She clocked the first one in the face with her elbow as he reached out to grab her. Before she could land a second hit, a sturdy pair of arms grabbed her from behind, pinning her arms to her side.

Brina's feet left the ground as the second meathead squeezed her. She gritted her teeth, closed her eyes, and whipped her head back as hard as she could. A sharp pain on the back of her head told her she had struck the man's nose. He let go of her with a howl.

"Enough!"

Versa's voice cracked through the air like a whip. Their impossibly tall figure loomed over all four of them as the innkeeper jumped on top of the bar. Their cloak seemed to wave in a nonexistent breeze.

Brina threw up her hands. Mattheus's goons stumbled backward, raising their own. Brina was pleased to see that both of them were bleeding heavily. *Hope it stings, dimwits.*

A sudden kick struck Brina's shin, forcing her to one knee. Mattheus had regained his composure.

His eyes were wide with fury, his mouth hung open, exposing multiple missing teeth.

"Nice trinket," he spat, holding up the pyramid. *Stupid, stupid, stupid.* It must have fallen out of her pocket as she lunged for the bastard.

She held out her hand. "Give that back, or you'll regret it."

Mattheus grinned. "You have damaged my property." He waved a hand at his wounded cronies. "I think I'll keep this as compensation." He scrambled to his feet with the grace of a spider that has been stepped on.

"Honestly, Springtide, you have your father's temperament." He shook his head in feigned disappointment. "I guess it's true what they say about you." One of the goons handed Mattheus his windup bow, which he held ostentatiously at his side.

Brina's jaw worked. *Keep your cool. He's fishing for an excuse.*

She considered the situation. She had a dagger tucked away in her boot. Should she take the chance? Mattheus was definitely slower than her, but the bow might go off and hit her, or worse, Versa behind her.

Still, there was something about that pyramid that made Brina reticent to part with it. Its flowing patterns drew her eye even now, with their curling waves and twists. They caught the light at an angle, creating the illusion of a red glow spreading from the center of the thing. She could almost feel the grooves on her fingertips. *It's just a piece of metal. Rule number one, don't get killed over stuff.*

As though by magnetic pull, Brina advanced on Mattheus, her hand stretched out toward the pyramid. She glared at the roamer, waiting for the flicker in his eyes that would give away his oncoming attack.

Instead, Mattheus drew back. His eyes widened, and Brina saw herself reflected in them. Two crimson orbs flared where her own brown eyes ought to have been, their glare refracting off the surface of Mattheus's blue eyes.

Brina felt powerful. Every muscle in her body jangled with untapped energy, as though she was on the adrenaline high of a lifetime.

She extended her open hand. Mattheus averted his gaze, then dropped

## CHAPTER 3

the pyramid into Brina's palm. He'd gone pale. Rivulets of blood ran across his lips where his knocked-out teeth had once been.

"That wasn't so hard, was it?" Brina slid the pyramid into her pocket.

Mattheus beckoned for his goons to turn around, and the three of them stormed out into the street. Just before the door slammed shut, Brina heard one of the meatheads mutter, "Demonic..."

When she looked back at Versa, the innkeeper's eyes were wide with terror behind the jester's mask. Their hand shook when it gripped Brina's shoulder.

"Listen carefully, Springtide, because I will never breathe another word of this. That thing is poison. Especially to you."

Brina frowned, unsure of whether she ought to be offended.

"So you're saying I should sell it?"

"No." The word fell with the definitiveness of an executioner's axe. "Toss it in the deepest well you can find, and forget it ever existed."

# CHAPTER 4

*24th day of the 10th cycle, 569KR*
**Home**

Brina gave a sigh of relief as the old mill came into view. The thick padlock on the front door was intact. That was a good sign. She never left the place for more than a single night at a time if she could avoid it. These days, however, Brina was forced to break her ground rules more and more frequently as she struggled to get food in her belly. She hadn't returned to the Ditch since the wampyr contract. The encounters with Huygen and Mattheus had left a bitter taste in her mouth that she didn't think would ever wash away.

Once, the mill had been one of a long series of them spread out through the hills surrounding Mallion's Depth. Back then, the hillsides were blanketed in golden fields of herz, a hard grain with kernels the size of a thumb.

Thousands of people had spent their entire lives trudging up and down the hillside in the tropical heat and humidity of summer on Hammerstroke. A lifetime ago, when she had visited what remained of the ancient library of Barangia with her father, Brina had seen a giant mural depicting the grueling work. In it, men and women carried large sacks up the steep incline, every one of them smiling contentedly as though they were living out their wildest dreams.

Now all that remained of that image was the dilapidated ruin Brina called home. Vines slithered up through the grooves between bricks, curling around the three rotting blades at the top like green serpents. The only new thing about the place was the lock Brina had installed when she discovered the ruin almost five years ago. So far, there had been no unexpected visitors, and she intended to keep it that way.

As the door creaked open, the scent of drying lavender and citrus grass

## CHAPTER 4

washed over Brina. She took a deep breath, trying to ignore the nervous anticipation of what was to come later that night.

The mill's lower floor was exactly as she had left it. Her favorite rocking chair stood beside the cast-iron stove. Bushels of herbs and roots hung from the wooden ceiling, swaying as the wind chased Brina through the open door.

A makeshift wooden rack underneath the staircase held her greatest treasure: two dozen leather-bound tomes she'd managed to salvage from the burned ruin of her father's house. Most of them chronicled ancient history from the days before the church had risen to power and were therefore highly illegal. Wouldn't want people to realize that everything was different once. Added together, the lot of it wouldn't fetch so much as a dozen shards. That was good. Once you had something of value, you spent the rest of your life glancing over your shoulder until someone inevitably pried it from your dead hands.

She flung her heavy pack, filled with over a dozen honey melons, onto her rocking chair. It squeaked and swayed merrily under the strain.

It was only when Brina reached the top of the winding staircase that she realized something was wrong. A draft. Her heart stopped. Across the circular bedroom, a lone window stood ajar. *I definitely closed that.*

Her fingers darted toward the dagger holstered at her ankle while her right foot dropped a step into a more solid stance. From where she stood, nothing seemed out of place. But if she were an assassin, she'd take care to make it look that way, too. *Don't get cocky. Nobody's sending an assassin after you.* A thief then. A good one. One who'd moved with restraint and purpose.

Inching her way up, Brina methodically cleared each angle of the room. She stuck her head out of the window to ensure nobody was standing on the ledge outside. Nothing. With a sigh of relief, she tucked away the dagger.

The latch on the window had been pried open with deliberate, almost artful, pressure.

With most of the immediate threat gone, adrenaline turned to dread. *Not the floorboard, not the floorboard, not the floorboard.* The mantra droned on in her head as she lay down on the floor and belly crawled underneath her bed. She stuck the tip of her pinky into a tiny hole in the third board on the left, carefully prying loose a foot-long section.

When her hand closed around the moleskin pouch inside, she almost cried. Inside, emerald, sapphire and a sprinkling of ruby shards twinkled in the twilight. She allowed herself to hold a large handful, eager to feel the weight of them, the undeniable proof that they were real and that they were still there.

Brina had no idea how many of them she had accumulated over the years. She had never counted them, and maybe she never would. The nest egg under the bed represented a dream, and dreaming was dangerous. *One day*, she told herself, *when things are different*.

With the pouch safely stowed away in its rightful place, the ramifications of that single bent latch started sinking in. Someone had forced their way in, only to leave empty-handed. That meant they'd been looking for something specific. Without conscious thought, Brina tapped her breast pocket, which had held the mysterious pyramid ever since she'd found it. That made no sense. Nobody knew she had it, except for Versa and Mattheus.

The former hadn't even wanted to touch it when it was right in front of them, and the latter was too dimwitted by a mile to execute such a precise operation. If Mattheus had been involved, the idiot would probably have broken an ankle trying to kick in the door and left a scarf with his initials at the scene.

No, this had been someone with both a specific skill set and a concrete goal. Huygen's cunning, watery eyes came to mind. What if he had found the pyramid in Brina's pocket when she'd passed out? If he'd taken the thing outright, Brina would've known it was him. This way, she wouldn't be able to prove a thing. It seemed like the sort of thing he would do.

Brina spat out of the window, equal parts angry and sad. Whoever the thief had been, they had taken one thing, the value of which couldn't be measured in gem dust. Brina's sense of safety in her own home. She had taken extreme care to keep the mill's location a secret, but now all of that was ruined. Someone out there knew exactly where she slept. *I should have listened to Versa and chucked the damn thing in the sea.*

Distant shouts echoed in the deepening dark outside, tearing Brina away from this unsettling realization. In the vale below, torches were popping up in all corners of Doorstep's Ditch. They spread in clusters from every square and hamlet, like exploding stars. This was how it started. Whether or not Brina was ready for it, the Scarlet Nocturne of 569 KR was taking place tonight.

*I'm not going. Let them go to Heil with it.*

## CHAPTER 5

Her guts churned as the incoherent shouts blended into a chant. Even though she couldn't hear the words, she knew them by heart at this point.

"Sway now, sway by the grace of the rope. Hooded man, hangman, avenger of our dying hope. Break, neck, break under the pull of the earth. Fade then, fade into the icy winter dirt."

*Bastards.*

The sheer glee with which they sang about the death of another human being made Brina's blood boil. Soon they would sing about her father like that. They would cheer as his last breath was ripped from his lungs.

Before she knew it, she had one foot across the threshold. If Azaria Oldenbreeze was to die tonight, she at least wouldn't die without one sympathetic soul at her side.

\*\*\*

Brina drew her hood as low as it would go. She made it a point never to make the trek from the mill to the Ditch after dark. It wasn't the wilderness she feared. The sounds and smells of the nighttime jungle were old friends to her. From the sickly-sweet twinge in the air that betrayed patches of devourer vines to the ghastly wail of a distant bargheist, Brina knew and cherished them.

The problem was people. Somehow, the problem always boiled down to people. Traveling through the Ditch at night was like playing dice with a troop of Biori. Eventually, someone got a dagger in the neck.

The sandy streets near the outskirts were deserted. Most of the outwalled were already at the Enclave, jostling for the best view of the action, or drinking themselves silly in one of the nearby taverns.

Brina roved through the familiar alleys and nooks with the silent grace of a cat. Get in last, get out first. That had been her plan for the past ten years, and it hadn't failed her yet. Though in reality, it was stupid to even risk attending the nocturnes.

Everyone in the area knew who she was. And even though most wouldn't dare attack her in broad daylight, the torches and excitement of the Scarlet Nocturnes had a way of bringing up old and dark feelings. Not a single nocturne had passed without blood in the streets. All Brina could do was hope it wouldn't be hers this year.

# CHAPTER 5

*24th day of the 10th cycle, 569KR*
**Doorstep's Ditch**

The hangman stomped onto the stage to raucous applause. Instead of the black hood that was common in the old days, the man's face was obscured by a grim leather mask that made him look like a bloated carcass.

Cheers and chants rose from the onlookers, exploding off the Enclave's stone walls like thunder. *They love a good show,* Brina thought bitterly. She'd found herself a spot on top of a rain barrel wedged between two storefronts. If the situation escalated, she'd be one of the first through the gilded gates.

From up high, the scene looked like something out of a satire on the dangers of excess. If it hadn't been for the gallows erected against the Enclave's far wall, one might have mistaken the occasion for a feast. Barrels of ale, a rarity provided graciously by the church, lined the outer walls. Loaves of sourdough bread were brought forth from within the city at regular intervals. It was the one time a year where Cardinal De Leliard, the empire's supreme ruler, dealt out anything other than punishment.

The hangman marched from the far end of the stage toward the gallows in the center, glaring at the crowd, who roared with excitement as he passed.

Brina shook her head in disgust. *Why do I even come here?*

Those first few years, it had been uncertainty which had drawn her out of her hiding place to witness the executions. The thought that her father might have to face death without his only daughter present, alone in the face of a crowd fiending for blood, had been too much to bear.

Over time, it had become clear that, as the leader of the Signum, Abrasax would have to suffer the additional torment of knowing his friends-in-arms

## CHAPTER 5

were dying one by one. Only when every one of them was gone would he receive the mercy of death.

Still, Brina had forced herself year after year to come here and witness the reality of the situation for herself. She had tried telling herself she only did it so she would be prepared when her father's appointment with the noose finally arrived, but, in truth, the nocturnes had become a twisted fuel to her.

A yearly reminder of exactly where she stood in life and what it would take to survive.

"... and through our purging of the dark, room shall arise for Heil's resplendent light."

The crowd cheered as a tall, heavyset Reynziel in majestic purple and golden robes read a message from Cardinal De Leliard to the outwalled.

"The death of Cardinal Estav II was both a terror and a costly blessing, for it revealed that even now there are those among us who would see us cast back into the wanton violence and chaos of the Primal Times."

Another roar drowned out the preacher's voice. From up high, Brina saw two red-faced women slamming their mugs together with such force that one of the vessels splintered, showering the drunk duo in shards of clay. The other woman, heaving with laughter, slugged down her remaining ale in one large gulp. Barely twenty feet to their left, two gentlemen leaned in close to each other, as though they were about to kiss. When they broke apart, one man hastily tucked away a small white ball of what was unmistakably cloud.

*Yep, it would be a real shame if we were to devolve into chaos and poor manners.*

The preacher droned on for what felt like an eternity. By the time he rolled up the scroll and motioned for the hangman to proceed, one of Brina's legs had fallen asleep.

Behind the stage, two dozen darkhelms in neutral black suits of armor formed a protective hedgerow near the inner gatehouse, which led into the city. They marched in perfect unison, as though controlled by an unseen puppeteer. When they were in position, the officer at their head knocked her mace into the golden gates thrice in rapid succession.

*It's happening.*

Near the front of the crowd, a restless jostling broke out as onlookers began climbing on top of each other and pushing others out of the way to get the best view possible.

The heavy gates inched open. For one heartbeat, there was the rattling of cartwheels against cobbles as the cage holding the sorceress Azaria came into view. Then the Enclave drowned in a flood of noise.

"Burn the hag!"

"Get it over with!"

Boos and cheers battled each other, melding together into a deafening surge of voices.

Azaria stood in her cramped cage, head held high. Her black curls were matted into clumps that ran down to her waist. She stared out at the crowd with dark, imperious eyes that reminded Brina of a wight she'd encountered near the King's Barrow one night. For the briefest moment, it seemed like Azaria's penetrating gaze locked upon hers. The sorceress's head gave a tiny nod. Then the moment dissolved.

*I imagined that. How would she know who I am?*

The cart came to a halt beside the stage. An uneasy feeling blossomed in the pit of Brina's stomach as the hangman stuck a pair of shackles through the bars of the cage. Why did she feel like she ought to do something? What could she even do if she wanted to?

*She nodded at me.*

That had been an illusion, a trick of the light.

*She saw me, then nodded at me.*

Azaria hobbled out of the cage, hindered by the irons weighing down her wrists and ankles. Eggs, handfuls of mud, and rocks sailed through the air from all sides. Somehow, all of them seemed to miss the captive by inches.

The hangman and an assistant each kept a hand on one of the sorceress's shoulders, guiding her firmly toward the gallows, where the noose awaited.

Azaria marched onward. Her face had grown slack, her eyes aimed forward, the sight of the gallows seemingly driving all distractions from her mind.

A hush fell over the scene as the hangman draped the noose around the woman's neck. The assistant stepped back, relinquishing his grip.

"Azaria Oldenbreeze, today you face judgment for the following crimes," the hangman spoke, unfurling a scroll of parchment. "Conspiracy against the common good of the realm, high treason, possession of demonic artifacts, robbery, kidnapping…"

Azaria's mouth curled into a faint smile as the list went on and on. By the Seven, it would take three lifetimes to do all that. As always, Brina marveled at the thought that the gentle, silly man she'd known as her

## CHAPTER 5

father had been in league with people who had committed every capital crime in the books.

"... and, most condemning of all, the murder of Cardinal Estav II." The hangman screamed these last words to make himself heard over the murmurs of the crowd. "Any last words?"

Azaria only smiled.

There was one heartbeat of perfect quiet. A wet snap. The hangman's head spun around at an unnatural angle, so that his masked face turned toward the crowd while he still had his back to them. His lifeless form slumped forward, revealing Azaria's grinning face. Her eyes radiated a bright blue light.

She lifted the noose from her shoulders, slowly and deliberately, like a noblewoman unbuttoning her corsage at the end of a long day.

The hangman's assistant stood frozen, only ten paces removed. Azaria was upon him in a flash. She grasped his head in both her hands and forced his forehead against hers. There was a flash of magenta, and the man whipped 'round, facing the troop of darkhelms storming up the stairs to the stage. He looked at once dazed and furious. The assistant let out a mad howl, then dashed toward the soldiers and hurled himself into their ranks at full speed, punching and kicking at every inch of them he could reach.

On top of her barrel, Brina's heart stopped. Was this it? Was this how a rebellion started? A horn resounded atop the Enclave's wall, and a second group of darkhelms flooded from the city to aid their struggling compatriots.

Azaria blocked a mace blow with her bare forearm. The heavy weapon ought to have snapped the limb like a twig, but Azaria didn't flinch. Her eyes flashed blue as she kicked one of her assailants in the chest, sending the armored darkhelm flying.

Then a quarrel flew from a darkhelm's windup bow from the top of the wall, plunging itself into Azaria's left shoulder. The sorceress buckled, and for a moment, it seemed like it would all be over. Then she got up, a dark stain spreading outward from the wound. Her eyes flared red. The exact tint Brina had first seen in the wampyr's and then Mattheus's eyes.

Brina jumped out of her hiding place and onto the cobbled square, then realized she had no plan. Did she really want to help someone who had committed just about every crime imaginable? Even if Brina wanted to help, she was a lone roamer with two daggers. One tucked away in her sleeve, the other in her boot.

The onlookers swept backward as yet another regiment of darkhelms streamed from the city. A burly, short-haired woman slammed into Brina's shoulder. Brina lost balance, and her knees exploded with pain as they collided with the cobbles. Everything grew dim as an ocean of stamping feet surrounded her.

A rough hand jerked at the back of her tunic, pulling upward. The assist gave her just enough leverage to regain her footing. Before she could utter a word of thanks, her savior had disappeared into the stampede.

Brina forced her way to a storefront. She jumped for an ornate wall sconce, which held the remains of a recently extinguished torch. The metal was hot to the touch, but this was no time to worry about burns. She pulled herself up and launched herself onto a first-floor balcony to get an overview of the chaos.

Against the far wall of the square, a gap had cleared around the stage. Darkhelms surrounded Azaria on all sides. Her mouth worked furiously as she screamed at the surrounding soldiers, the words lost in the crowd's panic.

A second bolt now sprouted from her chest, but against all odds, she was still on her feet. Though they outnumbered her dozens-to-one, the darkhelms kept their distance, content to contain their target without engaging. Brina looked up, scanning the Enclave's battlements for an unseen sharpshooter with a windup bow.

That's how she would have played it, keep the target distracted, then strike from the shadows. *If I take out the bowman, she may still have a chance.* Rushing into a stationary line of darkhelms was suicide, but if Brina got her hands on a bow, she might just be able to create enough confusion to give Azaria a fighting chance.

She couldn't explain to herself what compelled her to risk it all on account of a stranger she had nothing in common with. But something about seeing the woman surrounded, struggling to survive like a wounded animal, clicked with her. It was exactly how she'd felt all these years. Before Brina could act on the urge, however, a richly dressed Reynziel hobbled through the soldiers' line. His face was covered in a golden mask wrought like a face. He labored up the stairs to the stage, where he raised his hands in a gesture of peace.

The mood in the Enclave turned. Almost half of the crowd had flooded out through the gilded gates, back toward the Ditch. The other half

# CHAPTER 6

fell quiet. They had come here for a show, and they wouldn't leave until they'd gotten one.

The Reynziel's baritone carried across the square. "No more need to die." He took a step forward. "Promise us this, and we shall stand aside."

Brina's jaw dropped. Was this really happening? Again, her eyes wandered the battlements and balconies, looking for the glint of steel that would give away the darkhelms' ruse. The wall seemed deserted.

Azaria's eyes flared purple as the Reynziel took yet another step in her direction.

"I demand a trial," the sorceress cried out. A gasp rippled through the crowd. "I demand a chance to speak the truth with the people as my witness. I won't slink away into the night like a common cutthroat."

Azaria turned, facing the remaining thousand outwalled on the square.

"You have been lied to. You were lied to ten years ago, and you were lied to today. The second Sundering is upon us..."

The Reynziel's hand darted into his robe like a striking viper. There was a twinkle as he withdrew a long silver rod. Everything vanished in a flash of white. Brina felt her eyes burn and tear up. The merchant on the balcony beside her cried out in shock. Brina felt his hand close around her forearm for support as he wobbled. Brina swore. Not even a dozen silver lanterns should have been able to produce a flash like that.

Blurry shapes moved on the stage below. Soldiers. Azaria kneeled before the Reynziel, all light gone from her eyes. Where a second earlier, a confident sorceress had stood, ablaze with energy and fire, now lay a husk. Had the woman always looked this emaciated? She was barely more than a sack of gaunt skin pulled taut over lumps of bone.

The Reynziel jerked Azaria to her feet. Brina felt her eyes brim with tears of anger. They were doing it again. Brina had allowed herself a shred of hope, and now they were dragging it by the hair toward the gallows.

As the noose closed around Azaria's neck, the woman slumped forward, eyes closed. Her knees had already given way when the trapdoor swung open. It was like watching an empty robe sway on a clothesline.

Azaria's legs gave one final twitch. Then it was over.

And the outwalled cheered.

# CHAPTER 6

*24th day of the 10th cycle, 569KR*
**Doorstep's Ditch**

The Ditch was on fire. Columns of smoke were going up on all sides, twitching and writhing against the night sky like wraiths. Brina's lungs burned as she felt her way through the narrow alley behind The Wistful Chimera.

Doorstep's Ditch was a crate of kindling, always waiting for a spark. Every so often, the concentration of empty stomachs and liquor-soaked brains would reach critical mass and boil over into violence, looting, and destruction. But never like this.

The mobs that roamed the streets tonight were of a different caliber. The looting had started even before Azaria's corpse had stopped shuddering. Then the rest of the outwalled had streamed out of the Enclave with a volatile mix of adrenaline, alcohol, and bloodlust in their veins.

Brina reached the end of the alley and peered around the corner into Wicket Row. There was a tinkle of shattering glass as a hooded group of four flung rocks through the windows of a house to the right.

"Come out here, you Bladefin scum," a woman's voice bellowed from underneath a black hood.

The Bladefin were one of five major gangs in the criminal underworld of Hammerstroke, which meant that the hooded assailants were likely either members of the Auctioneers or the Satyrs. Both were embroiled in an ongoing territory dispute with the Bladefin; neither of them was to be messed with.

When it came to the gangs, Brina occupied a special neutral ground. She had ties with people in all five factions, and it was no secret that she sold to anyone who had gems. It was a precarious position, one based on

## CHAPTER 6

the mutual understanding that she was to steer clear of any gang-related conflicts.

Brina crossed Wicket Row and ducked into the opposite alley, turning her back on the masked group and its target. As she tiptoed through the narrow street, she caught a movement in the shadows just behind her. *Someone's watching.*

Pretending that she hadn't noticed, Brina took a detour into a wide hamlet surrounded by three-story tenements. If she was being followed, her pursuer would either have to reveal themselves or risk losing her.

Footfalls on the cobbles behind her confirmed her suspicion. She let the dagger in her left sleeve drop into her palm, careful to obscure the weapon. At best, she was dealing with an opportunist, looking for an easy target. At worst... Well, she'd worry about that when the time came.

There were two options for dealing with a tail. Either you disappeared, or you turned around and made them disappear. Nobody would bat an eye at one more body found in the streets after a riot like this, but a fight was a risk. Even a superficial slice could prove fatal if the rot got into it. It wasn't worth it.

As Brina slipped behind a series of forgotten sheets on a clothesline, a thought struck her. What if this was the same person who had broken into the mill earlier today? *That damn pyramid is proving to be a lot more trouble than it's worth.*

That changed things. For one, it would mean that simply vanishing wasn't good enough. They knew where Brina lived. What was to prevent them from following her up there in a few hours and slitting her throat while she slept? Second, if her theory proved correct, she needed to know who was after her and what it was they wanted.

Adrenaline spiked as Brina realized what she had to do. She took a deep breath, then turned sideways into a three-foot-wide gap between two rows of houses. *Now.*

With tremendous effort, she began pushing herself up in the space between the walls. She'd need to be high enough by the time her follower turned into the alley, or it wouldn't work.

Her palms turned into a pincushion of splinters as the flaky wood of the walls sank into her skin.

She was about fifteen feet off the ground when the sound of boots on mud approached. The spy had broken into a run to catch up. She got a good look at the man as he turned the corner.

He had to twist his broad shoulders to make them fit in the narrow pathway. Hairy arms like moldy tree trunks stuck out of a sleeveless leather vest, leaving the man's armpits exposed. There was a clumsiness to his gait that betrayed a weak right knee. A bristly dark beard was visible beneath a black leather mask.

Brina held her breath as Bristlebeard lumbered down the alley, careful to remain completely still. It didn't matter. The man didn't so much as glance upward once. *Idiot*. This was working far better than she could have hoped for. Fear gave way to excitement. The nervous anticipation of a well-laid trap.

"Aaargh," Bristlebeard cried out as Brina landed feet first on his shoulders. There was an audible *snap* as one of his arms slid out of its socket. The two of them crashed into the muddy underground in a tangle of limbs, Brina's fall comfortably broken by the meat shield underneath her.

Brina sprang up and kicked at the man's grasping hands.

"Ow, what'd you do that for?" the man wailed. His voice was dull, and a lisp suggested he'd bitten his tongue as Brina collided with him.

"Who do you work for?" Brina snapped, flashing her dagger.

"Work? I ain't worked a day in me life."

Bristlebeard tried to get up, but Brina was too quick for him. A swift kick swept his feet out from under him again. Brina grabbed the edge of the mask and jerked upward.

"You?"

Those dim, watery eyes and puffy cheeks unmistakably belonged to one of Mattheus's trusty goons. And if he was near, that meant...

*Crack.*

Something heavy smashed into the top of Brina's head with the force of a falling boulder. She felt her skull break under the impact as the ground rushed up to meet her.

***

"Told you she would do that, didn't I?" Mattheus's voice floated in the darkness above Brina. He couldn't have sounded happier if he'd just stumbled onto a mountain of diamond shards. "Honestly, it's like playing Galleons with a halfwit. You give them a barge, and they miss the schooner coming up behind them. I really thought this one was different."

Hot liquid pooled under Brina's head, but she didn't dare move to assess

## CHAPTER 6

the damage. The only way she'd make it out alive was if Mattheus thought she was already dead.

"My arm," Bristlebeard complained somewhere nearby. "It's all wrong. I can't get up."

"Oh shut it," Mattheus responded. "That's why I pay you, isn't it?" The tip of a boot poked Brina's ribs, followed by a kick. Brina's jaw clenched with the effort of holding in a scream. There was a silence. Had Mattheus noticed?

"Grab the trinket." Mattheus's command sounded lazy, almost disappointed.

Sour beer breath wafted over her as a pair of rough, calloused hands clawed at Brina's pockets. There was nothing in there but a handful of firebark twigs she'd planned to use on her way back to the mill. Now things seemed like she may never see the place again. *Just hold still, they think you're dead.* Maybe she was. Her limbs grew heavier with every passing second as blood gushed from her torn scalp. Even if they left her here, she was done.

"She's wearing it on a chain, you imbecile."

Beer Breath's hands shot up to her neck, then made to dip down the front of her shirt, where the pyramid rested against her bare chest. Brina stiffened. She'd endure a lot for a chance at survival, but not this.

Without thinking, she sank her teeth into the goon's hands. The man yelled, drawing back.

Brina struggled to her feet, forcing open her eyes. An immediate wave of nausea hit her, and she staggered sideways into the wall. Mattheus's blurry outline appeared in front of her. He hadn't bothered to disguise himself. The goon she'd bitten was staring at an oozing gash in his hand.

"Oh goody," Mattheus drawled, the corners of his thin mouth raised in a smirk. "I prefer when they fight back."

"Ambushing me three against one," Brina mumbled, her voice choked with the effort of staying conscious. "I see you've approached this with the same level of courage you apply to your other jobs." She snickered despite herself. A faint euphoric feeling was washing over her as the alley grew increasingly distorted around her.

"Ah well." Mattheus's smirk deepened. "I hear running around solo gets you killed. Care to weigh in?"

His fist slammed into Brina's gut. She doubled over, heaving.

"See that abomination earlier tonight? Sorcery of the foulest kind," Mattheus whispered in her ear. Fragmented memories of Azaria's blazing eyes, interspersed with the woman's ragged frame, swinging from the gallows to earsplitting applause. "That's when I knew what you tried to do to me back at the freak's pub."

"What?" It cost a tremendous amount of effort to get the word out.

"Don't. Lie." Mattheus spat. "I saw your eyes when I took your little pendant. You'd have had me crawling in the muck like a dog, wouldn't you?"

Brina swallowed. Was that true? Surely not. She'd have known if she had tapped into the supernatural. There would have been signs. But then again, hadn't she seen that red glow reflected back at her in Mattheus's eyes and in the wampyr's before that?

"You don't know what you're talking about."

"Just like daddy. Lying until the very end."

Mattheus got up close and landed another punch to her lower back. Brina dropped to the mud, landing on her side. Then she noticed the point of the dagger sticking out through the front of her tunic. She stared from the bloody piece of metal to the man who had driven it straight through her torso. Then the pain hit. A sharp burning that spread through her body like toxic shock.

Mattheus leaned over her, reaching for the pyramid necklace.

"What the..." He sprang up, his face illuminated with an orange glow.

Near the mouth of the alley stood a dark-skinned man, eyes radiating like flames. *A sorcerer.* Long black robes hung in tatters from his scarecrow frame. His face was obscured by the brightness of his eyes. The newcomer broke into a run, heading straight toward them. As he passed Beer Breath, the sorcerer's fingertips brushed the goon's coat. It lit up like a torch, causing him to roar in pain as flames licked his face and neck. He dropped to the ground, rolling in the mud.

Mattheus bolted. He bumped into Bristlebeard, knocking the injured man into the dirt. He didn't bother trying to help him up.

The sorcerer leapt over Brina with the silent agility of a sheikan. Bristlebeard held his hands up in surrender as the sorcerer approached.

"Please, I only do this for the money," he cried out.

The sorcerer bent low, and there was a flash of magenta.

"Your master has left you to die. I suggest you chase him down and plant that dagger of yours in his neck. Do it thrice for good measure."

When he replied, Bristlebeard's voice was a dull drone.

"He betrayed me. Must take revenge."

## CHAPTER 7

"Good boy." The sorcerer kicked the meathead in the backside as he got up to sprint after Mattheus, brandishing his knife.

A veil of drowsiness pressed down on Brina. Scalding blood streamed across her numb fingers as she tried to put pressure around the dagger sticking out of her belly.

The sorcerer's face appeared above her. The light in his eyes had gone out. His regular black eyes seemed dull and strange by comparison. His face and scalp were completely devoid of hair, giving the man a hardened look, as though he'd been carved out of a solid block of obsidian.

"Where is the script?" His voice was a low rumble.

Brina's heart sank. Of course. She should have known. This was Doorstep's Ditch. There was always a bigger fish. The only people around here who'd interrupt a robbery were better robbers.

It didn't matter. Her skull was cracked, and she was wearing a dagger for a bellybutton. She was done. It was a comfort to die knowing that Mattheus hadn't gotten the thing he desired after all.

"... neck," she mumbled, smiling at the thought of Mattheus being chased all the way to the beach by his own crony.

The sorcerer lifted the chain from around Brina's neck and placed a hand behind her head, forcing her to look up at him.

"There's not much time. You're losing a lot of blood."

He held the pyramid right in front of Brina's eyes. "Focus on the pattern. Let it draw you in. Give it everything you've got."

Brina looked at the silver surface, but couldn't make out anything other than blurry ripples. Her eyes slipped shut.

"No," the sorcerer muttered, a note of panic piercing his calm tone from before. "No, no, no. Not again." Forceful fingers pried at Brina's eyelids, forcing them open again. "Come on. Don't give up."

Again, Brina tried to force herself to see something she knew in her heart wasn't there anymore. Then, miraculously, a tiny red dot popped into life in the very middle of the pyramid. Her whole body tensed with the effort of staying awake. Brina watched as the dot started trickling down the grooves in the metal, like a drop of paint rolling around a maze. It split and curved until a complicated crimson symbol flared up in the dark.

Everything faded around her, giving way to that sharp red light. The symbol burned brightly in her mind for one glorious, euphoric moment.

Then the darkness swept her away.

# CHAPTER 7

*28th day of the 10th cycle, 569 KR*
**Barrow's Perch**

A pungent herbal smell filled Brina's nostrils. *Heil almighty, I'm alive.* Images of the ambush in that dark alley came swarming back like a flock of ravenous vultures. Her heart rate spiked. Blood. The tip of the dagger protruding from her belly. *My skull. The pyramid.*

She reached up, and her hand closed around the reassuring coolness of the artifact resting on her chest.

"Took you long enough," a gruff voice said.

Brina's eyes snapped open. The bald sorcerer was leaning over her. His eyes simmered with a faint orange hue. Behind him, Brina could just make out a low, curved stone ceiling and the flickering light of a single torch.

"Where am I?"

"This"—he threw up his hand nonchalantly—"is my home. Then again, that may be too strong a word. It's where I sleep."

Brina tried to sit up. White-hot pain exploded in her midsection. A whimper escaped before she could stop it.

"Bad idea," the sorcerer said. "You were stabbed, remember? Quite thoroughly, I might add."

*Mattheus.* As soon as she healed, that rat would pay. She'd drag him out of his own house in broad daylight if she had to. She didn't care. He wouldn't stand a chance in a fair fight, and he knew it. The idiot probably thought she was dead by now. By all laws of nature, she ought to be.

Only the sorcerer's arrival had prevented that from happening. He'd arrived just in time to conjure a spell. *And he used my pyramid to do it.*

"Who are you?" She looked at his gaunt face. He looked like a man who hadn't had a square meal in a decade. His cheekbones stuck out so far

## CHAPTER 7

that he resembled the skulls woven into a Biori warrior's beard. Countless thin, white scars contrasted with his dark skin to form something akin to a spider's web. He looked grotesque, like something out of a campfire tale, and yet there was a familiarity about the man. Something that pulled at threads from the past that Brina had been attempting to sever for years.

The sorcerer sighed. "You ask a lot of questions for someone who's spent the last three days floating between life and death. Makes me dread what you're going to be like when you've healed."

His matter-of-fact tone made Brina chuckle, causing a fresh series of stabs in her gut. She turned her head and noticed that the floor of the cavelike room was littered with dozens of ceramic urns. In the far corner of the room, mostly obscured by shadows, was a pile of what were unmistakably human bones. *This place better not be what I think it is.*

The sorcerer's mouth worked, pulling the scars tight across his face. "They used to call me Acheron."

"And you live *here*, in a barrow?" The thought alone made the hairs on Brina's neck stand up.

Acheron shrugged. "Nobody was using it."

Brina's stomach clenched. "But these are supposed to be cursed. The forefathers sealed them because..."

"... they were superstitious morons," Acheron finished. "I assure you, the only curses in here are the ones I utter when I run out of..." He pulled a face. "Well, that's neither here nor there. Point is, there's nothing to worry about."

Brina couldn't help but feel concerned that her health and safety were being watched over by someone who didn't see the slightest problem with living in a grave.

Acheron began rummaging through the urns, which he seemed to use as storage space. Muttering to himself, he retrieved a bottle with a muddy liquid, a dried-up vine with countless minuscule leaves, and a chunk of something white. He placed the ingredients on a stone surface which looked eerily like a sarcophagus. Over a dozen intricate metal devices stood side-by-side on top of it.

As Acheron worked, Brina struggled to remember all that had happened. One detail in particular made her uneasy.

"How did you know I had the pyramid?"

Acheron scoffed. "You basically rubbed the thing under my nose last week in the Chimera. Good thing you weren't more careful, or you'd have been dead. Funny how that works."

"Hold on," Brina said, trying to recall the day she'd clashed with Mattheus. "The Chimera was empty that day."

"Wrong." Acheron didn't seem to deem further elaboration necessary. Brina tried to recall the scene in the inn, but the dull throbbing near the back of her head wouldn't allow the memory to form. "Anyway, I tried to rid you of it the week after, but you kept taking it everywhere you went."

"How does it work? The pyramid?" Brina asked.

Acheron sighed. "It's what us sparkgazers would call a script. It has a sigil engraved on it, a shape that allows the human body to access its full potential."

"But how? I'm not a sorcerer," Brina said. "If I was, I wouldn't need to crawl into every dirty, dangerous cavern on the island to fill my pantry."

"There's no such thing as a sorcerer. With enough practice, anyone can use a script." A sad smile curled Acheron's lips. "Do you know why the church spends so much energy declaring the evils of 'sorcery' or 'demons'?"

"They say it will cast us back into the primal times," Brina said, remembering the fat Reynziel's words at the nocturne.

Heilinism told of a time before Heil, the so-called "Keeper of Balance," existed when the world was ruled by a pantheon of cruel gods who used humanity as pawns in their wars, each imbuing their human armies with their own divine powers. When Heil finally arrived, she banished the old gods and locked away what remained of their powers deep in the heart of humanity.

"They are right," Acheron said. "The only thing they've got backward is who the real oppressor in the story is."

There was a tinkle of metal on metal as one of the devices produced a puff of silver smoke. A sweet scent, like almond cakes, filled the chamber.

"Here." Acheron held a vial to Brina's mouth. She instinctively pressed her lips together. Drinking or eating anything you hadn't prepared yourself was one of the quicker ways to end up dead. She still didn't know why the sorcerer had brought her here.

Acheron let out an exasperated sigh. "Look, if I was going to poison you, I'd have done so by now. And, frankly, you wouldn't have been able to stop me."

"That's reassuring," Brina muttered sarcastically, warding off the vial with the back of her hand. "Why are you doing this?"

## CHAPTER 7

"Doing what? Keeping you from inevitably screaming your head off once your last dose of pain relief wears off? That, kid, is because I am trying to play the good guy for once. So drink."

He held up the vial again, and this time Brina gulped down the liquid in two mouthfuls, ready to pull a face. It tasted fantastic. Like molten pastries. Immediately, her rising headache and the stabbing in her chest were reduced to a vague tingling sensation, as though only the memory of the wounds remained. It was like sinking into a warm cushion.

"Does that mean you tend to be the bad guy?" Brina asked. She was suddenly rather enjoying herself. It was hard to remain alert when you felt this wonderfully comfortable.

"Judging by the way my old friend was treated in the Enclave, I'd hazard a guess that most on the island would see it that way, yes." He gave a wry smile, which made the scars on his cheeks whiten.

"You knew Azaria?" Brina winced as she remembered the way the woman had almost escaped before that Reynziel had flashed her with the silver torch. If Acheron was there, why hadn't he helped her?

"I knew her. Once." His face sank. Acheron walked away and began ordering and cleaning the devices on his workbench.

A sense of wonder overcame Brina. If Acheron had known Azaria...

"Did you know any other sorcerers?"

Acheron bowed his head, unwilling to meet her gaze.

"Yes," he said. "I knew your father. I considered him a friend. One of the best."

Brina's heart leapt. There was finally a chance. Preventing her father's rapidly approaching execution had been a distant dream, something she'd clung onto when everything had fallen apart around her. Deep down, she'd always known it couldn't be done. God's Maul was an impenetrable deathtrap. By herself, Brina didn't stand a chance.

But this changed everything. With a sorcerer on her side, anything would be possible. All she needed to do was to make Acheron see the possibilities.

He must have seen her face light up, for he immediately shook his head.

"Abrasax is gone. And I mean truly gone." He gave her a long, hard stare. "You know that, right?"

Brina's jaw clenched.

"But you're—"

"An old man and a coward," Acheron finished. "There were thirteen of us that night, not twelve."

He leaned down and plucked a tiny glass vial out of an urn behind him. From a distance, it seemed to be filled with smoke. A white substance, full of tiny glittering sparks, floated around inside.

Acheron pulled out the stopper and inhaled the stuff in one big breath. The dying orange ember in his eyes fanned into life at once.

"If you were there, then why weren't you rounded up with the rest of them? None of the others even made it out of the palace." Brina propped herself up on her elbows to get a better look at the man.

"Because I abandoned my brothers and sisters when they needed me most." The sorcerer looked Brina in the eye, and she saw he was telling the truth. "I had a source within the Cardinal's ranks who warned me, days before the attempt, that we'd been betrayed. The source claimed that one of our own had gone to De Leliard, who was High Inquisitor at the time, and sold us out for a chestful of gems."

The sorcerer's mouth worked as though he was trying to grind pebbles between his teeth.

"I went straight to Abrasax. I begged him to call it off until we'd rooted out the mole, but he wouldn't hear of it. He told me he wouldn't doubt anyone for even a second." Acheron shook his head. "Your father was a great man. He would've jumped down a leviathan's throat for any of us. Ironic how that loyalty ended up getting the entire tribe killed."

The corners of Acheron's mouth lifted as though he wanted to laugh, then the light in his eyes reached a new peak and his head slumped on his shoulders.

Brina didn't know whether to be concerned or annoyed. She stared as the sorcerer swayed on his feet like a sapling in a storm. Then it clicked. *He's a cloudhead, a floater.*

She had gotten herself dragged off into a grave hill that doubled as a cloud den. Another sickening realization followed. Hadn't she just drank a potion that was supplying her with a cozy, blissful feeling right now? Anxiety fluttered against that silky smooth chemical veil like a butterfly in a glass jar. The fear was there in concept. She noticed its presence, but found that she didn't have it in her to worry. Acheron had given her cloud. So what? It had subdued her pain, hadn't it?

She reached up and jabbed her index finger into the sorcerer's ribs.

"Hey," she called, snapping her fingers, "did you just drug me?"

# CHAPTER 7

Acheron's eyes snapped open. For a moment he seemed annoyed, then he looked at Brina as though he'd forgotten she was there.

"Oh. Right." He blinked rapidly. "Yes."

The trapped butterfly battered the walls of its jar.

"I trusted you." Brina tried to sound betrayed, but found it hard to convey anything other than detached joy.

Acheron waved a hand as though swatting at an invisible fly. "It's fine, it's fine. I gave you a smidge of water root to suppress your fever, four leaves of sinner's regret to dull the pain, and *yes,* a fingertip of cloud to negate any unpleasant side effects."

Brina opened her mouth to protest, but Acheron interrupted her.

"Are you seeing anything strange?"

"Yes, I see an ugly bald goblin with orange eyes stumbling around a grave babbling to himself."

"Highly amusing. How about if you take me out of the picture?"

"Then no." Brina shrugged.

"See, I told you it was fine. Anyway, I feel like we were talking about something or the other?"

"You were just trying to come up with an excuse for why you abandoned my father," Brina supplied. She pushed herself into a sitting position. The pressure in her head increased, but didn't quite peak into pain. Maybe cloud wasn't so bad after all.

Across from her, Acheron's face hardened.

"I deserve that."

"Did you ever find out who the traitor was?"

"No. If any of them had a deal with De Leliard, he didn't keep up his end. The inquisition rounded them all up that very night. At first I thought that was part of the plan, a play to keep suspicion off the double agent. Then De Leliard started having them executed in public.

"Azaria was the last possible suspect, but you saw what happened. All of them are dead."

"Except for one," Brina said, a hard knot forming in the pit of her stomach.

Acheron shook his head. "Your father was the only one of our brothers and sisters who I had complete and blind faith in. It couldn't have been him." He sighed. "Not that it matters much anymore."

"It matters to me," Brina said. "Because I'm going to break him out."

The words came out of their own accord. Brina hadn't intended to say it out loud, but realized she meant it. Thoughts she had been repressing for years surged to the surface under the cloud's influence. All her life, things had been taken from her. Everyone she had ever known had either died or turned on her at some point. She was tired of losing, tired of bending over backward to avoid ending up in a gibbet above Mallion's gate. She couldn't and wouldn't bear it one more day.

Acheron let out a deep sigh.

"God's Maul is a perfectly sealed stone box. Nothing goes in or out without the Cardinal's explicit orders. I'm sorry to say so, but Abrasax is lost."

Brina jumped up, spurred on by the chemical boost in her veins. Her feet felt squishy under her weight, like rotting stumps, but she stayed upright through sheer force of will.

"Together we could do it," she said, grabbing on to the front of Acheron's robe to keep herself from keeling over. "I have connections, more than we could ever need, and you've got sorcery. Actual sorcery. If anyone could do it, it would be us."

Acheron pulled back from her grip, causing Brina to stumble.

"No," he said, "those days are gone. The scepter has won. I died that night alongside my kin. This bag of bone and sinew is just the shell I left behind."

"So you're just going to leave him there?"

Acheron nodded. His eyes were wide, seeming to peer straight through Brina. "You would be wise to do the same. Gather some shards and go to Hawqal. They would welcome one with your talents. You'll be safe there. Don't ruin the life you have chasing after the one you lost."

"If you won't help me, I'll do it by myself." Brina looked around and spotted the gray slab that functioned as the barrow's door. It took every ounce of strength she possessed to wrench it open. Beyond the threshold, everything was pitch black.

"Don't." There was a pleading note to Acheron's voice. "At least stay until morning. You'll get yourself killed."

Brina scoffed. "I'd rather be dead out there than live on in a grave."

She took a few lurching steps forward, and the night engulfed her. When she looked back, she could see the old sorcerer lying slumped forward, head resting on the sarcophagus.

# CHAPTER 8

*6th day of the 11th cycle, 569KR*
**Home**

eventy-five, seventy-six, seventy-seven...

The sapphire shards tinkled merrily as Brina dropped them into a ceramic bowl one by one. Sitting on her bed with the window open, Brina's view of the bay was nothing short of spectacular.

The cloudless sky blended into the azure water of the Sundered Sea, making it impossible to spot where one ended and the other began. Waves swelled and tumbled as the earth breathed. Near the horizon, five pillars of black jutted out from the water's smooth surface like splinters of bone from a wound. God's Maul.

Eighty-three, eighty-four...

At a distance, the fortress felt like a figurine, a pentagonal chunk of rock and mortar. It was hard to imagine that people actually lived and died there. Even harder to comprehend was the suffocating reality that her father was right there, within view, but so very far out of reach.

Dozens of black dots crawled across the horizon. Trading fleets from Hawqal, escorted by convoys of skullbeard mercenary galleys. Then there were the redsails, vessels that belonged to the scepter. They patrolled the waters between Hammerstroke and God's Maul at all times. There wasn't a single ship that traversed the bay without the redsails' notice and approval. A disgruntled smuggler Brina had met in The Wistful Chimera had once spent the better part of an hour complaining about the redsails' tenacity in verifying the legality of every single crate carried across Hammerstroke's waters.

Ninety-one, ninety-two, ninety-three...

Brina smiled. It was looking like she had accumulated well over a hundred shards over the years she'd spent feeding her emergency fund. Most of them were sapphires and emeralds, but that wouldn't matter much to the people she intended to deal with. In fact, smugglers and mercenaries tended to be wary of anything ruby and above, as those shards were rare in the Ditch and therefore easier to trace back to the source.

One hundred and ten, one hundred eleven, one hundred twelve...

Even though she was pleasantly surprised by the pouch's contents, she'd still need to call in every favor and ounce of goodwill she'd cultivated over the years if she wanted to get anywhere near God's Maul.

There was one person in particular who she'd need to sway. One person without whom there was no plan. Unfortunately, it wasn't money she would need to convince them. No, the only person she knew who had ever set foot in God's Maul needed something else. To provide Brina with a map, Versa would need the courage to face demons no amount of shards could banish.

One hundred and twenty-one, one hundred and twenty-two, one hundred and twenty-three...

One hundred and twenty-four. The last shard dropped into the bowl, and then there was silence. Sadness overcame Brina as she stared into the mass of sparkling fragments.

This was what she had to show for a decade of filthy, dangerous, and illegal jobs. A bowl of colorful needles. A bowl that could take her down one of two paths.

Acheron's words had been droning on in the back of her mind, an unshakable chorus of doubt. *"Don't ruin the life you have chasing after the one you lost."*

One hundred and twenty-four shards would be more than enough to buy herself a false passport and a cabin on one of the dozens of Hawqallian ships that moored at the harbor in Mallion's Depth daily. Traders habitually sent out a sloop or two to the pontoons of Doorstep's Ditch's floating district to garner some off-the-books profits. Brina could probably make the arrangements before the week was out. She'd be able to leave all of this behind. The name-calling, the constant dread, being ripped off on half the contracts she took. She could have a brand-new life.

On the other hand, one hundred and twenty-four shards might also be enough to purchase the oldest and moldiest fishing boat in the Ditch. There would probably be enough left to buy a seal of passage forged with mediocre skill. With any luck, she could at least reach God's Maul's outer walls. It would be a shoddy attempt at jailbreak. One that was all but guar-

## CHAPTER 8

anteed to end in death. But it would be an attempt. Incontrovertible proof to herself that years of the church's oppression hadn't broken her spirit.

Brina replaced the pouch underneath the loose floorboard and edged down the stairs. She wouldn't be able to put off her decision for long, but in the meantime, she still needed to eat.

When she reached the front door, Brina's hands instinctively went for the windup bow on the hook left of the door. A herd of long-legged marsh walkers had been grazing on the grassy slopes of King's Barrow Hill for the past week. Picking one off would yield enough meat to last into next week, and the pelt might fetch a few sapphire nibs on the market. Brina paused, her hand resting on the weapon's smooth stock, then thought better of it. There would be plenty of nights to track game. She needed a change.

Brina closed the door and grabbed her fishing net off a low branch on a nearby oak. Even though it was bone dry and coarse to the touch from months of disuse, it still reeked of seaweed.

The smell brought back memories of simpler times when she'd trawled the beach for clams, crabs and other small critters as a little girl. Back then, the ocean had seemed like one giant treasure trove, always spitting out something interesting. Firejellies, mermaid's purses, carved pieces of ceramic, colorful shells, and everything else a child could dream up.

Now, the water was an obstacle. A wall between her and the only family she had left.

Spending time on the beach would give her an opportunity to think things over. Besides, she'd better start paying attention to the redsails' movements if she was to sail to God's Maul.

# CHAPTER 9

*12th day of the 11th cycle, 569KR*
**God's Maul**

The great fortress of the Cardinals loomed up before the ship's bow like a spectre in the night. The only lights visible from the outside were a series of beacons that shone from a dozen gargoyles hewn into the black rock of the outer wall. Their beams bathed the water surrounding the prison in an orange glare, creating a permanently lit circle around the base of the prison. Nothing could approach the island without passing through it, ensuring detection by the dozen guards stationed atop each of the keep's five towers.

Right in front of them was the gatehouse, a masterful piece of architecture that contained an archway so tall that entire ships, mast and all, could fit underneath it.

Solana stepped up to the bow and solemnly raised the device the Cardinal had given her. It was shaped like a golden scepter with a ruby the size of a child's fist embedded in the top. She pressed a button on the side of it, and the gem lit up, creating a bubble of crimson light on the dark waves ahead. The effect lasted a handful of seconds before the night closed in again.

Behind her, she could sense the crew's eyes on her. Throughout their, admittedly brief, journey, they had treated her with a reverence that was both foreign and uncomfortable to her. It was the sort of treatment that came with the expectation that, as the Cardinal's newest emissary, she possessed poise and dignity beyond those of mere servants.

Until now, it hadn't been too hard to play the part. She'd quite enjoyed strolling across the deck with her newly woven black and gold Reynziel's robes billowing in the wind. For a moment, in the privacy of her own cab-

# CHAPTER 9

in below deck, she had even allowed herself to take off the griffin-shaped helmet that came with her position.

Though the same breeze Solana had found so pleasantly soothing had caused significant troubles in keeping the ship on course, she hadn't been expected to lift so much as a finger. She hadn't objected.

Now the situation had reversed itself. All eyes were on her to lead them now that they had reached the outer wall of the black fortress. Solana's jaw clenched as the seconds ticked by. Shouldn't they have received the return signal by now?

Hesitant to risk seeming impatient, or worse, inexperienced, she kept the golden device at her side. She held the thing loosely to suggest that she was accustomed to holding objects worth more than the house she had grown up in and everyone in it.

After what felt like an entire tide cycle, two poison-green flashes erupted on the tower above the gatehouse. There was a metallic rattle as the gate's iron grate was pulled up. Barnacles and a layer of algae clung to the lower rungs. Solana marveled at the sheer amount of force that would be required to lift a gate of this size. She'd have to demand to see the mechanism once she was inside.

It seemed like an impossible task to steer a ship through the narrow archway, and Solana felt relieved that she would only have to give the order.

"Proceed." This time her voice was cool, with an imperious undertone. She liked this one. It had taken her a while to settle on what type of emissary she was going to be. In the end, the answer had been as simple as visiting home.

Her mother's condition had grown worse, and her treatment became more expensive as complications presented themselves. Solana couldn't afford to lose her position and the benefits that came with it, under any circumstances. There was no margin for error. There could be zero doubt about her competence and her ability to control any situation that threatened the scepter. Therefore, she would act the part.

Captain Morris motioned to her crew, and two dozen sailors began scurrying about on the deck, preparing the delicate maneuver through the gatehouse. In the hold below, the first mate barked orders at the rowers. As one, a dozen oars clattered into the water.

The ship slid into motion. Solana couldn't contain a gasp as they glided underneath the archway and God's Maul's inner court came into view.

From up close, the five towers surrounding the courtyard were colossal beyond anything she'd ever seen in Mallion's Depth. Every one of them was as tall as the spire of Heil's cathedral on Keeper's Square and as wide as Captain Morris's ship was long. The very thought of looking down over the parapet from such a height was dizzying.

Solana wondered where they'd have to moor. The courtyard consisted entirely of the rise and fall of the ocean's water, framed by the smooth black rock of the towers and their connective walls. There were no visible openings or irregularities in the rock.

Behind them, the grate splashed back into the water, locking them in. Solana's fingers tightened against the golden rod.

"Where next, Your Purity?" Morris asked. "Should I have the anchor lowered?"

Solana raised a hand, signaling for patience.

There was a clang as the heavy grate struck bottom.

At once, a section of the black wall in the northern tower moved backward, then sideways, revealing a passage ten feet wide and fifteen tall. A lone figure, dressed from head to toe in black, appeared at the entrance and beckoned.

"Lower me a sloop, Captain," Solana said.

With Captain Morris herself taking the sloop's oars, Solana floated over the eerily quiet courtyard toward the figure in black. The only sounds audible over the distant rushing of the waves were the rhythmic splashes of the oars as they dug into the water's surface.

Solana looked up and noticed she was being watched from the tops of the surrounding towers by dozens of black dots.

When the sloop reached the entrance, Morris jumped over the side to lend Solana a supporting hand as she transferred from the wobbly boat to the solid stone floor.

Solana had trouble suppressing a shudder as she took in her one-man welcoming committee. The prison's warden wore black leather armor under their cloak, reminiscent of the scaly underbelly of a large reptile. Not an inch of skin was visible, giving the impression that the figure in front of her had been woven from shadow rather than flesh and blood. To top off her unease, the warden's head was obscured by a silver mask shaped like a gargoyle. The eye-slits were hooded so that only dark circles were visible where eyes ought to be.

"Reynziel Solana," a cold, high-pitched male voice said from underneath the mask, "welcome to God's Maul."

## CHAPTER 9

\*\*\*
*12th day of the 11th cycle, 569KR*
**Barrow's Perch**

Acheron slumped against the smooth stone wall of the barrow. Every vein in his body burned red hot. The heat was comfortable and familiar, like embers glowing in the hearth of one's childhood home.

His head lolled sideways against a ceramic urn as the warmth traveled up his neck. *Free, finally free.*

The urn keeled over under his weight. The peaceful silence of the dead shattered as pieces of ceramic cascaded onto the floor.

He jolted upright, eyes snapping open.

She was there. Sitting cross-legged on the sarcophagus in the center of the room. Her eyes were milky white. Even without the irises and pupils, the fury in them was unmistakable.

"I tried!" Acheron screamed at her, his voice cracking. "What do you want from me? I tried."

"*But you didn't, did you?*" The voice in his head sounded just like hers, but the thoughts were his own. Or were they?

"You spent all day wandering the Enclave. You knew they were holding me in the gatehouse."

She sat up on her haunches, a sheikan ready to pounce. Acheron's hands scrambled for a piece of the urn, clawing for something to defend himself with.

"What could I do? There were so many of them."

His hand closed around a long shard. In his terror, he squeezed too hard. The sharp edge bit into his skin, drawing blood. There was no pain, just the dull sense of warmth dripping down his fingers.

"You convinced yourself that I was the traitor so you could let me die without lifting a finger, just like you did with the others."

"They would have captured me, too. I would have died." He was pleading now.

"Maybe you should have. Maybe you should have died a long time ago."

The warmth was pulling him under, as it was supposed to. Acheron didn't dare let it take him this time. What if she followed him down there, into that void where time and grief and joy didn't exist? He imagined Azaria clinging to him as they sank into the abyss.

Acheron shook his head like a wet dog. Out of the corner of his eyes, fresh horrors appeared. More figures crawled out of the urns, squeezed themselves from beneath the sarcophagus's lid, and glided in underneath the barrow's heavy door. They glared at him with those same runny, white eyes. He knew then that he was lost.

With a final, merciless tug, the world whirled away.

Abrasax stood before him on top of the ruined tower at Crow's Perch, north of Mallion's Depth, tears welling up in the corners of his eyes. Behind him, dozens of tiny islands bloomed in the azure blanket of the Sundered Sea.

"Please, brother," Abrasax said, grabbing him by the shoulders, "have faith. I know who my allies are, and I will need every one of them if we are to succeed."

Acheron's own voice resonated in his ears.

"I can't. It's madness."

*Madness.* The word echoed as he fell.

A horn in the distance. He watched from a rooftop as torches went up in the dark Cardinal's palace, signaling that the attempt on Estav's life had been detected.

*Madness.*

Acheron jumped from a crow's nest onto a slave galley's deck, carried through the impact by *Forte*, the sigil of strength. Abrasax landed right beside him, laughing.

*Madness.*

Acheron sat behind a grimy attic window. Below, the hangman pulled the lever, and Lagrima Soulsnake fell down the hatch, the snap of her neck deafening over the cheers of the crowd. The hangman pulled the lever again. Lagrima's body was replaced by Hammer Stoneblade's limp form. A sneer of defiance still lurked on the muscular Biori's face in death. One by one, Acheron watched the only family he'd ever had swing.

Madness.

He gasped. Dank air flooded his lungs as the barrow came into view around him once more. Then came the stinging. A violent burn on his face, chest, and arms. Acheron spat blood. He'd done it again.

His hands were stained with fresh blood, torn skin lodged underneath grimy fingernails. His forearms looked like a shark had mistaken them for a seal. Deep gouges ran up to his elbow. Luckily, there wasn't a single

## CHAPTER 9

mirror in the barrow. That way, he wouldn't have to worry about what his face looked like. It couldn't have gotten that much worse, anyway.

When he looked up, his heart sank. They were all still there, glaring at him.

"Go away." Salty blood dripped into his open mouth as he screamed. "It's over. Go away."

The ethereal shapes didn't budge. They were supposed to vanish. The dose he'd cooked up ought to have blasted them and every memory of them into the ninth sphere of oblivion. He'd used far more shaderoot than necessary. A deliberately dangerous amount of it. It hadn't been enough. To make matters worse, he'd sprinkled his last crumbs of cloud into the brew.

Acheron stared at the white stain on the bowl's bottom with the sort of grief a normal person might reserve for when a beloved pet got squashed under a passing cartwheel.

*"What's little Achie going to do now? Achie's happy powder is all gone."* He'd only been a boy when he'd last heard that cruel, mocking voice, but no matter how hard he tried, there was no getting rid of the woman who'd birthed him.

He closed his eyes and clamped his bloody hands over his ears. He needed to think before the inevitable spiral began. Usually the solution would be to mix up a second batch, which would knock him out long enough for the ceaseless hallucinations to simmer down to a manageable level. Now, with most of his shaderoot and all of his cloud gone, he might have to hunker down for the night and ride out the horrors the hard way. He didn't like the idea of that one bit. He'd given up the hard way long ago.

"Achie's pouting again." His mother tsk'd. "Useless brat. Always whining and moping."

This wouldn't work. He couldn't stomach another word of it. He jumped up, staring wildly around the cavernous room. There were more of them now. Every man, woman, and child he'd failed over the years. Dozens of them.

Acheron charged forward, darting between the shapes on his way out of the barrow. When the heavy door thumped shut behind him, he started running. He ran like his life depended on it, desperate to leave them all behind—only to see more white shapes spring into life between the trees ahead of him.

# CHAPTER 10

*12th day of the 11th cycle, 569KR*
**God's Maul**

"I wish the good Cardinal would have notified us of this visit in advance."

Solana nodded, unsure where exactly she ought to look when addressing the masked man in order to look him in the eye. The warden's tone was slimy enough to grease a cartwheel, but underneath he seemed irritated. Or nervous. Wilhelmus Bibber had been the head of God's Maul for four decades now, and he clearly saw the prison as an isolated state where he had total power. Solana would have to correct that little misunderstanding.

"As will become apparent, this matter could not wait." She followed the man up three flights of stairs. By the time the warden held open a heavy steel door for her, her forehead was beading with sweat. Years of skipping training in favor of prayer were taking their toll. The air inside the fortress was dank, hot, and devoid of oxygen. How the warden breathed at all underneath those layers of black cloth was a mystery.

Bibber's office took up an entire floor of the central tower. It was easily sixty feet in diameter, giving it a hollow atmosphere. Near the far wall stood a giant mahogany desk, laden with thick leather-bound ledgers and scrolls of parchment. Behind it, a series of bookcases held hundreds, if not thousands, of identically bound records.

The black walls were completely barren except for a single arched window that stretched from floor to ceiling. Thick metal bars blocked most of what would have been an impressive view of the ocean.

"So what *exactly* is it that brings you here, Your Purity?" The warden sat down in an ornate armchair behind his desk and gestured for Solana to grab one of three smaller and plainer chairs on the other side. She nodded,

## CHAPTER 10

but opted to remain standing. She wouldn't allow Bibber to tower over her like he'd obviously intended.

"I take it that news of recent events in the Enclave at Mallion's Depth has reached you?"

"It has." Bibber rubbed his gloved hands together.

"Then you know why I am here, do you not?" Solana took a step closer to the desk, leveraging the height she had over the man.

Bibber looked up at her, his masked face cast in shadow by the relief on that atrocious helmet of his.

"Azaria Oldenbreeze lived under your supervision for nigh on a decade. Yet, she was able to manifest not one, not two, but *three* shapes of power in front of almost two thousand outwalled. In fact, she would have gotten away had it not been for Brother Methusal's rapid response with a flash rod." Solana put both of her hands on the desk, leaning over the warden. "As a supposed expert on the capture and containment of sigilists, how do you think that was possible?"

Bibber's fingers tapped against the desktop.

"Well, Your Purity, it has been well-documented that accomplished sigilists can hold on to their power stores for some time after they have been placed into isolation."

"A decade hardly qualifies as '*some time,*' does it?"

"I suppose it is quite a bit longer than—"

"It is long enough to assume that there are holes in your security protocols." Solana had a hard time sympathizing with the weaselly warden. He'd ramble on until the second Sundering before admitting fault. "Has Miss Oldenbreeze's cell been investigated yet?"

The warden hesitated, then shook his head.

"Excellent." Solana smiled. "You will lead me there at once."

\*\*\*

*12th day of the 11th cycle, 569KR*
**Doorstep's Ditch**

By the time Acheron reached Doorstep's Ditch, he felt like he was the focal point of the world's most pathetic parade. Everywhere he looked, pale figures marched, crawled, and floated alongside him. It looked like he was storming the village with a translucent army.

He entered Wicket Row, then turned right toward the beach district. Decades ago, the Ditch's shanties had spilled off the beach and into the ocean. Improvised pontoon bridges made of empty barrels, driftwood, and a hefty helping of rope bobbed up and down a good two hundred yards into open water. Even by outwalled standards, it was a dangerous and miserable place to live.

Acheron's stomach churned as his feet left the reassuring solidity of the beach. The pontoon creaked as he placed his weight on it. The stink of saltwater and seaweed rushed up his nostrils. Even this close to shore, the walkway wobbled alarmingly. Acheron stared at the horizon, where dozens of floating houses stuck out of the ocean. He'd have to go all the way out there to find the man he was looking for. His stomach churned at the thought. *Now, now,* he reminded himself in an uncharacteristic moment of optimism, *with any luck you'll trip and stumble straight into a shark's open jaws before you get there.*

As he inched his way down a series of increasingly slippery wooden boards, he passed dozens of canvas huts. Most were simple structures, consisting of sloops with a piece of old sail on top. The only thing keeping them from drifting off to the edge of the world were ropes tied to posts nailed to the pontoons. Acheron suppressed the urge to loosen one of the knots, just to watch chaos unfold. No need. There'd be plenty of that where he was going.

The rising and falling walkways looked deceptively empty in the vague light of the chariots racing across the firmament. An inexperienced traveler might have missed the eyes and ears that clung to his every movement like barnacles to a shipwreck, but Acheron, having been on the other end of the game, knew exactly what was going on.

They were sizing him up, guessing the weight of his purse and the bite of his dagger. There would be at least half a dozen of them. On the bright side, they weren't likely to shoot him in the neck from a distance, lest he fell into the ocean, taking their loot with him.

A grin spread over Acheron's sunken face. He almost wished they'd try. Watching their dumb faces as he lit their crew on fire would certainly brighten his day. He glanced down and spotted Azaria's ghostly form, leering at him from a gap in the boards beneath his feet. Did he really want to add a handful of street urchins to the troupe of spirits that hounded him around the clock?

His amusement left as soon as it had come. Muttering to himself, he

## CHAPTER 10

burned *Forte* and kicked a suspiciously shaky barrel off the walkway just ahead of him. A squeal echoed in the night before it was drowned out by a splash.

Acheron laughed out loud as three boys, no older than fifteen, sprang from the roof of a nearby shack to aid their sinking comrade. Once started, he found it hard to stop. If you looked at it from the right angle, everything about his situation was laughable.

He was a forty-something who'd spent most of his life trying to forget what he'd done to his mother when he was nine, only to become all that she had told him he would become and worse. Now he was down to finding joy in kicking children into the ocean while on his way to visit the most dubious drug dealer in the Sundered Isles.

He was still chuckling when he arrived at the floating palace at the end of the walkway.

A duo of anchored galleons, interconnected by a series of ornate bridges that wouldn't have been out of place in the Cardinal's own gardens, bobbed slowly on the heaving waves. They loomed over the shanties around them like a leviathan amongst a swarm of firejellies. Both sails were painted with the same symbol: a skull with smoke rising from its empty sockets on top of a giant crab.

A rope ladder dangled over the side of the galleon nearest the walkway, flanked by two guards in gleaming leather armor.

"I'm here to see the maestro," Acheron said, holding up his right hand in salute. "My name is—"

"We know who you are, fire-eyes," the lefthand guard barked. "You're lucky. He's still up."

Acheron's stomach roiled as he hoisted himself up the ladder and onto the galleon's deck. He'd never liked heights much, especially not when his limbs were numb with the aftereffects of a double dose of shaderoot.

He found his target on the first bridge, looking out at the first chariot sinking into the horizon.

Even years after their first meeting, Acheron found himself surprised at how small the crime lord was up close.

If they were to bump into each other, the man's short, stumped nose would lodge itself neatly into Acheron's belly button. The man's bald scalp was offset by a long black beard.

The effect might have been comical, had it not been for the richly embroidered black and gold robes on his broad shoulders and the thick rings on each of his fingers. There were few in the Ditch who dared to wear jewelry openly, and Dimimzy Zot was certainly the most brazen of the lot.

Zot grinned as he noticed Acheron's arrival, baring a full set of golden teeth.

"Look who it is"—Zot smacked his lips—"my scarred friend, back again. Yet again." Condescension and glee intermingled in his words like vomit in a latrine.

Zot held out his left ring finger, exposing a ring encrusted with a ruby the size of a toddler's heart.

Acheron swallowed down a rising tide of stomach acid and his pride, then got down on one knee. Zot was so short that Acheron almost had to sink down on all fours to kiss the giant stone. The odors of sandalwood and cinnamon hung in a thick cloud around the man.

"Milord Zot," Acheron said, scrambling to his feet, "I have come to you with a proposal."

"Let me guess, it involves me giving you a substantial amount of product." Zot turned back toward the view he'd been admiring.

A jolt of anxiety shook Acheron as the second chariot sank deeper into the ocean. The dark window was rapidly approaching, and he was still here, bandying words with the tiny tyrant who held all the cards.

"It does." There was no use beating around the bush. There were two types of men who heard so many lies that they learned to read them like a second language: priests and drug dealers. To his clients, Zot was a bit of both. "However, it also involves you receiving a full keg of wampyr venom, which ought to be enough to produce, roughly calculated, an insane amount of high-grade cloud."

"Don't make promises you can't deliver on." Zot's tone grew cold. "You're swaying on your feet, you're sweating, you've licked your lips raw. I know what cloud sickness looks like."

Behind Zot, the second chariot definitively dipped into the ocean, dowsing the entire world in darkness. The dark window had started. At once, a servant rushed to hang a lit lantern on an iron hook above the bridge.

Acheron threw up his hands. "Of course I've got the sickness, Zot. What did you expect would happen when you sold me that rock last month? Did you think I would come back here with a fresh shave smelling like Heildamned potpourri?

"Now, I know for a fact that Karoling Huygen recently got his hands on a set of freshly caught wampyr. You know what he's like. I'd bet what's

## CHAPTER 10

left of my soul that he's been milking them raw. Right now, all that venom is fresh and waiting for us to seize it. If we wait another week or two, he's bound to have milked the poor creatures to death, and much of the venom will have spoiled."

Zot turned around. His face was hard, but there was a twinkle of greed in his squirrelly black eyes. He leaned closer, causing the scent of sandalwood and cinnamon to fill the air once more.

"What are you saying? That you're going to break into the Enclave and then run straight here with half the city's darkhelms on your tail?"

"I'm saying that tomorrow morning, Huygen will wake up to find an empty keg and a puddle beneath it. He will curse himself for not sealing it properly and chalk it up to an expensive mistake. He won't be any the wiser."

Acheron had rarely told a more confident lie. In reality, he would take everything of value he could find in the apothecary. Let Huygen go to the watch. They would never find his hiding place.

The corners of Zot's mouth curled. "Let's say, hypothetically, that you get me this keg. How much cloud would you, hypothetically, have me give you in return?"

"I'd say two fist-sized bricks is a reasonable start."

Zot's jaw tensed. He was clearly trying not to smile. The proposed deal was outrageously in his favor, they both knew that, but a man like Zot took care not to come across as too eager. That was good, because Acheron had a bucket of cold water to dump on his mounting excitement.

"I'll need one of those bricks in advance."

Zot's nostrils flared. "Out of the question."

"You just said it yourself. I'm reeling with cloud sickness. How do you expect me to be at my sneakiest when I have to throw up every five minutes?" Acheron flared *Rhetoris*. To Zot, it would look like he was just trying to underscore his proposal with a display of his unusual powers. Meanwhile, the sigil made his words supernaturally compelling. The effect wasn't unlike that of half a bottle of good kelp. It made everything sound like the greatest idea you'd ever heard.

Zot waved an irritable hand. "Fine, one brick in advance, but if you don't show up with my venom by sunrise, I'll find a keg of the stuff myself and make you drink it."

"It will be my pleasure"—Acheron smiled—"but I suggest we hurry this along. There's not much left of the dark window."

Zot beckoned to no one in particular, and the harried looking servant who'd brought the lantern reappeared. Zot whispered something in the man's ear, and moments later he emerged from the hold below the deck with a silver platter, which held the most beautiful thing Acheron had ever seen, a polished oval brick of cloud, so pure that he could almost see Zot's contorted face as he held it up in front of him.

Before Acheron was done savoring the moment, Zot clapped his hands. "Get off my deck, demon whisperer. I'll see you soon. Hopefully, it will be of your own free will."

\*\*\*

*12th day of the 11th cycle, 569KR*
**God's Maul**

The march from the warden's office to Locktower C was so disorienting that Solana wondered whether she would ever find her way back to fresh air should the navigator escorting her decide to abandon her.

Starting from the main tower, the journey had taken them from one dark, windowless corridor to the next. Each one of them had dozens of identical doors. Solana assumed that most of them lead to dead ends, though sometimes guards appeared from side passages, muttering to each other when they noticed Solana.

"How many of the staff know which doors lead where?" Solana asked the navigator marching beside her. The navigator, whose helmet was shaped like a horned satyr's head, stared straight ahead.

"Only the navigators and the warden." The woman's voice was low and pleasant to the ear, not at all like the satyr's bark Solana had expected. "It's impossible for the guards, or anyone else, to memorize the sequence, as the warden requires us to take a different route each time. Sometimes we make detours to make things even more complicated."

"Don't the guards resent being tricked by their colleagues?" Solana herself certainly wouldn't allow it.

The navigator shrugged. "It's not really a trick. They're well aware of what we're doing. Besides, this arrangement protects them as well. The inmates know the guards rely on us to move around the prison, which makes taking a guard hostage to escape useless."

Solana nodded. "Ingenious."

## CHAPTER 10

Another shrug. "Secrets breed loneliness."

The navigator held up her massive key ring with dozens of thick metal keys, carefully selected one, then opened a door that led to a narrow, winding staircase. She motioned for Solana to start upward.

As they climbed, the air grew increasingly stuffy. The smell of sweat and excrement came to the forefront as Solana stepped out onto a landing that held a single rusty door.

"We're here," the navigator said. She opened the door and stood aside, beckoning for Solana to pass. When the navigator tried to close the door behind her, Solana jammed her foot in the crack.

"Aren't you supposed to lead me back later?"

The navigator shook her head. "The warden ordered someone else to pick you up in an hour. Good luck."

The door clicked shut. Solana's heart raced. She was stuck. For at least an hour, she would be trapped in Locktower C. Doom scenarios formed on the edges of her mind. If she were in Bibber's shoes, would she risk making an emissary of the Cardinal disappear? The answer was more complicated than she liked to admit.

Was this how Lady Azaria had felt every hour of every day since her capture? It was a wonder the woman had stayed sane for that long. But to emerge from her cell with such powerful stores of sorcery intact? That kind of debacle could only be caused by something far more terrifying than wonders: complacency.

If the stink of human waste had been present in the staircase, it reigned over the central corridor of Locktower C with an iron fist. Solana was glad that her helmet obscured the faces she pulled as rank sweat and urine made her eyes water.

She stood in a circular room in the center of the tower, her back pressed against the door the navigator had so worryingly closed on her moments earlier.

The curved walls held one set of bars after another, behind which lay the dark prisoners' cells. It was like standing in the middle of a pie, with each slice representing a single prisoner's living space.

Four guards sat at a round table in the center of the room, playing Galleons.

"I swear, Dorian, you draw one more griffin, and I'm done."

Solana cleared her throat, causing the man named Dorian to drop a fistful of cards. They fluttered to the ground like a cloud of butterflies.

Dorian glared at her and opened his mouth, then his eyes locked on to the emblem on the front of her robes, and he closed it again.

"Your Purity," one of the others began, making a tiny bow that looked more like a nod. The woman's hair was woven into two black braids, and her helmet lay abandoned underneath her chair. "What brings you here?"

"I wish to enter Lady Azaria's cell."

All four guards shuffled nervously.

"I assure you, Your Purity, it was searched thoroughly, both during and after the lady's incarceration." The woman gave another bow, a proper one this time.

Not being fond of having to repeat herself, Solana gave the woman a glare that could have withered a rosebush in bloom.

"It's fine, Serene," the man named Dorian said. "Her Purity is welcome to confirm that we have done our due diligence."

He stood up and beckoned Solana over to a set of bars on the eastern side of the tower. Dorian riffled through a collection of seemingly identical brass keys, carefully selecting one. The lock opened with a pop.

"Take all the time you need, Your Purity." Dorian bowed and stepped back to allow Solana to enter the cell.

Solana's nostrils burned as she stepped onto a layer of soiled straw that covered the rectangular cell's stone floor. Old urine mingled with the sickly-sweet stench of rot. There was no bunk, merely a depressed section of straw where Oldenbreeze had slept on the floor night after night. Solana resisted the urge to dry heave as she spotted a wooden bucket in the corner, still half full of human waste. The entire prison was a breeding ground for every sort of plague imaginable. She wouldn't touch a single thing here.

"Was the straw searched?" she demanded, looking over her shoulder at Dorian.

He nodded. "We combed through it, but the warden ordered us to leave it where it was. He said we had to keep everything in its original condition until he'd contacted Mallion's Depth."

"Maybe he's not as stupid as he looks, after all." Solana grinned, but then realized that the man couldn't see her face underneath her helmet. "Anyway, I'd like you to remove it. Slowly. Handfuls at a time."

For a moment, Dorian looked like he might protest, but then he nodded. He summoned two of his colleagues. Under Solana's watchful eye, the guards began removing clumps of matted, moist straw from the cell and throwing it down a waste disposal chute on the side of the tower.

## CHAPTER 10

When the cell's stained floor lay bare, Solana crouched, examining the stonework for signs of the demonic symbols that made up power shapes. There was nothing to be found.

"So far, so good," she told Dorian. Her eyes roved the walls and ceiling. Nothing there.

She took a deep breath and mentally listed all the facts. Oldenbreeze had been detained many years ago, meaning any power that may still have been stored inside her mind ought to have fizzled out long before the Scarlet Nocturne. Besides, all prisoners were flashed with a silver rod upon arrival and at random intervals during their sentence. That meant Oldenbreeze had recharged her powers recently. Sometime close to the execution.

There had to be something they were missing. Solana's eye fell on the bucket filled with mushy excrement and instinctively wrinkled her nose. It had to be done. Just to be sure.

"Mr. Dorian, pour out the contents of that bucket on the floor."

"Excuse me?"

Solana jabbed a finger at the bucket. Repeating herself would make her look weak.

With a sigh, Dorian crossed the cell and dumped out the brown sludge.

An unbearable stench filled the room. Solana's eyes watered. Her meager dinner crawled back up her throat. Dorian retched openly. Solana steeled herself and bent forward to ensure no objects were hidden in the filth. Again, nothing. There had to be something she was missing, and she wasn't giving up until she had found it. There was no margin for error when it came to His Eminence De Leliard's trust.

"What's the protocol for emptying these?"

"Twice a week," Dorian said in between bouts of gagging. "They're poured down the trash chute along with the soiled straw."

"Demonstrate, please."

Dorian scurried out of the cell and made a show of tipping the already empty bucket down the chute. Then he turned on his heel and shoved the bucket through a small gap in the bars of Azaria Oldenbreeze's cell.

"That's how we do it. We never open the doors for anything less than a full search. We flash the prisoners before and after our entry into the cell."

Solana looked down into the soiled bucket. Though mostly empty, the sides and bottom of the bucket were caked in a thick layer of filth. She smiled. *Gotcha.*

She ordered Dorian to wipe the inside of the bucket clean with a rag. The man's protests withered under her glare.

As soon as the rag brushed away the grime on the underside of the bucket, thick grooves in the wood became visible. A wavy symbol with interlinking bends and circles.

"How did you know?" Dorian asked. His disgusted expression changed to horror as a second, and finally a third, symbol surfaced.

"It was the only place no one would ever look."

* * *

*12th day of the 11th cycle, 569KR*
**Doorstep's Ditch**

The dark window had all but run its course when Acheron reached the foot of the Enclave's wall. Aided by a healthy dose of *Forte,* he wriggled his fingers into the cracks between the large boulders that made up the twenty-foot-tall structure and began climbing.

He felt exposed, hanging from the wall at a height that few buildings in Doorstep's Ditch reached. Once the dark window was over, all anyone had to do was look up, and they'd be able to spot him from streets away. That just meant he'd have to get a move on.

When he reached the top of the wall, he peered over the edge and saw a pair of darkhelms marching his way. It took far too much of his *Forte* store to cling onto a narrow slit in the rock while he waited for the guards to pass. His forearms burned and a fresh wave of nausea hit him like a punch to the gut.

As soon as the guards had passed, he threw his legs up over the edge, skittered across the top of the wall, then blindly dropped himself over the other side. His feet hit the cobbles below with a force that would have shattered his legs up to the knee if it hadn't been for a last-second flare of *Forte.*

He felt the store extinguish as he straightened his back. That didn't bode well. He'd have to count on his own unaided strength for the journey back, which even an optimist would consider lacking. Those were concerns for the distant future, however. If he was spotted wriggling open the front door of Huygen's Herbs and Tinctures, the darkhelms' windups would find him in a heartbeat. *Let's pray for a fatal shot.*

Acheron crept along the edge of the Enclave, hugging the shadowy

## CHAPTER 10

inner side of the wall. By the time he reached the back of the apothecary, he'd counted eight guards in pairs of two. Each of them seemed to pay little attention to what happened behind them. They obviously expected any intruders to be caught long before they reached the inner courtyard.

Acheron crept along the apothecary's stone wall, then dipped into the portal that held the front door. Keenly aware that he was visible to any attentive eye, he knelt in front of the lock and retrieved his metal tools from his pocket. Lockpicking was a subtle art. It required full engagement of all the senses and continuous, thorough, study of technique. *Or* one could burn *Praece* and cheat their way through the process in moments. As a matter of principle, Acheron cheated wherever possible.

As he touched *Praece*, the complex labyrinth of its shape burst to life in his mind's eye. He withdrew his lockpicks and inserted them into the keyhole. As he moved his tools, sensing the lock's shape, a three-dimensional diagram appeared in his mind's eye. It took only a moment to identify a weak spring. Acheron forced a thin pick behind it and pulled on it. There was a snap as the spring jumped out of place. Huygen's front door opened.

He slipped inside the dark store. He burned *Lux,* making his eyes unnaturally sensitive to the faintest remnants of lights. Huygen's interior came into view.

*So much death.* To Acheron's left, a stuffed sheikan loomed over him from atop a marble pedestal. The creature's mouth was propped open, but nothing remained of the intimidating snarl it had worn in life.

With each shaky step, the floorboards creaked beneath Acheron's feet. He stopped for a moment to investigate a display of jars of ground up trihorn. Near the back of the store, a crate overflowed with fresh griffin feathers.

There were only five or six griffin nests a year on the island. Acheron hated to think how many chicks would be needed to fill a crate like this. Not to mention the fact that griffin feathers were, for all intents and purposes, useless.

There were rumors that they were lighter than air, or that they made anyone who consumed them see sharper. Neither of those were true, but that wouldn't keep an old miser like Huygen from exploiting the gullible and lining his pockets while the last remaining griffins on Hammerstroke died a silent death. On the plus side, Huygen's destructive greed made it all the easier on Acheron's already meager conscience to rob the man blind.

Acheron stepped behind the counter, where a dusty mahogany cabinet held rows upon rows of small glass trays, each of them labeled alphabetically with a thin strip of parchment.

He took all the shaderoot, five vials of water snake venom, an entire pouch of fleetleaf. Having ensured that he had enough ingredients to make months' worth of his special brew, he filled up his pockets with an assortment of random vials and powders. Most of them weren't especially useful to Acheron, but the thought that he might inconvenience Huygen by stealing them was all the incentive he needed.

He'd turned to leave when he remembered the deal he'd made with Zot. *The venom.*

There had been no sign of it in the display room, which meant that either the apothecary was still collecting it, or he had already sold it. Acheron's mouth went dry. He'd been so focused on convincing Zot to lend him a supply of cloud that he hadn't been concerned with whether he could actually deliver on his promise.

He knelt down behind the counter, his knee pressed painfully against the stone floor. There was a trapdoor here somewhere. Acheron had seen the apothecary vanish down it a few years earlier, back when he still bothered to visit stores when they were open and to pay for what he needed. Needlessly complicated, when you thought about it.

A smile spread across his face as his fingers curled around a steel ring. It took all his strength to lift the thick stone slab. Panting, he crouched to peer into the cellar underneath. The stench made him gag immediately. The air was ripe with the desperate sourness of animals made to live in their own filth. Then there was the screeching. A high-pitched wailing that tore the night like a dagger through flesh. *They think I'm Huygen, and they're terrified.*

There was no time to waste. The guards on the wall might've already heard the racket the wretched creatures were making. He had to get out of there *with* Zot's venom before the idiots put two and two together and came barging in. Acheron climbed down into the dark cellar, retching as the full force of dozens of uncleaned cages in a confined space hit him.

The wampyr were squeezed into cages that barely fit their bodies, let alone their limbs. They sat with their thin legs stretched out between the iron bars, which almost allowed them to lie down. All of them were screaming their misshapen heads off.

Acheron's heart skipped a beat when he noticed two sealed ceramic vases

## CHAPTER 10

in the corner next to the last cage. One whiff of the acrid liquid inside confirmed that they contained freshly tapped wampyr venom.

He raced up the ladder with the fullest of the two vases tucked underneath his arm. Just before he replaced the stone slab that sealed the cellar, he glanced backward at the pitiful creatures wailing in the dark below. They would die in that cellar, most of them before the week was out.

Acheron swallowed, then sealed the hatch.

Glass jars rattled as he sprinted past them toward the front door. He'd done it. He'd actually done it. One more stop at Zot's galleon, and he'd be back in his barrow, ready to brew up the meanest batch of...

"Hands up!"

The sudden light of a lantern scorched his *Lux*-enhanced eyes. Everything disappeared in a white haze.

Two pairs of powerful hands forced his arms behind his back before he could respond. The vase of venom shattered on the cobbles below. He blinked furiously, trying to regain some sense of what was going on around him.

The first thing he saw was a windup aimed straight at his chest. A darkhelm. Seven or eight of them. He tried to burn *Forte*, then remembered his store had run out. *Sigh*. The old-fashioned way would have to do. Acheron thrashed and jerked his arms free. His captors were knocked off balance for a split second. This was his chance. A tiny window of opportunity to—

A bolt penetrated Acheron's gut with a blunt thud. He sank to his knees.

"Enough with the nonsense," a gruff voice barked in his ear. The cool metal of a dagger pressed against his neck, right in the hollow underneath his jaw, where a single push would sever all his major arteries.

Acheron let out a long sigh. One moment it had seemed like the stars had finally aligned, the next he was kneeling in a puddle of stinking venom with a brand-new second belly button, courtesy of a loose fingered bowman.

He raised his hands.

"I told you the tip was good, didn't I?" a female voice piped up. "My mistress's source hasn't been wrong yet."

# CHAPTER 11

*13th day of the 11th cycle, 569KR*
**Doorstep's Ditch**

"Turn that smile upside down, Baron. You stick out like a Reynziel among honest men." Brina clutched her windup to her chest as the cart ambled down the last stretch of the trail. Ahead of them, a single muddy strip of road known as Wicket Row split Doorstep's Ditch down the middle.

"Excellent point, Miss Sabrina," said Baron Don Lonzo De Malheur in his cordial boom. "Truly a shame to see what our great nation has turned into, where one has to resort to mean mugging and petty threats to avoid harassment." He raised a dramatic hand to his brow, inspecting the driftwood and canvas shanties ahead as though they were his very own army camped out before a heroic battle. "Alas, alas. Gone are the days where one's noble blood commanded respect."

He sounded *almost* dignified. De Malheur's idea of what a nobleman sounded like came solely from the third-rate novels and sonnets he devoured as though they were honeyed strawberries. He wouldn't decline the strawberries either, if you offered him any. De Malheur had been born in Doorstep's Ditch just like everyone else, and despite his best efforts, he had never quite shaken the rum-and-hard-labor accent of his upbringing. That he would never be allowed to step one foot inside the stoneward didn't seem to discourage his efforts to portray himself as a man of noble blood. To him, life was one big adventure novel in which he was the main character.

Like his made-up dialect, De Malheur's dress was cobbled together from homemade replications of six-century-old illustrations and whatever scraps he had traded for that looked "royal" to him. He wore a doublet sewn from jute sacks over puffy black breeches, both of which fought hard to hold on to their buttons.

## CHAPTER 11

The most authentically kingly thing about him were his leather shoes with ridiculously curled tips with bells attached. Those might have belonged to an actual court jester once. To top it off, he insisted on wearing a crudely wrought iron crown. Put together, De Malheur looked like a ripe purse on legs.

In the past, Brina had often smirked behind the man's back, but over the years, he'd become a reliable source of generously paid work and something akin to a friend. Funny how these things worked out. Even budding rebels needed to eat. The floorboard fund would only stretch so far, and Brina would need every shard.

Brina had spent most nights this week sitting on the mill's roof, carefully marking down the movements of the lights drifting across the bay. It hadn't been until yesterday evening that something interesting happened. Just after dusk, she'd spotted a lone vessel entering God's Maul, possibly a galleon loaded with provisions. A few hours after its arrival, it had returned to Mallion's Depth. The gates to the fortress had remained closed since.

Nervous energy tingled in Brina's limbs as she mulled over her observations for the hundredth time. No matter which way she looked at it, the entire operation hinged on whether she could get past that gatehouse unseen. And even if she pulled that off, she'd have to locate her father, improvise a way to free him, *and* get past the gatehouse a second time with her father in tow. The more she thought about it, the worse the odds seemed.

"Oh my," De Malheur exclaimed. "What in Carralnar's crown is this?" Shaken from her daydream, Brina instinctively raised her windup. Then she saw what had rattled the baron.

Three children sat beside the street. The oldest, a girl no older than nine, was using a jagged hunting knife to gut the carcass of a stray cat, while the other two fed splinters of broken crate to a fledgling fire.

Brina lowered the bow, partly relieved that they weren't being ambushed, partly embarrassed that she'd allowed herself to get caught off guard.

"That, Baron, is called hunger," she said, watching the children squabble over who could roast the first piece of feline. "It's somewhat of a local tradition."

"Well, I find it quite distasteful."

Brina shrugged. "It's not that bad. Tastes like chicken."

De Malheur shuddered.

"I suppose that's the sort of insight into the world of the commoner I pay you for, but please, speak no more of the matter. I fear my stomach will rebel."

A chuckle escaped Brina. De Malheur had lived in these same streets as a boy, before he'd gotten lost in the jungle and stumbled into the ruin of an ancient tower house by accident. Inside, he'd spent three delirious days poring over what remained of the tower's library. By the time a search party had tracked him down, Geoff Mudbreeches had lost twenty-five pounds and gained the persona of "the Baron." No amount of pleading and reasoning could convince him to leave the ruins, and he'd lived in them ever since.

De Malheur described his ordeal as "divine intervention, calling upon me to return to the greatness of my forefathers." Brina called it "dumb luck." Emphasis on *dumb*. Despite his bumbling demeanor, De Malheur had gathered a small fortune over the years by acting as a middleman between traders from the North Settlement of Hammerstroke and the outwalled of Doorstep's Ditch. He specialized in commodities that required elaborate workshops and a skilled hand, such as expertly woven ropes and nets, cloth and mining equipment.

Driving a cart with two real, healthy horses through Doorstep's Ditch was equivalent to running through the streets naked while singing sea shanties at the top of your lungs. You were certain to draw every eye in a two-mile radius.

Brina rested an ostentatious hand on her windup, ensuring that the weapon was plainly visible to anyone entertaining unsavory thoughts. *Good thing only amateurs are looking for targets at this time of day.*

Then again, all it took was one amateur with the bright idea to inform one of the real gangs of their presence. They had no chance against a coordinated attack. Brina's connections might be enough to protect her life, but they wouldn't keep anyone from taking everything De Malheur owned and spilling the contents of his belly onto his pointy shoes. The man might be laughable, but he was harmless and, in his own way, a far better man than most in the Ditch.

The horses struggled to gain traction in the deepening muck, slowing their pace further. In the distance, Mallion's gate came into view. The yellow sandstone of the stoneward glittered in the morning sun, making the shoddy buildings that lined Wicket Row seem even more drab than usual. The Enclave was close now. If they could unload De Malheur's cargo at a lightning pace, they might still be fine.

## CHAPTER 11

When they reached the split in Wicket Row that led to Mallion's gate to the left and the Enclave to the right, Brina spotted a crowd gathered in front of the ward. At first she thought she must have missed the announcement of a new batch of outwalled to be sent into the Ditch. Then she saw people pointing upward. Though the spectacle was too far off to make out the details, it looked like something metal hung high in the air above the crowd. It swayed in the wind, reflecting the light of the sun in short bursts. Then it clicked. The old gibbets.

Though they had been out of use for as long as Brina could remember, a series of rusty cages hung all along the outer edge of the stoneward. For centuries, they had been a warning sign to wallfolk and outwalled alike, a scare tactic for those who considered committing the most grievous offense of all: heresy.

Brina put a hand on De Malheur's arm to make him stop the cart.

"I'll be right back."

De Malheur's protests were drowned out by the rising murmurs of a crowd that was rapidly expanding in front of the gate.

"They say he was with a sorcerer," a young girl told her little brother. The two of them gaped up, awestruck.

"Don't be silly," their mother snapped. "The last sorcerers were locked up a decade ago." She craned her neck to get a good look over the heads of the crowd all the same. Beside her, her husband shook his head with the air of a man who'd just stepped onto a slug with his bare foot.

"Zot must have finally put an entire foot over the line instead of his usual toe or two," he said. "The other fellow was probably in the wrong place at the wrong time."

Brina elbowed her way past the man and looked up. The small man in the left cage was undoubtedly Zot. He glared down at the crowd in silence. He looked at the same time horrified to find himself in the position he was in, and utterly furious. A young man wearing a sailor's cap yelled out at him: "Not so tough now, are you, little man?"

Zot raised his eyebrows, then spat a ball of phlegm right onto the kid's forehead with an accuracy the Cardinal's best bowmen could only pray for. Zot's cackling laugh worked infectiously on the onlookers, many of whom began spitting on the bewildered young man in a show of solidarity rarely seen among the outwalled. *Then again, they do love to spit on people.*

Brina was thinking of returning to De Malheur before he got himself stabbed, when the wind spun the other cage around and the face of the prisoner inside made her choke on her own spit.

Acheron. His scarred face was pale and caked with blood and dirt, but it was undeniably him. If it hadn't been for the occasional convulsions that seized his body, Brina would have thought him dead.

She forced her way through the crowd to get as close as she could. Her voice scraped painfully as she called out his name. She didn't care who heard or saw. There was a moment where it seemed like he heard. His eyelids twitched, and he tried to sit upright. Then another wave of convulsions rocked his body, and he went limp.

*He won't make it through the night if he has to spend it in there.*

Brina turned around, willing her heart to turn to stone. He was dead. She would just have to accept that. A dead squid twitches when you sprinkle it with salt. That doesn't mean it's come back to life.

Then she heard laughter around her. Hundreds of laughing, jeering voices poking fun at the suffering of one of their own. One moment they had righteously joined Zot in his assault on the kid in the sailor's cap, now they were back to taunting him. Brina knew how they felt.

It was the relief of knowing that, at least today, the axe had fallen on someone else. Tomorrow, any of the laughing and hooting outwalled around her could be face down in a puddle of mud with their throats slit, or hanging from the next gibbet. They knew that, and so they cheered. They might as well have chanted "Not me, Heil be praised, it's not me."

Before anything could change, that hopelessness, that feeling of life balancing on a blade's edge, needed to go. De Leliard's power didn't lie in blades, or quarrels, or cages. It lay in the minds of all those who believed that resistance was futile.

The outwalled needed a miracle. Heil, they needed a dozen miracles. They had to see before they would believe that things could be different. When they woke up tomorrow, that cage had to be empty. Brina felt it as clearly and surely as she had known anything in her life.

It wasn't about Acheron, not fully. Brina simply couldn't stomach standing by one more time as a life was stamped out in front of her. She had stood by and watched Azaria die. She wouldn't allow her father's last friend to suffer the same fate.

There was more to Acheron than he'd shown her, more perhaps than even he remembered. Whatever skulked behind those burning eyes, it wasn't allowed to fade. Not yet.

# CHAPTER 12

*13th day of the 11th cycle, 569KR*
**Doorstep's Ditch**

As the second chariot began its descent into the curling waves of the Sundered Sea, Brina's nerves jangled. It was almost time.

As soon as the dark window arrived, she'd have to jump into action. Dark clouds hung over the Ditch. The air outside was thick and oppressive. Left and right, people were boarding up windows and doors to prepare for what was predicted to be the most violent storm to hit the island this year. The clanking of hammers rang out in the night like the tolling of a hundred discordant alarm bells. *Just what I needed. More dread.*

Versa had been kind enough to let Brina stay in an unoccupied room on the third floor of The Wistful Chimera. She'd much prefer a night spent here over her own plans for the evening.

A bed with a straw-filled mattress and two cozy blankets was tucked away between the wall and the slope of the roof. Overhead, an oil lantern dangled from the rafters, casting a halo of quivering light on the wooden floor. Through the square window set into the inn's roof, Brina had a clear view of Mallion's gate and the two prisoners' cages rocking back and forth in the swelling breeze.

Acheron hadn't stirred in hours. It had taken Brina most of the afternoon to drop De Malheur off safely beyond the boundaries of the Ditch, after which she'd all but sprinted back to the mill to pick up supplies for what was undoubtedly going to end up being the most idiotic stunt she'd ever attempted. By the time she'd reached the Chimera, dusk had fallen, and Acheron's shape had gone eerily limp.

Brina leaned back in her chair. Her stomach growled, but she didn't dare eat. The nerves would make it all come back up anyway, and it would be a real shame if she got caught because she was spraying vomit like a gargoyle a hundred feet off the ground. Besides, she'd had roasted pheasant with the baron for breakfast, and that seemed as good a last meal as any.

There was a flash of sapphire light as the second chariot dove under the surface.

*Here we go.*

\*\*\*

In the complete blackout of the dark window, even the quick sprint toward the gate became a challenge. Then again, that was the entire point. For the next thirty minutes, she would be invisible in her black cloak. That would be enough to get her part of the way up. How she would get down with a fully grown, unconscious man draped across her shoulders was a worry for later.

Brina's outstretched hands reached the cool, rough surface of the stoneward. It was a good thing she couldn't see the sheer height of the thing. *Can't look down if I can't see.*

Scaling the smooth sandstone surface was very low on the list of things Brina wanted to do. She'd climbed plenty of cliffs to steal harrow-wing eggs or harvest stone stars, but nothing this sheer and never in the dark.

She retrieved a pouch filled with pitons and a hammer from the top of her pack, then threw it back over her shoulders. Something inside squirmed against her back.

"Shh, I know, it's scary, but you'll just have to cope for a while."

Brina reached up and wedged her fingers in a groove between two of the monstrous bricks that made up the ward. There was no way back now. As soon as her feet left the ground, she felt like she was climbing in a boundless void. She could be three feet from the ground or thirty. There was no way to tell. *Excellent. What I can't see, can't muddy my breeches.*

She worked her way up slowly and methodically, trying not to think about her rapidly passing window of opportunity. *One hand up, wedge it in, other hand up, left foot, right foot.*

With each tentative step up, the tips of her boots threatened to slip off the tiny edges between the bricks. Each grain of sand felt like a smooth marble, rolling back and forth under her sole.

After what felt like an eternity, Brina hit a dead end. She reached up blindly, her fingertips clawing at the smooth surface of the rock for an

## CHAPTER 12

edge or crack, anything at all to latch on to. There was nothing. The ward was entirely smooth, whichever direction she tried.

Panic welled up in her guts and spread to her limbs like the paralyzing sting of firejelly venom. Every fiber in her body tensed. Had that foothold always felt that slippery? Though she couldn't see the ground, she was certainly high enough for a fall to result in her immediate and gruesome demise.

*Think, Springtide, think.* With one sweaty hand wedged into a groove at her waist, she reached for a piton with the other. She planted its sharp end into a shallow pocket in the rock just overhead, then realized she'd need a second hand to hammer it in place. Great, she was going to be a mangled corpse on the cobbles below.

She could almost see it, a tangled knot of bones and guts with a nice little halo of useless pitons scattered around the squashed watermelon that had once been her head.

Brina sighed. She'd made peace with the fact that she had a one in a hundred chance of making it through the night alive, but she'd pictured the end to be just a smidgen more... *glorious* than this. There was supposed to be a melancholy beauty to dying for the cause. One last roar before storming into a hail of arrows. That sort of thing. As far as she was aware, rebel heroes rarely died because their hands got sweaty.

More out of desperation than ingenuity, she began twisting the piton's point, trying to drill it deeper into the pocket. A trickle of sand rained down, sticking to her sweaty arms and crawling down the back of her neck. When she felt her other hand slipping from the hold at her waist, she launched herself up with one final desperate lunge. It held. The damn thing actually held.

Before the seven patron saints of the outwalled could change their minds about sparing her, Brina reached for the hammer on her belt and gave the piton three solid whacks. Each impact echoed loudly off the wall, but the relief of not suffering an excruciating end trumped any other concerns.

When the first chariot reappeared at the horizon, casting its tentative light over Hammerstroke, Brina found she was within touching distance of the heavy metal rods that held the cages in place.

From the ground it had looked like the gibbets hung right up against the wall; up close they were at least six feet too far away for Brina to reach.

"Acheron," she whispered, "wake up, I'm getting you out of here."

It wasn't Acheron who responded.

"Well, if that isn't the most pleasant surprise I've ever laid eyes on." Dimimzy Zot grinned. He sat with his hands clasped around the bars of his cage. A wicked gleam twinkled in his black eyes. Though he clearly hadn't shaved or washed in days, he looked otherwise completely at ease in the situation.

Brina ignored him. She called Acheron again, but couldn't get him to wake up.

"I'm afraid that one's a little worse for wear," Zot said, his voice ripe with sarcastic concern. He crossed his eyes and circled his temples with his fingers. "The cloud's gotten to him."

"Shut up," Brina hissed. "The darkhelms will hear."

"Wouldn't that be an absolute shame?" Zot's voice grew louder. "I would hate to impede your plan to rescue Floaty over there while leaving me to rot. I have so much to lose by alerting the watch to your presence... oh wait—" He threw up his hands, eyes widening in theatrical shock. "I don't."

Brina stared into those malevolent eyes, wishing she had her windup with her so she could silence the rat before he could do any more damage. As it stood, however, he had a point. He had nothing to lose and everything to gain.

"Fine, I'll let you out after—"

Zot clucked his tongue. "Do you think I'm stupid? You'll free me first, or I swear to the Seven that I will sing like a sailor on his third bottle of kelp."

Brina's jaw clenched. Nobody talked to her like that. But there was no time for pride now. The first chariot was climbing the firmament at a breakneck pace, its light growing more distinct as it went.

She loosened her pack and plunged a hand into it. Her secret weapon squirmed and fought as her fingers closed around its scaly skin.

"What's *that*?" Zot's voice shifted up a pitch.

The tinhead's metal scales clicked softly as it coiled its serpentine body around Brina's forearm. Its head was wide and flat, shaped like a horse's hoof.

"This is your key out of here, and you best hope it's still hungry after I'm done getting you out."

Brina swung one leg over the steel rod and began pulling herself across with her free hand. The tinhead immediately began writhing against her forearm, struggling to get to the metal.

When she reached the cage, Brina extended her arm. The tinhead unfurled its long body and sank its razor teeth into the nearest bar as easily as if it were an apple.

"This better not be an attempt to poison me. I know who you are, Springtide."

"Don't worry, it doesn't eat rat."

Zot chuckled and sat back as the tinhead did its work. The serpent chewed through the bars in minutes.

"Amazing. Bring me a dozen of those, and I'll reward you handsomely," Zot said, his eyes lighting up. He picked up a loose piece of the bar and tucked it into his waistband. "I'm getting out of here. Good luck getting the cloudfiend down in one piece."

Without another word, Zot scurried across the metal rod and began his descent.

By the time Brina reached Acheron's cage, Zot was already halfway down.

"There's someone down there." A carrying whisper on the battlements overhead made Brina's heart freeze. The clock had run out. She squeezed the tinhead's body, urging it to chomp through the bars quicker. The snake hissed and snapped at Brina.

"Nonsense, let me see." A wild face appeared over the side of the wall.

Brina's terror turned to confusion as she noticed the traditional metal skulls woven into the man's foot-long ginger beard. The warrior's milky skin seemed to glow in the night. *Since when did the darkhelms enlist Biori?*

She pulled free a loose bar and used it to jab Acheron in the ribs as hard as she could. He groaned, his hand swatting uselessly at the air.

"Wake up, you useless sack of squid ink." Brina didn't bother keeping her voice down anymore. If they weren't out of here by the time the darkhelms on top had fetched an archer, they were done. Another jab of the bar accomplished the impossible. Acheron's eyes snapped open.

"Sabrina," he said. "No, no, no. Get out of here." He looked down and swallowed. "I'm not worth it."

"Nice of you to remind me that my heroic last-ditch effort was futile."

A second bar tumbled from the cage, slipped through Brina's outstretched fingers and clattered down the sloping surface of the ward, ringing like a bell.

"Keep it down, morons," the Biori man called down. "We'll have the entire Mallion's Depth garrison on our tails with that racket."

Brina frowned at the man. If this was a trap, it was the strangest one she'd ever encountered.

There was a rustling overhead. Brina instinctively moved out of the way as something streaked past her. *A rope.* Whatever was going on above them, Brina had no intention of sticking around to find out. They needed to get moving now.

Still hanging above three hundred feet of nothing, Brina set down the tinhead in the cage. She used her free hand to pull Acheron into a sitting position. His limp weight threatened to pull her off the metal rod she was holding onto as he immediately sagged backward.

"Leave me," he croaked. "I'm already dead. My body just doesn't know it yet."

Brina slapped him across the face. "Get up or I'll make your body remember all kinds of unpleasant things." The impact seemed to knock some of the bleariness out of his eyes. He gave a gurgling chuckle and pushed himself up onto his knees. "You really are you father's daughter."

The rope creaked as it went taut. Brina glanced over her shoulder, just in time to see a thin man glide down the rope as though this was something he did for fun every weekend. On the ramparts, the Biori warrior held the rope in place with his bare hands. The glare of the second chariot reflected in his eyes, making them seem luminescent.

The thin man stretched out a hand and gestured toward Acheron when he reached Brina. He had a thin, pointy face, which reminded Brina of a hedgehog. A meager tuft of black fuzz resided on the tip of his chin, as though he'd been dipped into coal dust. A similarly thin coating of black ran across his scalp. His most prominent feature, however, were his eyes. They radiated blue in the dusk as though he'd had his original pair replaced by sapphire globes.

*There are more of them. Sorcerers.*

Whoever these men were, they weren't with the darkhelms. Brina helped Acheron out of the cage, and the stranger put a thin arm around his waist. With an inhuman amount of controlled strength, the stranger slung Acheron over his shoulder. The Biori at the top began pulling up the rope hand over hand.

Panic stabbed at Brina. *The bastards are leaving me behind.* She spun around the metal rod and scooped the tinhead, which was blissfully chomping away at the bars, up out of the cage. The creature had been the key to her success. She wouldn't leave it behind, even if it ended up costing her.

The end of the rope slithered past her. Soon it would be out of reach. In a moment of panicked impulsivity, she let go of the metal rod and dove

## CHAPTER 12

for the rope with both hands. The rope's course fibers seared the palms of her hands as she slid down a full foot before she could twist the rope around her forearm to keep herself from falling. Her feet dangled over the abyss as the Biori's great heaves pulled her to safety, one foot at a time.

"What'd you do that for?" the thin man exclaimed when all three of them had their feet on solid stone. He stared at Brina with a mixture of disgust and incredulity. "Could've broken your neck, you could have."

"Then again, it *did* look spectacular," a woman's voice drawled. Brina hadn't noticed her in the excitement of clinging onto the rope for dear life, but now it was hard not to look at the woman gliding toward them from the shadows.

Two feet of pitch-black hair flowed down to her middle, framing a regal face with thin lips. Her deep brown eyes were streaked with black stripes that circled the pupils like the grain in a slab of polished mahogany. They were at once warm and fueled with the sort of sharpness that was rarely seen in Doorstep's Ditch. Brina felt the urge to bow before the woman, but caught herself right before following through.

"You tried to leave without me," Brina snapped, rounding on the thin man to shake off the impression the unknown woman had made on her.

"I did no such thing," the man protested, waving his hands up and down like he was fending off a swarm of wasps. "In case you hadn't noticed, I had my hands full." He jabbed a thumb at Acheron, who sat with his back against the stone ramparts.

"Easy, Sneak," the woman interrupted. "You can scarcely blame the lady for worrying if you can't even introduce us properly."

Brina was glad that the dusk obscured the sudden blush on her cheeks. She had never been called "lady," but coming out of this woman's mouth, she rather liked the term.

"Again," Sneak said. "Hands. Full."

Brina shrugged. "Don't worry about it. I didn't plummet to my untimely death. What more can we ask for?"

"Hear, hear," the Biori man rumbled. "Now let's bail before we end up with our heads on pikes."

"How many times do I need to tell you, Bron? They don't do that here." Sneak shook his head wearily.

"Don't want to risk it," the man named Bron retorted. He stooped down and slung Acheron across his broad shoulders.

As Bron and Sneak crept toward the door of the nearest tower, Brina turned toward the mysterious woman.

"I still feel like I'm missing an important piece of the puzzle."

"I would say that is an accurate assessment," the woman's clear voice chimed. Her hair whipped around her as the winds picked up speed, giving the woman an aura of bubbling energy. "My name is Saphara Al Noor, but you can call me Saf. Me and my friends have been watching you for quite some time."

Brina immediately opened her mouth to demand elaboration on this outrageous statement, but Saf put a hand on her shoulder to silence her.

"All in due time. For now, let's try to make it back to headquarters before this storm blows us off the wall."

# CHAPTER 13

*13th day of the 11th cycle, 569KR*
**Mallion's Depth**

*ang.*

The door to the gatehouse slammed shut. Brina whirled round to see Bron pushing against the door with all his might. Every muscle in his trunklike arms stood out like interwoven ropes.

Sneak, dragging along a semiconscious Acheron, sprinted back toward Brina and Saf. His eyes were wide with terror.

"So..." he began. "We might be in trouble. A decent amount of it, judging by the procession of darkhelms stomping up the staircase."

Saf straightened up. She wore the look of a Galleons player who had just watched her opponent make a risky move.

"They'll have the other tower barred as well," she said, glancing back at the door leading to the second tower. "At least the seal will hold them off the ramparts on that side."

"Seal or not, they've got us pinned down," Sneak said, clawing at the black fuzz on his chin. "There's no way we're getting out of the city."

"Then we go in."

Saf peered over the edge of the wall, into the sea of tiled roofs and white walls that was Mallion's Depth. She looked up at the rumbling sky. Droplets of ice were already sleeting down from a thick blanket of thunderclouds. "And we better make it quick."

"Might I remind you that the watch has us completely blocked in?" Sneak yelled over the moan of the incoming storm as he ran to support Bron's attempts to keep the watch on the other side of the door.

"Perfect." Saf smiled. "Let them believe that. By the time they realize their mistake, we'll be long gone."

Desperate to do something, Brina picked up the abandoned coil of rope, knotted it around the battlement, then flung it down into the city. It barely reached halfway down. A series of hollow thumps resounded as the darkhelms battered the blocked door, each impact accompanied by increasingly strained grunts from Sneak and Bron. They were losing ground, one inch at a time.

Saf knelt down beside Acheron, who lay flat on his back on the cold stone. He opened one bloodshot eye.

"We're going to make a fortified jump. Can you pull it off?"

Acheron let out a gurgle that could have been a chuckle or a death rattle. "Sure, just lob me off the wall. Gravity will do the rest."

"Excellent."

Saf gestured at Brina to put her fingers in her ears. As soon as Brina did so, Saf righted herself and whistled. Her eyes turned a dark purple as she held the same high-pitched note. The sound changed in midair, like a thought evolving into a scream. It penetrated Brina's bones, rattling them to the marrow. She felt a sudden, deep-seated urge to get as far away as possible from the source of that unnatural wail.

As soon as Bron and Sneak heard the noise, they let go of the gatehouse door and ran back toward the group.

Saf's whistling rose into an earsplitting crescendo. The door to the gatehouse burst open. Two dozen armor-clad darkhelms charged onto the ramparts. The first two ranks stumbled to their knees as Saf advanced, her eyes shining like a pair of stars pulled straight out of the heavens.

Brina ducked to pull a dagger out of her ankle holster. She got into a fighting stance, ready to jump into the fray. Sneak grabbed her elbow, shaking his head.

"Saf'll handle them. You're with me." He turned around and crouched. "Get on my back."

Despite the acute threat, Brina couldn't help barking out a laugh. "That's a joke, right?"

"Dead serious for once. Unless you think you can make that jump yourself." He pointed at the thirty feet gap between the wall and the tiled roof of the nearest building.

Feeling like a toddler, Brina put her arms around Sneak's bony shoulders. It was like hugging a sack of rocks.

As Sneak stepped onto the wall's edge, Brina's stomach lurched. It was one thing to climb up on her own strength, but to look into the abyss, relying on someone else not to drop her, was something else entirely.

## CHAPTER 13

Before she could change her mind, Sneak hopped over the edge, holding onto the rope as he walked down the inside of the stoneward. Brina watched the countless streetlights shiver in the dark, mirrored by the stars above. Never in her wildest dreams had she imagined setting foot inside the ward, and now here she was, officially a criminal with the entire city watch on her heels. *Like father, like daughter.*

"Hold on to your backside," Sneak yelled as he reached the end of the rope, still a good hundred feet above solid ground. "I'm going for it."

Brina felt the muscles in Sneak's shoulders harden as he took on an almost completely horizontal squatting position. Then he launched himself sideways into an absurd arc.

The paved street passed underneath them. An additional garrison of darkhelms clattered their way toward the gatehouse in full suits of plate. Before they could do more than yell out in surprise and point upward, Sneak's momentum carried them out of view above a large marble building.

"Puke and pus, I've done it again," Sneak cursed as they overshot the first slanted roof. They began plummeting toward a finely trimmed garden in the building's courtyard, which was lined on all sides by a gallery of marble columns.

"It's going to be a close one," Sneak yelled.

They crashed into the top of a squat tower, sending the both of them tumbling head over heels onto a flat roof beyond. Sneak's head slammed into the heavy stone tiles with a sickening crack. Brina let go at the last second and tumbled sideways. The wind got knocked out of her as her back hit the ground hard.

The first drops of rain spattered against her forehead, and howling winds picked up speed around them, whistling through the streets below.

"I thought you said you had this?" Brina asked in between gasps.

"Technically, I didn't make any promises." Sneak rolled himself over and sat up on his knees. His forehead had split open down the middle, causing a wave of red to flood into his open eyes and mouth. He was in shock, carried onward by the sheer adrenaline of the landing and the light that was still burning in his eyes. Beside him, the stone slab he had fallen on had cracked.

Brina rushed over to keep him from collapsing.

"Here, take this. You're supposed to look at it or something." She reached down the front of her shirt and held the engraved pyramid up to Sneak's eyes.

It was this minuscule piece of metal that had been the catalyst for everything that had happened to her over the past month. She had been living her life, trying to ignore the dismal reality of life in the Ditch. She hadn't been happy, but she had been as safe as any outwalled could be. Then this thing had fallen into her lap, and it had all gone upside down.

Sneak swayed against Brina's grip, his eyes focused on the pyramid for a moment, then went wide. The remnants of the blue light in his eyes turned red.

"Good," Brina said. "Hold it. It'll help."

In front of her eyes, the bleeding slowed from a steady trickle to a drip. Sneak shook his head like a wet dog, causing the blood to spread on his face like war paint.

"Heil on a stick. This thing burns smoother than a sparklizard in a haystack. Where'd you get it?"

"Long story."

Behind them, Bron and Acheron soared through the rain, arms interlocked, their glowing eyes casting thin beams of light out into the downpour.

On top of the stoneward, only Saf's thin outline was visible, a smear of black with two purple dots against the gray canvas of the building storm. On the opposite side, huddled against the tower's entrance, the watchers seemed to have run into a solid wall.

Bron landed beside Brina with a heavy thunk, followed by a mild tap as Acheron touched down. The Biori raised an eyebrow as he saw the rapidly healing cleft in Sneak's forehead.

"Idiot boy never learns," he said, shaking his head solemnly.

"It's harder with a passenger," Sneak protested.

Bron put a hand on Acheron's shoulder, an expression of sincere confusion on his face. "Worked fine for me."

Sneak opened his mouth to reply, but froze in horror halfway through as a bone-shattering howl rippled through the night.

*Bargheist.*

Recognizing the threat just in time, Brina flung herself to the ground, her fingers jammed tightly in both ears. The others weren't so lucky. They collapsed like rag dolls, one after the other, just as Brina's warning left her lips.

Acheron crashed to the ground beside her, his wide eyes staring straight through Brina into a slice of horror only he could see. "I didn't know..."

## CHAPTER 13

Acheron convulsed, the words dying on his foaming lips. "The source... I didn't mean to..."

*Where did they get that thing?* Bargheists were as rare as they were deadly. The only way to hunt one was to shoot it from a distance before it realized you were there. It was absolutely crucial not to give it a chance to unleash its wicked howl. But then, how had the watch captured and trained one alive?

Brina sat up, fingers stuffed in her ears. Behind Acheron, Sneak and Bron lay shivering, the stars overhead becoming specks of dust in the glassy surface of their staring eyes. Rain pattered onto their frozen faces and into gaping mouths. By itself, the beast's howl wouldn't be fatal, but if left unbroken, the trance could drag on for hours as the beast used its victim's own memories and every ounce of hurt they'd ever been through against them. By the time the watch clamped them in irons, they'd be grateful.

Then realization set in. *Saf.* She'd been up there on the ramparts, within touching distance of the bargheist. Brina swallowed. It took every drop of courage she had left to look up to where Saf had been standing.

Most of the watchers had withdrawn into the tower, overwhelmed by the power of their own secret weapon. Only two helmed figures remained, standing beside the bargheist, which rose a good foot above their heads. They tugged at the beast's leash, trying to force it to pounce, but it just stood there, rooted to the spot.

In front of the bargheist, two beams of flickering sapphire light blocked its path. Inside of this shield of light, Saf crouched, eyes ablaze. She seemed to have summoned the barrier out of instinct rather than conscious effort. The blue shield seemed awfully close to collapsing.

Torn between who to help first, Brina kicked Bron in the ribs. He blinked. Brina drew back for a second kick, but the man held up his hand.

"Easy, wild girl, I'm back."

"Wake up the others and run. Don't look back."

Leaving behind the bewildered Biori, Brina ran across the flat rooftop toward the tower she and Sneak had crashed into. She'd need to get as close to the bargheist as possible for this to work. In a handful of adrenaline-fueled movements, she soared up the cracks in the masonry.

The top of the tower was still a good fifty feet below the ramparts atop the ward, but it would have to do. Not wanting to give herself a moment to doubt her plan, Brina threw back her head and howled. It wasn't the best one she'd ever produced, but it was close enough to the real thing. The bargheist shook its head and jumped onto the battlements, its yellow eyes flicking left and right. Brina waved her hands over her head as she let out a second howl. Bargheists were fiercely territorial. Even a trained one wouldn't suffer an invasion of its hunting ground.

As the sound split into a hundred echoes against the stoneward's massive surface, Brina saw the plan had worked. With a great lunge, the bargheist flung the darkhelm holding its leash to the ground, dragging them behind it as it bounded toward the gatehouse.

With the bargheist's influence no longer oppressing her, Saf's protective sphere gained a new level of solidity. She stood up, wagging her head as though she had just woken up.

*Come on, clock's ticking.*

Brina whistled. Saf's head snapped toward her. *She's back, by the Seven, she's back.* In one fluent movement, Saf jumped onto the battlements and flung herself into open air, her arms held wide as though they were wings.

Brina's mouth fell open as she watched the woman's graceful flight. Saf arced through the air with the precision of a hawk diving toward its prey. Moments later the woman landed beside Brina, panting.

"What is that *thing*?" Saf's eyes dimmed to their regular deep brown. "I've never come apart like that." The aftereffects of the bargheist's trance were still visible in the creases of her face. She looked like she'd aged a decade, but she was on her feet, and that was all that mattered.

"Bargheist," Brina said. "Nightmare eaters."

There was a rush of shouts and clinking armor on the street below as the beast charged out of the ground floor of the gatehouse, still dragging its handler behind it like a human wrecking ball. The man's limbs twisted in unnatural angles as he bounced off the uneven cobbles of the street.

"Run." Brina grabbed Saf's shoulder. "It's locked on me. It won't go after the group. Save Acheron. Tell him he'll need to finish the job without me. He'll know what that means."

Saf looked as though she had a mind to argue. Then her expression hardened, and she nodded. Saf thumped a fist to her chest in a gesture of respect, then disappeared down the side of the tower.

Brina's jaw clenched as the bargheist came flying across the corner of the street. The long black hairs on its back stood on end in a show of vicious rage. Its razor claws drew grooves on the cobbles as it skidded to a halt.

The creature snarled. Its hollow yellow eyes found Brina's.

*It's just me and you now, you drooling furball.*

\*\*\*

## CHAPTER 13

The whole situation seemed distinctly unfair to Brina as she stood atop the decorative tower turned improvised fortification. The bargheist growled, revealing a row of teeth, each of which was at least as long and twice as thick as the single dagger Brina had dug out of her boot. It was like a naval battle between a galleon and a raft.

*Go on then, sing me a song.*

Brina whistled, waving her hands above her head to keep the beast distracted for as long as possible. She had to give the others a head start, or the beast might pick up their trail once it had dispatched Brina.

The dagger's hilt was slippery with sweat. There would be one chance. A fraction of an opportunity to strike with complete accuracy. She'd have to get close, though. Close enough to feel the monster's breath on her cheeks.

Agitated by Brina's taunts, the bargheist lurched forward. It crawled up the base of the tower with its front paws, its claws sinking into the sandstone blocks as though they were made of wax.

Though Brina had expected it would try to climb, had even hoped it would, she was horrified at the sheer speed with which the heavy creature lurched up the stonework toward her.

*Any second now.*

The foot-long snout came first. A huge, wet nose, jaws slathered in thick white strands of slobber. Brina's fingers tightened against the dagger. *Not yet.*

Two front paws the size of dinner plates curled around the edge of the battlements ahead. The bargheist's eyes locked on to hers.

Brina stared into those bottomless pits of darkness. Their pull was magnetic. Her feet grew unsteady beneath her, as though she could tumble straight into those gates to the beyond, never to be seen again.

The beast unhinged its jaws and howled.

Brina never felt the dagger leave her hand. She watched the beast lunge at her as though all of it was happening to someone else. There was a glint of moon on steel as the weapon soared toward the bargheist's throat, then its rancid breath engulfed her. Iron teeth closed around her skull like a vise.

# CHAPTER 14

*14th day of the 11th cycle, 569KR*
**Mallion's Depth**

"By the Seven, she killed that thing *by herself?*" The voice was Sneak's. Brina groaned as a pair of muscular arms lifted her.

"A deed worthy of a golden skull, if ever I've seen one." The proximity of the voice told Brina it was Bron who was carrying her.

They had come back. They weren't supposed to.

"Idiots," she muttered, the air burning in her lungs like molten tar. "The darkhelms will have you all hung."

"You've got a funny way of saying thanks, kid," Acheron said. Brina opened her eyes to find the old sorcerer jogging along beside them. He was on his own feet once more, and though he looked ancient in the blossoming light of the oncoming dawn, there was a newfound alertness to his eyes.

Wind and sleet battered the group as they hurried out of an alley and into a street paved with slabs of white marble. Bron jerked sideways right before a windswept roof tile shattered on the ground beside them. As they sprinted from one slippery street into the next, houses of white stone and dark wood flitted by on both sides. In the storm's gloom, they became almost indistinguishable from one another. Their facades were decorated with expertly carved curls and floral patterns, reminding Brina of illustrations she'd seen depicting the golden age of Mallion's Depth. She had thought those images to be exaggerations, nothing more than nostalgia for a bygone age, yet here they were in all their glory. Turns out, one had only to look beyond the wall to find things of beauty.

"On the left. Here." Acheron gestured toward a mossy alleyway wedged between two gilded storefronts. Only the store to the left, "Witherby's Botanical Boutique," still seemed in business. Its counterpart, "Malperteus's

## CHAPTER 14

Clash of Curiosities," looked forlorn when contrasted to the finely kept establishments that surrounded it. The gilded lettering was peeling, and a decade's worth of dust and cobwebs coated its front windows, making it impossible to see the wares on offer.

About twenty feet down the alley, Acheron stopped at a rusty door set into the wall. He rapped his knuckles against it.

"I don't think that's right," Sneak piped up, joining Acheron in hammering his fist against the door. "See, it's more of a *tap* than a *thump*."

Acheron's mouth thinned.

The door opened a slit, and a woman's head poked out of the crack. She looked like something halfway between a dried prune and a recently bathed cat. "Oh, good. Look who decided to show up. It's not like I've got a..." A pause. "What happened to her face?"

Brina's guts churned as Bron carried her over the threshold and down a set of stairs into a dimly lit earthen basement stuffed with bunk beds. About half of them were occupied by the most diverse crowd Brina had ever seen. They ranged from heavily muscled sailor types to an elderly woman with waist-length gray dreadlocks who leered at Brina as though dinner had just been served. The only thing they had in common were the suspicious scowls on their faces as they watched this motley crew enter their sleeping space.

It was only after Bron had laid her down on a musty, straw-filled mattress that Brina realized someone was missing.

"Where is Saf? Is she safe?"

Bron nodded. "Upstairs. Making arrangements."

"Grouchy Zelda wanted to kick us out when we told her we had to go back to fetch you," Sneak said, a grin plastered across his face. "Saf almost ate her."

He chuckled. "It was great."

Brina managed a weak smile, which caused a bolt of fire to shoot through her cheek.

"Is it bad? I can't open my eye."

Everyone around her shuffled uncomfortably. Silence dragged on for a season.

Finally, it was Acheron who crouched down beside her. There was a forced undertone to his cavalier attitude.

"Listen, kid, there's no easy way to tell you this. We won't be able to save your eye."

"What do you mean, 'won't be able to save it'?" Brina's fingers shot up to meet a lumpy mass of swollen and burning flesh. When she drew back her hand, it was smeared with sticky, drying blood.

"One of that thing's teeth was still jammed into the socket when we found you." Acheron's features folded, in what might have been his version of a sympathetic smile.

"We kept it, if you want it," Sneak said enthusiastically. Without waiting for a reply, he stuck a bloody fang, double the size of Brina's thumbs, under her nose. "Crazy how big it is, eh?"

"Yes," Brina muttered as reality sank in, "crazy."

She looked at Acheron. "I won't be able to learn to use the sigils now, will I?"

Acheron refused to meet her eyes.

"I don't know."

\*\*\*

It took until the following afternoon for Brina to even attempt to drag herself up from the mattress. Using the basement's earthen wall for support, she forced herself up. Her knees wobbled as though she were wading through quicksand.

Her head was swaddled in a heavy cocoon of bandages that Acheron replaced every few hours. Whenever he did so, he smeared a thick brown salve on the inside, which smelled like a mixture of smoke and citrus. Whatever was in it made the pain almost bearable. In exchange, her night had been fraught with bizarre half-dreams and sleep paralysis. Over and over, she'd watched herself slogging up an endless spiral staircase, only to end up at the bottom again.

Most of the other bunks in the cellar had emptied overnight, leaving only a pair of elderly Hawqallians who needed two bunks each to fit their lanky eight-foot frames. Their hairless, sunken faces were like wax masks, their skin at least three tones darker than even Brina's. Neither of them moved a muscle, but Brina knew they weren't sleeping. Hawqallians rested by going deep into a meditative trance, which allowed them to stay aware of their surroundings at all times. Brina had tried to learn the technique on a handful of occasions but had soon discovered she possessed less patience than a drunk waiting for her next mug.

When she neared the staircase, heated voices traveled through the wood-

## CHAPTER 14

en boards from the floor above. One was definitely Acheron; the other sounded like a stranger. There was a thump, followed by Acheron's yelling.

In her hurry to storm up the stairs, she misjudged the height of the second step and only barely avoided crashing teeth first into the stone steps. At the top, she reached for the handle of the door and missed it, tricked by her distorted depth perception. It cost every ounce of stubbornness she had left not to burst into tears. How was she supposed to get her father out of an airtight fortress when she couldn't even save herself from an unlocked room?

"Tell him to go drown himself in a bucket of squid ink," Acheron yelled, now clearly audible through the door on the opposite side of the landing.

Brina opened the door to find Acheron standing nose to nose with a tall, elegant woman in exquisite emerald robes. Her unnaturally red lips curled into a self-satisfied smile as Acheron continued shouting in her face.

"While you're at it, maybe you could give the little weasel back the dagger he left buried in my back."

"As I stated earlier," the woman said in a tone that wouldn't have been out of place inside a courtroom, "Master Zot had nothing to do with the circumstances of your unfortunate detention. Might I remind you he too fell victim to this betrayal? From that perspective—"

"From that perspective, Zot can kiss my inexplicably hairy behind." Acheron threw his head back and laughed at his own comment like a madman.

The woman's smile briefly wavered. She opened her mouth to offer another rebuttal, but Acheron simply waved his hand in her face.

"Goodbye."

With that, he turned around and walked past Brina to hold open the door leading into the alley. He repeatedly gestured at the door until the woman finally stepped over the threshold.

"Sorry about that." He turned toward Brina, still grinning at his own wit. "Did I wake you?"

She shook her head and pointed at the clump of bandages covering her eye. "This did."

Acheron's smile faltered. Up close, there was an unmistakable orange glare in his eyes.

*He's back on the cloud already after he almost died over it.*

Brina had a hard time caring. Of course, nothing had changed. Had she even believed it would? Looking back, her whole nighttime rescue operation seemed little more than a teenager's tantrum, a reckless outburst of rebellion, born out of spite rather than purpose.

Acheron lingered for a few uncomfortable seconds. He looked like a frog sitting in a pot of slowly heating water.

"Where are the others?" Brina asked.

"Out. They're making arrangements to get us out of the city once you…" He got stuck. "You know." He waved a hand in the general direction of her mangled face.

Brina's hand traveled to her bandaged eye. In the jungle, wounded animals were culled from their habitat by fitter, stronger specimens. Doorstep's Ditch was no different. From now on, Brina was playing the game at a disadvantage, and everyone would be able to read it on her face.

"Can we trust them?" she asked.

Acheron gazed at her with those watery cloud-misted eyes, and Brina's mood took a further dip. Would a reassurance from this miserable figure really make her feel better? *Father trusted him*, she reminded herself.

*And now look where he is.*

"Seeing how they broke about a dozen capital laws to prevent me from dying a slow, agonizing death, I'm inclined to give them the benefit of the doubt." Acheron shrugged.

"But why?" Brina asked. "Why did they risk it all?"

"Why did you?" Acheron asked. He suddenly seemed very interested in the woodgrain of the floorboards.

Brina opened her mouth, then closed it again. Now that she was being put on the spot, it was hard to put into words what exactly had driven her attempt to free her father's oldest friend. She wished she could say she had acted out of altruistic care for Acheron, but that would be a half-truth. She had only met the sorcerer once before, and that occasion hadn't exactly ended on a positive note.

"Is this some kind of trick question?" she asked, buying time.

"No tricks." A sad smile played on Acheron's lips. "Just making a point."

"I did it because what they were doing to you was wrong. It angered me."

"There you go," he said. "Maybe that's explanation enough."

Brina scowled, unsatisfied with such a shallow answer. People never did anything without an angle. Especially not when death, or worse, imprisonment, was on the table.

"Anyway," Acheron said before Brina could voice this opinion, "I'd better go prepare some more of that salve." He nodded, then scurried back down

## CHAPTER 14

the staircase into the basement. When the door closed behind him, Brina noticed it was covered in a layer of tiles. When the lock clicked shut, it was indistinguishable from the rest of the wall.

To distract herself from the throbbing pain in her empty eye socket, she began wandering aimlessly around the shadowy front room. The wooden floorboards were bent with moisture. They creaked under Brina's weight. Strips of light filtered in through the boarded-up store windows, illuminating the most bizarre collection of wares Brina had ever seen.

Shelves stacked with glass jars lined the walls. Some of them were filled with ground up powders in colors ranging from murky brown to glimmering gold, while others held dead creatures suspended in transparent liquid. The acrid scent of decay hung over the store's many aisles. One jar labeled "thirteen-headed serpent king (Untar Province, Hawqal)" held a tangle of snakes that were knotted together by the tail, creating a slimy ball of intertwined scaly bodies.

Near the front door, Brina's eye was drawn to a six-foot-tall creature with countless tentacles floating in a huge glass tank filled with a murky liquid. The thing was dead, but it had been preserved so well that Brina couldn't shake the feeling that it might smash through its container at any moment to wrap those slimy appendages around her neck. Its single purple eye was the size of Brina's head. It was an unsettling sight, but somehow she couldn't bring herself to look away.

"Be careful with that." A sharp voice, like rusty knives rubbing together, echoed from across an endless, dark cavern. "Even when dead, a mistling's eye retains its hypnotic properties." What felt like an aeon later, a beautiful era of complete mindless peace in the void, a clawlike hand fell on Brina's shoulder and pried her away from the glass. She turned around to find herself almost face to face with the woman who had let them in yesterday. Grouchy Zelda.

"What is this place?" Brina asked, a little more aggressively than necessary. She couldn't help but feel annoyed at being removed from the mistling's grasp. The afterimage of that purple circle popped back into view with every blink of her eye. It had been so peaceful.

"Exactly what it says on the tin, dear," Zelda croaked. "This is Malperteus's Clash of Curiosities."

"And this man, Malperteus, doesn't mind harboring a band of fugitives?" Brina sat down on a stark white chair labeled "Meltwood (Northern Settlement, Hammerstroke)." At once the solid wood began shifting under her weight until it cupped her form perfectly, creating the most comfortable seat Brina had ever experienced.

"My dear husband has been sleeping at the bottom of the bay for quite some years now. I doubt he cares about what I do with the place." A wicked grin spread over Zelda's ancient face. Brina couldn't help but wonder how Malperteus had ended up in the ocean.

"And what exactly is it you do with the place?"

"I help people disappear. For a price."

"And nobody ever noticed that the store has been boarded up for years?" Brina frowned.

"Nobody notices anything in these parts of the city, dear." Zelda waved a dismissive hand. "We're in a blind spot."

"Why is that?"

Zelda tittered. The sound made the hairs on the back of Brina's neck stand up straight. "Heil almighty, you're even greener than you look, girl. The way Al Noor talked about you, I would've expected..." She stopped and tittered again. "Not that it matters, of course."

Brina clenched and unclenched her jaw as though she were chewing on a solid rock. She was tired of feeling like everyone around her knew things she didn't. It had been a decade since she'd relied on anyone else for anything, and she wasn't about to pick up old habits.

"Not needling people again, are you, Grizelda?" Acheron's voice broke the silence.

"Don't have to get all protective," Zelda chortled, eying Acheron with malicious glee. "Must be that godfather instinct."

Godfather?

Acheron leaned against the doorframe, holding a new jar of the stinking salve and a roll of clean bandaging. He was as cloud-addled as Brina had ever seen him. His wide eyes blazed like two miniature suns, and there was a visible stumble to his gait as he approached them.

"Just having some fun, Spider. You remember what that's like, right? Fun?" Zelda grinned, baring a set of pointy yellow teeth.

"Vaguely," Acheron muttered. "Now, if you don't mind, I need to tend to Sabrina's wounds. Kindly find another victim."

"What happened to you?" Zelda prodded. "You used to be such an exciting companion."

"I used to be a lot of things."

Zelda let out a cackling laugh before vanishing into the hallway.

## CHAPTER 14

"You're my godfather?" Brina hissed as soon as Zelda had disappeared from sight. "When were you going to mention that little tidbit?" She didn't know why she was so angry; she just knew that she was.

"I didn't think it would help to bring it up," Acheron grumbled, as though that settled the matter.

"I don't believe it," Brina said. Her knuckles turned white against the chair's armrest, causing the meltwood to ripple underneath her fingers. "All this time I had to do it all by myself, and now you're telling me I had a godfather living a stone's throw from my house?"

"You turned out fine," Acheron said, his voice thick with the effects of the cloud. "You were better off without me."

"I was a child." She was shouting now. It felt great, like pus gushing from a lanced boil. "That first year I slept under the open skies in a cloak I pulled off a dead man. I ate rotten fish guts the inns chucked out. Everything I had, I stole. How is that fine? How is any of this fine?"

Acheron remained silent for what felt like a century. His face looked hollow and sunken in the stripes of sunlight that filtered in through the cracks in the boarded-up windows.

"I messed up, kid," he said finally. "I could have done more. I should have done more, but at the time I didn't see a way forward. The last thing you needed was the target that my presence would place on your back." He brushed a tear off his scarred cheek. "And then, before I knew it, you were such a capable and fierce young lady that I figured it was too late. I assumed you wouldn't want anything to do with me once you learned the truth about how I let your father down. Not once, but twice."

Brina swallowed. She wanted to keep yelling at him, to tell him everything she had been through because nobody had ever been there for her. Then she took one look at the shrunken, tearful man in front of her, and all of that anger fizzled out like a wet log. It wouldn't make her feel any better to burden him with her hurt. *No good to dwell on what's done.*

"Zelda said this place is in a blind spot," Brina said, her tone making it clear that they were done with the godfather mess. "Do you know what she meant?"

Acheron nodded. "You can get away with quite a lot in the outer quarters of the city if you're careful."

"But we're inside the ward. This place is crawling with darkhelms," Brina said, her scowl pulling at her injuries.

"That's the thing," Acheron went on, seemingly keen to keep the conversation rolling now that no one was yelling. "Mallion's Depth is an illusion." He wandered over to the boards covering the front windows and beckoned for her to follow.

"How many cities do you know where the streets are deserted at two in the afternoon?"

Looking through a slit between two boards, Brina saw what he meant. The slabs that covered the road were too white. There was no trace of dust, mud, tracks left by cartwheels, nor any other sign that the road had recently been used. Across the street, a series of three-story houses with facades of white marble were frozen in a state of unnatural neatness. None of the windows were open; all curtains were drawn.

"Nobody lives here?" Brina's mouth fell open as she pondered the ramifications of this discovery.

Acheron nodded. "The city's population has been dwindling for more than a century. Turns out that banishing your citizens by the boatload empties your ranks faster than you can replenish them.

"The church grants members of the watch and their families free access to housing in the city's periphery to keep up appearances. The remaining citizens are lured to the center by the markets, theaters, and temples. They have no reason to wander too far from Keeper's Square. The same applies to visiting merchants and emissaries. They arrive at the docks and see the thriving heart of the empire, never uncovering the greatest lie in the history of the Sundered Isles.

"The church says they banish the worst ten percent of people to keep the other ninety percent safe. In reality, it's the opposite."

The ground under Brina's feet turned to jelly. She leaned back against the boards for support as Acheron's words sank in. *Ninety percent versus ten.* All her life, Brina had thought herself the mouse. What if she, and the rest of the outwalled, were the cat?

"We could take the city through sheer force of numbers alone." She almost shouted her conclusion.

Acheron smiled. "You're starting to see what your father was first to see all those years ago."

"Then why did you go the assassination route? You didn't need to. The outwalled could stand against the scepter's armies directly if they organized."

"Let me put it this way," Acheron said. "If I gave you a spear and told you to charge a dragon with it, what would you think?"

## CHAPTER 14

"I'd think you were insane," Brina said. She rubbed her temples. It was all so much to take in.

"But what if I took you to see the dragon in question and showed you that one of its wings was lame and that it had lost its ability to spit fire? What if I removed a scale from its armor while you watched?"

Brina nodded as the puzzle pieces fell into place. "Cardinal Estav was the scale."

"Precisely."

Brina peered out at the empty street. The sun ricocheted off the white marble surfaces like a quarrel against steel. It all looked so smooth, so clean, so solid. Could it really be that it was all just a thin veneer over a cracked pot?

She glanced at Acheron's scarred, weary face. The orange cloud was still raging in his eyes, but there was something else there. An ember, buried deep under the refuse of years spent trying to forget. No matter how much he tried to sound like someone who had given up, that spark didn't lie.

"I'll ask you one more time," she said, staring up at him. "I'm going to free my father, no matter the cost. Will you help me?"

Acheron averted his gaze. His jaws clenched and unclenched as the moment stretched on. When he finally spoke, his voice sounded strained.

"You really are his, you know that? Yes. I will help you."

# CHAPTER 15

*14th day of the 11th cycle, 569KR*
**Mallion's Depth**

olana spotted the black carriage rolling down the paved street minutes before it turned onto the smooth marble of the priory's courtyard.

"Pack the satchel, bring everything," she directed Medina. "Unless I'm much mistaken, we won't be back here for a while."

The apprentice jumped up from her armchair and scrambled around the office, collecting inkwells, a set of feathers, and the pile of scrolls they had spent the afternoon preparing. Solana stared into the hearth. The soothing heat of the embers cast an orange glow on her face. She took a deep breath, steadying herself against what was to come.

Outside, the carriage swayed as it hobbled toward them. With each turn, those black wheels brought trouble a little closer to her doorstep, but it wouldn't do to tarry now. They would need to face this storm head on.

*It will be fine. He needs you,* she reminded herself. She wished that sounded more credible. Cardinal Augustine De Leliard had outwalled far more important clergywomen for far less egregious mistakes. *But not me. He wants this job done. He knows I'm trying, and how close I was last month.*

"I'm ready, mistress." Medina stood in the doorway, two heavy bags draped over each shoulder. The girl's dark curls were tied back in a sleek ponytail, a new style, which certainly wouldn't have been allowed back when Solana herself had apprenticed under Reynziel Othara. Might as well cut the girl some slack before the trouble begins.

"What did you forget?" Solana asked. She sounded harsher than intended, her building anxiety spilling over into frustration.

"I—" The girl looked stricken.

"We never reveal our faces to those whose title differs from ours." Solana

## CHAPTER 15

jabbed a finger at the two silver helmets that stood side by side on the windowsill.

It still irked her to see the two of them standing next to each other. The apprentice's arrival had been an unforeseen and unwelcome complication. Getting used to her new role as emissary was hard enough without having to explain every little step she took to an inquisitive novice.

One would think that after years of dedicated study and unspeakable tasks, she would be exempt from having to mentor mere initiates. Then again, the church's traditions ought to be kept in high regard. Even if some of them were bothersome. They had kept the empire together for a thousand years, longer than any of the heathen kingdoms that had popped up across the isles in the past centuries could claim. Entire nations had risen and fallen while Heil's teachings endured. That winning formula had to be preserved at any cost.

Solana's helmet, shaped like a griffin's head, shone brighter than it had on the day she had received it out of the hands of the Cardinal himself. At least the apprentice's cleaning skills were on par. She made a mental note to praise Medina's work *later*. *If* she still felt like handing out compliments after tonight's audience.

Solana sat down, allowing the apprentice to lower the heavy helmet over her eyes. As always, the world looked different from the griffin's point of view. It was narrower, more black and white, and therefore clearer. The pit of worry she had been silly enough to entertain melted away. *He will understand. He must.*

When she was done, the apprentice picked up her own helmet, a plain model with a single slit for the eyes and no opening at the mouth, and draped it over her head.

"*Now* we are ready."

\*\*\*

Solana had entered the palace of light many times, but never under a mood so grim. Four watchers opened the main gate just wide enough for their carriage to maneuver through. A metallic rattle behind them told Solana that it had been shut again immediately behind them. *No escape.*

Just ahead, the nine towers of Heil flickered with the flames of a thousand candles, sticking up into the dusk like a circle of flaming swords raised in a salute to the Keeper. In its center, a decorated dome rose.

Dozens of sculpted figures told the story of the Sundering. The day when the world ought to have ended had it not been for Heil's selfless descent from the heavens.

It was a magnificent sight, one that had brought a tear to Solana's eye on more than one occasion. Today, however, it felt ominous. It was a reminder of who she had failed when those heretics had vanished into Mallion's Depth. This wasn't about Cardinal De Leliard, or his image. She had disappointed the Keeper herself. Solana gritted her teeth as the driver steered them through the exquisite palace garden. She had to make this right. She would make the Cardinal give her one more chance. There were no alternatives.

A garrison of watchers surrounded the carriage in a box formation as soon as it came to a stop in front of the palace.

A young officer held out a hand to help Solana descend onto the gravel underground. Solana ignored him, striding straight past him and toward the twenty feet high archway she knew led to the throne room.

"Patience, Your Purity." The youth jogged to keep up with her, beckoning for his soldiers to follow. "My name is Captain Hogeveen. The Cardinal has ordered us not to let anyone in without a thorough search."

Solana turned on her heel and gave the officer a look that could have evaporated the Sundered Sea. The man took an involuntary step back.

Over his shoulder, Solana could see Medina struggling to keep one of the other soldiers from removing her helmet. Solana's leather satchel had fallen to the ground. Solana's heart skipped a beat. If that was opened, the odds of leaving here as a free woman would shift from bad to catastrophic.

"Tell your crew to stand down," she hissed at the child in front of her. "If His Eminence takes issue, he can take it up with me."

Hogeveen looked uncertain, glancing from Solana to the holy towers looming over them. Finally, he sighed and raised a hand. The scuffle stopped.

"Change of plans," he shouted at his soldiers. "We'll only be escorting Her Purity tonight."

Solana beckoned for Medina to pick up the satchels, and together they marched into the hallway with the watchers in tow. Their armor clattered in the arched corridor as they strained to keep up. On either side of them, pillars as wide as millstones supported the vaulted ceiling.

"Wow." Medina let out a sigh of admiration as they strode between two rows of marble statues depicting the succession of Cardinals spanning the

## CHAPTER 15

church's entire history. There were one hundred and three in total, De Leliard being the 104th Cardinal.

Solana opened her mouth to chastise the apprentice for her lack of restraint, but then remembered her own reaction when she had first walked these hallways. Perhaps a little wonder couldn't hurt on a night like this.

When they reached the double doors that led into the throne room, the officer went inside first to announce their presence. Moments later, the double doors opened again.

"Send them in, send them in," De Leliard's voice boomed in the distance.

"Yes, Your Eminence, at once." Hogeveen exited the room. His hands trembled slightly as he held the door open.

Without a second glance, Solana strode past the captain and into the throne room.

The circular room was dominated by the dome above, which was covered by a mosaic that consisted entirely of interlinked geometrical symbols. Legend dictated that within those curves and angles, a secret message from the Keeper was hidden. It was considered improper for anyone but the rightfully elected Cardinal to look at them for too long, a rule that even Medina had remembered. Not that there wasn't anything else to draw the apprentice's wandering eyes.

Alongside the curved walls, dozens of statues glared down at them. Some of them were human; others, beasts. All of them were symbolic representations of the stories encapsulated in the holy scriptures. There was Helena, a common woman who had offered Heil a loaf of bread and a drink of water upon her landing on Hammerstroke. There was Gidarna, the monstrous serpent of the depths, which Heil had summoned to traverse the waves of the Sundered Sea.

Each statue was larger than life-sized and so impressively detailed that even the staunchest heathens would be unable to refute Heil's greatness if they were to behold them.

Cardinal Augustine De Leliard sat on his throne at the opposite end of the room.

Compared to its majestic surroundings, the throne itself was a rather modest piece. It consisted of nothing but polished mahogany topped with plain white pillows. It looked like something suitable for the captain of a middle-sized fishing barge, but for Heil's flesh-bound delegate, it was meager.

A long rectangular table stood before the Cardinal. It was laden to the breaking point with silver dishes that held whole roasted peacocks, jars of raw honey, a pile of fresh squid, and a host of other delicacies.

"Reynziel Solana," De Leliard boomed, "welcome."

*Why is he so happy?*

The ruler of the Heilinist empire wore a white robe that was stretched tightly across his barrel-sized belly. A row of golden buttons fought valiantly to stay in place as he sat up. De Leliard was completely bald and clean shaven, with a small round nose, making him look faintly like an overgrown baby. Solana had met the Cardinal several times now, and every time she was taken aback by the nonchalance with which he displayed his face to those beneath him. It was like seeing an elder naked.

This time, however, it was his crown that drew Solana's attention. De Leliard's previous crown, a tall golden band heavily laden with emeralds and rubies, had been replaced by a familiar iron circlet with only a series of spikes for decoration.

"Heil almighty," Solana muttered as she realized where she had seen it before. *Estav was buried wearing that.* Had De Leliard really seen fit to dig up his predecessor to rob him of his crown? Solana shook off the thought. Where he'd gotten the crown didn't matter, at least not while her existence balanced on the edge of ignominy.

She knelt before the man who held her fate in his hands. Beside her, Medina did the same.

"Your Eminence."

De Leliard waved his hand. "Oh, come on, don't give me any of that formal nonsense." He let out a laugh that sounded like someone tickling a gorilla.

The Cardinal got up from his throne and stretched out his hand toward Solana to help her up. She took it hesitantly. Something was off. He had no reason to be cheery, and all the reason in the world to have her thrown out of the city. Yet here he was, smiling and laughing.

De Leliard helped up Medina, who giggled.

"Let us dine, shall we?"

He sat down at the head of the table and gestured for them to do the same.

Solana nodded and took the seat to his right. Without hesitation, De Leliard began loading up a porcelain plate with a large helping of mashed yuca, an entire leg of the roasted peacock, and two boiled turtles with the shells still attached. Solana noted each dish De Leliard touched. They were least likely to be poisoned.

## CHAPTER 15

"What are you waiting for?" The Cardinal laughed again, then picked up a turtle with his bare hands. He sniffed it once, then bit off an entire leg. The crunch made Solana's stomach lurch.

From the other end of the table, Medina looked at her through the slit in her helmet. Solana knew they were both wondering the same thing. In order to eat, they would have to take off their helmets, which was out of the question in the presence of one ranked so high above the both of them.

*A drink.* She poured herself a cup of banana beer and raised it in a half-hearted toast. She poured a conservative sip into the steel griffin's beak of her helmet. Most of it dribbled down her chin. Medina's eyes went from scared to terrified as they searched for any sign of direction from her mistress. Solana looked away. She couldn't guide the girl through this situation any better than a blind man could steer a ship through a reef. Surely, the head of the church wouldn't push them to forsake one of its key tenets.

Meanwhile, De Leliard munched on his turtle with oblivious satisfaction. Fragments of bone and shell crunched between his stubby teeth as he devoured the creature whole.

"Not hungry?" he remarked, looking at both of his guests. Slimy juice dripped from the corner of his mouth and down both of his chins.

"The food looks delightful, Your Eminence." It was important not to upset the man's sense of hospitality while Solana's career hung in the balance. "But our vows of modesty forbid us from eating in the presence of one so enlightened as yourself." Solana conjured up her most winning smile, then realized it was invisible behind her metal mask.

"Bah," De Leliard scoffed, "the whole covered-face thing really is one of our more inane traditions, don't you think?"

Solana stiffened in her chair. *It's a trap, it's a trap, it's a trap.*

"I agree, Your Eminence." Solana's heart sank as her apprentice spoke with wholly inappropriate enthusiasm. "What could be immodest about displaying the features gifted to us by the Keeper herself?"

"Then free yourself, child," the Cardinal said, an expression of fatherly kindness on his face.

"Thank you, Your Eminence, I think I will." With a flourish, the girl removed her helmet, leaving Solana stunned.

"There you go. Turtle?" The Cardinal raised the dish in her direction, and Medina took one of them gratefully. She smiled at Solana as she draped her ponytail over her left shoulder and dug into the boiled creature.

"And you, Reynziel?" De Leliard wagged the dish back and forth.

"I would rather get to business, if you don't mind, Your Eminence." She sounded more confident than she felt. "I imagine we have pressing matters to discuss, do we not?"

"What could be more pressing than a celebration of all the delightful creations our lady has granted us?" The Cardinal's voice remained light, but there was a hard undertone to his voice that even doe-eyed Medina seemed to catch. The apprentice's eyes flickered nervously between her mistress and the man who occupied the center of the universe.

"I suppose nothing, Your Eminence." Solana swallowed, then took the gamble. Taking care to disguise her trembling hands, she lifted the heavy griffin's helmet and set it down on an empty stool beside her. She tried to put on a smile, but it died on her lips as she saw the Cardinal's reaction.

De Leliard's eyes roved across her features hungrily, as though she were a wounded sheep stumbling across a famished wolf.

"Excellent," he muttered, allowing his gaze to linger unapologetically. "Quite excellent."

Solana reached for the roasted peacock, grateful for the excuse to look away. It melted away in front of her knife, and when she brought a slice to her mouth, she couldn't help but savor the rich flavors of the meat mixing with a glazing of raw honey and cinnamon.

"Enchanting, is it not?" The Cardinal smiled. The strange look that had taken over his face moments before had vanished. "Anyway, Reynziel, perhaps it would befit us to insert some form of business talk into our pleasant dealings, lest the enlightened council accuse me of having my priorities in the wrong places."

In her eagerness to respond, Solana nearly choked on her next bite of peacock.

"Of... course... Your Eminence," she spluttered, spraying chunks of meat onto the gilded plate in front of her.

"Your plan to use the one sorcerer we had in custody to draw out others has failed catastrophically." His tone was conversational, as though he were commenting on the statues behind him.

"I do not deny the trap did not yield the results we'd hoped for, but there were unforeseen circumstances we could not have anticipated."

"Is it not your job to take all possible outcomes into consideration?" De Leliard reached for a pyramid of oysters dressed with various fruits and snatched up the one at the very top. He jammed an overlong thumbnail into the crevice between both halves of its shell and pried it open slowly.

## CHAPTER 15

"There was a third party involved. A woman. She wasn't part of the group our informants identified."

That wasn't exactly true, but Solana thought it wiser not to disclose her suspicions surrounding the woman's identity. Or the fact that Medina had failed to take care of her in Solana's absence.

A loud slurp interrupted her as the Cardinal inhaled the gooey oyster.

"She somehow tricked the bargheist," Solana went on. "Not even the beast's trainer could call it off. The others got away in the commotion."

"You assured me a bargheist could incapacitate any sparkgazer that crossed its path."

"It would have done so, Your Eminence," Medina butted in. "We had Al Noor cornered until the stranger showed up."

The Cardinal favored her with a brief smile. It was exactly how Solana imagined a spider would look upon a fly trapped in its web.

"And do you think you would recognize this stranger if you were to see her again?"

"Without a doubt, Your Eminence."

Damn the foolish confidence of youth.

"Excellent." De Leliard looked from Medina to Solana and back. "You, my dear, will have the highly important task of delivering this stranger to me. Preferably alive. Dead if need be."

The apprentice seemed uncertain whether to look shocked or pleased.

"Me? But Lord Cardinal, certainly my mistress would be better suited to..."

"You will do, child." De Leliard waved her off with a flick of his ham-sized hand. "Now go, I must speak with Reynziel Solana under four eyes. My guards will accompany you to your new lodgings."

He whistled, and immediately the doors to the throne room burst open. An escort of four watchers strode in. They had clearly been waiting in the wings since the conversation had started. They marched up to the young apprentice and bowed in sync. None of them dared look at Solana's uncovered face. Instead they pretended like she wasn't there.

Medina's eyes locked on to Solana's for the briefest moment. Then the girl averted her gaze, put on her helmet, and marched out of the room without another word. Solana knew the girl hadn't had much of a choice but to obey, but she couldn't help feeling betrayed.

"*Now*," De Leliard said, finally dropping the pleasant uncle act. "Did I not tell you that there was zero margin for error in this case?

"We already had one sigilist running amok on the other side of the ward. Now you allow a whole hive of them to slink away into the crevices of *my* city?"

Both of the Cardinal's chins jiggled with rage. He reached into his robe and retrieved a scroll of parchment, which he unfurled on the table. Solana barely had to glance at it to know what it was. She'd seen it before.

Outlined in thick black were the countless islands and archipelagos that made up the Sundered Isles. In the very center lay a round island that was larger than any around it. Hammerstroke.

Dozens of red crosses littered the map, marking strategic positions that the order of the watchful had identified.

"Look at this." The Cardinal traced a greasy index finger around Hammerstroke and the dozen surrounding islands that made up the Heilinist empire. "This is what remains of a once almighty powerhouse. A seed, a pit. Less than a shadow of the tree that once bloomed so proudly.

"Heathens dwell in the ruins of Alpa Barangia. The Temple of Gaunt has been reduced to a pigsty. Everything our forebears died to build has been wheedled from the limp fingers of a line of lesser rulers. Estav may have been the worst of the lot, but he was far from the first to let the reins slip. We are a disgrace to the Keeper. She who sacrificed all to spare us above all others from certain destruction now looks upon us with shame."

Globules of spit rained down from De Leliard's mouth onto the map, creating dark stains. To Solana's shock, tears of anger welled up in the corners of the Cardinal's watery eyes.

"This decay can no longer be tolerated. It cannot.

"Soon, things that have been brewing for decades will be set into motion. The great machine of our advancement will whir into action to take back what is rightfully ours.

"The last thing the scepter needs is for a bunch of heretics to go around reigniting old fires."

Solana watched with a mixture of awe and horror as the man's voice turned into a screech. There was an unhinged quality to that manic face that she hadn't seen there before.

"Surely a handful of sparkgazers are no match for the might of our watch-legions?" Solana said.

"And the thousands of drunk, violent criminals that wriggle in the dirt on our very doorstep. What about them?"

Solana swallowed. *Did he say thousands?* Of course, Solana had caught

## CHAPTER 15

glimpses of the slums on the other side of the wall now and then, but she had never entered that Heil-forsaken cesspool. Could thousands really survive in such animalistic conditions? If so, they might outnumber the watch by a significant margin. If a rebellion were to erupt, it would be like having an army appear in front of the city gates overnight.

"I'm glad your limited brain is catching up." De Leliard sneered.

"I will see that the heretics, and any who support them, are made examples of, Your Eminence," Solana said.

"Oh, it's too late for that. My faith in your capacity to handle this crisis has suffered a mortal blow."

Solana felt her cheeks go red as the floor began sinking beneath her feet.

"You are to travel to the Everberg Abbey. Tonight. Further instructions await you there. Let's hope you will make yourself more useful in your new role."

"Everberg?" *That's where the blind order dwells.* Solana had only ever met one monk from the abbey, but the image had never left her. The gaunt skin, the empty eye sockets set in a grisly helmet with sharpened spikes. "But, Your Eminence, my mother is ill. She needs..."

"She will be notified of your failings."

Solana sprang to her feet, adrenaline pumping in her veins like molten lead. This couldn't be happening. Her fingers subconsciously sought the comfort of the leather satchel attached to her belt.

De Leliard whistled, and before she could break out of the state of frozen terror that rooted her to the spot, two pairs of powerful arms marched her out of the throne room and into the dark corridor beyond.

# CHAPTER 16

*15th day of the 11th cycle, 569KR*
**Mallion's Depth**

"What'd you discover?" Brina was the first to her feet when Sneak trotted down the stairs and into Grouchy Zelda's earthen basement. He was the last of them to report back, and the atmosphere in the room had grown tense as afternoon had slipped into evening while they waited for him.

"It's a bleak situation, *Cap'n*." Sneak came to a stop in front of Brina and gave a mock salute.

"What?"

"You know," he muttered, going red, "because of the erm..." He pointed at the patch of cloth tied in front of Brina's ruined eye.

Brina gave him a dark scowl, then burst out laughing when Sneak took a step back.

"I like it," she said, clapping the man on the shoulder.

"Get on with it," Bron growled from atop his bunk near the back of the room. "What did you see?"

"Right." Sneak nodded. "The good news is that they probably don't know we're here. I broke into a building across the street to watch Bron and Saf return. Nobody was tailing them."

"How do we know you were not followed when you came back?" Saf asked.

Sneak gave her a skeptical look, as though she had just suggested that the ocean was filled with rum.

"Anyway, the bad news is that the city is swarming with darkhelms. There are more patrols in the streets than warts on Bron's mum's back." He gave the Biori a grave nod. "I'd say it would be near impossible to get the lot of us out of the city without running into a herd of darkhelms."

"And yet we will need to find a way," Saf said. Her voice carried through

## CHAPTER 16

the group's sighs and mutters like a fog bell, drawing their attention. She got to her feet, and Sneak wordlessly changed places with her.

"I spoke with Grizelda at length earlier tonight. Her position is unwavering. She wants us out of here by Friday. In the meantime, however, she was gracious enough to allow me to pay for all available beds. We will have absolute privacy here for one week. Every day counts. After Friday, we will be on our own."

"Simple," Bron said. "If we can't avoid them, we fight. There can't be *that* many darkhelms at the gate."

"We don't have the stores to attack them," Sneak butted in. "We haven't been able to imprint for days. I can barely feel my power stores anymore."

"Who said anything about stores?" Bron's voice rose. "My spear is worth a dozen sigils on its worst day."

"He has a point, Bron," Saf said. "Without our stores, we are just a more poorly equipped and less thoroughly trained version of the darkhelms. They will have the advantage."

Bron scoffed. "Speak for yourself. I was trained by the mighty Bahov himself, long before I so much as touched a script." He ran a hand through his beard, causing the dozens of metal skulls that were woven into it to tinkle against each other. "Each one of these is a confirmed kill. I still have room for a few more."

"They will expect us to show up at one of the major passages through the ward," Sneak said. "I say we look for some distant stretch of the ward far away from either gate, then we just wait until nightfall and climb across."

"Won't work." Acheron sighed, shaking his head wearily. "You can bet your last sapphire nub that De Leliard will have every square inch of the ward and the docks locked down. For now, we'd best stay put. There's plenty of vacant real estate at our disposal around here."

"That just reinforces the problem," Saf said. "Every day we're stuck in here, our stores drain even further. Besides, we can't leave our headquarters in Doorstep's Ditch empty much longer. Everything we've collected over the past few years is in there. If someone were to break in..." She grimaced.

"I've got a plan that might work," Brina said. She flinched when all eyes turned on her. As a rule, she avoided being the center of attention. There was more wiggle room in the shadows. In fact, her entire plan relied on said wiggle room. "But if I tell you, I want some answers in return."

"What answers?" Sneak asked, throwing up his hands. "We don't know any more than you do, do we?"

"I want to know why you've been watching Acheron and myself." She stared at Saf, whose face was adorned with a peculiar little smile. "Yesterday, you told me an explanation would have to wait. I'm done waiting."

Bron's and Sneak's furtive glances at Saf were everything but subtle. Saf nodded. "Of course. It was never a secret. Not from you, anyway."

"Then we have a deal," Brina said.

"So, what's the plan, Cap?" Sneak leaned back against a straw-filled pillow on the floor.

"What's the only group of people that travels through the main gate on a weekly basis without so much as a backward glance from the darkhelms?" Brina could almost see them, a motley band of fresh rejects shambling into Doorstep's Ditch for the very first time. Clothes as colorful and diverse as their backgrounds. Most of the time, the darkhelms simply drove them out in front of them like a herd of sheep hurrying toward the slaughter.

"Of course," Sneak exclaimed, "the outwalled. Nobody even wants to look at them."

"That's what I'm banking on," Brina agreed. "It's the last place they'll expect us."

Acheron let out a throaty chuckle. "They'd literally be holding the door open for us. No violence or sigils required."

"I suppose," Bron said. He ran a finger along the handle of one of his spears, giving the weapon a wistful look befitting a lost lover.

"It's risky." Saf tapped the tips of her fingers together as she considered the suggestion. Though her eyes were aimed at Brina, she seemed to stare straight through her. When Saf finally spoke, a smile appeared on her face.

"Yes," she said, "I think you're right. Blending in with the outwalled is our best bet. No blood needs to be shed, and with any luck, we can save a handful of them in the process."

"You'd risk exposing us to protect *wallfolk*?" Brina frowned. "They're the ones who are hunting us."

"As you said yourself," Saf replied, still smiling benignly, "those men and women have been outwalled. They are part of us."

"Not until there's mud on their boots." Brina's voice rang out louder than she'd intended. An unexpected surge of anger spiked through her veins like a firejelly sting. The thought of helping the very people that had watched the outwalled suffer for decades without so much as a single outstretched finger of aid made her guts crawl. Everything of value she

## CHAPTER 16

had lost had been taken in the scepter's name. In their name. Her fingers toyed with the string that kept her eyepatch in place.

"Let them feel what it's like. Let them get their hands dirty and calloused and torn. Then they can ask me for help, but not a moment before," Brina said.

"Frankly, Saf," Sneak butted in, "I've got to side with the Cap on this one. I spent some time in the market square today, and most of these people are walking clouds of perfumes and fabrics transported from halfway across the Hawqallian desert. I bet most of them haven't suffered through so much as a bee sting. For all we know, they'll turn around and report us as soon as we take their place."

To Brina's surprise, it was Acheron who offered a rebuttal.

"Who do you think is most likely to be outwalled these days? The vapid puppets who fall in line behind every one of the scepter's decrees or those who dissent?"

Brina grumbled. It was a fair point, but she'd rather choke on a tinhead egg than admit it.

"Let's set that debate aside for another time." Saf stood up and began pacing the room. "If we're to pull this off, we'd best begin preparing straight away."

Brina cleared her throat. "Not so fast. I was promised answers, remember?"

"So you were," Saf agreed. "It's probably for the better to fill you in as soon as possible."

"Might as well make things interesting," Bron rumbled. He reached for the pack that stood at the base of his bunk and pulled out a large, round bottle with a thin neck. When he removed the stopper with his teeth, a dense plume of blue-green smoke rose out of it. "Biori smokewater. I 'found it' in an inn near the docks. Snatched it right from underneath the innkeeper's greasy nose."

The five of them sat down in a circle on the cool floor. Brina's first gulp of the smokewater was cloaking her in a warm embrace that dulled most of the aches in her face and shoulder. The basement was lit with a handful of oil lamps in brackets on the walls, which cast everything around her in a pleasant, blurry light.

"Why bother with salves when this miracle exists?" she asked Acheron, raising her empty cup at him. There was a trace of a list to her voice.

Acheron grunted. His eyes had lost their orange sheen, and he seemed to get grumpier as the evening progressed. Not even a double helping of Bron's liquor had elicited anything but a scowl from him.

"For one, I'm not a Biori brewmaster. Second, I'm trying to keep your eye socket from rotting from the inside out. But who knows? Pour some smokewater in there and see what happens."

Brina couldn't help but laugh out loud at the sheer amount of unwarranted vitriol, which only deepened Acheron's annoyance.

"Actually," Bron said, reclining against the side of his bunk with his arms behind his head, "the angry scarface will be pleased to learn that smokewater is commonly used by shamans to treat war wounds." He pulled up his sleeve to reveal a nasty scar that ran from his elbow up to his shoulder. It shone white in the lamplight, as though someone had sewn a bowstring on top of his skin. "Works like a charm."

The bottle traveled around the circle one more time before Saf set down her cup and waved a hand at Brina. Her usual regal and dignified demeanor had taken a hit. She grinned from ear to ear as though they were lodging in Mallion's Depth's finest inn rather than Grouchy Zelda's dank basement. Brina couldn't help but like this version of the woman. Her smile was infectious.

"So, what was it you wanted to know?" She held out her arms. "We're an open book. Mostly."

"You said you'd been watching us," Brina began. The revelation that she'd been spied on seemed less worrisome than it had half an hour earlier. "What did you mean by that?"

"I meant we got wind of a certain incident that occurred in The Wistful Chimera a few weeks back," Saf said. "We put two and two together and realized there was another sparkgazer in Doorstep's Ditch. So Sneak set out to make your acquaintance. When we found out your name and realized who your father was, we couldn't believe our luck. Unfortunately, the events at the Scarlet Nocturne and the riot that followed obscured your trail.

"We had known about Acheron for a long time." Saf nodded at him. "But it turns out you're a slippery man to get a hold of."

"That was the idea." Acheron looked like he was being forced to chew a lemon.

"But why?" Brina asked.

"Isn't it obvious?" Acheron's temper flared up again. "They think they're the second coming of the Signum. Champions of the people, born anew." He waved an invisible flag with a mock sycophantic expression on his face.

## CHAPTER 16

"I bet they've even given themselves a cool name. What is it, '*The Undying Flame of Hope Arising*?'"

Saf raised her eyebrows. Though the smile didn't leave her lips, something in her eyes changed. Was it sadness or disappointment?

Bron glared at Acheron with danger in his eyes. He took a gulp of smokewater, then pointed the thin neck of the bottle at Acheron.

"You will respect my chieftain." It wasn't a threat, nor an expectation. It was a statement of fact.

Acheron looked him straight in the eye and yawned. He looked so perfectly bored that Brina was convinced he'd practiced the expression just to be extra flippant. *I should have let him stew in that cage for a few more days.*

"Actually," Saf began, an edge of frost to her voice, "you are very close to right. Just like you once did, we believe that the only way to return stability to this miserable nation is to make knowledge of the sigils as accessible as it once was.

"Almost a thousand years ago, before Heilinism spread across these lands like a cancer, every fireplace had the *Gnis* shape scripted into it. Common workers amplified their stamina and strength with scripts provided to them by their employers. Potent healing was available to all. Can you imagine such a world?"

Brina swallowed. It was hard to believe that such a thing could be true. Who would ever allow a life like that to be taken away from them?

"Neither can I, unfortunately." Saf rubbed her hands together. "Centuries of the scepter's rule have all but erased every memory and relic of that time. But not all of them."

Saf's hand reached out toward Brina, who instinctively flinched backward.

"May I?" Saf pointed at the leather string of the pyramid, just visible above Brina's collarbone.

She nodded. Saf leaned in, and her warm hands grazed Brina's neck as they lifted the pyramid over her head. Brina's cheeks burned red, and she was grateful for the dimness of the light.

"It's magnificent," Saf said, holding the artifact up in front of her. "I've never seen anything like it." Her eyes widened as a red ember flared in them. Saf's mouth fell open. "The pattern continues on all sides. Zero imperfections. No wonder it's so powerful."

She blinked, and her eyes returned to their usual mahogany hue. "Here." She replaced the string around Brina's neck.

"Do you really think this thing is that old?" Brina asked.

"There's no doubt about that. Once there may have been many copies just like it, but we're lucky that just one of them survived. Imagine what we could do if we figured out how to reproduce it?"

"And you think we can help you do that?" Brina shook her head. Something heavy dropped into her stomach. "I can't even burn it anymore since I lost my eye."

"Among other things," Sneak said. "Some of our other activities are a little more '*hands on*,' if you know what I mean."

"Like breaking people out of cages?" Brina stuck a thumb in Acheron's direction.

"Depends on who's in the cage, doesn't it?" Sneak shrugged, then took a swig of the bottle of smokewater.

"Let's say, hypothetically, that it was Abrasax Springtide behind the bars. Would he warrant an attempt?"

Acheron hissed a warning in Brina's ear.

Sneak's eyebrows threatened to move all the way to the back of his head. Beside him, Bron spat out a mouthful of liquor, coughing vehemently.

"Calling God's Maul a cage is like calling a leviathan a squid," Saf said. She eyed Brina with a mixture of curiosity and apprehension.

"Well, I'm going fishing with a net on a stick, so I could use a hand."

"Are you saying what I think you're saying?" Saf asked.

"No. No. No," Acheron whispered with the subtlety of a horn in a library.

"Yes." Brina's gaze locked on to Saf's as she tried to gauge the other woman's reaction. "I'm going to break out my father."

Bron let out a low whistle.

"Awesome," Sneak muttered, grinning from ear to ear, until a sideways glance from Saf made his face fall again.

"That is a dangerous thing to think about, much less say out loud," Saf said after a prolonged silence. "Your goal is little more than a death wish with a veneer of valor."

"No." Brina's sharp retort made the others glance in her direction nervously. "I spent over ten years pretending I didn't exist to keep the church off my back. I allowed myself to be bullied, cheated, and cursed, all because I was afraid. *That's* a death wish."

"You gotta admit, Saf," Bron said. A liquor-fueled blush that almost matched his beard had spread across his face. "The woman's got fire."

"It's not the fire that concerns me, so much as the burns," Saf replied.

## CHAPTER 16

She righted her back against the post of her bunk and looked from Brina to Acheron and back, as though trying to weigh something.

Brina pushed the discussion into terrain she knew would entice the three sparkgazers. "You lot know he's only in there because of what he represents."

"Sure," Sneak replied, unable to keep a smile off his face, "that and his instigation of a tiny little scuffle that ended with the High Cardinal of Mallion's Depth sprawled on his back like a strangled rooster."

"He had it coming," Bron grunted. "We Biori haven't forgotten his invasion of the Bay of Bones. Many noble warriors were lost. Many more were enslaved, and for what? To see us bow before his stone god?" Bron concluded his statement with yet another gulp of smoking liquor, an expression of deep melancholy falling over his rough features.

Brina pushed the advantage.

"Exactly. The scepter has been obliterating lives it deems 'sinful' for generations. I bet there isn't a single person present here who hasn't suffered at their hands." Her eyes roved over the others ostentatiously, daring them to refute her.

Bron raised the bottle at her in a toast. Only when he put his lips to it did he realize it was empty. He looked at the glass disappointment in his hands with a sigh, then chucked it over his shoulder where it shattered against the earthen wall. Shards of glass rained down on his mattress and sheets, which didn't seem to bother him.

"All of us would see Abrasax Springtide roam free if the choice was up to us," Saf said, "but it isn't." She spoke with the slow deliberation of a guide leading her passengers through a patch of quicksand.

"I vowed to do whatever I could to return the shapes of power to the people they belong to. In the long run, thousands of lives change. All injustices perpetrated by the scepter could be erased.

"If we allow ourselves to be taken or killed in the pursuit of a suicide mission, none of that will come to fruition. That is a great deal to risk."

Brina clenched and unclenched her jaw. The cold and methodical way in which Saf spoke made her blood boil. Her father wasn't just some weight on an imaginary scale that tipped in the opposite direction. This wasn't about playing the odds; it was about sending a message. And maybe, deep down, it was about a little girl who had kissed her father goodnight, never to see him again.

"Opportunity lies at the end of a broken chain." Acheron's raspy voice rang out.

The old sorcerer got to his feet, his eyes fierce and fixed on Saf. He seemed impossibly tall as he towered over the rest of them. His cloak rippled as though caught in a sudden gale. Every scar on his face glittered white, like a dozen lightning bolts.

"That's right," he went on. Shock passed over Saf's face. "I remember. My brain isn't that far gone yet."

Saf stared at Acheron as though she was only now truly seeing him. After a long moment of silence, she too got to her feet.

"Is this it, then?" Her voice was clear, but brittle, like a sheet of ice. She extended a hand toward Acheron.

"It is." Acheron nodded and grabbed Saf's forearm. The two shook.

"Then it is decided." Saf let out a deep sigh. She turned toward Sneak and Bron, who looked as dumbfounded as Brina felt. "I expect neither of you to follow me in this, but my course is set. I will aid Miss Springtide. For better or worse." A sorrowful note lingered on the last word.

"Are you kidding?" Sneak shook his head vigorously. "You'd expect me to twiddle my grimy thumbs while you go off to break into the most dangerous prison known to mankind? Not a chance. I'd miss all the fun! I was on board from the start."

"The little man speaks true." Bron clapped his compatriot on the back so forcefully that Sneak toppled forward. "Sneaking around and stealing are fine, but it's about time I got my spear wet, lest it lose its appetite for blood."

"So be it." Saf extended a hand toward Brina, who grabbed her forearm as she'd seen Acheron do.

"Once my father is free," Brina said, "I'll be behind your cause until the bitter end. You can count on that."

"And I daresay Abrasax will make himself more than worth the trouble," Acheron said with a maniacal gleam in the corner of his eye. "He still has a grudge or two to straighten out with the scepter."

"And you?" Saf asked him. "Where do you stand?"

"In a frankly awful smelling basement in a city where every man, woman, and child wants my head."

# CHAPTER 17

*18th day of the 11th cycle, 569KR*
**Mallion's Depth**

"Name?"

"Versarro, Rosaldo Versarro," Sneak announced, using his best approximation of the honey-and-lavender accent he'd overheard in the streets over the past few days. Coming out of his mouth, it became more of a jaw-locked-with-toffee kind of sound.

"Pardon me?" The darkhelm bent forward as if it had merely been the extra foot of space between them that had made Sneak sound like his tongue had swollen to the size of a grapefruit.

They were standing in front of "The Scale," the seat of the highest judicial authority in the entire Heilinist empire, the quadrumvirate. The courtroom rose from the marble flagstones of Keeper's Square like a spear tip protruding from an armored back. Built entirely out of glistening black marble, its smooth, windowless facade seemed to ripple in the light of the beating sun.

A small crew of four darkhelms stood in front of the arched front gate. One of them was growing increasingly irritated with Sneak.

"Ver-sar-ro," Sneak said in tones that were dangerously close to reverting to his natural manner of speaking. Having grown up in the crooked alleys of the port town of Merkede, he doubted it would blend in with the well-dressed crowd of wallfolk around.

"Ah, yes," the darkhelm said, nodding with slow and exaggerated motion, as though explaining something to a halfwit. "You *are* on the list, Murio Versarro. You may go in now." He added a quite unnecessary wave at the gate ahead. Relief surged in Sneak's chest at the confirmation. Grouchy Zelda's connections had come through once again. For all her talk, that woman had a heart of... maybe not gold, but definitely something like rusty bronze.

Sneak nodded toward the darkhelm to avoid having to thank the man verbally. If he was to get out of here on his own two legs, he'd be best off keeping his mouth shut at all times. He had just begun debating the merits of playacting being a mute, when the woman in front of him turned around on the obsidian staircase that led to a torchlit corridor on the first floor.

*Great, more talking.*

"Forgive me," she cooed, "but I do not believe we have met. My name is Cerise D'Hautefagne." She looked at him expectantly with a set of dark green eyes that caught Sneak off guard. Her hair, as dark as the black marble walls around them, was braided in an elaborate pattern on top of her head.

"Rossaro Versaldo," he said. He put an arm on the staircase's smooth railing in an attempt to look natural. Only then did he register what he'd just said. "Versarro, I mean, Rosaldo Versarro."

Cerise's eyebrow rose a fraction of an inch before she got it under control again.

"Nice to meet you, Murio Versarro." She pronounced each syllable with care, as if to remind Rosaldo Versarro of his own name. "Do you perform the judicial duties frequently? I do not recall seeing you here before."

"It is my first time, Muria D'Hautefagne. My father's a silverhelm, you see. I was born and raised in the far province of Bior. My ship only arrived a handful of days ago." Sneak cursed himself inwardly. His mouth had run away from him again, and now he'd be running to catch up.

"Truly? How fascinating," Cerise tittered. "Are *they* as filthy as the stories say they are?"

"I'm afraid so, Muria," Sneak said with as much gravitas as he could muster. "They are as hairy as the mammoths the Hawqallians ride, and the smell is about the same." A grin escaped him as he thought about what Bron would say if he could've heard that.

Cerise seemed to love it. "That's what I imagined they would be like," she said. Her hands fluttered around like a set of drunk butterflies. "Come on, we'll be late."

She pulled him by the arm into a series of black corridors. Sneak hobbled to catch up, half enjoying the attention, half terrified of the inevitable moment when he would say or do something that gave the game away.

A few minutes later, they arrived at a set of heavy steel gates, beyond which lay the heart of the building, the Scale itself.

## CHAPTER 17

The Scale was a circular room with ebony bench-rows all along its outer edges. It was like stepping into a giant bowl. Three more tiers of seating towered over them on all sides.

When his eyes reached the ceiling, Sneak let out an involuntary gasp. Stars. Thousands of stars twinkled against a dome of smoothened obsidian. Once, Bron had told him a legend shared among the Biori about a woman who had clung to a griffin's claws until both beast and woman had disappeared into the great void that lay beyond the night sky. Sneak felt as though he had just stepped into that same endless blackness among the stars.

"Over here." Cerise beckoned to a row right in front of the balustrade that separated the first floor from the courthouse's ground floor, where a long stone pew stood for the judges to take their places. Set into the wall behind it stood a brazier filled with a roaring fire that lit the entire ground floor.

Though the hall was impressive, there were only a good three dozen other people spread out in small clumps around the room. It gave the place a hollow, soulless feeling.

When they'd gotten seated, Cerise leaned close to him and whispered, "I hear they've got quite the case today. My brother told me it's almost guaranteed to go to a draw."

She seemed excited about the prospect, though Sneak could hardly imagine what would be so interesting about annoying snags in the course of bureaucratic proceedings. He gave her a nod and a smile he hoped conveyed tacit agreement.

"Here they come." Cerise slapped his forearm in excitement and pointed as a section of the stone judge's pew slid aside to allow four Reynziels to take their place. All four of them bore gilded masks instead of the commonly worn griffin helmets. Their black, hooded robes made them look like wraiths as they swept into the room. Sneak imagined booming, authoritative voices echoing off the gleaming black walls.

He was, therefore, thoroughly thrown off when a dusty squeak arose from the leftmost judge.

"Muria, Murio, I bid you welcome to today's proceedings. As always, the scepter thanks you for your unwavering fulfillment of the judicial duties. It is your efforts that keep this court a just, fair and benevolent one." The masked Reynziel concluded his speech with an impatient gesture to a duo of darkhelms guarding a door set in the wall opposite of the judges' pew.

"That's Jozep Methusal," Cerise whispered into Sneak's ear. "He's our resident Keeper Chosen. They say he's a hundred and three years old, but he presides over every case that passes through here."

Sneak nodded politely, as though everything she had said made complete sense to him. His lips, however, remained tightly sealed. Cerise hadn't punctured his bubble of weak lies just yet. Even the worst gamblers know the best time to quit is when you're ahead. But just like the worst gamblers, Sneak already felt the looming temptation to take it just one last step further.

Each of the three leftover judges took turns stating their names and credentials. Sneak reached into his coat pocket to reach for a square scrap of parchment he'd hidden away in there. He had it in his hands when he realized how suspicious it would look to his new friend if he began scribbling down everything.

*I'll just have to memorize it,* he told himself. He went over the judges' panel in his head, ticking them off on his fingers. *Methusal, Baringich, Ghelbar... No, that's not it. Gerardo? No, not it either. Heil's plague-ridden body. This is a disaster.*

He had to get rid of Cerise.

"Apologies, my dear lady, but I think I see an old acquaintance over there." He made to get up, but Cerise stopped him with a hand on his forearm.

"Who is it?" she asked excitedly.

"Oh, you probably wouldn't know him," Sneak said, trying for a casual smile.

"You never know." Cerise waved a finger at him. "I do tend to be somewhat chatty."

*Of all the people at all possible moments, why her? Why now?*

"It's the man in the navy-blue robe," Sneak improvised, pointing in the general direction of the upper tiers on the opposite side of the room.

Cerise made a face as though she'd just sniffed a rack of drying garroter's weed.

"Hermes? I can't begin to understand how a perfectly pleasant gentleman such as yourself would find himself keeping that brute's company."

"It's more of a business relationship," Sneak muttered. He extricated himself from Cerise's clutches and began shuffling his way around the hall toward the opposite end, inwardly cursing himself, Cerise, and whatever trickster gods had put him in this position to begin with.

## CHAPTER 17

He could still feel the woman's eyes pricking at the back of his neck as he reached a flight of steps that led to the second and third tiers of seating. Now he'd have to pretend to greet the man he'd pointed out. About halfway up, the hem of his robe caught on his shoe, and he stumbled.

There was a loud bang as his outstretched palms thumped against the wooden steps, earning him reproachful looks from about a dozen dignified citizens seated nearby.

When he'd located the man named Hermes, Sneak took a seat two rows behind him. From a distance, it ought to look convincing enough.

Moments later, the doors to the courtroom clanged open, and four darkhelms entered, escorting a wild-eyed woman in a disheveled gown of emerald satin embroidered with gilded roses. Her black, curly hair stuck out wildly in all directions.

"Lena Vance," the Keeper Chosen squeaked from his eerie golden mask, "you have been brought before the court today on charges of undignified conduct in the first degree, blasphemy, and public drunkenness. How do you plead?"

"Guilty, Reynziel Methusal," Lena Vance replied, her legs quaking. "But I swear, it was only a brief lapse of judgment. I didn't mean to besmirch the honor of the almighty Keeper. I wouldn't dream of it."

A darkhelm stepped in to hold up the terrified woman as her knees gave way completely.

Methusal held up a scroll of parchment and read in tones drier than a bucket of sawdust.

"Here follows the report of Lieutenant Matthew Fillepleur, commander of the fifty-seventh squadron of the Enlightened Watch.

"On the morning of the first Friday of the third moon cycle of the year 569, I, with my own eyes, witnessed Muria Lena Vance squat down behind a marble statue inside the sacred cathedral of Heil, after which she promptly, and vigorously, urinated.

"Upon her detention, it became clear that Muria Vance was severely inebriated. Officers of the watch will detain Muria Vance until a formal court hearing can be arranged."

Methusal leaned forward over the edge of his pew to look down upon the quivering woman in front of him.

"What do you have to say to that?" he droned.

"It's true," Muria Vance sobbed. "Oh, Heil almighty, it's true. My sister... she brought this cask of wine from—"

"Stick to the facts pertinent to this case," Methusal interrupted.

Muria Vance opened her mouth one last time, then simply gave up, hanging her head.

"You have severely and irreparably damaged not only your own dignity, but that of our innermost sanctum. Your conduct has proven you unworthy of the title of Muria. The council will now vote on your reformability."

High above them, Sneak withdrew his scrap of parchment and a stick of charcoal and noted down Vance's name and offense. The callous rigidity with which the poor woman was being treated made his nerves tingle. If this was how they approached a stray piss, he didn't like to imagine what they would do to a full-on outwalled caught spying.

On the courtroom floor, the four judges rose from their seats. Each of them held out a fist.

"In the case of Muria Vance, guilty of undignified conduct in the first degree, blasphemy, and public drunkenness, the council votes," Methusal croaked.

Three thumbs extended downward, including Methusal's own. The fourth judge, Wyzensk, or something of that ilk, retracted his fist.

"Irreformable." The word whizzed through the giant hall with the finality of a quarrel striking home in a heaving chest.

Muria Vance cried out once before a nearby darkhelm forced his gloved hand over her mouth to stifle the wailing.

"Miss Vance, you are hereby stripped of your citizen's title. All of your possessions within city limits will revert to the scepter's treasury to be redistributed among your betters."

With a careless wave, Methusal had Lena Vance dragged out of the courtroom.

The next case, a merchant named Erich Winter, accused of evading city taxes, took significantly longer. There were scrolls upon scrolls of proof to be read and ledgers to be cross-referenced. By the time Murio Winter was declared "reformable" in a unanimous 4-0 verdict, Sneak had been staring at the star-strewn ceiling for so long that he nearly toppled out of his seat in shock when the heavy steel doors fell shut behind Winter, who was allowed to walk out without a detail of darkhelms.

Next, there was Everard Silner. Voted "irreformable" on account of his nasty habit of slitting his opponents' throats if the cards didn't play out in his favor. *Silner, bald, double chin, bit of a temper,* Sneak wrote.

Over the following two hours, another eight cases were heard, seven

## CHAPTER 17

of which resulted in "irreformable" judgments. Sneak jotted down names and descriptions for each.

"The court will hear one last case before we adjourn for the day," Methusal announced. He sounded exhausted. "Bring in Murio Harrod Wane."

A collective gasp sprang forth from the onlookers as the doors flew open, revealing a thin boy with a mop of dirt-colored hair and a set of huge blue eyes.

The two darkhelms escorting Harrod Wane each had a hand on one of the boy's shoulders. Under different circumstances, it may have looked like a fatherly gesture.

"Murio Wane," Methusal began, "you have been brought before the court on suspicion of theft with a value exceeding one hundred sapphire shards. How do you plead?" Nothing in the judge's tone or posture suggested he had so much as noticed that he was speaking to a child.

"I'm guilty, Reynziel Methusal," the boy said. He sounded on the verge of tears. "But I only did it because of my sister's wedding. I just wanted her to have something pretty and special to wear."

"And so you helped yourself to a ruby necklace worth more than a year's proper wages?" Methusal asked in that same maddeningly uninterested tone. Sneak's fingers curled around the edge of his seat to contain his anger. It was like watching a younger version of himself being bullied.

"I honestly didn't know how much it was worth. I didn't really think about it," the boy replied. "It was pretty, and I thought Marala would like it."

"Hardly an excuse. No further questions will be necessary." Methusal stood up to initiate the vote.

Methusal's thumb instantly flicked downward. Sneak felt the edge of the wood bite into his palm as he squeezed harder. He'd like nothing better than to march down there and slap the old man's mask inside out. Only the knowledge that it would mean the certain and swift death of not only himself but of their escape plans kept him glued to his seat.

*If you only knew what we've got in store for you, you bastards,* he thought bitterly. He couldn't wait to see how many heads would roll in the Cardinal's ranks when they proved that none of the scepter's defenses were impenetrable.

The second judge withdrew his fist, indicating a counter-vote. The third judge's thumb turned downward slowly, as though they were savoring the moment. Now it all came down to Wyzensk. The courtroom went so quiet that an ant's footsteps would have resounded like a war drum.

*It's all part of the show,* Sneak realized. The ominous black ceiling looming high above them, the sparse torchlight, the judges seated in their pew like griffins, lecturing their prey on their corrupted morals before casting them out into lawlessness. It was mummery, and the citizens lounging on the surrounding benches were the target audience. Justice and showmanship meshed together so tightly that it was impossible to tell where the fiction of it all began.

Wyzensk's withdrawn fist was a boulder cascading into a still pond.

*"It's a tie,"* a woman to his left gasped. Similar exclamations rose from the sparse audience all around Sneak. He remembered what Cerise D'Hautefagne had told him as they had taken their seats. She'd been told in advance there would be a tie, as though that was something to look forward to.

In the judge's pew, all but Methusal sat down in a single fluid motion. The Keeper Chosen spread his arms wide.

"All rise," his voice rang out with sudden vigor.

As one, the citizens in the stands got to their feet. Sneak hastily followed. *Just do what they do, and you'll be fine.*

"Citizens of Mallion's Depth, once again this court has need of your judgment. When the proper course of justice is unclear, we rely on you to tend to the garden of our blooming civilization. It is up to you to weed out that which threatens to overturn the ideals we stand for and to nurture that which has the potential to blossom once more."

There was a deafening clap as dozens of hands snapped together at the same time.

"Murio Wane knowingly stole from one of our hardworking brothers and sisters. You have heard his plea. The facts are yours. Do you see fit to restore his place among you?"

Cloaks ruffled, and shoes scraped as people raised their fists all around Sneak, who did the same. Suddenly being involved, however perfunctorily, in the boy's fate, put him on edge.

With an outstretched arm, Methusal pointed at each of the onlookers in turn, counting their votes aloud. All along the edge of the hall, thumbs pointed downward. Some did so with looks of gravitas, others outright smiled when their turn came to pile onto Harrod Wane's impending doom. Not one vote to spare the boy was counted.

As Methusal's pointing arm moved closer, like the arm of a clock nearing midnight, a pang of panic hit Sneak. He was going to have to vote, and by

## CHAPTER 17

the way things were going, they would expect a thumbs-down from him as well. Would it look suspicious if he was the only one to vote "reformable"? Would it even matter? With twenty-three votes to zero, there would be no turning the tide.

In front of him, the man named Hermes jerked his thumb downward instantly when he was called upon.

Methusal's finger landed on Sneak. He could feel eyes burning on his skin. The trembling in his outstretched fist peaked. *Just turn your damn thumb down, you idiot. It doesn't matter anymore. The kid's gone, and there's nothing you can do.*

People in the rows in front of him were turning around in their seats to see what the delay was about. Frowns and scowls appeared as yet another handful of seconds passed without his vote cast. He tried looking away from the courtroom floor, but found that he couldn't look away from the child in chains, staring up at so many downturned thumbs in horror.

*I'm sorry, kid, but there's no point in drawing attention to myself.*

A flutter of indignation reverberated through the hall. Sneak looked down to find his fist withdrawn, his thumb still locked firmly in place.

"Twenty-seven to *one*," Methusal called, emphasizing the last word with displeasure.

Sneak sighed. The citizens in front of him turned away, their own thumbs still extended. He hadn't been able to do it. His heart sank at the same time as the relief hit him. *Bloody idiot.* Since when did he let petty emotion endanger a job? Everyone had noticed him now. *In and out like a ghost, no traces.* That had been the plan. Now everyone present here would remember the oddball in the lime-green top hat who had wanted to let a thief walk free. As a few final votes were counted, Sneak stared at his shoes, defeated.

"Thirty-two to one. Irreformable," Methusal said, finally lowering his finger. "Harrod Wane, you are hereby stripped of your citizen's title. All of your possessions within city limits will revert to the scepter's treasury to be redistributed among your betters."

*Kid's probably got three spinning tops and a stale pastry to his name.*

Harrod Wane sobbed quietly as the watchers dragged him out of the room. As soon as the doors had clanged shut behind the kid, the four judges rose without warning and disappeared through the hidden door in the back of their pew.

# CHAPTER 18

*18th day of the 11th cycle, 569KR*
**Mallion's Depth**

"Why in the world did you do that?"

Sneak turned around to find Cerise D'Hautefagne's face dangerously close to his own. Her drawn-on eyebrows curled into a formidable scowl.

"Do what?" Sneak asked, feigning obliviousness. A nervous glance over his shoulder told him they were among at least a handful of stragglers still making their way down to the ground floor. Their footsteps pattered against the black granite steps of the staircase. Every word either of them spoke would be overheard.

"Your vote," Cerise urged, struggling to keep up with Sneak's quickening pace. "You went against the Keeper Chosen. Why?"

*Because he's a crooked snake with a stone in his chest,* Sneak thought.

"I did?" Rosaldo Versarro's hand shot to his mouth in shock. "But I retracted my fist, did I not?" He mimed the gesture.

Cerise's eyes narrowed, as though trying to determine whether he was pulling her leg or just plain moronic. Sneak could almost see the connections forming behind her eyes. There was only one thing for it. He began sobbing. They were dry, tearless sobs that sounded like a small dog being stepped on.

"I don't belong here, do I?" He let out between heaves. "I knew it, once a provincial man, always a provincial man. All those hours studying etiquette, wasted on an oaf like me."

"So you truly did not know what you were signaling?" Cerise asked. Her posture softened.

"I must have mixed them up in the excitement of the moment." He threw up his hands in despair, making the pompoms on his sleeve bob

## CHAPTER 18

up and down like a school of firejellies. "In the provinces, we use a much cruder verbal system."

"I see." Cerise was smiling now. "I thought you were one of those *troublemakers.*" She whispered this last word like it was a scandalous request.

A muscle in Sneak's shoulders tensed. He subtly slowed his pace to let those behind him pass.

"There's been trouble in the great city of light? I can hardly believe such a thing."

Cerise sighed. "For the past few years, there has been a minuscule, but loud, contingent of citizens who want to undermine the Cardinal's rule. They believe that the leader of the empire ought to be elected by the people, not Heil. So when you voted against the Keeper Chosen, I assumed you might be one of them."

She shook her head with a giggle, as though the idea was ludicrous.

"And then just last week," she went on, "I heard the watch tangled with a gang of stargazers. Sergeant Bonnehelme all but confirmed it to me in person. He was really worried. I bet those protestors hired them to scare people. Remember what happened to poor Cardinal Estav?"

"Vaguely," Sneak said. He'd managed a straight face throughout Cerise's staccato ramble, but he was sure his furiously beating heart would give him away at any moment.

"Are you well, Murio Versarro? Your visage is growing rather red."

"Quite well, Muria, quite well." Sneak gave her a nod. "I was just thinking back to the horrible faux pas I made just now. It will pass."

"You've only just arrived from the provinces. We can't expect your etiquette to be up to par just yet, can we?" Cerise gave him a light tap on the shoulder. Though she'd obviously meant to encourage him, Sneak had to bite back a smirk at the sheer unintentional condescension. She'd essentially called him a provincial boor. Which suited Sneak perfectly. It explained away his less than complete knowledge of the various ways wallfolk made their daily lives unnecessarily complicated.

"Just so I don't make any more embarrassing gaffes," he said, "do you know when the convicts will be transferred to the stocks on Keeper's Square? I understand it is tradition for the citizenry to pelt them with a variety of spoiled goods." He'd made that up on the spot, but given how much they loved to feel superior, it seemed like the sort of activity local citizens would partake in with gusto.

Cerise giggled. "Oh my, your etiquette master wasn't the most youthful character, was he?"

"Master?" Sneak exclaimed, disappearing in his role as Rosaldo Versarro. "All I had were dusty books, Muria." He leaned in conspiratorially and whispered behind his hand, "There weren't even any sketches."

Another bout of giggles.

"Someone ought to show you around, straighten you out," she said. A radiant smile appeared on her face, which made both Versarro's and Sneak's own stomach twinge. He didn't hate the feeling.

"I would like nothing better, Muria D'Hautefagne, but I'm afraid I have urgent matters of business to attend to," he replied with what he hoped appeared sincere regret.

They were almost at the base of the final staircase. Both of the heavy steel doors stood open, allowing the midday sun to flood the entrance hall with light.

"I understand," Cerise nodded. If she was disappointed, she hid it well. "At least allow me to correct you on one last point, then. Consider it a parting gift.

"The stocks on Keeper's Square have been out of use for nearly fifty years. These days, they are a tourist attraction."

"But then, what about the prisoners?" Sneak asked. "Where are they being kept?"

"Right here, of course," Cerise said. She giggled again, as though meeting someone who didn't know about the intricacies of the legal system was the most amusing thing that had happened to her in the past decade. "It's much safer that way. No need to transfer them until it is time to purge them from the city."

"Of course." Sneak smiled. "That *does* sound much safer." *And like a giant problem.*

A sudden idea struck him like a snort of wakeroot after a long night's drinking. It would be risky, but once he exited the building, he wouldn't have the opportunity again. Sneak began patting the pockets of his coat, conjuring up the best horrified expression he could muster.

"My timepiece," he gasped, slapping a hand to his forehead, "I must have left it in my seat."

He bowed toward Cerise D'Hautefagne while backtracking up the stairs again. "Nice to meet you, Muria D'Hautefagne."

She nodded, taken aback by his sudden departure. There was an unidentifiable gleam in those huge brown eyes. Was it annoyance? Or disappointment? "Likewise, Murio Versarro. Perhaps we shall meet again someday."

"I would like nothing better," Sneak said, realizing it was true.

He stole one last glance at the blue sky above before striding back into the darkness of the Scale, heart thumping violently.

# CHAPTER 19

*18th day of the 11th cycle, 569KR*
**Mallion's Depth**

Sunlight crept through the boarded-up front window of Grizelda's doss house in icy slivers. Brina sat back in the meltwood chair, feeling the armrests and back support give way to envelop her form to perfection. It was like floating. Had it not been for the scrap of metal in her hand, it might have been a relaxing afternoon.

She took a deep breath and held the pyramid at eye level yet again. *Follow the pattern,* she told herself. *Just follow the damn pattern.*

As the pyramid turned on its chain, Brina's eye traced every minute curve and bump of its shape. The pattern spread out in exact replications from the middle of each side of the pyramid. She'd at least figured out that much.

*Come on, focus. Make it flow. Make the light flow from the center.*

The sunlight caught on the pyramid's surface, reflecting a sharp glare right into Brina's wide-open eye.

"Plague and pus," she yelled out, pressing her palm into her stinging eye. She flung the pyramid away and heard it collide with the wooden floor on the other side of the room.

Her one good eye teared up, only partly because of the glare. She'd spent the past three days forced to sit out the action like a child on a time-out. To pass the time, she'd glared at the pyramid for so long that she'd wished her other eye would go blind too more than once. So far, she was no closer to burning the sigil than she was to pole vaulting over the stoneward.

"You dropped something."

Though she could hear Acheron, only a blurry stain vaguely resembling a human being was visible through the tears in her eye. *This is what he must look like on the inside.* The thought made a brief grin re-appear on her face.

"Oh, don't worry," she said, "I threw it. I would have swallowed it whole

## CHAPTER 19

if I wasn't so afraid I would choke on it. On second thought, that just might be preferable to languishing here like a potted plant."

"And here I thought *I* was the cardinal of self-pity." Acheron sat down on an ebony stool across from her and leaned back against an apothecary's cupboard stocked with jars brimming over with ground herbs.

"Last time I checked, you had twice the number of eyes I do." The nervous tapping of Brina's leg confused the meltwood chair, causing it to ripple beneath her.

"True," Acheron admitted, "but my face looks like something a sheikan spat out, I might be the lowest coward in history, and everyone I ever loved is dead."

"Not to mention the cloud." Brina circled her temple with her finger.

"Yes," Acheron said. "Don't mention that." Though he attempted to sound annoyed, the corners of his mouth lifted. "Either way, you're getting worked up over nothing. It's only natural that you can't burn such an advanced shape as your first one. This thing is complicated." He traced one of the pyramid's lines with his index finger. "It's like wanting to fly without learning to jump first."

"I burned it before. In the alley, when you saved me." Brina stared at a stuffed griffin's head on the wall behind Acheron to hide her embarrassment. Though they may be even after the gibbet incident, Brina didn't like the fact that she was ever in his debt to begin with. That it had been Mattheus who had gotten the better of her only made things worse.

"True, and a good thing that you did." Acheron yawned. "But in life-threatening or highly emotional situations, we may find ourselves capable of things that ordinarily would be just outside of our reach."

"We are in a life-threatening situation," Brina replied. Though she did her best to keep her tone matter of fact, an undertone of anxiety was clearly audible. "We're stuck between a million darkhelms and the greatest fortified wall ever built, and I'm useless."

"Useless?" Acheron chuckled. "Out of all of us, you're best suited to deal with the tornado of excrement we find ourselves in. You haven't learned to use sigils, so you're not reliant on them. I bet every one of those wannabe heroes in the basement feels like they're lugging about a body filled with cement and a head full of sawdust. I know I do."

"Sorry to tell you this, Ach, but there may be more than one reason for that."

"I'm serious, kid." He pelted her with a snail shell from the jar behind him. "The single greatest danger of sparkgazing is how quickly we forget what we are underneath, just another mortal sack of bones and muscles.

"I've never met a gazer who didn't fall into that trap to some degree. It begins with burning just a smidge to get up a long flight of stairs. Next, you're enhancing your vision to keep working in the dark. Before you know it, it becomes like breathing. Imagine suddenly only getting a fraction of the air you're used to. That's what all of us are going through right now. Except you. That's why we need you."

Brina picked up the shell and threw it. It arced over Acheron's head and dropped neatly back into the right jar.

"Sounds like a lot of words to say I'm ordinary."

"Exactly." Acheron nodded. "Which is infinitely harder than getting to take shortcuts whenever things get uncomfortable."

Brina still wasn't sure whether he was patronizing her.

"I'll take the shortcuts," she said. She glared at the pyramid in Acheron's palm as though it, personally, was working against her. Then the question that had been burning in her mind burst from her mouth.

"Is it because of my eye that the pyramid won't work anymore?"

Acheron sighed, then made a face halfway between exasperation and sympathy. "I see your mind is not to be diverted."

"It rarely is."

"Look, I'm working on purely theoretical grounds here," Acheron began, waving his hands to stress the point. "I've never met anyone in your particular, erm... situation. But I don't see why you wouldn't be able to burn shapes. The eyes are merely the gateway of the shape. It's our brains that turn it into power, and I daresay you've got at least a modest set of those."

He extended the pyramid toward Brina, and she took it.

"How does that work, then? I thought the sigil *was* the source and we store it, kind of like how a sponge holds water."

"A sigil is a key, nothing more, nothing less," Acheron said. He leaned back in his chair with his arms behind his head. "As the story goes, humanity was created by a handful of fledgling gods now only remembered as 'the chaotics,' whose youthful overzealousness led them to gift each of their creations with a piece of their own supernatural abilities.

"For a time, humanity thrived. Civilizations rose faster than the trees needed to fuel them. Entire mountains were leveled and turned into pyramids and spires that reached for the sun. Rivers were diverted and lakes drained. Then the fighting started."

## CHAPTER 19

Acheron grimaced, causing his spiderweb scars to whiten.

"As it inevitably does when people get a taste of power, conflict tore across the known world like a manmade hurricane. Entire nations, built with the sweat of a hundred generations, were razed in half a century. To put an end to the chaos, an elder god banished the chaotics and placed a lock on humanity's mind, restricting our access to the divine for good."

"This sounds a lot like what the Heilinists preach," Brina said, unable to keep an edge of distaste out of her voice.

Acheron smiled. "Good. I'm glad you picked up on that. For what happened next has been the subject of boundless doddering and diddering amongst an entire era's worth of philosophers.

"Today, the Heilinist church, as you mentioned, teaches that no stability can exist in a world where humanity wields forces they consider divine." Acheron picked something out of his teeth with his thumbnail. "Bunch of sanctimonious wafflers."

Brina shuffled uncomfortably in her seat. "Sounds sensible though, given everything you've just told me."

"Which is precisely what they are banking on," Acheron replied, jabbing a finger at Brina. "But, as just about every other thinker since Methron Albich has pointed out, our world has been the domain of conquerors, slavers and oppressors for as long as written records date back.

"So, sigils or not, we are doomed to slaughter each other until the last two humans on earth die with each other's daggers buried in their throats."

Brina thought back to all dagger-burying, bottle-clubbing and plain old thumb-strangling she'd witnessed in the Ditch over the years. "Sounds about right."

"Which is exactly why a scholar by the name of Methron Albich took matters into his own hands. 'If humanity's gifts have indeed been locked away,' he reasoned, 'there must be a way to pick that lock.' He was right."

"What do you mean?" Brina asked. She was beginning to question whether this history lesson was just another attempt to distract her.

Acheron pointed at the pyramid and gestured for her to hold it up.

"Albich was the first to discover that, given the right stimulus, our minds still have access to the parts that were hidden away."

"So the pattern on the pyramid..." Brina hesitated. "It tells my brain what to do?"

Acheron nodded. "Sigils only enhance that of which we are already capable. Take the fire sigil, *Gnis,* for example. It simply condenses our body heat into an extreme version of itself. The psycho-sigils Saf specializes in all draw upon the natural charisma and guile of the wielder. Meaning, their effects will be shaky when I burn them, while Saf could make a panther think it's a lobster and vice versa."

"So my pyramid uses my body's natural power to heal itself?"

"Exactly. When we conjure up the shape in our mind's eye, we break through the barrier that keeps us from the divine. Which is why I think your eye shouldn't trouble you too much, though I could be wrong."

"Still, it'd be a comfort to know it's possible," Brina said, staring at the jars behind Acheron. "Can't you just draw an easier sigil from memory for me to practice on?"

"If only it were that simple." Acheron sighed. "We could have distributed scripts by the box and let the rest sort itself out."

"What's stopping us?"

"Nuance. As always, the problem is nuance. A script isn't just a copy of a sigil, created by the nearest painter or blacksmith. It's an art form on its own. Every line and twist needs to be perfect, down to a level of detail untraceable by the naked eye. Sigil scribes spend their entire lives studying a mere handful of shapes before they master them sufficiently to create scripts. If I were to sketch a shape, it would be imperfect."

"So it wouldn't work?"

"Most likely, or, even worse, it could work in unforeseen ways."

"Won't you try?" Brina asked. "It would just be for practice, nothing I would actually use in a life-and-death situation."

A long sigh escaped Acheron. Their eyes met. "You know, it continues to astound me how much you resemble your father. He too needed to feel the scorpion's sting before he would leave the damn thing alone."

He stood up and retrieved a sheet of parchment and a charcoal stick from a drawer in Grizelda's dusty counter. A minute or two later, he returned, holding up a torn scrap holding a triangular shape, with dozens of smaller triangles within it.

"This is *Gnis*," he said, "one of the most basic and widespread sigils. If you're so keen to begin, you could try imprinting on it, but be warned, there's every chance that nothing will happen."

Brina held up the scrap with the widest smile she'd managed in days. The *Gnis* shape looked simple, dull even, compared to the countless whirls and angles of the pyramid. Now all she needed to do was imprint it on her mind's eye. How difficult could that be?

## CHAPTER 19

Half an hour passed while Acheron studied Grizelda's collection of oddities, muttering to himself. Meanwhile, Brina leaned back in the meltwood chair, trying to make all distractions and stray thoughts float away. It was harder than it sounded.

Every time she found herself locked on to the shape, a floorboard would creak or someone on the street outside would yell, and she'd have to start over.

Whenever this happened, she forced herself to return to the task at hand. *Spike, angle, slanted line, spike, angle...*

At first, she thought it was another ray of sunlight caught on the parchment. Then she felt the heat. With a yelp of surprise, she let go of the parchment as it suddenly burst into flames.

A searing pain struck her left hand, which was curled around the chair's armrest. Then her legs followed. She jumped up to stomp on the burning parchment before the floor beneath it could catch fire. When Acheron's improvised script had been reduced to a pile of powdered ashes, she turned around to find a smoldering handprint scorched into the chair's smooth finish. A thin string of smoke rose from the place where she had sat.

"I did it," she yelled, waving her burnt hands. "I did it."

"And you only *almost* burned down the place," Acheron said, impressed. "And here I thought that script would be a disaster."

# CHAPTER 20

*18th day of the 11th cycle, 569KR*
**Mallion's Depth**

Sneak crept down yet another flight of smooth, obsidian stairs. Though the courthouse's deliberate lack of windows made it hard to gauge, Sneak guessed he must have descended below ground level multiple floors ago. The icy draft cut through Rosaldo Versarro's woefully thin doublet, making Sneak's teeth chatter. A moldy scent intermingled with smoke from ensconced torches, making him want to sneeze.

*What in the Seven are they doing down here?* Locking up a dozen prisoners required a single room. Two, if you felt generous. The Scale had dozens, all of them tucked away behind reinforced metal doors.

Sneak swallowed as the stairs evened out into the narrowest corridor yet. Gleaming steel doors lined the black walls on either side of him, almost a dozen of them in total. Gilded placards marked each one with a coded combination of numbers and letters similar to those he'd observed on the floors above. His chances of locating the prisoners' quarters were growing slimmer with every door he passed.

In the gaps between rooms, larger-than-life statues of Reynziels, wearing spiked, eyeless helmets, stood in vaulted alcoves. A ripple jerked across Sneak's back each time he passed one. They seemed otherworldly. A wicked and twisted version of the priests that ran the empire. He felt their presence pricking at the back of his neck.

Once he neared the end of the hallway, he squeezed himself into the narrow space behind one of them, hastily marking each door on a scrap of parchment he'd brought. The thin charcoal lines carved across the document, connecting to the crude representation of the floors above this one.

Sneak had hoped a map would help the order in figuring out the next

## CHAPTER 20

step of their plan, but after seven floors, thirteen landings, and twice that number of black corridors, he'd be lucky if the tattered thing could lead him back up to the daylight.

Sneak's finger traced the doors on the floors above. If even a fraction of the rooms behind them were in regular use, the Scale ought to have been bustling with bureaucrats and other vermin, and yet, he hadn't seen or heard anything since his descent into the courtroom's underbelly except for his own pulse hammering in his ears. It didn't add up.

When a hovel in Doorstep's Ditch lacked visible security measures, that meant there was nothing worth stealing inside. When a highly prestigious scepter institution seemed devoid of security measures, that meant he'd missed something. *Nothing to be done about that now,* he reminded himself as he folded up the map. *Your feet are already wet. Might as well go for a swim.*

A metallic groan ruptured the silence as a door opposite the alcove opened. Two darkhelms stepped out, locked in a heated debate.

"You're growing soft, Ignatio," a woman's voice accused. "They're convicts. Doesn't matter how young they look. None of them are harmless, or they wouldn't be here."

The man named Ignatio muttered something Sneak couldn't discern.

"Of course, that's what he would tell you." The woman gave a weary sigh that hinted at a long history of similar disagreements between the pair of them.

"What I do with my own bloody rations is my business." Ignatio's tone made it plain that he considered the conversation over. "If Trango's got a problem with it, he'll have to take it up with His Purity."

Sneak peered around the edge of the statue as the woman's glittering armor disappeared up the stairs.

Ignatio watched her walk away, his expression obscured by the closed visor on his helmet.

*Come on,* Sneak urged the man internally, *get a move on.* He suppressed a curse as the darkhelm leaned back against the closed door, arms folded. Trapped behind the statue, Sneak slid down the wall into a seated position. His jaw clenched and unclenched as the darkhelm retrieved a small bread roll from a pouch on his belt and began tearing at it as though it had insulted him.

Every passing second turned to an age under the imminent threat of discovery. A single glance into the alcove was all it would take.

Heart racing, Sneak risked another peek into the corridor. The staircase at the far end might as well have been a mile away. There were two options. Either he'd wait until it was too late, or he could act now.

There was a clank as Ignatio set his raven's head helmet on the floor beside him. A mane of tangled gray drooped down his shoulders, framing a thin face carved with age.

*Bad move, my friend.*

Sneak closed his eyes. He took a slow, steadying breath as he dug for his remaining sigil-stores. A handful of his core shapes still drifted around in the crevices behind his eyes. They were weak, blurry replicas of what they should have been. Forte's pale blue square flickered in and out of focus in his mind's eye.

One reinforced punch to the darkhelm's temple was sure to knock him out, but it would unquestionably be the death of the store. After that, he'd have to rely on his own, embarrassingly lacking, strength. The idea inspired little enthusiasm. It felt like chucking your last oar into the sea right before drifting into a storm.

*Hollow-brained bastard,* he cursed himself. Just like him to get himself trapped in the worst place on this side of the stoneward. If only he'd allowed Saf to come in his place. She had offered multiple times, but no, he'd had to insist that spying was his specialty. That nagging voice in the back of his head wouldn't allow it any other way. It droned on even now. *Useless, useless, useless.*

He smiled ruefully as he imagined how easily Saf would have handled the situation. She could have walked out from behind the statue and manipulated Ignatio into believing that *he* was the one out of bounds. The man would probably have given her his helmet as a keepsake.

Then something clicked. Before he allowed himself to think it through, he'd hopped to his feet.

Ignatio's head jerked up as Sneak stepped out of the alcove, his hand darting toward the mace on his belt.

"Stay down," Sneak growled. He burned what little *Lux* he had left, willing it to make his eyes crackle with the shape's energy. "Nobody needs to get hurt."

"Who are you? What do you want?" Ignatio's voice quivered, his wide eyes trained on Sneak's own.

If he'd gotten up and swung the mace, Sneak would've been defense-

## CHAPTER 20

less. But the darkhelm didn't. He just sat there, transfixed. "*It's all about suggestion*," Saf had said once.

"As for your first question, I think you have a decent clue." He dipped Lux, just to flare it again for effect. He took a menacing step forward. "As for the second, I want to not have to turn you into a pile of bloody bits of bone, Ignatio."

He could do nothing of the sort, but the threat seemed to suffice.

The darkhelm's mouth worked, terror and fury warring across his lined face. "The Keeper will have your soul for this."

"She's had it for a while." Sneak gestured toward the locked doors on either side of the darkhelm.

"Slide me your keys."

Ignatio's eyes flickered from Sneak to the stairs on the far end of the hallway, where his colleague had vanished minutes earlier.

"Don't make me ask again," Sneak growled. He sounded about as menacing as a hungry pup, but Ignatio seemed to think it impressive enough.

There was a sigh, followed by the tinkling of two dozen keys skidding across the floor. Sneak picked up the heavy key ring and riffled through the keys with a bony index finger.

"What's in here?" He pointed at the smaller door to Ignatio's right.

"Storage room," Ignatio grumbled, the muscles in his caved cheeks working hard.

"Excellent." Sneak smiled. "And which key might we need to enter?"

Ignatio's face hardened as he realized what Sneak was about to do. "You go too far," he spat. The darkhelm rolled over, getting to his knees to spring up. Sneak darted forward and cut him off with a quick kick to the ribs.

The darkhelm hit the floor with a thud laced with an unpleasant popping sound. "Curse you and all your kin," the man yelled, clutching at his dislocated shoulder. "You'll die here. Today."

Sneak winced as he watched the man writhe in silent agony. This wasn't how he'd wanted things to go. It was bad enough to kill a darkhelm when they were storming you in full plate. To harm a defenseless one while they were looking you in the eye took a special kind of guts. The kind Sneak didn't possess.

"I'm sorry," he muttered. "I could look at that if you want..."

The darkhelm gave him a glare that dissuaded Sneak from getting into arm's reach of the man. His ears rang with the echoes of the man's shouts.

Adrenaline flooded Sneak's bloodstream, making him jittery. For all he knew, a dozen of Ignatio's colleagues had heard him.

"Which. One. Is. It?" He emphasized every word with a jangle of the key ring.

"The heavy one." Ignatio breathed a resigned sigh that turned into a grunt of pain.

Sneak opened the door at the man's shoulder with the swift turn of a large wrought-iron key. Behind it lay a square room, about fifteen feet wide. Piles of jute sacks filled with oats lined the walls. Multiple bales of straw were piled against the back wall, the dust of which itched in Sneak's nostrils.

He gave Ignatio a curt nod to get in.

The man dragged himself across the floor with his good arm, the other one hanging at his side at an awkward angle. Sneak was about to lock the man in when a stroke of brilliance hit him.

"You're not going to like this," he said, looking down at Ignatio with a sudden flicker of amusement. "I'm going to need you to strip."

\*\*\*

The darkhelm's leather breastplate, studded with gleaming steel spikes, clanged against the smooth black floor at Sneak's feet. Only the man's raven helmet remained now. Ignatio clutched it to his chest as though it was his firstborn.

Sneak waved an impatient hand.

"Here with it. The sooner this is over, the better for the both of us."

"I can't." Ignatio's face was growing paler as the pain in his mangled shoulder built. Beads of sweat clung to his forehead like boulders on a hillside. Whatever remained of the adrenaline in the man's system would soon give way entirely. *Poor bastard.* No matter Ignatio's stubborn pride, soon he would scream. By that time, Sneak needed to be long gone.

"Losing the helmet is a first-degree offense," Ignatio breathed through gritted teeth. "They'll have my title. I'll lose everything. You can't take it. I won't allow it."

Sneak swallowed. A vain attempt to suppress the growing disgust he felt for his own actions. *You owe him nothing. He's the enemy.*

"What were you arguing about?" Sneak blurted out before he could stop himself. "Just now, with your colleague?"

"Hosana was right. I've grown soft. I'd forgotten who I was dealing with." Ignatio's voice had dimmed to a hoarse whisper. He spoke as much to himself as to Sneak. "That's a mistake I'll never make again."

## CHAPTER 20

He spat at Sneak's feet. Sneak sidestepped the volley with a frown.

"What did you do?"

"Gave the kid, Wane, my bread and beans. Thought he needed them more than I did." He shot Sneak a look that could have felled an erymanthian mid-charge. "Little did I know."

"You're a decent man."

The order's plan, to collect names and data of the new batch of outwalled so they could take their places in the line, was ruined. Sneak had seen to that. As soon as the darkhelms found Ignatio, the Scale would become a fortress to rival God's Maul. Every darkhelm in the city would receive his description. Assuming he could even make it back out of the Scale's front gate in time. Dread squeezed his chest.

"Where are you keeping the kid?" Sneak asked.

Ignatio chewed on his bottom lip. "Door to the left. The one I just came from."

An involuntary smile curled Sneak's lips. At least he'd gotten something out of this ordeal.

"Murio Versarro?"

Sneak's stomach plummeted from malaise into sheer despair. He knew who it was, even before he turned to look at her.

"Muria D'Hautefagne? Oh, thanks goodness, I must have taken a wrong turn somewhere on..."

Ignatio took that as his cue to scream for help. Sneak instinctively kicked the door shut, turning the key with a smooth motion. The steel door muffled most of the darkhelm's voice, but the damage had been done.

"I knew something wasn't right." Cerise's voice rose. Sneak dropped *Lux*, hoping to ease her fears, but the sudden shift in his eyes made her jump back. "I waited outside for you, you know. I wanted to ask—" She waved a hand to chase away the thought. "I thought you'd gotten lost or something, but you're not lost, are you? You're *this*." Her index finger waggled between both of her own regular eyes.

"I can explain," Sneak said, dropping Rosaldo Versarro completely. He could feel the edges of his frayed nerves unraveling.

"No need," Cerise snapped. She inched backward, the way you would disengage a wild animal. "I've got the measure of things."

Sneak followed her, each one of his strides covering two of Cerise's. The woman's eyes widened in terror as he neared.

"Wait," Sneak tried desperately, "I don't want to hurt anyone. It's the opposite. I'm here to set people free. That's all I want. Freedom for all."

He could hear the scream building in Cerise's guts long before it escaped. Helplessly, he watched the sharp inhale, the stiffening in her posture, and the unconscious clenching of both her fists.

He caught her with a hand over the mouth just in time. The screech turned into a terrified whimper against the palm of his hand. It might as well have been the death-squawk of whatever tension between the two of them had made his stomach flutter so pleasantly not half an hour earlier.

Before he gave himself a chance to think, he wrapped his other arm across her stomach, pinning her arms to her side. Cerise fought to get away from him, but even without sigils, panic had turned Sneak's grip into a vise.

Icy horror flooded his system as he began dragging the struggling woman back toward the storage room.

"Listen." His fingers found the heavy key still in the lock. "You're safe. I won't harm you. I just can't allow you to get me caught. Too much depends on it.

"You're being lied to," he continued, unsure of what he was hoping to achieve. "There are thousands of us outside the wall. A bright woman such as yourself can't possibly believe that each and every one of us is scum, can you?"

His forceful grip on the woman's face might undercut the point somewhat, but he couldn't stop looking for excuses. The thought that Cerise would live on thinking about him as some kind of monster was unbearable.

The storage room swung open, and Sneak shoved Cerise forward, gently but firmly. She turned to glare at him, face frozen in an inscrutable expression. The tears in the corners of her eyes struck Sneak like a windup quarrel.

"I'm sorry," he said. "I've got to finish what I started here. See if you can help ol' Ignatio over there with his shoulder, will you?" He nodded at the darkhelm, who lay on a bale of straw near the back of the room.

The man glared at Sneak, still clutching his helmet.

"Don't worry." Sneak sighed. "Keep it."

*I must be the worst bloody criminal on this entire sphere.*

# CHAPTER 21

*18th day of the 11th cycle, 569KR*
**Mallion's Depth**

With his cover shattered and his plans ruined, Sneak felt the dungeon close in around him. He looked up at the vaulted ceiling, picturing all those floors above him. A crushing amount of stone and steel stood between him and fresh air. He leaned back against the door that led to the prisoners' quarters, taking deep steadying breaths.

He was in no mood to return to Grouchy Zelda's under these circumstances. He could all but hear Bron's delighted chuckles as he recounted the disastrous denouement of his mission. Not to mention the jabs that old bastard Acheron would come up with. Disappointing Saf would merely be the foam on his pint of misery. He wouldn't prove himself a failure. Not again. Never again.

Resolve settled in his chest. Before his newfound courage had a chance to cave, he turned the key and set off toward the prisoners' quarters.

He was silent at first, tiptoeing down the torchlit corridor. Flickering shadows blended into the vaulted ceiling, making it impossible to tell which was which. As the corridor dragged on, he sped up, pushed forward by the knowledge that Ignatio and Cerise could be found at any moment.

A muffled scream resounded just beyond a corner up ahead, followed by a series of thumps, each accompanied by the creaks of splintering wood. Each impact hammered in Sneak's chest.

"Stay back, Silner," a gruff voice called out, tainted by fear. The only response was another volley of battering.

Sneak peered around a corner just in time to watch Silner, the throat slitter, kick down the heavy door to his cell. Silner blinked as he stumbled into the well-lit guards' quarter, looking as surprised as anyone at his triumph over the wood and metal barricade.

In the middle of the square room, their backs turned to Sneak, two darkhelms stood side by side. Each of them bore a heavy rectangular shield, complemented by thin, unusually long swords. On the opposite side of the room, almost a dozen identical doors were set into the smooth black wall, one of which hung at a slant from torn hinges.

"Last warning, Silner," one of the darkhelms, a brawny woman standing over six feet tall, called out.

For a moment, Silner hesitated. Now that he had successfully forced his way out of his cell, his plan seemed to be at an end.

"What's going on?" a voice called from behind one of the other cell doors. "Let us out," another yelled.

"Shut up," the armored woman shouted back, "or I'll whip every one of you raw."

The threat had the opposite effect. A renewed chorus of shouts emanated from the cells, interspersed with deafening crashes that made the doors rattle.

Silner shook his head like a mad bull, disoriented by the growing chaos around him. When the two darkhelms took a step toward him, he charged. The two-man shield wall braced for an impact that never came. At the last second Silner darted sideways, out of blade's reach, grabbed an abandoned stool from beside a round table, and flung it right into the smaller guard's face.

There was a clank as the stool bounced off the man's helmet. The darkhelm staggered backward, hands clutching at a dent on the top of his head. His long blade clattered to the ground, forgotten.

The other darkhelm jabbed forward as Silner lunged for the weapon. A deep gash opened on Silner's upper arm.

A second thrust went over the prisoner's shoulder, inches away from the exposed flesh of his neck.

Sneak clutched at the smooth wall, frozen between a desire to remain unseen and the realization that more darkhelms could enter the passage behind him at any moment. His fingertips rubbed at Ignatio's armor, which sat loosely on his scrawny chest. If only he'd had the stones to make the man give up his helmet, he could have posed as a darkhelm, and in the battle's aftermath, he might have been able to blend in long enough

## CHAPTER 21

to escape. Luckily, the Seven had granted him one more chance to learn from his mistakes.

Back in the guards' quarter, Silner looked more fired up than weakened by the wound he'd sustained. He danced around the darkhelm's long swipes with the sort of wooden efficiency that betrayed years of experience dodging pointy objects swung his way.

In one smooth motion, Silner dipped down and pulled the unconscious darkhelm on the floor into a chokehold.

"Drop the cutter," he snarled at the remaining guard, "or I'll wring his neck like a cloth."

The guard hesitated, circling Silner like a predator sizing up its prey. Silner tightened his grip, eliciting a groan from his captive.

"I said drop it."

"I don't negotiate with the likes of you," the woman snarled. With a flash of steel, she lunged at Silner's exposed flank. Surprised, Silner dropped his hostage as his hands shot up to shield his face. It was a bad reflex. The type that got a man killed. Silner knew it, the guard knew it, and Sneak knew it.

The darkhelm's long blade swept toward Silner's chest, primed for a lethal blow. Right before it made contact, she let out a squelched shout. The blade swung upward, missing the prisoner by inches.

"I'm sorry," Sneak whispered in the woman's ear, his arm wrapped around her neck. "It was the only way."

The guard kicked and struggled, but under the influence of his last ounce of *Forte,* Sneak's arm may as well have been made of Pylaean silver.

"Excellent," Silner muttered in between heaving breaths. "For a second, I thought it was all over."

When his store of *Forte* ran out, Sneak lowered the limp darkhelm to the floor. The woman would wake up with a mammoth of a headache, but at least she'd live. Or so Sneak hoped.

"You want to squeeze some more, my friend," Silner said conversationally, bending down to pick up a discarded sword. "Just to be sure."

Sneak frowned. "There's no need to—"

There was a wet squelch as Silner drove his blade through the smaller darkhelm's leather armor and into his chest. Blood spurted from the opening like a hot spring, spattering the black armor with crimson stars.

"No!" Sneak stared down at the convulsing man in abject horror. Before he could stop himself, he'd lunged at Silner, pushing the giant backward just as he raised the blade for a finishing blow. The sword crashed into the stone floor with a grating wrench.

"What's your plaguing problem?" Silner roared.

"We have to get out of here," Sneak improvised, trying to hide his unease as the giant towered over him. In a fair fight, Silner could tear him to pieces with one hand tied behind the marble slab he called a back. "There's no time to mess around. Besides, how are we going to look when we stride out of here covered in gore?"

Silner frowned, his piggish face screwed up in thought. It looked painful. "Fine."

Sneak bent down to steal the unconscious woman's helmet. He pretended to fiddle with the leather strap just long enough to search for her heartbeat. He could have cried with relief when he felt a weak, rhythmic thrust against his fingertips. At least one of them would survive the ordeal.

"What are you doing?" Silner scowled, a glint of greed in his piggy eyes. "I did most of the work. Loot's mine."

"We need a cover. You're going to pretend to be my prisoner."

"Hey, what about us?" a muffled voice shouted from one of the cells at the opposite end of the room.

"Yeah," another called, "you can't just leave us here."

"Yes we can," Silner barked, rushing over to the cell doors and banging his fist into the wood. "Shut up."

Sneak was already fiddling with Ignatio's key ring. He might as well accept that he was too soft to leave any of them behind.

A short bronze key did the trick. Before he could fully open the door, Muria Jarnethe z'Ondael, convicted of fraud, stormed out. She made to rush into the corridor, but Sneak grabbed her by the arm.

"Not yet," he said. "They'll pick us off one by one. We'll go as a group."

She nodded.

Moments later, nine recently outwalled prisoners stood clustered together in the guards' quarter, each of them torn between excitement and terror. Only one was visibly absent.

"Where is the kid?" Sneak asked the group at large. "Harrod Wane. Where did they take him?"

"I'm here," a small voice croaked from the last cell to the right, the door of which stood ajar.

"Come on," Sneak called. "What are you waiting for?"

"I'm not coming."

## CHAPTER 21

Silner let out a demonstrative sigh, tapping an imaginary timepiece on his wrist.

"Wait here." Sneak shot the man a threatening look.

He found Harrod Wane sitting on a thin layer of straw, knees drawn up to his chest. The kid's blue eyes were red with tears.

"You don't want to come with us?" Sneak asked.

The kid jerked away from him, backing further into the dark corner.

"Oh. Right." He lifted the helmet's visor, revealing his face.

Wane's whole body sagged with relief. "You're not with the watch?"

"Not even a little."

"Then how did you..." He mimed turning a key.

"It's a long story," Sneak said, "but right now, we have to go. Time is running out."

"Nuh-uh." Wane shook his head like he was trying to get water out of his ears. "They'll kill me. I'm fast, but weak. Like a hare."

Sneak swallowed. The kid was right to be scared, but with his age and build, his chances weren't much better in the Ditch. Between the gangs, the cloud and the violence, there were plenty of ways for a kid to disappear.

"I'll protect you," Sneak said, extending a hand. "Just stay close to me, and we'll be just fine."

"But how?" Wane asked, looking skeptical. "There's one of you versus the entire Enlightened Watch."

"I'll let you in on a little secret." Sneak burned *Lux*, creating a brief flash of starburst light. The store sputtered and went out as soon as he touched it. *That's two down.* He'd be working with scraps from here on out.

Wane's eyes went big as goose eggs, a smile tugging at the corners of his mouth. "You're a—"

"Shh." Sneak held a finger to his lips. "It's a secret, remember?"

Wane nodded excitedly. "Okay," he said, "I believe you. I'll come with you."

As the kid sprang up, a guilt unlike any Sneak had felt that day overcame him. Trapping Ignatio and Cerise had been bad. Giving Silner the opportunity to murder an innocent man had been worse, but flat-out lying to a child, that was the worst. If it came down to it, he wouldn't be able to protect the kid.

"Where'd they go?" Wane asked, looking from the empty guard's quarter to Sneak.

"Pus, plague, and piss," Sneak shouted. "When I find that bastard, Silner, I'm going to make him eat his own—" He stopped himself as Wane giggled.

"Madame Arturia says you're not supposed to say *piss*. Or *bastard*."

"It's not ideal," Sneak agreed. He shoved Wane toward the empty corridor ahead. "We better run, kid."

\*\*\*

Sneak didn't know which was worse, the fact that he could lead Harrod Wane back up to the Scale's ground floor by simply following the racket the other prisoners made on their way up, or the trail of bloodied darkhelms that marked the path like ghastly cairns. It made him glad he'd broken his promise to release Cerise on his way out. The mere thought of her running into a bloodlusted Silner made his teeth chatter. It was better for her to be stuck in storage for a little while longer.

When they'd passed the first body, Sneak had tried to cover Wane's eyes to spare him the horror. By the tenth, there had been no hiding the carnage.

"We're here, kid," he whispered at Wane when they reached the final landing, where a set of bronze doors guarded the way to the Scale's main hallway. They stood ajar just far enough for the din of a battle to reach them. "Hide behind that vase. *Only* come out when I give you the signal, understood?"

The boy nodded.

"Remember, I'm the one with the bent spike." He pointed at the top of his helmet, which had struck the ground of the dungeon when its original owner had collapsed.

Beyond the double doors, chaos reigned. Silner stood in the middle of the hallway, atop the marble stairs that led to the outer gatehouse. He was surrounded by five remaining prisoners, each of whom had scavenged darkhelm maces. Both above and below the desperate group, the darkhelms had formed a shield wall, barring all paths of escape.

The panic that had been simmering in Sneak's gut boiled over. *What have I done?* He peered over his shoulder, toward the vase where Harrod Wane sat hidden. Sneak had promised that he'd keep the kid safe. That had been the only reason Wane had agreed to leave his cell. If they were caught now, the kid might be slain in the fray. Or worse.

*Think, idiot, think.*

"Cowardice is a grievous sin." Sneak's throat closed up with terror as

## CHAPTER 21

a familiar high-pitched drone resounded from the staircase behind him. Methusal, the Scale's Keeper Chosen, trudged up the staircase, his gilded mask exchanged for a wicked steel helmet covered in spikes. There was no visor, nor any other way for the man to see. Yet he knew Sneak was there from two dozen feet away.

"My apologies," Sneak intoned, deepening his voice to something he imagined a generic darkhelm would sound like, "I was sent to fetch you, but I see you have already been alerted to the present situation."

Methusal's head twisted left and right. A deep, rattling breath escaped from underneath that wicked helmet, as though he was trying to taste Sneak's presence on the air.

"Name?" the Keeper Chosen croaked.

"Ignatio," Sneak muttered, his throat drier than a Doorstep's Ditch inn at sunrise. "Ignatio Fillepleur."

He slapped a hand to his forehead as the made-up last name rolled off his tongue. Why did he always have to improvise?

Methusal clicked his tongue.

Then, without warning, the old man lurched forward, arcing through the air like a hawk diving for its prey. Only an instinctive flare of *Veloce* allowed Sneak to twirl out of the way right as Methusal's outstretched hand brushed his throat.

"Oh-ho." Methusal let out a mirthless laugh. "What have we here?"

*What have we here indeed?* Not even a top-tier athlete in his twenties should have been able to cover that much distance in a single leap, never mind a decrepit old man of Methusal's stature. Before Sneak could ruminate further on the matter, the sightless priest flung his palm outward, and a wave of bone-splintering cold engulfed Sneak.

"What the..." The rest of his curse died on his lips as they stiffened beyond all use. He let out an involuntary rattle as his chest contracted, squeezing the frozen air out of his lungs. The muscles in his arms and legs ground to a halt mid-dodge, causing him to topple onto the smooth floor.

Instinctively, Sneak flared *Gnis* with all his might, desperate to keep the last remnants of warmth from evaporating from his blood. The sigil bloomed in his mind's eye. A seed of heat dropped into his stomach, a molten core in a body of hardening steel.

"Your hollow tricks will not save you, heretic." Methusal limped over to Sneak with the slow confidence of a spider that knows the fly is irrevocably ensnared in its web. "Want a taste of what real power feels like?"

Methusal's fingers twisted into a complicated gesture, and a new stab of cold pierced Sneak's chest, extinguishing his store of *Gnis*. As the sigil vanished, Sneak's world descended into darkness.

Somewhere high above Sneak, Methusal let out a delighted cackle.

"You fire-eyes run around with clay mugs, trying to steal a gulp or two from the Keeper's stream. Meanwhile, *we* control the tides."

There was a dull *crack* as Methusal's booted foot thumped into Sneak's stolen helmet, tearing it off his head.

"I know someone who is going to be happy to see you, my sacrilegious friend, very happy indeed."

Through blurry, glazed over eyes, Sneak watched as the dark figure loomed over him, the spiked helmet drawing a black outline against the torchlight behind it. Terror such as he had never felt seeped into every vessel of his being. *On the bright side, if I piss myself, at least I'll be warm.* A smile tugged at his rigid lips, splitting the skin.

"You and your friends have troubled His Eminence greatly of late," Methusal muttered, "but now we will finally get to the bottom of your antics, won't we?"

Methusal knelt down beside Sneak and held two wrinkly fingers to his frozen mouth. There was a flash of heat as Sneak's skin burned and blistered. His lips became mobile once more.

"Who are you?" Methusal demanded. There was an unnatural depth to his voice, a sonorous drone that bored into Sneak like a drill.

"Yuranes," Sneak croaked. "Yuranes Hole." He let out a weak chuckle. Sticky liquid ran down his chin as the blisters on his lips broke.

"That won't do." Methusal clicked his tongue disapprovingly, like a disgruntled elder might chastise a bawdy child. "I asked you who you were."

The unnatural ring of the priest's voice deepened until the words seemed to echo from within Sneak's own skull, a coercive, unrelenting drone. *My name is Sneak.* As the thought forced its way into his consciousness, he felt his lips move in tandem, hearing the words bounce back at him from a distance.

"I'll need a real name."

"No. No. No. Don't think," he told himself out loud, "think about nonsense."

"I doubt much else goes in that shell of yours on the best of days," Methusal sneered. "Who do you work for?"

## CHAPTER 21

"We're called the Order of the Prism." Sneak cursed himself and all the world around him. *Keep your mouth shut, you useless idiot.*

The harder he tried to keep a grip on his own treacherous mind, the more his thoughts flickered toward Saf, Bron, and, worst of all, Brina Springtide. He mustn't tip the scepter off about her or... *No.* A scream escaped him as he bit down hard on his own tongue, the pain forcing any thought of Brina and God's Maul out of his mind.

"What are you doing? Idiot boy." Methusal cuffed him around the ears with a leather gloved hand.

Sneak was spared the effort of coming up with a sufficiently snarky response when a hail of pottery shards clattered down from above.

Methusal stumbled sideways, then collapsed into a heap.

Where his black form had loomed over Sneak, a second, much smaller shape stood grinning.

"I bet he's not going to like that when he wakes up," Sneak said.

"Run," Harrod Wane yelled, still holding the handle of the vase he'd conked Methusal over the head with. He kicked the Keeper Chosen in the temple with surprising ferocity. Then he broke into a sprint.

Sneak struggled to keep up. His lungs were on fire and with every breath, droplets of blood sprayed everywhere. When they burst into the main entrance hall to the Scale, chaos greeted them.

Three prisoners were embroiled in a life and death struggle with two darkhelms trying to block their escape. Harrod Wane slithered through the fray like an eel. Using the path the boy had made, Sneak followed, dancing between flailing arms and kicking legs. None of the combatants seemed to have eyes for either of them.

Moments later, they found themselves in the square outside. Sneak lowered his visor, blending in with the legion of darkhelms swarming toward the courtroom. The scuffle inside the Scale's portal was drawing a growing crowd. On the other side of the square, an entire squadron of reinforcements plowed through the crowd toward them.

"Over here."

Sneak looked over his shoulder and saw Wane beckoning from an alley to the right. The kid led him down a series of ever narrowing alleys that ran in the crevices between rows of identical sandstone houses. They jumped a wooden fence, slipped through an open gate and ended up in a small but well-kept garden in a hamlet surrounded by three houses.

Wane ushered him in through the back door. On the other side lay a cluttered kitchen with a round table and six chairs.

"Harry!"

"Madame Arturia," Wane said, giving a bald woman who was built like a draught horse a deferential bow, "this is my friend..." He looked back at Sneak.

"Abel. My name's Abel."

# CHAPTER 22

*18th day of the 11th cycle, 569KR*
**The Sundered Sea**

"and ho!"
Solana gripped the edge of her writing desk when the dreaded call came from overhead. It was time. She went over the letter one last time, her eyes tracing every syllable with longing. She had spent so long perfecting every curl and wave that the journey from Hammerstroke had felt like mere hours. Now they were here and everything would soon be different. Would she still be able to write once it had been done? It seemed unlikely.

She rolled up the parchment and sealed it inside a wooden case with rose-scented wax from the candle next to the small bunk in her cabin. When she was done, she tucked the case away in the inner pocket of her Reynziel's robe, donned her helmet, and strode out of her door.

Captain Joanna Morris stood leaning on the starboard railing.
"You call that hoisting, Higgins?" she barked at a petite woman who was pulling in rope in quick jerky motions. "Put some starlight into it, for Heil's sake."

"How long until we arrive?"
The captain looked over her shoulder as Solana approached.
"Three hours, maybe four, Your Purity," Morris said. "From there, it'll take you half an hour behind the oars to reach the abbey's dock."

"Excuse me?"
"Did our officers not inform you?" The captain's head tilted with amusement. "Our ships never anchor at Everberg. Not even to deliver such an imminent personality as yourself."

"And why is that?" Solana snapped, glad to hear her regular icy tone had regained its punch. "Have you not been tasked by the office of the

Cardinal to bring me to Everberg? Not 'almost to Everberg' or even 'very near to Everberg.' No, you were sent out to bring me to its very doorstep if I so desire."

The captain's crooked smile sagged. She tugged at a golden button on her doublet. "It can't be done. Not by us, nor anyone else with full eye sockets. The abbey is surrounded by reefs that chew up a ship's hull faster than a priest can..." She broke off when she realized who she was speaking to.

"The point is that only the eyeless ones know the secret to steering ships safely to their own shore, and only the Keeper knows how they manage it. So, begging your pardon, Your Purity, but I will not risk this ship and everyone on it."

"Fine." Solana leaned over the rail beside the captain and peered at the growing black bump on the horizon. A low mist hung over the calm sea like a mourner's veil. The knot in her stomach tightened. "Do you have a spyglass aboard, captain?"

"Aye, Your Purity. In my cabin."

"Fetch it."

Morris's eyebrows jumped up. It had clearly been quite some time since anyone had given her a command on her own ship. Solana didn't care. Before nightfall, she would be a novice once more. She might as well leverage what authority she had while it lasted.

The captain barked an order at Higgins, who returned moments later with a gleaming wooden case that held a solid silver spyglass. Solana leaned her elbow on the railing to get a steady view.

It was an excellent instrument. Even from this distance, she could make out acidic green splotches of algae and vines on the outer wall of the abbey. Everberg had been built on a hill that stuck out of the ocean like a small island. At the very top of it stood a mighty cathedral with three spires. Even in this cloudy weather, its sandstone facade seemed to emanate white light of its own. It seemed ironic that the only living souls who ever got close enough to admire its details couldn't see it.

Maybe that was the point, she thought. Beauty constructed in the Keeper's name, destined only for her, never to be marveled at by mortal eyes. A lightness came alongside the realization. Such a magnificent tribute to the Keeper would surely carry some blessing with it. This was all part of the path Heil had laid before her, even if she couldn't see the end herself.

Solana lowered the hourglass and interlocked the knuckles of her fists at chest height in prayer. *Heil, keeper of souls and intentions, grant me strength*

## CHAPTER 22

*in the face of tribulation. Give me the fire and conviction to build on the foundation you have laid for me and all of humanity.*

\*\*\*

"Gotta hand it to you, Your Purity," Captain Morris said as her crew bustled about to lower a sloop into the water. "Your nerves are firmer than my own. I wouldn't go near that island if it were made of gemstones."

Solana was grateful that her helm obscured her expression. Her heart thumped in her throat as she stepped over the ship's railing and into the sloop. The crew's solemn faces did little to bolster her failing courage.

"When the Keeper lights your path, there is no room for the shadow of fear," she quoted. It was taken word for word from the memoirs of Cardinal Catalina III, but she doubted the sailors were familiar with the work. Best to keep up appearances for as long as possible.

As soon as the sloop dropped toward the water, Solana's posture drooped. There would be no more reprieve, no more windings in the path, just the bubbling foam of the sea and the inescapable call of her uncertain destiny.

Her first pull on the oars was like stirring quicksand. She yanked on those wooden torture devices with all her might, only to find the sloop pulled sideways by a strong current. Just another part of the given path.

As she fought her way through this barren and unruly waterscape, doubt seeped back into her mind alongside the sour burn that invaded her arms and shoulders. The dark outline of Everberg loomed up ever larger in front of her, a spectre in the mist. It wasn't too late. Not yet. Past the island, almost invisible in the distance, lay the gold and green shore of Merkede. She could still allow the current to drag her past the abbey, toward a life in exile. A life outside of the Cardinal's long reach, away from the lasting consequences of her own failures.

A mad, giddy sense of relief took hold of her. She could see him now, De Leliard, the gluttonous slob, sitting behind his overladen table like a greedy spider in its web, pulling her strings only to find out she was no longer at the end of them. *He's Heil's emissary,* a guilt-ridden voice in the back of her head warned, *you owe him your allegiance as if he himself were the Keeper. To stray from him is to stray from the given path.*

Something glimmered in the water ahead, distracting her from the impossible ambiguity of it all. She peered over the side of the sloop and felt her jaw drop. Reefs. It was like gazing into a different universe. Intricate formations of coral in red and green, sprawling out like cities with towers, walls and cathedrals of their own. A school of rainbow-colored fish split before the sloop's bow, only to find each other again when it had passed. They danced this way and that in the clear water in perfect synchronization. They simply flowed. Hundreds of tiny luminescent crabs skittered across the seafloor, like stars shifting in the night sky.

"How could I have doubted you?" Solana muttered, subconsciously interlocking her fists against her chest. Guided by the current, she drifted toward a series of pontoons that bobbed up and down in front of Everberg's gatehouse.

She would never forget that first unstable step onto the floating dock. She looked down into the water, soaking in the elegant grace of the Keeper's creation one last time.

Then she reached for a heavy steel knocker and rapped it against the dark wooden door.

# CHAPTER 23

*18th day of the 11th cycle, 569KR*
**Mallion's Depth**

"Are you sure we can trust this man?" Brina asked, peering through the boarded-up windows at the rundown carriage that stood in front of Grizelda's storefront. Even while standing still, the vehicle creaked and groaned like the old horses that were drawing it.

"As much as we can trust anyone in this miserable city," Sneak said. "That's Gardo, the kid's eldest brother. He'll bring us to the docks, where one of their associates will sail us out to sea."

"Also," Acheron said, his voice cold and irritated, "since *someone* thought it necessary to facilitate a full-blown jailbreak in the highest seat of justice in the empire, we don't have any other choice. It's a matter of hours before the darkhelms begin kicking in every door north of the palace."

"We were going to break them out regardless," Sneak reminded him, face growing red. "That was the plan to begin with."

"The plan was to swap ourselves in, smoothbrain. The whole point was to keep the scheme low key. You know what's not low key?" Acheron looked around wide-eyed, as though genuinely curious. "Getting Keeper's Square and everything around it locked down by a thousand darkhelms."

"Easy for you to say. You weren't there. That place had a million identical hallways and staircases. Where would those prisoners have gone once we released them?"

"Fair point," Acheron grumbled, "but enough with the pleasantries. Let's get ourselves smuggled."

Saf greeted Gardo Wane with an outstretched hand. The man shook it, glancing at the countless windows on either side of the street. It couldn't be plainer that Gardo had never even stolen so much as a boiled squid on a stick, much less faced the pressure of smuggling five highly wanted criminals past the entire mobilized might of the scepter. Brina's already lacking confidence in the undertaking waned further.

"Please excuse the smell," Gardo said. He pulled back the jute tarp that covered the back of the cart, revealing a gruesome assortment of squid, giant clams, and three-foot-long sun sharks. All of them were far past edible. "There's a second tarp underneath the cargo for you to hide under."

"I'm not getting in *that.*" Bron gagged louder than was necessary.

"Bye then," Acheron snapped at him, one foot already in the squishy mass of rotting seafood. Before their eyes, Acheron disappeared from view with a squelch.

The others stared at each other with expressions ranging from distaste to "sudden death wish."

"It was the only way to ensure the city watch wouldn't investigate too closely," Gardo said. His eyes jumped from window to window as though he was afraid a manticore would burst through one of them at any moment. "Please hurry, Phillipina will be waiting."

Brina sighed and clambered over the side. Icy slime coated her arms up to the neck as she wormed herself underneath the second tarp, which was already soaked through with filth.

In the end, Saf and Sneak had to force a retching Bron into the cart.

"I hate getting dirty," he whispered. "You best hope I get this stink out of my beard, little man."

"I wouldn't bet on it," Brina said, wrinkling her nose. As a roamer, she had experienced filth in untold forms and quantities, but even she had trouble keeping her sparse dinner down.

The cart set off at a hobble. Every bump in the road felt like a kick to her legs and arms. Come morning, she'd look like a walking bruise, but that was nothing compared to what would await them in the Cardinal's dungeons. She imagined being thrown into a cell alongside her father and smiled. *Hi, Dad, I'm home.*

"Barricade up ahead," Gardo whispered from the coach box. His voice was steeped in dread. Brina swallowed as the cart came to a stop. *He's not up to it. He's going to fold like a cheap playing card.*

"Halt," a woman's voice to Brina's right snapped. "Nothing goes in or out of the seventh district without approval."

"Feel free to take a look, madam watcher, but I'm afraid you won't find

## CHAPTER 23

my cargo much to your liking." Brina was pleased to hear a smidgen of confidence in Gardo's tone.

The cart rattled as the tarp on the top was lifted. There was a shuffle of retreating footsteps.

"This is trash. Rotten beyond all use," the woman said. "Why, of all times, does it need to be moved now?"

Gardo's reply came so smoothly that Brina assumed it must be true.

"My sister's a fisherwoman, Muria watcher," he said. "We use our leftovers as bait to catch monkfish. They're much easier to lure at night."

A moment of silence passed, then the woman sighed.

"Fine, get that stinking mess from under my nose."

"Will do," Gardo replied. "Have a good night."

As soon as the cart was out of earshot from the barricade, Brina whispered to Acheron, "Reckon she was talking about you?"

\*\*\*

*18th day of the 11th cycle, 569KR*
**Everberg Abbey**

"Sister Solana, we've been expecting you."

Solana hesitated, unsure of how to address him. The man who stood before her was wearing neither the helmet of his order, nor the customary white and gold robe that signified one's status as a Reynziel. Instead, he was clad in a worn-out black robe that hung off his frame in tatters, its hood drawn so far over his face that it was entirely obscured. An unpleasant, sickly-sweet stench like rank roses emanated from him. Not knowing the man's rank, she decided to play it safe.

"Thank you, Reynziel." She added a shallow bow, enough not to cause offense should the man prove to be of a higher rank than herself, but not overdone either lest the opposite be true.

"We of the abbey have little use for titles." He cackled. His voice sounded like a rusty hinge. "As I am sure you will soon come to grasp."

Beyond the gatehouse lay a corridor with a vaulted ceiling carved out of plain sandstone. Her nameless guard closed the gate behind her, and darkness took over at once. She expected the man to give her a jelly lantern, or another way to navigate the path ahead, but no such accommodations were made. The monk's dragging footsteps and the rustling of his robe were her only guide. The experience was at once disorienting and intensely claustrophobic. Even in the confines of this straight corridor, Solana felt lost in the absence of the sense she relied on most. Soon, that would be her life. Better get used to it.

Even amongst those ascended to the rank of Reynziel, little was known about the blind order. Some thought them mad, a group of radical outliers, barely more refined than the heathens of Bior. Others saw in their willingness to forgo their sight a noble quest to attune their minds to the worship of the Keeper. Then there were the rumors. They ranged from miraculous healing performed by the order's abbot to the blood sacrifice of heretics in Heil's name. If there was one thing everyone agreed on, it was that Everberg was nothing like the other orders.

"In here," the monk whispered in her ear. Solana jumped. The monk let out another ghastly cackle.

Feeling the rightmost wall of the corridor fall away, Solana turned into a doorway. The space beyond was just as dark, disorienting her.

"Welcome, sister Solana," a second voice said. The woman who had spoken was so close that the warmth of her breath brushed against Solana's neck.

"Thank you," Solana replied, omitting the title this time. "Where are—"

Something cool and slick clamped shut around her wrist. Manacles. Two pairs of hands grabbed hold of her shoulders, dragging her further into the room.

"Wait," Solana shouted, "what are you doing?" The tentative courtesy she'd wished to extend to her new hosts went out the window when her back slammed into a smooth stone slab.

"We're inducting you," the woman hissed at her. "Once one has set foot across the threshold, the customs must be observed."

"No," Solana snapped, trying to elbow her assailants anywhere she could reach them. "I thought there would be more time. I'm not ready."

A dozen hands clamped around every inch of her flesh they could grab, struggling to subdue her. Solana bucked and fought, swinging her arms blindly into the dark as dread turned to panic in her chest.

Then she thought of the majestic beauty of the reef just outside this abbey's front doors and stopped fighting. "It's part of the given path. All part of the given path," she murmured to herself, trying to find peace in the words.

"Yes, I did come here to be inducted on the orders of Cardinal De

Leliard himself," Solana croaked, "but you can't just ambush me in the dark like this. I'm not ready."

"It is always dark in here," the woman replied, her voice cold and emotionless. "That is the sacrifice all of us make to serve the Keeper. Your resistance is a slap in the face of the almighty."

Solana deflated and allowed herself to be held down. She had made her decision when she gave up her last chance to escape. The only way out of the burning building that her life had become was to walk through the flames.

Chains rattled as she was fastened to the icy stone.

"The given path," she whispered frantically to herself, "all part of the given path. Heil, keeper of souls and intentions, grant me—"

Then the screaming began.

# CHAPTER 24

*18th day of the 11th cycle, 569KR*
**Mallion's Depth**

The trick with the fish worked a second time as they passed the gates of the dock district, making Brina wonder how motivated these darkhelms actually were. Half of what was in the wagon would've been considered a fancy meal at most of the inns in the Ditch. Nevertheless, she was all too eager to vacate the cart when Gardo finally announced their arrival.

One at a time, they slipped out from under the tarp. When Brina's turn came, she found herself momentarily awed by the view.

The dock they were standing on was just one of eight long quays where over a hundred ships lay moored. They ranged from tiny fishermen's vessels to two monstrous galleons that could have fit half the shacks in the Ditch. Stars littered the black velvet sky above, their reflections bobbing up and down with the breathing ocean. Pinpricks of light clustered on the horizon where the city of Barangia lay across the bay.

Gardo Wane pointed her toward the gangplank of one of the more sorry-looking vessels in the vicinity.

The *Adversity's University* was about thirty feet long and covered in a layer of bright green algae and barnacles. The ship's sail hadn't been white for at least half a century and the hoisted nets had been repaired so often that only scraps of the original webbing remained.

On the ship's deck, Sneak beckoned for Brina to join him and the captain in the cramped cabin. Phillipina was a stocky woman in her late forties with bushy salt-and-pepper hair. She greeted Brina with a firm handshake. The calluses on her fingers told her all she needed to know. Here was a woman who knew the value of an honest day's work. Her light brown eyes found Brina's.

## CHAPTER 24

"Thank you." Phillipina had a voice like a whisper.

"I wasn't really involved..." Brina began. She looked from Phillipina to Sneak.

"Excuse us a moment, Captain Wane," Sneak said, tugging at Brina's sleeve. As soon as he'd pulled her out of the cabin, he made an apologetic face.

"So..." He hesitated. "To convince the captain to risk smuggling us out of the city, I sort of had to promise her we'd take care of her little brother."

"You what?" Brina choked. "I better have misheard that."

"Look," he urged, "it's all my fault to begin with. I encouraged to kid to escape, and then he ended up rearranging the Keeper Chosen's brains to save me.

"I might as well have brought rope to hang him myself, Cap. He's a dead man—or kid, whatever, I don't know—walking."

"Hey! I heard that." Brina jumped and looked down. A set of hazel eyes, identical to the captain's, glared up at them from the metal grid that covered the ship's hold.

Brina slapped a hand to her forehead. "Real subtle," she whispered at Sneak.

"Nobody's going to hang you, kid." She attempted a reassuring manner, but it was like rouge on a pig.

"Yes they are," Harrod replied, giving her a look as though he thought she was slow. "That Methusal guy isn't dead. I saw him twitching when we ran away. He saw my face. He knows I tried to kill him."

Brina looked from the kid to Sneak, willing him to burst out laughing and say that this was all a joke. Sneak shrugged, throwing up his hands.

"Was it your intention to kill?" Brina asked, eying Harrod Wane's soft features.

"Yes," the kid began, "I mean, no, not really. But between master Sneak and Methusal, it was an easy choice."

Sneak grinned broadly, then reined it in when Brina shook her head. With the kid listening in on their every word, she struggled to express her feelings regarding this turn of events in child-friendly terms.

"And once we reach the Ditch?" she asked Sneak. "Where will the kid go then?"

"He'll come with us to headquarters, won't he?" Sneak said. There was a defiant edge to his voice. Brina liked it. The slender man needed a little more backbone. That still didn't mean she liked the idea of dragging along a child into certain danger.

"But that just means that the kid ends up outwalled, anyway," Brina whispered, trying to cut Harrod out of the conversation. "He's worse off now than he would've been in his cell."

"He's got us now," Sneak said. "We'll keep him safe, teach him to protect himself, and when all of this dies down, we'll smuggle him back into the city."

"Into the city? Into it?" Brina gaped at him.

"Hey, keep it down. There are watchers about." Wane's voice drifted up from the grate.

"You do realize we're in this whole mess because we wanted to get *out* of the city, right?" She leaned against the deck's railing, trying to keep herself from shouting.

"Almost getting strangled by a deranged Reynziel who could burn sigils kind of drove the message home, yes," Sneak bit back. "I went in there by myself to keep all of your butts out of the inquisitor's chair."

He broke off abruptly. There was more he could have said, had maybe wanted to say. *Where was Brina when it all went sideways?* It would have been more than fair to throw that back in her face, but he hadn't.

When the bargheist had all but finished her, Sneak had returned to bring her to safety even though she was a stranger to him. He'd had nothing to gain and everything to lose. Brina wasn't sure that she would have done the same.

"I trust you," she said finally. "If your gut tells you this is the way, that's how we'll do it."

Sneak grabbed her by the shoulder. "Thank you."

"I told you they'd come around," Wane butted in. "Wait until they see my special bond with locks."

Brina knelt on one knee beside the grate. "Do you ever shut up when others are talking, kid?"

A mischievous grin spread across Wane's face. "Rarely."

\*\*\*

As soon as Captain Phillipina's ramshackle vessel squeaked into motion with all of them tucked out of sight in the hull, Sneak resumed his desperate attempts to convince the others of his plan to take Harrod Wane back to headquarters.

Bron saw no problem with the proposition.

"Twelve circles is plenty to make a man. I speared a five-hundred-pound erymanthian in my tenth circle." When he extended a bottle of kelp rum

## CHAPTER 24

toward Harrod to welcome him to the crew, Saf stepped in and confiscated it. The boy gave her a reproachful look but seemed not to dare say anything.

*At least the kid knows what's good for him.*

"With all due respect," Acheron began in a tone that implied the opposite. Brina shot him a warning glare. She didn't love the idea of letting the boy in on their plans, but subjecting the kid to one of Acheron's trademark rants would be unnecessarily cruel.

"I, erm, believe it would be wise to consider the ramifications of what you are suggesting before making any definitive decisions," Acheron said, taking care to exaggerate every syllable. He gave Brina a sanctimonious smile that conveyed his annoyance better than any insult could have.

"Young master Wane, self-reliant though he undoubtedly is, is a child. The affairs we are entangled in do not mix with childcare. We cannot in good conscience risk any harm befalling him on our account."

A giggle drew everyone's attention away from Acheron's mumbling. Harrod Wane sat on a barrel behind him, wiggling something shiny between his fingers.

"How about a trade? I'll give you back your white pebble, and you let me join your gang?"

Brina froze in shocked glee when she saw the nugget of cloud between the kid's forefinger and thumb. Acheron, however, didn't think it funny in the slightest.

"You give me that back, you rat," he roared, jumping to his feet. Then, realizing that everyone was watching, he fixed a false smile on his wrinkled face. "That's nothing for anyone your age to be playing with." Harrod stood up on the barrel, holding the lump out of Acheron's reach.

"Tell me I can come with you." He laughed. "I'll earn my keep. My hands are like vipers." He wiggled the fingers on his free hand.

"Fine," Acheron said through gritted teeth, "get yourself killed. See if I care."

Wane dropped the cloud into Acheron's outstretched hand.

"Deal."

After that, Saf seemed too distracted to worry about whether their little group would be joined by one more. Her eyes kept lingering on Acheron and the inside pocket of his robe. Just like that, while they were jostled by the waves and with tensions running high, Harrod Wane became one of them.

Brina shared what remained of the kelp rum with Bron, trading increasingly unlikely tales.

"Its fangs were *this* long," Bron growled, spreading his hands two feet apart. "I had to jump onto a boulder to get high enough to reach its throat with my spear."

"You harvested the venom, right?" Brina demanded. "Even the stingiest alchemists pay a shard a drop."

"I drank it." Bron roared with laughter.

"Not a chance." Brina slapped him on the shoulder, grinning. "But I like your imagination."

"Cheers to that." The Biori slugged down enough rum to sedate a horse.

Footsteps thumped on the deck above before the hatch opened and Captain Wane's face appeared against the type of inky black sky that only occurred during the dark window.

"It's time," she said. "This is as far as I can go without drawing suspicion."

One by one, they ascended the ladder to the deck. Fresh air swept against Brina's face like a bucket of icy water after a hard night's work at the inn. Both chariots hung side by side like a pair of eyes glaring down on them.

In the pale light, the massive outline of the stoneward dwarfed the low dark fuzz that were the countless shacks of Doorstep's Ditch. It was all rather far away.

Captain Wane stood at a distance near the railing of the deck, her right arm draped around the shoulders of her brother. Their conversation was lost to the rush of the ocean.

"I thought you said the ship would bring us to the beach?" Saf whispered at Sneak. She stared at their destination in the distance. "This is open sea."

Sneak scratched his hair. He looked less than pleased with the state of things himself.

There was a thunk as the hatch that led into the hull slammed shut.

"My bad," Acheron raised a hand. He looked unsteady, as though one good roll of the waves below could send him flying. "Slipped out of my hands."

He righted himself and stumbled to the edge of the deck. He looked from the too-distant shacks of the Ditch to Brina. Their eyes locked, and he burst out laughing.

"Excellent," he howled. "Truly, spectacularly, excellent."

Saf rounded on him.

## CHAPTER 24

"This is funny to you?" she demanded, losing her natural poise for a moment. "We're almost a mile from land."

"Stop," Acheron heaved between bursts of high-pitched laughter. "Stop. You're only making it better."

"You're useless," Saf snapped at him. She stalked past him to speak to Captain Wane.

Brina shook her head, unable to keep a smile off her face.

"You're going to drive that poor woman mad one of these days."

Acheron shrugged. "Maybe she'll lighten up once she's cracked."

"Listen up," Captain Wane called out. Her words carried over the waves unhindered. There was an undeniable authority to her voice. On this piece of wood and canvas she was queen, and it showed.

"This is the farthest I can go. Not only because of the lighthouse but because of the alteria malliona current, which flows toward the beach. Once caught in it, the ship will be forced all the way to the shoreline, destroying all hope of your return going unnoticed. Not to mention the consequences for myself and Madame Arturia's orphanage, should I be seen offloading a shipment of fugitives." She shot a pained glance at Harrod Wane, whose face was set into a determined scowl.

"The upside is that the current will do most of the work for you. I brought hydra bladders. They will help you float. Lock arms. It's safer to drift toward the beach as a unit."

"This is madness," Bron growled. "You just want to get rid of us. No crack in your shield if we drown, right?"

The captain's face hardened. She took a step toward Bron, and Brina reflexively braced herself. Even sober, the Biori wasn't known for restraint. With half a bottle of kelp rushing through his veins, he was a brawl waiting to erupt.

"That's my little brother you are taking with you, Biori. You think I would let him touch even a drop of seawater if I didn't believe this was the best course of action?" There was a wounded danger in her voice.

Bron looked from the captain to Harrod, then nodded.

"My apologies, captain."

Minutes later, each of them had a flotation device strapped to their chests. It was made of a blown-up hydra bladder the size of a coconut, which could be fastened to the wearer's body with a leather strap.

Brina stood on the railing of the deck, looking down into the inky black. The jitters in her guts had nothing to do with the prospect of swimming.

Long ago, after a disastrous nighttime hunt for a water serpent, she had promised herself never to touch another drop of water after sundown, not even in the inn. Too many unknowns. Who was to say what creatures lurked just out of sight beneath the surface? Out here they would be a floating treat to anything that deigned to give them a nibble. Best not mention that to the others. *Not like there's anything we can do about it.*

With a final look at their destination, she jumped. The water rushed up to meet her, then swallowed her. As soon as she hit the water, the hydra bladder yanked her toward the surface. Brina spat out of a mouthful of water. The salt and seaweed smell of the ocean made her nose run.

Shadows rained down around her, spraying her face with splash after splash. A spark of fear lit up in Brina's chest. There was no way back now. They were floating in the great nothing under a void of stars. She had never felt this tiny.

Bron's muscular arm locked around her elbow, and Brina reached out to Acheron with her other arm, forming a chain. Together, the flotation devices kept them from sinking, allowing Brina to rest her paddling legs for a while.

On the deck of the ship, Harrod Wane was the last to step onto the railing. He turned around, hugged his sister, and then let himself tumble gracefully backward. He spun in the air just in time to hit the surface in a dive.

"What are we waiting for?" Bron roared. "Start swimming."

It took some practice, but after a handful of minutes of slow progress, they fell into a rhythm. Already, the cold water was numbing Brina's fingers and seeping into the muscles in her kicking legs.

As they drifted on the swell, Brina stared up at the stars, trying to forget about the exhaustion in her limbs.

It was the squealing that tore her away from her trance. A low hum like a recently kicked beehive. She strained to get her head higher out of the water to get a better view.

Then an incoming wave carried them upward, and her heart stopped. Pink lights. Thousands of them. Hundreds of thousands. The firejellies covered the ocean ahead like a slimy luminescent blanket.

Brina had seen jellies form these "islands" on countless occasions, but out here in the open sea they looked bigger than she had ever dreamed. There must be more here than she had seen in her whole life. A single sting could paralyze an adult human for close to an hour. Certain death when swimming in open water.

# CHAPTER 24

"We've got to turn back," she called over the rushing of waves and wind.

"What?" an indistinct voice to her right replied.

"We've. Got. To. Turn. Back."

There was a lot of back and forth as the message traveled across the six-man line.

"She says we need to swim backward!" Harrod Wane shouted.

"Why?" Saf's voice barely registered over the tumult of the sea.

"I don't know," Wane shouted back. "Hey lady, why do we need to swim back?"

Brina suppressed a roar of frustration as the island of jellies neared. "Those lights. They're firejellies. One sting could be fatal. We need to swim around."

This got everyone's attention. The chain broke as the others turned and jerked their arms free to struggle against the waves that carried them ever closer to the mass of pink blubber ahead.

Brina tried to do the same, but found her right arm still tightly locked with Acheron's. He alone hadn't let go.

"It's too late," he yelled. "These waves can't be conquered by human strength."

"This isn't the time for your nihilistic meanderings," Brina screamed, salt flooding her open mouth. A monstrous wave swelled beneath them. Brina briefly felt as though she was flying before she reached the tipping point and the immense weight of the water began yanking her back down.

"That's not what I mean. I'm saying if we can't go around—"

The sea roiled, spitting up a sheet of white foam that cut Acheron off mid-sentence. There was a forceful yank, and Brina lost touch of Acheron's arm as she was dragged down into the icy depths. For a moment, she kicked and flailed against the overwhelming weight of the ocean. Then, realizing she was burning precious energy and air fighting a literal force of nature, she ceased her wriggling and gave in.

For a single drawn-out minute, she resigned to the fact that she might never feel the breeze on her face again. A lightheaded sense of peace filled her. Would it really be so bad to sink into the void and leave it all behind? What was out there for her anyway, if not suffering, anguish and a hopeless future? Then, just as it had swallowed her, the ocean spit her back out with vigor.

Brina heard the firejellies' high-pitched buzzing before she could shake the water out of her eyes. Through blurry eyes, she saw the glow all around her. She was surrounded.

Acheron's voice echoed off the waves, supernaturally loud over the roar of the sea.

"Under. Go under, idiots. Go. Under."

# CHAPTER 25

*19th day of the 11th cycle, 569KR*
**Crab's Cove**

Brina clung to the wet sand of the beach like a child to its mother's leg. *Alive. I'm alive.* Her lungs burned with every breath. Her soaked clothes clung to her like a straitjacket spun out of ice. As she tried to get to her knees, her stomach convulsed, and she threw up what felt like a washtub's worth of saltwater.

"Smooth ride, all in all," Sneak spluttered beside her. He lay on his back, shivering. "Nice touch, those jellies. Really broke the monotony of swimming through open water."

Every muscle in her body protested as Brina forced herself up. They had overshot Doorstep's Ditch by about two miles. The section of beach they had stranded on was known as Crab's Cove because of the swarms of diamond scale crabs that took over the entire shielded inlet every year during the height of winter. Tonight, however, the beach was littered with dark, lifeless bodies of a different kind. There was no telling who was who in the oppressive dark.

She stumbled over to the nearest body and found Saf stirring, clenching and unclenching her fist.

"Come on, we've got to get out of here before the cold takes us." Brina pulled Saf into a seated position. Saf rubbed her face with her hands, moving clumps of wet hair out of her eyes.

"Right. Let's find the others."

"Not necessary," Bron said. "We're ready."

Brina looked over her shoulder to see the heavily muscled Biori stroll up to them with a squirming Harrod Wane slung over his shoulder. If he hadn't been dripping seawater everywhere, there would have been no way to tell that he'd just narrowly escaped a watery death. If anything, he seemed refreshed.

"Where's Acheron?" Brina asked, scanning the beach.

"Over there." Bron pointed out a slender figure standing in the surf a hundred feet away. "Said he needed a moment to himself."

Brina shook her head in annoyance and strode over to him.

"Let's go," she yelled.

Acheron just stood there with his back to the beach, staring off into the distance. When she reached him, she saw what had drawn his attention. A group of torches that seemed to float over the dark water. God's Maul. The place she visited every time she closed her eyes. A labyrinth of blackened corridors and staircases leading nowhere.

"Doesn't seem that far away from here," Acheron said, more to himself than Brina. "Like we could just reach out and pluck it from the horizon."

"If only it were that easy," she murmured around the lump in her throat. The reality of their encounter with the firejellies suddenly hit her. Guilt wrenched at her insides when she thought back to the peace she had felt as the oxygen ran low. *I can't die. I'm not allowed to. Not yet.* As long as he was a prisoner, her father's life was linked to her own. She couldn't let him down.

"For years, that place has haunted me," Acheron muttered. He sounded uncharacteristically sincere. "Everyone I loved disappeared behind those walls. I often wished to be there with them." He spat into a withdrawing wave. "Instead, it's just me out here. Me and the millstone of my own cowardice around my neck."

"We'll pay them a visit soon," Brina said. Her jaw clenched. "One they will speak about for generations."

Acheron reached out and squeezed her shoulder.

\*\*\*

Constrained by their wet clothes and the surrounding darkness, the hike to the Ditch took them twice as long as it should have. Given their exhaustion and laughable lack of equipment, they were forced to take the longer way along the shoreline instead of cutting through the treacherous jungle slopes of Barrow's Perch.

Neither Brina nor Acheron spoke a single word the entire time they slogged through the loose sand. Brina would have liked to claim that

## CHAPTER 25

she was filtering the screeches and howls of the nighttime jungle, listening for threats. In reality, she was struggling to banish those distant fires from her mind.

Three hours later, Saf led them into the slums on the outskirts of Doorstep's Ditch. With only a handful of hours to spare until sunrise, even the uneven, muddy alleys of the Ditch had gone quiet. The patchwork shacks had gone dark, though here and there the sounds of clinking bottles and stomachs being violently emptied onto dirt floors escaped through windowless holes in crooked walls.

Brina's heart leapt as something seized her ankle in a dim nook between two rows of houses. She yanked back her leg to find the shadowy outline of an emaciated woman lying slumped against a barrel of rainwater.

She beckoned Brina with bony arms.

"Ello, missz," the woman slurred, "won'z you help a poor gal in need?" In the glow of the chariots above, Brina saw the white fog glossing over the woman's eyes. *Another one taken by the cloud.*

"What do you want?" Brina took a step back, expecting another grab.

"Just one shard. A small one. Tiny one." She held her thumb and forefinger half an inch apart. "Thaz all."

As she spoke, the tip of her tongue was visible for a flash. Brina suppressed a grimace. It was glassy and white, the tissue dead and rotting at the edges. That could only mean one thing. *She's a licker.* Most dealers kept a separate chunk of cloud on hand for their most desperate clientele. For a nib, they were allowed a single lick of the chunk. It was a fifteen-minute superficial high that people pawned, stole, and murdered for. Once someone had sunk that deep, they were as good as dead.

Brina swallowed as she stared down at the woman, who was already holding her hands out hopefully. Brina's desire to help clashed furiously with the knowledge that the woman would run straight to the nearest cloud-peddler as soon as she got her hands on so much as a grain of gem dust. If there was anything Doorstep's Ditch had taught her, it was that some people were simply too far gone, no matter how you wished it were otherwise.

She looked over her shoulder at Acheron, who had spent half the walk from the Crab's Cove digging through his pockets with increasing desperation as he looked for any crumbs of cloud that the ocean hadn't washed away. "How about I introduce you to my friend?" Brina said. "I bet you two have a lot in common." She grabbed him by the shoulder and gestured a summary introduction.

"Who—" Acheron began.

"Your future."

Brina strode off, a duel between amusement and utter sadness raging inside her. *It had to be said. Before it's too late.*

It took Acheron almost ten minutes to catch up with them, by which time the group had crossed Wicket Row into the northern side of town.

"What took you so long?" Brina asked. A twinge of guilt stirred in her guts as the image of the decrepit woman forced itself to the front of her mind.

"Nothing. I lost you guys for a moment, that's all."

"You didn't give her any money, did you?" Brina asked. His casual, almost cheerful, tone plucked at Brina's suspicion like a foot stumbling across a tripwire.

"No," Acheron said. His gaze locked with Brina's, exposing glowing orange eyes. "Nothing like that."

For the rest of their journey, Brina refused to so much as look at him. Acheron didn't seem bothered. Saf finally led them up the slopes of King's Barrow Hill. As they climbed, the houses and huts became sparser. They stopped at the very last house on the right side of the path. It looked like a cross between the farmsteads scattered across the western coast of the island and one of the ramshackle warehouses near the beach district.

The bottom floor consisted entirely of sandstone bricks, with a second wooden floor underneath the thatched roof. Once, it might have been an impressive dwelling by outwalled standards, but those days were long gone.

The place looked like it routinely played host to a herd of enraged tri-horn. Not a shred of glass remained in the windowpanes, the woodwork had more holes than a fishing net, and what remained of the thatch on top had rotted half a century ago.

"Quickly now," Saf said, gesturing at an empty doorframe to the side of the building. "Wouldn't want to be seen."

Brina allowed herself to be herded inside along with the others. She wrinkled her nose as mold, rust, and an undertone of decay engulfed her. Sneak grabbed a lantern from a hook on the wall. As the lantern light bloomed, a dusty workshop appeared around them.

Four huge stills with dozens of valves and pipes protruding from them lined the far wall of the room. Each of them was at least twenty feet high,

# CHAPTER 25

reaching all the way for the crooked roof above them. Brass pipes ran along the floor and walls like the threads of a spider's web. A mouthwatering number of rum casks were stacked into the nearest corner.

What had looked like a second floor from outside was little more than a walkway that yielded access to the distillery's many valves and switches.

"Mind your heads." Sneak angled the lantern upward, and Brina cringed. Dozens of black shapes hung upside down from the pipes, the roof, and even the barrier of the walkway above. Silver claws gleamed in the lantern's beam. The creatures' leathery wings were wrapped around them like a shroud, leaving only a pair of long fuzzy ears visible.

"Put that light away," Brina whispered at Sneak. "Those are sickle fleders. You agitate one, you agitate them all." By itself a fleder was nothing to worry about, but put two dozen of them in a locked room and they'd strip a leviathan to its core before the key was fully turned.

"That's the idea, Cap'n," Sneak grinned. One of the fleders lazily flapped a two-foot-long wing. Acheron took one look at the nightmarish creatures, then turned on his heel and walked out, drawing further snickers from Sneak and Bron.

Saf sighed and muttered something that included the word "childish." She raised her hand to her mouth and blew on it softly.

Chaos. A hurricane of black leather wings whirled around them. Panicked screeches filled the distillery as the fleders crawled all over each other to escape through holes and cracks in the roof. Not ten seconds later, the place was abandoned.

*Of course.* Brina smirked.

"Where'd you get it?" she asked Saf, who gave her an approving nod.

"In the bottom of a barrel of rubbish a merchant from Hawqal was trying to palm off before returning. The blessed woman couldn't be rid of it fast enough."

"I suppose there's not much demand for wailers around those parts," Brina said. "May I see it?"

"Professional interest?" Saf asked with a sly grin, handing Brina a tiny silver flute.

It was an elegant instrument, no thicker than Brina's pinkies and only twice as long. In the dusk, it was hard to make out the decorative engravings along the edges, but those were of little importance. It was all in the tone. Brina inhaled and blew the flute. Nothing. Not so much as the rustle of breath on silver. It was perfect. Inaudible to humans, but a deafening screech to all sorts of vermin with sensitive hearing.

"I used to have one," Brina remarked as she followed Saf through the dark distillery, "but that one was plain wood and a pain in my own ears to boot."

"Think you could still find it? I've been trying to find a spare."

"Not unless you're motivated to take a swim in Turncoat's Marsh." Brina shook her head at the memory. A week of tracking an adult female kukulkan had turned into the fight of a lifetime when the winged serpent's enormous tail swept the wailer straight out of her hands and into the bog below.

"Shame."

The grinding of metal on stone tore Brina's attention away from the kukulkan debacle. Sneak and Bron were each holding one side of the rusty still in the corner. Even with Bron's considerable strength, they shouldn't have been able to budge it a fraction of an inch. And yet, the still slid forward smoothly, as though it stood on ice.

A trapdoor appeared behind it, which Sneak held open. When Brina made to descend, Sneak bowed with mock decorum.

"Welcome to our humble abode, Cap'n."

# CHAPTER 26

*19th day of the 11th cycle, 569KR*
**Everberg Abbey**

"How are you feeling, sister?"

"Miserable," Solana groaned. She bit down on her lower lip to keep from screaming.

Part of her wanted to maintain the facade of stoic poise she'd so carefully built up over the years, but she didn't see the point. She was a novice again. Any authority her name had held before had faded along with her eyesight.

Her cheeks were scabbed with dried blood, filling her nose with the acrid stench of rust. Both of her empty sockets burned like they were being worked with a red-hot poker.

She still lay on the hard, straw mattress she'd woken up on hours prior. It was a strange sensation to open her eyes, only to find a void crowding in around her. It was the deepest darkness she had ever experienced. There were no shimmers creeping in underneath doors or through slits in a roof; there was no halo of moonlight to break the drab shadow of night. There was only nothingness. For all she knew, dozens of her new brothers and sisters could be watching her.

"My name is Brother Wilhelm," the man said, sliding a gentle hand underneath Solana's head to help her sit upright. "As the abbot of the Stigmata, it is my privilege to care for you until your wounds have healed."

A feeling of nausea overcame Solana.

"Where you present when they..." She pointed at her face.

"It is my solemn duty to help you transition from the profane sight of your past to the sacred vision that will be your future from this day onward."

Solana stiffened as she realized what he meant.

"You did this to me?"

"Does that anger you?" Brother Wilhelm replied as he held up a cup of water to her lips.

"Yes." It seemed imprudent to start her relationship with the abbot on a lie.

"Good," Wilhelm said. "It wouldn't be a proper sacrifice if you hadn't lost something dear to you."

The abbot helped Solana stand and placed a hand on her shoulder.

"Where are you taking me?" Solana asked as the abbot steered her through a narrow doorway and out into what felt like a drafty hallway.

"Yesterday, I took something from you. Today, the Keeper will reward you tenfold."

The creak of rusty hinges was followed by a sweet acidic smell. Solana's fresh wounds stung, weeping with renewed vigor.

"Enter," the abbot's voice echoed from ahead.

Solana shuffled toward the sound, sliding one foot in front of the other, feeling as though she were walking a tightrope over a cliff.

Smoke forced its way into her nose and throat with every tentative breath. That acrid herbal stench soaked her entire being, like wine spreading across white lace.

"Kneel." The abbot's voice grew louder. It circled her, enveloped her, the sound woven from the very smoke burning in her lungs.

Solana's knees pressed upon smooth marble. Inches ahead of her, waves of heat emanated from a fissure in the tiles. She jerked her hand back, feeling the throb of seared skin across her fingertips. It didn't hurt as much as it should have. The burning seemed diminished somehow, distant, as though she was merely remembering something that had occurred years prior.

"Welcome to the hall of dreams," the abbot droned in the back of her mind. "You will enter this place only once in your lifetime, but the memory of it will be with you for as long as your blood flows."

Solana's fingers searched the floor around her and rested on a series of tiny bumps in the marble, like gooseflesh, but deliberately structured. Geometrical flows that transitioned effortlessly from one shape into the next. As though controlled by invisible strings, her hands traced the patterns. It soothed her. Energized every fiber in her body.

She was levitating, whirling through the air, adrift on the smoke that surrounded her. Only those tiny bumps remained.

"We of the Stigmata have existed for centuries," the abbot said. "Our bond with the Keeper runs deeper than any who claim the faith. By sacrificing our profane windows to the world, we are elevated by Heil into the tightknit circle of those she deems worthy of her own vision."

"I don't understand," Solana muttered.

"Think back to yesterday. What did your eyes show you?"

The memory of those rainbow-colored reefs surrounding the abbey flooded back. She could see them, swirling around her, woven from vapor. Thousands of tiny fish in every shape and size, traversing endless underground cities.

"I saw life," she said. "Fish, crabs and jellies dwelling amongst towers of red and yellow and purple. Weeds and algae blossoming in between."

"In other words, you saw the facade of life," the abbot said. "Muscle, bone, pigments, and fibers.

"To connect with the Keeper of Worlds, we need to look, as she does, into what lies beyond.

"We, the Stigmata, see not bright colors or the beauty of shapes. We see flow and balance, the careful alignment of energies that keeps the world from tilting. Our senses are not limited to one moment. Instead, we observe the timeline of what has been, what is, and what shall be. A palimpsest, ever folding over unto itself, never striving toward an end, always turning on its axis, maintaining stasis."

As he spoke, his words turned to shapes around Solana.

She watched from a bird's-eye view as forest, desert, and ocean formed around her. Snow fell, ice bloomed against white shorelines. Before she could reach out, white gave way to a flood of lush green, the swell of herds of mammoths traversing the endless waves of the desert and the flight of birds across vast stretches of forest. Then everything turned hard, hot, and brittle, before crumbling away into the slow decline of autumn, with its dying leaves and creatures burrowing into the dark nooks and crannies of the world. The process repeated itself, speeding up with every cycle.

"We are tiny. Unimportant. Our job is not to preserve our meager bodies, or anything we can touch with our shallow skin. Our job is to keep the circle round.

"Whom have you served in this life? Think."

Solana watched herself, a mere child with the overconfidence of youth, receive the raven helmet of the Enlightened Watch. She saw Argideon, her first commander, put his sandal on her back as she completed a series of pushups. Every time she forced herself up with trembling arms, he leaned harder, until, finally, she collapsed into the dust.

Argideon's face melted away, changing into Her Purity Lusana, who had taken her as an apprentice as she sought to fight her way up the ranks. She sat on her knees, reciting prayers from memory in the grand temple at Mallion's Depth as dawn turned to dusk behind the stained-glass windows. The enlightened council sat on the pews behind her, listening to every word, judging.

The raven helmet turned into the griffin, which turned into the leering face of Cardinal De Leliard, who grew until he towered over her the way he did in each of Solana's recent nightmares.

Then she understood.

"I have served the church. Not the Keeper."

"Good." There was approval in the abbot's tone. "The Stigmata care not for such trifles as titles or crowns disguised as helmets. Our dedication runs deeper."

"Then why did the Cardinal send me here as punishment?" The words escaped her without thought. In Mallion's Depth, it would have been enough to have her whipped for insubordination. The Cardinal did not punish; he only executed the Keeper's will.

The answer only deepened her shock.

"Because he does not understand what we are," the abbot said. His voice betrayed no hint of fear at this blatant disrespect to Heil's physical vessel on earth. "He sees us as pawns. Pieces to be moved in pursuit of his profane ambitions. We aid the church, but only insofar as its goals align with ours. We do not follow orders; we chase balance.

"To a man like De Leliard, optics are everything. That's why he will never comprehend what we gain through our sacrifice.

"You will. I see it growing in you even now. Though there will be many hurdles along the path."

Solana bowed her head, her fingers still roving over the shapes on the floor around her like a Hawqallian automaton stuck in a loop.

"You are ready." The abbot's voice grew louder. "Open your eyes."

"But..."

"Open. Your. Eyes," he screamed. "Awaken. Now."

The sudden violence in his voice triggered something within her. She opened her eyes.

Gray shapes came into view around her, woven from the smoke that filled her lungs. She first saw the vaulted chapel ceiling, then the plain circular walls that closed in around her. Finally, the abbot's shadowy out-

## CHAPTER 26

line appeared in front of her. Though she couldn't make out his face, she knew he was smiling.

"Yes," he urged. "Hold on to it. How does it feel?"

"Sensitive." It was the only word she could think of. Every cell in her body had come alive. She could feel the warmth of her blood vessels traversing thick patches of muscle. She could hear the pounding of the abbot's heart from ten feet away, could taste the silty air of the ocean beyond Everberg's walls.

Panic built in her chest as the impulses threatened to overrun her consciousness. "What is this?"

"This is how the Keeper perceives the world. How you will perceive the world from this day forth.

"Through prayer, we will teach you to move boulders with the touch of a finger. You will hear truth and deceit in the voice of others. You will predict the movements of enemy soldiers before their earthbound minds have conceived of them."

"But that sounds like the heresy of the ancient days. Like what sigilists do."

"They use shortcuts. Tricks, not arts. They are foam, we are the wave."

Solana's heart tumbled into a gallop, as her senses were pushed beyond their breaking point by the flood of sounds and sensations. Mammoths trumpeted in the distance. Bloody iron filled her mouth and nose as her wounds wept. Her mind expanded, tearing patterns of thought formed over decades of discipline and obedience. Her memories shrank, becoming mere etchings, mementos of ages past.

Then, as rapidly as it had expanded, the balloon of the world contracted, swallowing her whole.

# CHAPTER 27

*26th day of the 11th cycle, 569KR*
**Doorstep's Ditch**

It took Brina less than a week to admit to herself that the Order of the Prism's headquarters had its advantages over the mill she had called home all these years.

The old storage vaults of the distillery had been out of use for nigh on two centuries. Unless you knew they were there, you had as much of a chance of stumbling across the entrance as a windup bolt had of striking an innocent man in a crowded Doorstep's Ditch inn. Add a swarm of thirsty sickle fleders to the mix, and you had a recipe for a peaceful night's sleep.

This reality had been driven home to her on the fourth night, when she'd dozed off in an armchair by the hearth. How long had it been since she had simply fallen asleep like that? No triple-checking locks and latches, no tripwires on every entrance, not even a single dagger tucked away under her pillow. Afterward, she'd woken up in a flurry of panic and fury at her own carelessness, until the low snores of the others had reminded her of where she was.

Safe.

For now.

The vaults were laid out like a five-leaf clover. In the center lay a circular room with an impressive teak and ebony table. Its domed ceiling was painted to look like a canopy of trees, granting the illusion that you were sitting in a forest clearing. The order called this "the bell jar."

Saf spent most of her waking hours there, surrounded by stacks of scrolls and maps covered in handwritten notes that only made sense to her. The only moment she'd grudgingly clear them away was when they'd have their communal dinner, which Bron insisted they ate together. The

## CHAPTER 27

Biori proved to be an unlikely talent with a stove, turning anything even slightly edible into delicious dishes that never lasted the night.

"The secret is in the spices," he'd told Brina one night while sucking contentedly on his pipe as he watched the last of his snake and mango stew vanish down Brina's gullet. "Only wild saffron from the slopes of Mount Ach-Dra in my homeland can bring out that smoothness in snake meat. Shame I'm down to my last pouch."

Five alcoves branched off from this central room, each just large enough to function as a room of its own. On the right side of the bell jar, there was the library and an adjacent sitting room, which had the smallest fireplace Brina had ever seen. The library, if it could rightfully be called that, contained a handful of roughly constructed shelves that tilted inward near the top because of the alcove's slanted ceiling. There must have been close to a hundred manuscripts, a small fortune's worth of parchment and tedious but delicate labor. A ledger lay on a small reading table, detailing every title the order possessed, alongside Saf's summary notes about the contents.

Brina had only briefly perused a handful of books before conceding defeat. Losing her eye had amplified her frustration with the tiny squiggly lettering tenfold. That most of the books chronicled political controversies and military gaffes from centuries ago didn't help. She had enough to worry about in the present as it was. The sitting room, with its cozy armchairs and well-stocked liquor cabinet, was a much preferable place to pass the time.

The three alcoves on the opposite side of the bell jar served as bedrooms. Motley curtains shielded low bunks from view, granting a thin illusion of privacy. The sudden doubling of the group had been a source of tension when it came to sleeping arrangements. Bron, Sneak, and Saf, who'd grown accustomed to the comforts of having a bedroom to themselves, now found themselves being forced to share with three newcomers. The first night, three of them had slept on the floor after drawing the short straw. The next day, Brina and Sneak had spent most of the morning cobbling together three new bunks from the empty casks on the brewery's main floor.

Comfortable though their lodgings may be, Brina's favorite thing about their return to Doorstep's Ditch was Acheron's renewed lessons on the use of sigils. Now that they finally had access to the order's collection of scripts, Brina began seeing the first traces of results.

She could finally practice using a true script containing *Gnis*, a glyph shaped like an uneven triangle, to control her body temperature. Or more precisely, her body's warmth. *Gnis* concentrated this heat, while its inverted counterpart, *Pruine*, diluted it. Both had their uses, though Brina was a long way off fully controlling either.

During their first lesson in the headquarters, Acheron had demonstrated Gnis by holding his index finger to the wick of a candle placed on the bell jar's antique table. When it caught flame as easily as if he had struck a match, Brina's excitement had overtaken her better judgment. She'd struggled to replicate the effect, only to get sweaty and nauseous before a wave of cold hit her and she'd needed a blanket and a quarter bottle of kelp to remedy the effects.

Acheron thought this extremely entertaining. "You're a long way off from making fire, kid. And perhaps that's for the better. A spark can cause as much wreckage as a blaze, but is less likely to do so by accident." This piece of wisdom hadn't much impressed Brina. A spark was a spark, but a blaze... now that sounded like the kind of thing she'd want to call upon when the need arose.

Then there was the God's Maul problem. Though their return to Doorstep's Ditch had gone unnoticed, their efforts to observe the comings and goings at the island fortress were hamstrung by the constant need to look over their shoulders.

To Brina's increasing frustration, her injuries bound her to around-the-clock care. Contact with the salty water of the Sundered Sea had left the wound around her eye red and throbbing. She didn't need Acheron to tell her that spelled trouble.

Meanwhile, Sneak and Harrod Wane spent most of their days in a hidden cave near Crab's Cove taking turns peering through a spyglass as they noted down the movements of guards and ships in and around God's Maul. Their nightly reports over dinner were the undoubted highlight of Brina's days. Finally, they were taking steps. Small though they may be, each one brought her a little closer to her father.

\*\*\*

"I wonder how those God's Maul darkhelms do it," Sneak sighed on their seventh night in Doorstep's Ditch. They sat in the bell jar, fishing the last scraps out of a ceramic dish that had been full of pineapple curry and rice half an hour prior. The burn of the dried pepper lingered on Brina's tongue.

"Maybe they have a good cook too, eh?" Bron said. He leaned back in his chair with a satisfied grin on his face, one hand resting on his belly.

## CHAPTER 27

"Or generous rations of drink," Brina added. A pleasant glow was spreading from her stomach to her fingertips.

"Let's hope so. It'd make things a stretch easier for us if we could just slit their throats while they're sleeping it off," Acheron said.

There had been a bitter edge to his voice ever since the group had voted to keep him out of sight in the headquarters for at least a few more weeks. At the time, he'd agreed that his outstanding business with Dimimzy Zot made him far too recognizable in the Ditch. In a moment of unexpected selflessness, he'd accepted that his return risked exposing all of them. But he seemed to have forgotten all about this the very next morning, and tonight his vitriol was reaching new heights.

"Do you have to say things like that in front of the kid?" Saf bit at him. Her tolerance for Acheron's moods had taken a sharp dive as the week went on, which secretly amused Brina. Acheron's jabs could be quite funny if you didn't take them to heart. She doubted whether even Acheron himself took half the things that came out of his mouth seriously.

"Hey," Wane interrupted, "watch who you call a kid. I speared three mud eels for lunch." He crossed his arms as though this decided the matter once and for all.

"See," Acheron prodded, pointing at Wane, "the kid's fine. I bet when the time comes, he'll make a fine cutthroat."

Wane grinned and pulled a finger across his own throat.

"I was being serious," Sneak said, pulling their attention back to the matter at hand. "We've been watching that place for a week now, and the gate has opened only once. They receive supplies, and they're stuck there for another week. Not to mention the insane shifts the guards on top of the walls and towers pull. They're only relieved twice a day, at noon and midnight."

"That's twelve hours per shift," Saf mused, running a hand through her black hair.

"Glad to hear you've mastered basic math," Acheron said.

"What I was getting at is that they're probably tired toward the end of their shift," Saf replied through gritted teeth. "Which we could use to our advantage."

Acheron didn't reply, but couldn't keep a smug grin from his face. Brina cuffed him around the back of the head to keep him focused, drawing a chuckle from the old grump.

"Sure," Sneak went on, "it could be useful once we get that far. Right now, all we're seeing is how impossibly locked down the place is. Let's say we somehow smuggle ourselves in with the supplies. Then what? We have no clue what's behind those walls."

Brina nodded. "I've been wondering about that. They've kept some of the most powerful sparkgazers in recent history in there—that has to require specific security measures, doesn't it?" She looked around the table for input from the only sparkgazers she knew.

"Well, I suppose they'd have to make sure the prisoners can't imprint. So they'll have regular cell searches to make sure no scripts are smuggled in," Acheron said.

"Wouldn't stop all of us," Bron said. "My old mentor, Bahov, told me about an ancient legion of elite warriors who had power shapes inked into their very skin. Those tattoos were done by a trained scrive. They can't take away someone's skin in a cell search."

Brina winced as various options to do just that crossed her mind.

"I don't see why they couldn't just burn them off." Acheron shrugged.

"But what about containing a scrive?" Saf replied. "Some of them can replicate scripts from memory, can't they?"

Acheron's mouth twitched. He suddenly seemed highly fascinated by the bottom of his empty cup. "They can. I've seen it. Azaria and Ghar-Ul from the old Signum could both reproduce over half a dozen scripts from memory." He swallowed. "I don't really want to think about this." Before anyone could intervene, Acheron stood up and disappeared into the sitting room.

"But let's say you've somehow imprinted," Brina insisted. "What's your path of escape?"

"You could use a guard," Saf said. "I can be extremely convincing when I need to be. I'd force one to escort me out."

"Why bother when you could rip the doors straight off their hinges?" Bron asked, his calloused fingers drumming on the tabletop. "They'd need an army to stop a truly powerful gazer."

"Why bother fighting?" Sneak shook his head. "With a delicate hand, you could blend into the shadows and disappear."

Brina hummed her appreciation. "Let's assume the warden has thought about all of those scenarios. That ought to bring us closer to guessing what we might face, right?"

"We need someone who has seen it," Acheron said, slamming down

## CHAPTER 27

a bottle of kelp rum and six glasses onto the table. He filled them and handed them out, starting with Saf.

As soon as Wane could reach one of the glasses, he raised it and gulped half of it down before anyone could stop him. He gave Saf a sly glance, as though expecting her to snatch the drink out of his hands. For the moment, however, she was distracted.

"Like who?" Saf asked. "No prisoner ever leaves God's Maul save for when they are executed. And I doubt the darkhelms will draw us up a floor plan." The muscles in her jaw tensed as she looked at Acheron, who shrugged.

"I provided an idea. I didn't say I had a plan ready to go."

"He has a point, Saf," Sneak said, rubbing his hands across his face. "As long as our intelligence ends at that gate, our plan will do the same, and I don't feel like improvising on this one."

"Agreed," Acheron said. "We've seen what happens when you improvise."

Sneak opened his mouth, but then cast a sideways glance at Harrod Wane and closed it again.

Brina reached for her glass of rum and downed it in one. They were right. Without information, they might as well charge in there blindfolded. At least that might give the darkhelms a laugh.

Something about Saf's words had sparked an itch in Brina's mind, though. *No prisoner ever leaves God's Maul.* That wasn't true. Not entirely. Someone had made it out. Someone who had sworn never to breathe a word of it. Versa. Brina's stomach churned. What were the chances that they'd find someone else in time?

She held her tongue. Even if she didn't give the others Versa's name, it still felt like a betrayal of the innkeeper's trust to even mention them. There would be pressure on Brina to get them to talk, and she didn't think she was up to that just yet.

The meeting wound down soon after. As the group scattered, Brina sank into her favorite chair in the sitting room. A candle and the clay Gnis script stood on a table beside it. She had gotten a lot better with the shape, having been able to light the wick without melting the entire candle on three separate occasions now. Tonight, her mind wasn't in the right place. Every time the sigil appeared in her mind's eye, it morphed into Versa's masked form, then faded away.

# CHAPTER 28

*5th day of the 12th cycle, 569KR*
**Order of the Prism's Headquarters**

As days crept by, Brina grew restless. Being unable to leave the vaults under the distillery was part of it. Her wound still stung and throbbed ceaselessly, no matter how many salves Acheron applied or how much kelp she gulped down from the moment she woke until she passed out in front of the hearth.

The script on the pyramid around her neck would lighten her discomfort significantly, if only she could build up the focus to imprint on it, but the harder she tried, the further away it slipped. Acheron and the others had tried to assure her that it was a complex sigil, one many experienced sparkgazers would have trouble with. That didn't help her impatience one bit.

The second part of her growing unease was the complete lack of progress when it came to the God's Maul question. Days of repetitive observations were stretching into weeks without any new leads. Every way she looked at the task ahead, Brina found nothing but dead ends.

One morning, after the others had left headquarters for the day, she gathered up her courage and stepped into the bell jar, where Saf sat reading Hendrikus Draek's *The Heilinist Revolution and the Rise of Post-Sigilism*.

"I know someone who has been inside God's Maul," Brina said.

Saf's eyes narrowed behind the heavy tome. She marked her page with a scrap of parchment and closed the book with a flourish. "Go on."

"They've always refused to speak a word about what they saw in there. Said the memories are too painful."

"And? Is that supposed to stop us?" someone barked from behind them.

Brina sighed. Of course, Acheron, who spent days on end in his bunk, had to choose this moment to stomp into the bell jar. She'd considered confiding in him first, but his recent mood swings had made her reconsider.

## CHAPTER 28

He was rapidly turning into a cynical sack of misery, and she doubted his ability to feel empathy for anyone but himself.

"They were tortured, Acheron. Tortured." Brina's face flushed with anger. "Besides, it's not like we can force them to tell us anything they don't want to."

"That's not exactly true," Saf said delicately. "There are sigils we could use, but they'll only work if the target is unaware of what's happening. If we tip them off in any way, it could become impossible."

"So what are you suggesting?" Brina asked, eying Saf with apprehension. She would have expected something like this from Acheron, but Saf?

Brina looked into those vehement brown eyes and realized that she knew nothing about this woman. Nothing except what had come out of her mouth over the span of a few weeks. Promises and high-minded rhetoric. She had no idea what Saf was capable of if the stakes were high enough.

"I'm merely laying out the situation," Saf said, raising her hands. "We can all but guarantee success if we plan thoroughly, but it will come at a cost."

"Being that we'd be no better than the church?" Brina looked up at the vaulted ceiling and began counting the colorfully painted birds. *Breathe. Stay calm.*

"Partially. But our primary concern is what happens afterward. Once the effects of the sigil wear off, the target will know they were supernaturally compelled to speak. How they respond to that realization could have a serious impact on the order's secrecy. Do you think this person could pose a threat to us?"

"I don't think so." Brina hated herself for answering. Hated herself for even entertaining a conversation this vile. Versa maintained the order in the Chimera with a firm hand, but that was breaking up spur-of-the-moment brawls between drunks. Against a group of sparkgazers, or even someone with Brina's experience wielding sharpened steel, the innkeeper would be outmatched. Add to that the fact that Versa was an outsider, and the conclusion was that they would be as safe a target as any in the Ditch. Thinking about it in those terms made Brina's insides squirm.

"The sigil wouldn't harm them, if that's what you're worried about," Saf said. Her tone was matter-of-fact, as though they were merchants weighing spices. "I could use it on you, so you could feel what it's like firsthand."

"No." Brina never showed anyone the back of her tongue, let alone allowing someone of Saf's caliber to dig around the dark crevices of her mind. Who knew what might be dredged up. "Use it on Acheron if he's so keen to coerce others into talking."

He cast a side-eyed glance at Saf. "Don't even think about going for a tour in my brain, Al Noor. You couldn't handle half the stuff that goes on in there."

"Fine," Brina said, thumping both hands against the table. "Then we agree that forcing our way into someone's thoughts using sigilistic coercion is despicable. I'll find some other way to get them to talk."

"What other way?" Acheron snapped. "If there was another way, you'd have come up with it by now."

"Give me two weeks." Brina jumped to her feet, her legs buzzing with nervous energy.

Saf's expression was illegible. "Sooner or later, you'll have to decide what's more important to you, Brina, the cause or your moral lines in the sand. There's a reason men like De Leliard always float to the top of the cesspool. Remember that."

"I said, give me two weeks."

# CHAPTER 29

*10th day of the 12th cycle, 569KR*
**Doorstep's Ditch**

Brina marched down Wicket Row, naked as the day she was born. At least, that was how she felt as she maneuvered her way through the throng of beggars and drunkards lounging in the ankle-deep mud. It was the first time she'd shown herself in public since the bargheist had torn out her eye, and people noticed. That was the trouble with being a roamer, she thought bitterly as yet another distant acquaintance stared at her from a nearby alley. She gave the man a curt nod. *Too much notoriety.*

She was keenly aware of her newly limited field of vision. Her neck whipped back and forth as she tried to monitor what was going on around her. As she was looking over her shoulder, a group of urchins whipped past her, gibbering and laughing at a red-faced man with a potbelly who limped after them. The man yelled something about "thieves" before doubling over in the middle of the street to catch his breath.

Brina's jaws clenched. *They were close enough to touch me.* A single blade combined with ill intentions was all it would have taken. Her heart pounded in her chest.

She wondered how long it would take before some piss-for-brains amateur decided to roll the dice on a wounded target. Her trusty windup slung over her shoulder provided only a meager bit of comfort.

The Wistful Chimera's sign creaked in the breeze. Brina took a moment to steel herself before entering. She was a frequent guest at the Chimera, and she wasn't looking forward to the unavoidable questions her mangled face would draw like flies to a sun-ripened carcass.

Before she could reach for the rusty door handle, however, the front door swung inward of its own accord.

"Next time you see me, I'll be covered in feathers and laden down with gems," Mattheus Fortuyn shouted over his shoulder to a roar of laughter and jeering from the patrons inside. He almost bumped straight into Brina, who refused to budge so much as a hair's breadth.

"Hey, watch where—" His face went pale when he saw her. He took an instinctive step backward, pinning himself against the door he'd pulled shut behind himself. His hand strayed toward the dagger on his belt.

"Keep that needle in your pants," Brina said. Oddly, she found herself smiling. "If I'd wanted to shoot you, you'd be an ugly doormat right about now."

"What do you want, then?" Mattheus asked, his eyes darting from Brina's scarred eye socket to the windup that rested on her back.

"Rum, Fortuyn, a lot of it. Some asshole tried to kill me a while ago, if you can believe it." She took a step forward and was pleased to see Mattheus squirm backward against the inn's door. "My nerves could do with some steadying."

"But they said you were..." He swallowed.

"Dead?" Brina supplied. Mattheus's grimace was answer enough. "Not yet, but thanks for your concern."

"Hey look," he began, "about that business on Scarlet Eve. They paid me to do it. It wasn't personal, just another job."

She placed a hand on the roamer's shoulder, smiling magnanimously. Mattheus relaxed. Then she burned *Gnis*, taking care to flare the sigil slowly and steadily. "I think it *was* personal, Matty."

Mattheus's eyes widened as an orange glow appeared on his face. The fabric of his cloak smoldered. A quick look at the street revealed no one was close enough to see what was going on.

"I knew it," he mumbled. "You are one of them. You're a heretic."

Brina dug her thumb underneath Mattheus's clavicle with all the force she could muster and flared the shape. "Glad you're catching on."

Mattheus let out a scream as the heat reached his bare skin. The stench of burning flesh filled the air between them. Brina let go and shoved him aside. Mattheus gasped as his fingers touched the scorched skin on his shoulder. He was petrified.

"I left you a little mark. It should help you remember to stay out of my way." She tapped a finger against his forehead. "Am I making myself clear?"

"Yes." Mattheus grimaced as though he'd swallowed a gulp of sewage.

## CHAPTER 29

"Good." Without another glance, Brina turned the door handle and stepped inside, unable to wipe the grin off her face.

\*\*\*

A tense atmosphere had taken over The Wistful Chimera since Brina's last visit. The place seemed at the same time rowdier than usual and yet devoid of joy. The closest comparison was the mob mentality brought about by the Scarlet Nocturne each year. It was the low whistle of a kettle reaching its boiling point.

A group of dirty, but well-armed gang members, Auctioneers by the looks of it, had laid claim to the entire front end of the bar. Only a handful of empty tables remained near the boarded-up windows on the street side.

Versa shuffled from one end of the bar to the other, continuously pouring generous swigs of rum into rapidly draining mugs. They wore a roughly hewn wooden mask made to look like a traditionally bearded Biori man. Their outfit, a long-sleeved fur tunic and breeches, matched what a Heilinist theater troupe thought the Biori looked like, though Bron wouldn't have touched it with three spears tied together.

When Versa noticed Brina, they stopped dead in their tracks. A handful of cups tumbled off the platter they were carrying and onto the bar.

"Oi," one of the Auctioneers shouted as rum spilled over the edge of the bar and onto his trousers. Versa's momentary distraction was enough to make all twelve of those sitting at the bar turn around in their seat.

"Well, have I ever," a woman in the middle barked. Her black hair was woven into numerous thin braids that stuck outward like a spider's legs. "It's Springtide."

"Mahrovia," Brina said, nodding. Under the watchful eyes of Mahrovia's comrades, Brina stepped forward and grabbed the woman by the shoulder in greeting. Mahrovia grinned.

"I knew that Fortuyn idiot was lying," she said. "He told us you'd gotten yourself eaten by that griffin that's been terrorizing Barrow's Perch."

"Not yet," Brina replied to raucous laughter from the mercenaries. *A griffin, here?* Things really were getting stranger every week.

"I'd hurry if I were you," Mahrovia said. "Fortuyn claimed he'd have the beast tracked down and slaughtered by sundown."

"The only way he's killing that thing is if it chokes on his fancy armor," the man soaked in Versa's spilled rum boomed to another round of howls.

Brina sighed. If only she'd known that money-hungry moron was planning to slay such a magnificent creature five minutes earlier. *I should've crippled him.* It would have been more than fair, given what he'd done. *Why didn't I?* Not out of some newfound sense of forgiveness. No, she had just enjoyed terrorizing him too much.

Mahrovia slapped Brina on the shoulder and pulled up a stool beside her.

"I used to have one, you know," Brina said as she sat down. "A griffin, I mean."

Mahrovia's eyes became skeptical slits.

"It's true," Brina said. "I found a chick underneath a bush near the edge of the mountains. Must have fallen out of its nest or something. It was no bigger than a lamb."

"And you thought it'd be a good idea to take it home?"

Brina shrugged. "It would have starved or frozen. I couldn't leave it. Not when so few griffins are born these days. So I took it home. I fed it, kept it warm. Before I knew it, it was the size of a pony."

"Then what happened?" The inn had gone quiet as people leaned in to catch the end of Brina's story.

"It grew too large and restless. They're not meant for human company. They need open skies and rocky mountain peaks. I set it free in the woods." Brina shrugged. "Anticlimactic, but true."

There was the rustling of disappointment as people went back to their drinks.

Mahrovia shook her head. "Maybe Fortuyn was right, Springtide. You are a little cracked."

"So what happened to you then?" Mahrovia went on between gulps of rum. She smacked her lips. "Nobody's seen you around in two weeks. People were talking."

"I got bogged down in a very long, very good, book," Brina said in a tone that implied no further questions were necessary.

"Fair enough. Read your books then, Springtide, more power to you." Mahrovia waved a hand at Versa. "Hand her a mug of that on me."

"Coming right up."

As an Auctioneer passed Brina a mug, she took in the rest of the patrons seated around the barrels against the far wall. A hooded man nursing a pipe and a full mug of ale sat staring out of the window at the alley behind it. Brina's hackles rose.

Either this hooded stranger was inebriated enough to find amusement in staring at a patch of mud, or he was trying to hide the fact that he was

## CHAPTER 29

listening in on their every word. Brina suspected the second, though she could only guess at what he was hoping to hear. He'd already been in here when she arrived, so he couldn't have been following her. And everyone else seemed surprised at her unannounced arrival. So why was he so interested?

Brina raised her mug at Mahrovia and took a calculated sip. Then she beckoned for Versa to step aside for a moment.

"Do you have a room to spare?" she whispered, so the stranger in the corner wouldn't hear. "I'll need to stay at least two nights."

"Anything you need," Versa said. Then, in an even lower voice, they added, "I can't believe you're back in one piece—I mean, sort of." They nodded at Brina's eye. "The rumors I heard. Each one more incredible than the last. It didn't help that Zot and that unfortunate stranger disappeared from their gibbets without a trace as well."

"I kept your room empty for as long as I could," Versa said. "I expected you to be back." There was the merest hint of accusation in their tone.

"I'll tell you all about it once the racket in the common room dies down," Brina promised. A quick glance over her shoulder told her that the stranger in the corner had abandoned the window strategy and was now full-on gaping at her. "Could you let me in through the back door? That bloke in the corner seems to suffer from wandering eyes and ears."

Versa nodded, then in a louder tone said, "Fine, then. Guess I'll see you next week."

\*\*\*

Brina exited the inn with a casual wave to Mahrovia and her band. She then swiftly squeezed herself into the two-foot-wide gap between the Chimera and the house beside it to reach the back door. It was already open.

"Here." Versa handed her a brass key with the number five engraved on it.

The place looked familiar as she traipsed up the creaky oaken steps toward the second floor. The cast-iron chandelier still held a dozen stumps of molten wax, the old painting of a jester in a pre-Heilinist court still hung just a touch too far to the left, and the panicked scurrying of the mice in the attic still pattered on the ceiling.

And yet something was different, as though someone had torn the old place down in her absence and built a perfect copy in its place. It was more feeling than conscious thought, the unsettling squeeze of realizing that she no longer belonged here. She'd always felt safe here, but today her nerves jangled at the thought of sleeping with nothing but the slanted oak door as security. She shook her head, as though trying to get water out of her ears. *I'm becoming as unhinged as Acheron.*

As she reached the landing, Brina paused on the top step, listening. The faint scratching of quill on parchment escaped through the slit under the door to number three. Aside from that, all was quiet. For now. A renewed round of laughter from the common room startled her into moving on.

She locked the door of number five behind her as soon as it clicked shut. It was the same room she'd occupied the night she'd set out to rescue Acheron. The same view of the imposing stoneward and Heil's Gate greeted her, except this time the gibbets were empty.

A pouch of dried herbs hung beside the window, spreading a lavender scent that struggled to cover up the pipe smoke that drifted through the floorboards from the common room below. A puff of dust sprang up from the straw-filled mattress as she flung herself down on it. After the improvised bunks in the vaults below the distillery, it was dangerously comfortable. *No sleeping, there's work to do.*

She reached down from the bed and opened the travel sack she'd brought with her. Inside were water, a scroll of parchment, ink, and a small stone tablet, wrapped in an old tunic. Her fingers trembled as she remembered what Saf had said as she'd slipped the thing into Brina's sack. "You never know. You might change your mind." She hadn't wanted to take it, and she probably shouldn't have. *It's just a backup, just so I know it's there.*

Curiosity got the better of her, and she unwrapped the tablet. The engravings on it shimmered and flashed in the light. It was a complex shape, more difficult than *Gnis* by miles. Dozens of loops branched off from each other in a sunflower pattern, only to reattach to each other seemingly at random. There was an entrancing quality to it. Brina found her breath slowing as her eye traced those curls and twists automatically. *Consol*, Saf had called it. It replaced the target's sense of self with a warm fuzzy state, which made them highly suggestible.

She lay back down on the bed, holding out the script above her. The longer she stared at it, the more doubts sprang up. Why was she so drawn to this thing? It called out to her, as though the script itself wanted to burrow deep in her mind and never let go.

She should have left it in the headquarters, where it belonged. She wouldn't use it, anyway. Like she'd said, she would rely on her own wits and the honest relationship she'd formed with Versa over the years. They'd

## CHAPTER 29

known her since she was a kid. Once they realized what was at stake, they would help on their own accord. *Then put it away.* She didn't.

Another horrific thought rose from the fringes of her mind. If misapplied, power shapes could have an adverse effect. She'd seen as much in Grizelda's store, when Acheron's hand-drawn script had caused her to burn herself. If such a simple shape could so easily go awry, she hated to think about what might happen if she messed this one up.

Between the raucous patrons in the common room below, the hooting and hollering of passing pedestrians, and her own intrusive thoughts, it ought to have been impossible to imprint. The mere buzzing of an astringent fly was usually enough to ruin an entire session. Not today. Not with this shape. Before she knew it, Brina fell back down onto the dusty bed, eyes tracing the pattern over and over and over.

The first chariot was sinking over the Ditch's roofs when a brief flash of pink raced across the script. Startled by this unexpected change, Brina dropped the script, causing the stone tablet to crash into her ribs.

"Muck and ash," she shouted, rubbing the rapidly expanding sore spot on her chest. She picked up the script as quickly as she could, but by the time she regained her focus, she'd lost the shape.

Embarrassed at how easily the shape had eaten up an afternoon, Brina wrapped the script up in a spare tunic and tied the package around her waist, so it was hidden from view. If anyone came snooping in her room while she was gone, they'd find nothing but some scraps of laundry and a handful of bananas she'd plucked off a low-hanging branch on her way to the Chimera.

With nothing to do but wait until the common room emptied, Brina settled herself behind the desk near the window and watched as passersby scurried about their business. From up here, everything that played out on the street below seemed somehow magnified and exposed. She watched as a woman with a cane bumped into a young lady carrying a baby. As the target struggled to regain her balance, a youth swiped her purse from behind.

Across the street, two men were watching a fisherman ride by on a wobbly cart drawn by a mule, hungry expressions clouding their faces. A little way to the right, a hooded man leaned against a wall, his face obscured by shadow. He was staring intently at The Wistful Chimera's front door. Brina's jaw tensed.

*He's still here, still watching.* Whoever that man was, Brina would have to think thrice about each step she took while he was out there. It was all but guaranteed that someone was paying him. There was a rehearsed casualness to the way he leaned back against the windowsill, arms crossed. The man might not be a good spy, but this certainly wasn't his first time surveilling the Chimera either.

There were only two types of people in Doorstep's Ditch with the funds to pay someone to stand around all day. Gang leaders and scepter-lackeys. The former could be ruled out. If the gangs wanted to know something about Brina, they knew where to find her. The latter option, however, came with a set of additional questions. The most burning of which was why the church was suddenly so interested in her. Then it hit her. The bargheist. Brina's stomach sank. Of course. How many people on the entire island of Hammerstroke knew how to handle a bargheist? Half a dozen at most. From there, it wouldn't be difficult at all to check names off the list.

Brina glared at the spy. *I'm going to need to ask you a few questions soon, my friend, and you're not going to like them one bit.*

# CHAPTER 30

*10th day of the 12th cycle, 569KR*
**Doorstep's Ditch**

o," Versa asked, running a gray towel through a series of drying mugs, "am I going to hear all about your wild adventure now?"

The common room of the Chimera was deserted. Those who had hired lodgings had retreated to the second floor, and Versa insisted on locking the inn's front doors from midnight until dawn.

"Not much to tell." Brina shrugged, keeping her eyes focused on the dregs of ale in her mug. "I wasn't gone that long, after all."

Behind their motionless mask, Versa's eyes narrowed. "I may be discreet, but I am not a fool, Sabrina Springtide." They abandoned the towel and began stacking the mugs to be used the next morning. "You disappear from the room you rent here in the middle of the night. The following morning two prisoners are missing alongside yourself. Do you expect me to believe that to be a coincidence?"

"Who else has made that connection?" Brina asked, inwardly cursing. A room overlooking Heil's Gate had seemed like the perfect hiding place, but that plan, of course, had assumed she would be back in bed by dawn with no one any the wiser. Now, with the image of that spying hooded figure still fresh in her mind, it had become a dangerous loose end.

"Don't worry. This secret, like all others, is safe with me." Without question, Versa slid a sealed black bottle from underneath the bar and placed two glasses beside it. "But first, let's celebrate. This has been gathering dust for years, saved for a special occasion, and what more can we hope for than the safe return of a friend thought lost?"

Brina smiled as Versa tilted a copious amount of black liquid into both cups. A drop of it splashed onto their white glove, where it soaked into the fabric. For a moment, Versa's gaze remained fixed on the spreading bloodlike stain.

"What is it?" Brina asked, lifting her glass.

"Oh." Versa's head snapped back up. "It's wine from Hawqal made from a special type of berries that only grows in small clusters in the desert. It's supposed to be exceedingly rare."

"Heil's mud-soaked breeches. Where'd you pick that up?"

"A friend gave it to me a long time ago, when things were different," Versa said mildly, raising their glass into a silent toast.

It was sweeter than Brina had expected, and thicker. Complex flavors vaguely resembling strawberries and wild honey mixed with a smoky undertone. The taste lingered on her lips even after she gulped it down. She could feel the liquor dissolving in her stomach, granting an instant lightness. It gave her just enough courage to go through with step one of her plan.

"Want to go for a walk?"

Versa stopped wiping down the mugs. Their head tilted sideways as they considered Brina. "You know I hate to leave the Chimera alone for too long. Especially at night..."

"Oh, come on." Brina waved the concern away with a lazy flick of her hand. "If I know you, and I think I do, every lock in this entire building gets checked thrice a week. No one's getting in here. Besides, we'll only take a quick stroll to the beach and back. I could really use the fresh air."

With a sigh, Versa dropped the rag and reached for a heavy key ring that hung from a hook underneath the bar. "Fine," they said, placing the bottle of wine in the inside pocket of their cloak, "but I'm taking this with me."

Brina grinned. "The more the merrier, I say."

"I suppose one favor warrants another," Brina said as Versa locked the Chimera's back door. They set off across Wicket Row and toward the beach district. "I did free that stranger from the gibbet, but things went awry, and I ended up taking cover in the city."

Versa chuckled. "I knew it was just a matter of time before your kettle boiled over."

"What's that supposed to mean?" Brina was unsure whether she ought to be offended.

Versa shrugged. "You've never quite learned to accept life as it is in Doorstep's Ditch, that's all."

"I'm sure I'm not the only one who hates getting screwed over."

## CHAPTER 30

"You are not." Versa laughed. "But the difference is that most who sit down at my bar complain about what happens to them, and only them. You, on the other hand, can't look away from the suffering of others, no matter how much you may try to pretend otherwise."

Brina didn't know what to say to that, so instead she drank some more of her wine in silence.

"How was it?" Versa asked. "The city?"

"Empty." It was the first word that came to mind when she thought back to all those white stone houses with their red clay roofs. Houses, but not homes. "It's like half of the city is just decor for those in the center to perform in front of."

Versa nodded. "It was like that twenty years ago. I can't imagine the situation's improved since De Leliard took over. Batches of outwalled have been arriving weekly the last few years. One wonders where they keep finding them."

"All of that space," Brina muttered. "Hundreds of houses are decaying from disuse while we're putting up driftwood shacks by the dozen. If only that damn wall didn't stand in our way."

She glanced at her own wobbly reflection in a shard of broken glass that lingered in a smashed window. *I look terrible.* Her hair was matting to the point of turning into unintentional dreadlocks. Dark scarring encircled her missing eye. It was a miracle that people even recognized her in this condition.

"We both know it's not the wall that keeps us out, but our acceptance of it. It's a symbol, nothing more," Versa said, breaking a silent spell that had fallen between them.

"I don't know. It feels pretty solid when you're clinging to it by your fingertips fifty feet off the ground."

Versa burst out laughing. "You scaled that thing by hand? You're even more cracked than I thought. "

"Thanks." Brina chuckled. "I'll admit it wasn't one of my better plans."

"So what's next?"

Brina looked over her shoulder, eying Versa with a mixture of amusement and weariness. Why did they always seem to know just a touch more than they were supposed to? Then again, she needed to nudge the conversation in the right direction somehow.

The image of *Consol* drifted into her mind's eye, and her mood dropped like a brick. Now that she was face to mask with Versa, after all they had done for her, all the reasons she'd objected to Saf's plan stood out all the clearer. *That's Plan B,* she told herself. *For when I run out of options.*

"I'm thinking about taking on a different challenge. Something bigger," she said with false nonchalance.

"I figured." Versa sighed, stopping at the crossing between two alleys to pour another round of wine. They glanced at the cracks in the surrounding boarded-up windows before turning those piercing eyes on Brina again. "I know who that stranger in the gibbet was, Brina."

"You do?" This time, Brina's surprise was genuine.

"When I was young, they called him 'The Spider.' I don't know what name he goes by these days, but I know who he used to run with. When I... returned to Doorstep's Ditch, I was surprised to find him still roaming the island." Versa's tone told Brina they were aware of more than they were letting on.

"Why do I feel you're always two steps ahead of me?"

Versa let out a mirthless laugh. "I suppose I see a lot of myself in you. Or rather, of who I used to be. It doesn't hurt that an innkeeper hears all. Liquor makes loose tongues."

*Excellent point, old friend.*

Brina downed the remains of her wine. She was pleased to see Versa mimic the gesture as they trudged toward the beach through increasingly muddy streets. Another round of refills followed.

Brina took an intentional detour, regaling Versa with the tale of all that had transpired on the other side of the stoneward, though she kept the Order of the Prism out of the story, making it sound like it had been just her and Acheron.

All the while, she was careful to nudge the bottle of wine in Versa's direction whenever their cup was running low. By the time bottle's contents dipped below the label, Brina was struggling to avoid slurring her words. Versa, however, remained rock steady, even if their eyes had grown red behind the mask.

"... so we swam all the way to s-shore," Brina concluded.

Versa shook their head. "You were born under a lucky star indeed, Springtide." As they dipped out of a final alley and onto the beach, Brina could see her target in the distance. The shivering lights of God's Maul, the black fortress.

"Your story explains a lot," Versa mused, unaware of where they were going. "There's been talk of undercover darkhelms blending in with the

## CHAPTER 30

outwalled, asking questions. That man in the inn this afternoon, he's been in at least four times this week. All he does is sit and listen. Now, normally, that sort of thing wouldn't stir my suspicions, but given the commotion you caused, I'd say better safe than sorry."

"Which is exactly why I wanted to talk out here. The walls have ears." Brina paused near a cluster of boulders, then sat down on top of the flattest one. Versa groaned, their ruined joints clicking and popping as they sat down. The bottle of wine tinkled as they set it down beside them. *Empty.*

This was it, as perfect a window as Brina was going to get. It all came down to this. Without a description of God's Maul's internal structure, the Order may as well deliver themselves at Mallion's Gate in a cage. "*There is a way to guarantee we get what we need.*" Saf's words rattled around Brina's mind like the tail of a venomous serpent sticking out of a patch of grass. "*The target needs to be unaware or it won't work.*"

"So," Versa began, "is this when you're going to tell me about your grand purpose?"

Brina's stomach dropped. Had she been that transparent?

"You've been dancing around it all night," Versa said, nodding to the beat of a song only they could hear.

Brina took a deep breath, then pointed toward the sea, where God's Maul fell outline broke the horizon.

"There it is. That's the purpose."

A silence fell. The type of silence that stretches on for aeons as the ocean swells and retracts, eating away at the brittle boundaries of all it touches. Silence in which everything is said, heard, and digested all at once. The type of silence that splits the world into a before and after when it breaks.

"How I wished you would have said anything else," Versa muttered. Their voice had changed. It was at the same time higher, softer, and yet clearer than it had been. Brina knew instinctively that it was the voice of who Versa had once been. "That fortress lies in another world, Sabrina, one we mortals cannot, and should not, touch."

"It's a pile of stone," Brina answered, gesturing wildly at the boulders scattered on the beach around. "One which holds the only family I have left."

"Your father is lost, Sabrina. As painful as that truth is, you must accept it, or it will destroy you." Versa turned away, casting their porcelain mask in shadow.

"So what would you have me do?" Brina's veins tingled with a sudden surge of grief and anger, fueled by the wine and pain built up over years. "You want me to watch as they drag my father into the Enclave to be murdered?"

"Go north," Versa pleaded. "Leave Doorstep's Ditch until it is all over with. It's the only way."

"The way to what? I don't need twenty more years of slogging through jungle, marsh, and mountain passes to provide our noble neighbors behind the wall with every trinket and substance they desire in exchange for a pittance."

This was not how this was supposed to go. Brina's guts wrenched. *I'm messing up our one chance. Our one key into God's Maul.*

"That's not so bad a life, Sabrina. Not compared to what most of us have to settle for. We were born on the wrong side of history. There's nothing we, or anyone, can do to change that. Don't make them break you to make you understand that."

"We can do something," Brina said, using every ounce of willpower she possessed to sound calm. "I met some people. Skilled people, who are on our side. With their help, we can do it. We can break into God's Maul and release my father. The old rebellion would rise again."

"No one who enters through that gate comes out again."

"You did," Brina urged. "You came back."

"No," Versa snapped. "I did not."

They raised one of their gloved hands in front of Brina. The white fabric shone in the reflected light of the chariots. With slow, pained movements, Versa began pulling it off. When it finally slipped loose, Brina let out an involuntary gasp.

Underneath was something that more closely resembled a claw than a human hand. The skin was a mixture of red and gray scar tissue, and two fingers had been sliced off at the middle joints. The pinky was missing completely. What remained looked like it had been chewed up and spit out.

Versa flexed the fingers and tried to make a fist, but the hand wouldn't fully close.

Before Brina could say anything, Versa put the glove back on.

"Whatever entered that cesspit of human cruelty, I am not it. Not anymore."

Brina swallowed. Her heart was racing from the shock of what she had seen and the sinking realization that things were only veering further away from the outcome she'd hoped for.

## CHAPTER 30

"But you have seen it, right? You know what it's like in there."

"I remember little of it. Even if I did, I would not breathe a word of it to any living soul."

"I don't expect you to help," Brina pleaded. "I just need to know what I'm walking into."

"It's not about that," Versa snapped. "I left everything to do with that place behind the day I stumbled into Doorstep's Ditch as an outwalled. To force myself to relive what came before would threaten to erase all the work I've done since then to move on. I can't go back there. Not even in my head." Versa was wheezing now, refusing to look at the ocean and what lay at the horizon. "Even if I could, I would not tell you anything. It will only goad you into a false sense of security. You cannot enter that place and expect to make it out. I will not help you uphold this illusion that your plan is anything more than suicide."

They got up, swaying on their feet. Panic overtook Brina's spiraling thoughts. *They're leaving. My one chance is about to walk away.*

"It will be fine," Brina said, her voice low and soothing, like a mother taking care of a startled child. She burned *Consol*, feeling the sigil's unnatural authority roll off her tongue with every syllable. "You're stronger now. You can handle it."

Versa stopped. Their back turned toward Brina. The low pink burn of the shape mixed with the white light of the sinking chariots as it reflected off Versa's black cloak.

"See, there's nothing to worry about," Brina went on, flaring the shape as intensely as she could. The glowing curves and waves sliced through her retina as though she were staring directly into the noonday sun. *I'm doing it. It's working.*

Alongside the unexpected rush of power she felt, a second, smaller feeling reared its head. Disgust. As soon as she'd burned that shape, she had crossed a line. One from which there would be no coming back. *What's done is done.* She clung to the shape with all her might. *I need to get to the truth now.*

"When you sailed past that front gate, what was the first thing you saw?" Brina struggled to breathe as the immense authority in her own voice hit her ears.

Versa stood with their head bowed, shoulders twitching.

"The maze. Door after door after door," they mumbled drunkenly. "Door after door after door."

"Good," Brina encouraged. "Where do the doors go?"

"Nowhere. Doors go nowhere." They began shaking like they'd just clambered out of a tub of ice. "Nowhere. Doors go to the nowhere. The pain world."

"Is that where they kept you? The pain world?"

"... pain world..." Versa mumbled, "... pain..."

Brina's heart jumped up in her throat. She could see the shape growing dimmer in the corners of her vision. She tried to speak again, but found she couldn't. Something was pressing on her throat, squeezing until no words would come out.

Versa turned around, bones clicking and snapping. Their mask was obscured by two bright rays of white light where their eyes ought to have been. *They're a sparkgazer too.*

Brina watched as Versa's hunched shape shuffled closer. Her throat was closing up further. She only realized she was choking when her knees sank into loose sand.

"I told you," Versa howled hysterically. "This will break you. It's already broken you."

The sigil's hold on Brina was so forceful she felt like she was back underneath the ocean's surface, being squeezed by an unspeakable weight from all sides.

"You are one of them," they babbled. "Just like them."

Versa's dark shape loomed over Brina in the night like an ill omen. Their arms twitched and writhed at their sides. With every movement, it became clear that they were no longer in control of themselves. Versa would kill Brina, and there was nothing she could do.

"... never hurt me again... never..."

Those beams of white roved over Brina, blinding her. There was one last shudder from the innkeeper. Then the shape evaporated, leaving only dark slits in the mask.

Without another word, they turned and hobbled away into the treeline.

The hold on Brina's lungs fell away. She heaved once, then began sobbing uncontrollably.

# CHAPTER 31

*21st day of the 5th cycle, 537KR*
**Rothmoor**

Acheron pulled a moth-eaten ankle-length cloak from a hook above his head, then shuffled back into the deepest, darkest corner of the wardrobe. The familiar smells of rot, pipe smoke, and rat piss closed around him like a nauseating blanket.

A sliver of wobbly firelight fell through the slit between the closet's doors. He resisted the urge to peek out into the room beyond. Mother had warned him not to.

First there was the creaking and the banging of solid wood against the apartment's hollow walls, a rhythmic tap like a drum. Slow at first, then quicker. Louder.

Then the yelling began. Somehow, it always coincided with the banging of the wood. The louder the bangs, the louder the yelling. High-pitched screams and angry grunts, like discordant singing on an unsteady beat.

As it always did, the urge to rush out of the closet to help his mother pulled at Acheron's limbs. She would be angry if he did. He was not to show himself. That would "ruin it," his mother had said. Whatever that meant. So he obeyed and stuck his fingers in his ears as far as they would go. It wasn't deep enough.

A spider, large as the palm of his hand, skittered up his folded leg and under the cloak. Acheron closed his eyes, focusing on the gentle prods of the creature's eight legs as it worked its way up his arm. It was almost enough to take his mind off what was happening. He had always felt a kinship with creatures most people considered vermin. No spider, rat, or snake had ever kicked, burned, or spat on him. People, on the other hand…

There was a bang, louder than usual, followed by the sharp slap of skin on skin. Acheron froze.

"Ow, what the..." A second slap interrupted his mother's outburst.

"Shut up, woman." Acheron recognized the voice at once. Mr. Holloward. A fat, angry man who showed up once or twice a month, always grumbling about money. Like the other kids in the building, Acheron feared him. Not only because of the cuffs around the ears he'd hand out if you forgot to hand him a chair or stood with slouched shoulders, but because of the mood his mother would be in after he left. When she had one of her bad days, Holloward's cuffs seemed like pats on the head by comparison.

On the other side of the wardrobe, the noise peaked, the way a street quartet sped up toward the end of a song. Only, this time, it was different. There was a clatter, as from a chair sailing through the air. His mother's yelling had changed. It had gotten somehow "realer."

Mr. Holloward sounded angry. Even angrier than he'd been when Acheron had accidentally stepped on his new shoes months earlier. Before Acheron could decide whether he ought to burst from the closet and "ruin it," the noise died as suddenly as it had erupted.

The door slammed, rattling the wardrobe and the floor beneath it. Acheron breathed a sigh of relief. It was over. For today. His fingers were still lodged in his ears when the wardrobe flew open.

A hand grabbed of a fistful of his short, black hair and he was flung out onto the splintery wooden floor. He raised a hand against the light of two oil lamps hanging from the wall, blinded.

"Get up, useless boy." Before he could sit up, his mother slapped him across the face, knocking him back down. "And what'd I tell you about wearing my clothes?"

The cloak was jerked off his shoulders. The black and yellow spider tumbled from its folds. For a moment Acheron thought it might skitter back toward him, then the heel of his mother's boot stomped down on it.

She looked livid. Her long, dark curls were tangled and disheveled like a patch of brambles. Tufts of it were missing. The seeds of bruises encircled her furious brown eyes. She was only twenty-six, but the angry lines in her hollow face made her look twice that.

"Mother—"

"Don't call me that," she bit at him. "Never call me that."

He got to his feet, taking care to stay out of arm's reach.

"Make yourself useful for once and get the ledgers."

He nodded and sat down on the overturned chair near the room's only

## CHAPTER 31

window. Closing his eyes in front of her made him feel vulnerable, but he knew she wouldn't hit him while he was accessing the ledgers.

"We now owe Mr. Holloward two fewer shards. How many does that make in total?"

Numbers and lettering appeared on the back of Acheron's eyelids, loose clumps of mathematical glyphs floating through his mind's eye like driftwood on a receding tide.

It was all here. Every detail of everything he had ever seen, lodged in the crevices of his brain like barbed fishhooks. No matter how hard he tried to forget some of it, it would always be there, as real as the moment it had occurred. His mother often said it was the only useful thing about him. Acheron hated it.

He rummaged through piles of mental debris until his mother's ledgers moved to the forefront, momentarily wiping all else from his mind. There were almost two dozen names she had made him memorize, all of them belonging to people they owed money. He deducted two shards from Mr. Holloward's tally.

"We owe Mr. Holloward another nineteen shards."

"What about Garulon?" his mother demanded. "Do we have credit left there?"

"He won't lend us any more without collateral," Acheron said, rewinding the fight between his mother and the Merkedian loan shark. "Not unless we can pay back the thirteen shards we owe him."

"What thirteen shards? I paid that greedy mammoth-licker back every last nib."

Acheron winced at her tone, shrinking away from a blow that hadn't come yet.

"It says here we borrowed fifteen, two months ago. You didn't tell me what for."

"Because it was none of your business."

The chair was jerked out from under Acheron, causing him to topple sideways onto the floor. A bolt of lightning shot through his temples as his head slammed into the side of the desk.

He watched through blurry eyes as his mother sat back on the bed. She was holding the only thing she loved in the entire world, a battered tin goblet stained black with soot. A triangular rune was engraved in the front of it. Inside lay a white sliver the size of a fingernail.

Thick white and gray vapors rose from the goblet, which she breathed in greedily, her furious features relaxing with every heave of her chest.

Acheron leaned closer, trying to get a whiff of the pungent, but sweet, smoke. He didn't know why, but the smell always seemed to cheer him up. It smelled like home.

His mother shot him a bored look, as though she had forgotten he was still there.

"Here." She flung a pack of playing cards at him. "Don't bother coming back empty handed."

Acheron nodded. He knew what to do.

***

*11th day of the 12th cycle, 569KR*
**Doorstep's Ditch**

Acheron awoke shivering, his sheets damp with rank sweat. His heart thundered in his chest as though he had just run two miles with bloodhounds at his heels. It had been that way for as long as he could remember.

A talon raked across his lungs with every shallow breath. He delayed opening his eyes, half-convinced that he would find his mother sitting at the foot of his bed. Instead, he saw only the vaulted stone ceiling of the Order's cramped headquarters and the motley curtain which shielded his bunk from the main living space. It was a convenient storage location, very space efficient if you wanted to hide some trash from sight.

The ripe stench of fresh bread and fried bacon wafted toward him from the bell jar. Acheron gritted his teeth, grateful that his stomach was empty. The very notion of food made his guts squirm. He needed a different kind of sustenance.

*Coward. Rat. Useless boy.*

"Good morning to you too," he muttered out loud, rubbing his hands across his scarred face. He lifted his pillow and gazed upon the most wondrous vista the Sundered Isles had to offer. A fist-sized chunk of misty white resin lay pressed into the straw mattress.

A wide grin cracked Acheron's face as he held it up to the light. He still couldn't believe his luck. Acheron grinned as he wondered whether Zot had already found out one of his cronies had been robbed of a chunk of cloud worth a brand-new wagon and two mediocre horses to draw it. *I hope he's angrier than a Reynziel in front of a closed brothel.*

## CHAPTER 31

*Achie's brain is all misty and numb,* his mother cooed, *Useless little boy.*

"Technically" he hadn't been "supposed to" leave this damnable place, but after a week of being locked up and isolated like a diseased pig, he'd found nothing but joy in roaming the nighttime streets of Doorstep's Ditch in search of prey. Let them recognize him. He'd survived as a ghost for a decade. They wouldn't do him in so easily.

Acheron reached for his patchwork robe, which hung on a wooden peg, and retrieved a soot-stained tin goblet. An absent finger traced the crude, triangular pattern on the rim. It had all seemed so real. His crystal-clear memories often replayed in his mind as he slept, and in those moments, it felt like he had never grown up, had never moved away.

With every blink of his eyes, she returned to him. Her ashy visage, limbs sprawled at unnatural angles as blood seeped from a scarlet wound on the back of her head. He looked down at his hands and found them covered in black gore.

No matter. Soon, all of that would vanish. All he needed was a little chemical push to help him let go of it.

He forced himself to his feet with a groan. A quick peek behind the curtain informed him the bell jar was deserted. A lonely plate of breakfast stood on the opposite side of the table, untouched. The others had left without waking him up. *They don't need you. Nobody does.*

As he strode into the bell jar, familiar shapes crowded in him around him. Azaria, Ghar-Ul, Hosana, his mother... The list went on and on. Their twisted faces snarled insults, inches from his own. "*It should have been you.*"

"Yeah, yeah." He waved an impatient hand as though trying to dispel smoke. He put his feet up on the richly decorated table, leaning back on two chair legs. "Any other wisdoms to impart before I blast you all into the abyss?"

"Borrowed time. We will be waiting on the other side." Ghar-Ul leered at him, his tall Hawqallian frame towering over Acheron. "Nowhere to go, old friend."

Acheron shrugged. He held up the cup in one hand and broke off two flakes of pearly white oblivion with the other. A small touch of *Gnis* turned the goblet red hot. He bent closer, inhaling every wisp of pure, loving smoke.

As soon as he exhaled, everything shifted. It was as though he became a mere third-party spectator to the pitiful, emaciated husk he piloted through the mortal world. His limbs grew heavy and numb, as though he were suspended in a tub of honey. He watched with satisfaction as his mother's hollow face dissolved in front of him, giving way to the forest mural behind her.

He wasn't happy. No. Never that. He just didn't care anymore. Didn't care that his entire life had been a disastrous sequence of tragedies manufactured by his own actions. Didn't care that he had spent the last decade of his life cowering in the grimy crevices of the world. Best of all, he didn't care about all the damage his existence had caused others from the very moment he'd been born. For Acheron, this was as good as it got.

"I knew it."

Acheron's perfect peace shattered like a vase chucked out of a third-floor window. Saf stood underneath the arch leading to the library, eyes wide in disgust.

Her trademark black gown fluttered about her as she strode toward him. "I don't believe it. Acheron of Rothmoor, Thirteenth Pillar of the Return, Library of the South, hopeless floater." She shook her head. "And to think I believed you would save us. Elevate us."

Acheron instinctively clutched the smoking goblet to his chest, protecting it from a lunge that hadn't come yet.

"I didn't make up any of those fancy nicknames," he said, trying to soak up as much of the fumes as he could. Where he was concerned, wasting cloud was worse than death. At least with death, you were supposed to find peace after you snuffed it. "Not my fault people like you get carried away with the whole savior-of-humanity nonsense."

Saf stood over him. Her face seemed carved out of ice. "Where did you get that?"

"None of your business."

"Oh, it damn well is my business, you pathetic sack of fleder pellets." She swallowed as though trying not to spit fire. "You left headquarters. You broke our agreement."

Acheron stared back into those round brown eyes, unable to feel so much as a twinge of regret, or anger, or... anything really. He imagined he would've been annoyed with the woman, had any part of his brain still functioned as it should, but as it stood, it was all he could do to look back at her blurry outline and conjure up the illusion that he was listening.

"You didn't understand a bloody word I just said, did you?" Disappointment dripped from every syllable, like piss spilling over the edge of a chamber pot.

## CHAPTER 31

Acheron saw the movement in his mind's eye a fraction of a moment before it happened. Saf reached for the cup of bubbling resin in his hand, but he was quicker. He reflexively burned *Testudo*, and her hand slammed into his rock-hard forearm. One of her fingers bent back at an unnatural angle, and she yelled out in pain.

*See what you did,* that dirty voice inside him balked. *The only thing you bring is pain.* A fist closed around Acheron's heart. They weren't supposed to be back. Not yet. Not with thrice the amount for a lethal dose still simmering away in his hand.

Saf stepped back, her eyes wide. She looked at him as though she was seeing him for the first time, as though she finally saw what he truly was. Her index finger stuck out of her clenched fist, dislocated.

"So that's how it's going to be?" she shouted at him. With a crunch and a grimace, she forced the finger back into place. "You're going to hide behind the cloud like a coward and float through the rest of your life?"

Normally *the* C-word would have sent Acheron over the edge, but vapors were still rising from the cup in his hands and into his brain, a salve for all injuries, mental or otherwise. He heard the words only vaguely, as if she had shouted them from the top of an endless ravine while he languished at the bottom in a bed of stone.

"That's exactly how it's going to be," he slurred back at her. "You don't know. You don't know what it was truly like back then."

"No?" Saf reached for the sleeve of her robe and jerked it up to her elbow, revealing a series of angry scars running from her wrist to the crook of her elbow.

*Slave brands.* Acheron's jaw clenched. Of course. That memory, too, was forever seared into his memory.

Without wanting or planning to, he began rambling. "I told them. I told them it was a bad idea, that someone had been leaking information to the darkhelms. Yet none of them wanted to believe one of our brothers or sisters would betray us. All of them swore by their oaths."

Saf didn't look at him. Her eyes kept flickering back to the smoking cup in his hands.

"I begged them not to go through with it, Saphara. I really did, but they persisted. That is why I didn't go with them that day. That's why I am here and they are dead." He raised his mother's cup of cloud and inhaled as deeply as he could. He needed every wisp of consolation he could get.

"Not all of them are dead," Saf said. "Abrasax lives. We can still get him out of God's Maul before the time comes."

A lump swelled in Acheron's throat at the mention of the name. Abrasax, The Viper. The only man Acheron had ever known who could call a brick a gold bar and make it glimmer in front of you. He smiled despite himself.

"Abrasax got me off the streets, you know." Why was he telling her all of this? "He found me a few weeks after my 17th year, when I got by hustling people playing Galleons. Abrasax convinced me to leave that life behind. He said my talents were wasted on petty crime. I didn't even know I had any." He forced himself to stop talking.

Experience had taught him not to go down this road when he was floating. For once it started, it was impossible to stem the flow of memories oozing from his mind. Besides, it wasn't anyone's business.

"He was right." Saf said. Her eyes flared crimson as she massaged her injured finger. "Do you want to know how I got started with all of this?" She gestured at the stacks of books, scrolls, and artifacts on the bell jar's round table.

"Fourteen years ago, I was stuck in the hull of a ship from Snake Island, bound for the mines of Onderheem. I was three years into a decade of hard labor I was condemned to by head-inquisitor De Leliard. No trial. No jury. Torture in a dark room, followed by me telling him whatever he wanted to hear to make the agony stop.

*"Possession of forbidden scriptures with seditious intent,"* they called it. All I had was a statuette my grandfather left me when he passed. It was engraved with a handful of scripts, but I didn't know. I thought they were mere decorations. That thing must've been worth a fortune.

"I was chained hand and foot alongside three dozen others. The darkhelms hadn't given us food or drink in two days. There was barely any air left. Some had died, and many more of us were close. They only want the strongest for the mines. Even those who make it arrive with their spirits conveniently broken. Mine had already bent further than I thought possible."

Acheron tried to speak, but Saf held up a trembling finger.

"That's the way the church operates once they've got the condemned isolated. Technically, they aren't putting anyone to death, so Heil is okay with it. That's what a Reynziel told me years later, anyway. He changed his mind rather quickly when I gave him a taste of his own medicine. It took less than an hour to break him."

## CHAPTER 31

Acheron shuddered. He'd known life had hardened Saf. It was plainly visible in the intensity of her glare. Takes one to know one. But to hear her describe the torture of a Reynziel without so much as a shred of emotion, drove home the point in a way nothing else could. Beauty and ugliness, warmth and cold, love and hate, all living side by side in one person. "How long did it take?"

Saf frowned.

"Until the Reynziel died."

"I don't know. I left him there."

Acheron let out a hiss of cloud fumes. *Maybe we ought to send our demons on a play date.*

"There I was, a simple blacksmith, starving amongst rebels, spies and other "disloyals" deemed too dangerous to release outside the ward," Saf continued. "I was praying to die in my sleep when the sound of splintering wood exploded over our heads. Moments later, the trapdoor flew open, and moonlight shone down for the first time in days."

Acheron's stomach lurched. In his mind's eye, he followed the beam of his own *Lux*-enhanced eyes down into the dark belly of the slave galley. The stench of death and stale urine drowning out the bitter cloud vapors.

"Your hair was short back then," he said, "and your face was covered in blood and grime. You looked so different."

He could see her now, standing in front of him as clearly as the contemporary version of her had been just a moment ago. Dressed in jute rags, heavy chains weighing down bony wrists and ankles. Her face was hollow, but those eyes stared back at him unwaveringly.

"I had heard the rumors," she said. "A band of heretics roaming the night, wielding weapons wrought by the hands of the old gods. I recognized you instantly: Acheron, the spider of Rothmoor. At first I thought I was hallucinating. There were only three of you against so many."

Acheron's heart swelled at the memory. He saw both of them beside him. Abrasax, shrouded in his trademark cloak, and Cassandra, posted atop the crow's nest like a bloodhawk. She was already showing. It had been one of their last raids before the kid was born. After that, she had taken a step back from the Signum, insisting that they couldn't risk the kid losing both parents. Little did she know. There's always another plague just around the corner in these doomed lands.

Unaware of his inner turmoil, Saf went on, "... you knelt down beside me and broke my chains with your bare hands. And you said, 'Remember tonight, my friend,'..."

"For tonight you are reborn," Acheron muttered. "You have died at the word of Keeper and Cardinal. Now you are resurrected by the hand of the people. You have seen your god's true face and felt the sting of his whip across your back. Freedom lies at the end of these broken chains." Tears ran freely down his scarred cheeks. He made no effort to stop them.

"You invoked these words to remind me of my debt. I heeded the call, because I owe this second chance at life to the man who risked it all to free me. A man who inspired everything I have worked tirelessly to achieve since." Saf walked toward him and knelt beside his chair. "Don't tell me that man is dead."

The cup of cloud went out, burnt to ashes. Saf put her arms around his shoulders. "Don't tell me that man is dead," she repeated. Acheron tried to respond. Instead, he sobbed.

*Freedom lies at the end of these broken chains.* The cup of cloud slipped from his hand and clattered against the tiled floor.

He bent down to pick it up, when a disturbance overhead announced the arrival of a newcomer. There was only time to straighten himself in his chair before Brina climbed down the ladder, looking more distraught than he had ever seen her.

# CHAPTER 32

*15th day of the 12th cycle, 569KR*
**Everberg Abbey**

eeks after the initiation, the wounds still oozed. Blood trickled down Solana's cheeks like iron tears. She wiped at her face with the sleeve of her tattered black robe, wincing.

"Why have you stopped your exercises, Sister Solana?"

Her heart skipped a beat as Brother Burke's frog's croak of a voice rang out behind her. Her hearing had improved dramatically since she'd lost her vision. Almost unnervingly so. And yet, her newfound brothers and sisters of the Stigmata had a way of sneaking up on her that made her wonder whether they did it on purpose. Multiple times a day, she'd be scared half to death by sudden hands falling on her shoulder or someone's breath hissing in her ear.

"My apologies, Brother Burke."

She held her left palm over the candle in the center of the prayer table in front of her, then traced the bumps and ridges on the prayer tablet with her right hand. The candle burst into life at once, the heat of it radiating back onto Solana's palm. She allowed herself a brief smile. She was getting good. *That's what fourteen hours of dedication a day will do,* she told herself.

Her fingers traced across a second tablet, and a wave of cold extinguished the candle like the icy breath of a winter storm. For the past week, she had been focusing exclusively on the prayers of heat and frost. Each week, Brother Burke assigned a new pair of prayer tablets for her to pore over. So far, she had gathered six in her very own prayerbook, which she was to keep on her person at all times.

Though some of her brothers and sisters had mastered many more of the prayers throughout their years of service, the weight of those stone tablets in a fortified pocket inside of her robe made Solana feel powerful.

Heil's power, which she had prayed for all these years, now sprang forth from her fingertips as freely as water from a hot spring.

Just yesterday, she had ignited a pile of logs in the dormitory's hearth with one hand, and instantly put it back out with the other. From a distance of six feet. She could hardly believe it herself. This place, and the things that her brothers and sisters could do, was like something out of a dream.

For a decade, she had been trained and indoctrinated to fight against the heretics and their illicit use of the forbidden powers, only to find out that Everberg Abbey housed dozens of previously titled Reynziels who could do far greater things than any heretic had ever managed. The trickery of the fire-eyes seemed petty now. Barely more than children fighting with sticks, unaware that swords exist. The Keeper, in all her wisdom, had foreseen the rise of heresy, and so she had given her servants the tools to keep it at bay.

Every night, she spent an hour before bed reciting the prayer of healing. Solana could feel it pulling at her hands even now. The mere thought of the shape forced her fingers into the right position. She could feel the metallic bumps of the prayerbook prick into her fingertips, verging on the point of breaking skin.

Solana shook herself to avoid falling into the prayer completely. That would have to wait until after today's prayer study. She shook her head and relit the candle. Without touching it, she extinguished it by reciting the right-hand prayer. Thus she continued, lighting and extinguishing. Lighting and extinguishing.

Heavy footfalls approached through the hallway outside. Solana felt the rattle of knuckles rapping against the door reverberate through her limbs and sensed Brother Burke glide across the prayer hall to open the door.

"Is Sister Solana present for prayer?" A deep voice she recognized as the abbot's scribe, Brother Engelbert, intoned.

"She is."

"The abbot needs to see her in his office. Immediately."

"Sister Solana is to be engaged in prayer from six in the morning until dinner is served at eight tonight, as the abbot surely knows." Burke's voice rose in pitch. "The Keeper does not take kindly to disturbances when it comes to her worship."

"The abbot foresaw that I might find you less than flexible. He instructed me to tell you that if your position as master of prayers is dear to you, that you shall obey his command."

## CHAPTER 32

Shoes shuffled back and forth against the stone floor. Clearly, Brother Burke didn't dare openly oppose the abbot, but he was annoyed. Angry even. Solana could smell it on him.

Even before Burke gave the command, Solana had risen and closed her wooden prayerbook. In Everberg, the abbot may as well have been the Cardinal himself. She maneuvered between the rows of benches to the exit.

Over the past weeks, a curious thing had started to occur. As soon as Solana had mastered the prayer of hearing, the world had taken on gray and black hues around her. It wasn't vision exactly. It was more of an echo, painting a rough sketch of objects around her. She had once read that certain creatures in the colony of Bior could fly with great accuracy at night, by producing sounds to gauge the distance between objects in their way. With her prayer-enhanced hearing, Solana now seemed able to do the same.

She followed the abbot's scribe through the hallways, trying to keep the faint outline of his form straight ahead of her to avoid losing track of him. The more experienced of her brothers and sisters could maneuver the world as well as they had prior to the sacrifice, but Solana still had a long way to go.

When they reached the abbot's office, the scribe knocked twice and stood aside. When the door creaked open, Solana could smell that it wasn't the abbot who had opened it. Instead, a heavily perfumed woman stood on the other side. The Stigmata did not allow perfumes or any other cosmetics, and after weeks in the musty air of the abbey, the smell of roses and cinnamon was overwhelming. Solana stifled a cough.

The woman stepped back from the door, allowing it to slide open. There was a gentle push in Solana's lower back as the scribe shoved her inside, then snapped the door shut behind her.

"Brother Wilhelm," Solana said solemnly. She bowed before the abbot.

"Please, Sister Solana, take a seat."

Solana, never having been inside the abbot's office, felt her way through the room. The auditory feedback in the room indicated a great deal of clutter. Everywhere she turned, fuzzy objects on spindly legs stood in her way. She didn't dare step forward for fear of knocking something over. Her heartbeat thrummed in her ears, distorting her sense of her surroundings further.

"Brother Wilhelm, I'm afraid..."

"Of course," the abbot said at once. "Allow me to guide you."

Before the man could stand up, a small hand fell on Solana's shoulder. The fingers were small, but strong, like a vulture's claw digging into her neck, guiding her to a hard wooden seat. Solana could feel two people's breath on her skin as she sat down. The abbot's flow was cool and low, while the unknown woman breathed out in fierce bursts of warmth. Solana shuddered.

"I have summoned you here, sister, on account of a message that reached us from Mallion's Depth." There was a definite undertone of irritation to the abbot's voice. It was subtle enough for the strange woman not to pick up on it, but present enough for one of the Stigmata to recognize it. The abbot was sending her a signal.

"But Reynziel Catharyn"—he waved at the woman—"has instructions to only deliver this message to you in person. She is aware that there can be no secrets between our brothers and sisters. Thus she has agreed to read this message in my presence, so that we can discuss its implications together."

"Exactly so," Catharyn said. Her voice was soft, but firm, like a pillow pushed over a sleeping babe's face. With the crinkling of fresh parchment, the woman unfurled the scroll and read.

*To Solana Winterbloom,*

*I trust that this message has reached you well in the hands of our esteemed sister Reynziel Catharyn.*

*Upon receiving this message, you are to set sail to Mallion's Depth at once. Arrangements have been made for your passage aboard the same vessel that bore our emissary to your doorstep.*

*Further information regarding your assignment will be distributed once you have left the islands. This in to ensure secrecy in what is an exceedingly delicate matter. No further assistance shall be required of the Stigmata, and Cardinal De Leliard has dictated that you, and only you, possess the required expertise to aid the scepter in this matter.*

*Yours in faith,*
*Medina Khayin*

*PS: His Eminence wishes to inform you that your mother's condition is being carefully monitored by our best surgeons.*

## CHAPTER 32

The abbot's energy shifted. There was a tremor in the air as he scraped his throat. "This is highly unusual. Sister Solana is still in training, and has not yet attained the standards of skill that we require of our brothers and sisters to become full members of our order. She is not in a position to leave the abbey."

Solana remained silent, grateful for the old man's attempt at salvaging her freedom. He, like her, had seen through the meaning of the Cardinal's request for her. He wanted to isolate Solana. So he could have an Everberg-trained puppet all to himself.

A wave of nausea engulfed Solana's guts as she thought of her mother, alone in that cold, oversized mansion in Mallion's Depth. Though neither the abbot, nor Reynziel Catharyn, understood its true meaning, De Leliard's reminder that he still had Solana's mother close at hand in Mallion's Depth was as close to an open threat as he could get. The implication was clear. Fragile old women perished every day.

"My orders were quite transparent," Catharyn droned. "I am to return to Mallion's Depth alongside Miss Winterbloom, or I am not to return at all. This is a direct order. Nonnegotiable."

Solana's hands trembled. Though the abbot claimed the Stigmata followed their own set of guidelines, she doubted it would go over well if he outright refused a direct order. To make matters even more complex, since Medina's letter had contained no specific orders aside from the summons, there were no reasonable grounds to object to it.

The abbot could not, and should not, jeopardize centuries of cooperation by undermining such a banal order.

"I assure you," the abbot said, "that a multitude of our fully trained brothers and sisters will serve the Cardinal much better than a mere apprentice. Sister Solana has only learned the very basics of those skills we deem essential. The time she has spent attuning to the Keeper's presence on this island has been much too short to pry her away. Especially at such an important time in her training."

"I am not fond of repeating myself," Catharyn said. "The Cardinal's office has provided me with alternative means of persuading Miss Solana to fulfil her duty. I beg you not to make me employ them."

Solana could feel the woman stiffen beside her and heard the dry squelch as Catharyn swallowed her growing frustration. Clearly, this woman, like Solana, was in a dangerous position. The Cardinal had some leverage over her, which ensured that this woman would rather burn Everberg to the ground than return without fulfilling her mission.

"I will do it," Solana said. She bowed toward the abbot. "I know it's unconventional, but if the Cardinal requests it, it is not my place to refuse him. I will not have you or our brothers and sisters fall out of his grace on my behalf."

Just speaking the words made her sick. Once again, her back was up against the wall. Once again, De Leliard was making it plain that she was a rag doll in his clenched fist. He could fling her from one end of the empire to the other on a whim, and she would have to obey.

"Very well." The abbot bent his head and let out a resigned sigh. "So be it. I shall pray for your speedy return to our ranks, so your training can be completed. We shall have need of every one of our brothers and sisters soon."

Solana stood up, heart racing. She wouldn't even have to return to the dormitories before setting out. The only physical possession she was allowed to keep on her person was the small wooden prayerbook, which contained the prayer tablets she had been training with. She could feel its comforting weight in the designated pouch on the inside of her robes. It was still far from complete, however, as it only contained six tablets at the moment.

Reynziel Catharyn marched over the door and held it open, gesturing for Solana to exit.

"Wait, sister." The abbot's voice rang out close behind her.

His wrinkly hand closed around Solana's own as he handed her something heavy. It was the size of a prayerbook, but much thicker than her own. The abbot bent closer. His whisper was so low, that even with her sensitive hearing, Solana had trouble making out the words.

"Take this. Continue training on your own. Something is wrong. I can feel it. Age and power have made De Leliard too bold for his own good and that of the church. Protect yourself. Protect those who need it, and lack our power."

Solana nodded. Her throat closed with emotion. A full prayerbook. She could hardly believe it.

"Thank you, Brother Wilhelm."

She exchanged her smaller prayerbook and stashed the full one in her pouch. A sense of calm overcame her. Whatever happened, she was a force to be reckoned with now. She could do things that ordinary clergy could

## CHAPTER 32

only dream of. She turned on her heel and strode past Reynziel Catharyn, ignoring the woman completely.

On their way out of the abbey, Solana passed by the armory, where she donned the spiked helmet of the Stigmata and the accompanying suit of light armor. Finally, she strapped on a pair of fortified, spiked gauntlets. When Solana exited the armory, Reynziel Catharyn instinctively stepped away from her. Solana could smell the stench of fear emanate from the woman. *Good.*

As they stepped out onto the docks in front of the abbey, Solana felt a rush of anxiety at being cast into such a wide-open environment. After the narrow corridors and vaulted chambers of the abbey, the Sundered Sea felt like a great void, ready to suck her in. The faint black and gray shapes that had allowed her to navigate on her own dissipated in the open air. She was blind once more.

*It's all part of the given path. All part of the Keeper's plan.* For her entire life, she had served the Keeper loyally. In return, Heil had granted Solana powers beyond anything she had deemed possible. It would be all right. There was a bigger plan, one Solana just didn't see yet.

A sloop awaited them at the far end of the dock. Solana, guided by Reynziel Catharyn's hand on her shoulder, put one foot in front of the other, taking deep breaths to keep the seed of panic in her chest from spreading. When they reached the sloop, she could make out just enough of its shadow to lower herself from the wobbly dock onto a wooden bench.

This time, she wouldn't have to row. Two short, but stocky men sat at the boat's bow and stern. They stank of sweat, poorly wiped behinds, and strong alcohol.

"Your Majesty," one of them said, his voice a leering growl. "How nice to make your formal acquaintance."

Solana's stomach roiled as the stench of tooth decay filled the inside of her helmet.

"Shut up and row, you pirate scum," Catharyn barked. "We pay you to work, not to blabber."

"Aye, aye. Back to the fleet it is, then."

# CHAPTER 33

*16th day of the 12th cycle, 569KR*
**Doorstep's Ditch**

"Like I said, they wanted nothing to do with it. I tried everything." Brina sighed. She stared at Acheron, jaws clenched. For close to a week, she'd avoided questions about her meeting with Versa. She had almost begun hoping that she may have gotten away with it, when Acheron cornered her as she sat between two shoulder high stacks of books in the library nook at headquarters. She took a slow sip from yet another glass of kelp rum, savoring the silty burn as it hit her nostrils.

Acheron frowned. He slumped in his red-velvet chair, looking wary. "But what did they say? Did they give you a reason? If we know what's bothering them, maybe..."

"It won't work. Nothing will. They made it very clear they don't want to remember God's Maul." *And yet I tried to coerce them into doing just that.* A guilty weight stirred in her chest. She looked down, feigning interest in *The Withered Empire: Heilinism's Second Age* by Celeste Verdunia.

There was a glint of suspicion in Acheron's eyes, as though he were trying to stare through her eye and into her brain behind it. "So you're saying there is nothing we can look into?"

"They mentioned something about doors. There's supposed to be a lot of doors, but they all go nowhere," Brina mumbled, refusing to look up and meet Acheron's eyes.

"So there's a lot of dead ends and wrong turns an outsider could take?" Acheron nodded. "See, this is good. I bet it wasn't all for nothing."

"I don't think that's what they meant." Brina's fingers ruffled the corners of the book. "They spoke about it like it was an actual place, but I didn't get many details. It sounded like a torture chamber or something."

## CHAPTER 33

"But how could all the doors lead to a torture chamber?" Acheron asked. "Unless they were referring to the different cells or something like that."

Brina shrugged. "That's all I got."

Acheron gave her a shrewd look, and for a moment Brina was sure that he knew exactly what she was thinking. That he was watching Versa's broken profile hobble off into the dark like she had over and over these past days.

"What's bothering you, kid?" he asked. Even though there was no accusation in his tone, a flash of worry hit Brina. She didn't know exactly why the thought of telling the others what had happened repulsed her so thoroughly. Saf had been the one to suggest it, and the script she'd used had come straight out of the Order's collection. *You don't want to hear it out loud,* a voice in the back of her mind said. *If you tell someone, it'll all become real.*

She looked back down at the book, turned a page, and shook her head. "Nothing's bothering me. Unless you count old farts nosing through my business while I'm trying to do some research."

"Fine." Acheron sighed, looking over the faded volumes that surrounded them. "What are you looking for, anyway?"

"Anything," Brina replied. "That fortress was built by human hands. Someone designed it. Hundreds must have worked on it. Who knows how many retired darkhelms kept diaries about their time there?" *Doors after doors after doors.* Versa's hoarse voice resounded in her head. *Doors to the nowhere, to the pain world.*

"And you're expecting those diaries to magically appear in the bookcase by rooting through it over and over again?"

"I don't know what I expect," she snapped. "But there has to be something in here. A single clue that tells us where to go."

"Maybe," Acheron said, "but there might just be another way to look at this problem."

Brina looked up. Acheron smiled faintly when their eyes locked.

"When you're looking to snatch something stored away in a locked chest, what are your options?" Acheron asked.

Brina narrowed her eyes. "I'm afraid I've always earned my shards the hard way."

Acheron rolled his eyes. "How noble." He put his fingers to his lips and whistled, causing Sneak and Bron, who were dozing off in the sitting nook, to jump up in their chairs. Acheron waved them over.

"Gentlemen, let's say I asked each of you to retrieve an item from a locked chest. How would you approach that?"

"Depends on the chest," Sneak said, rubbing his chin. "If you've got a standard lock with two pins, a basic skeleton key should do the trick. If we're talking about something more complex, I'd need more time." He pulled a ring of steel lockpicking tools out of his pocket and jangled them together.

"Little man likes fiddling with shinies." Bron chortled. "I haven't yet seen a chest that could withstand a good whack with an ax."

Acheron's eyes lit up. "See where I'm going with this, kid?"

"No." Brina gave him a belligerent, fake smile.

"We've tried studying the lock. I say it's time we sharpen our battleaxes." He tapped the side of his head and mimed an explosion.

When Brina still didn't get it, he sighed and mumbled something about *"... taking all the fun out of it."*

"Fine. I'll spell it out," he said. "Back when me and your father worked together, I spent a lot of time traveling the Sundered Isles in search of new sigils we could use to aid the rebellion. I found quite a lot of them."

"And you're only mentioning this now?" Brina veered up from her chair. "Do you have them here? What sigils?"

"They're still in my humble barrow," Acheron said. "But there's a minor kink in our proverbial rope." His tone became delicate. "I may have torn it all to shreds in a moment of mild frustration."

Brina gaped at him, not bothering to close her mouth again. "This may be the worst thing you've done."

"... so far," Acheron added with a wicked grin. "But the good news is, most of the pieces should still be there. I think."

# CHAPTER 34

*16th day of the 12th cycle, 569KR*
**Barrow's Perch**

"I definitely heard something that time," Brina whispered. She put a hand on Acheron's shoulder to stop his rustling footsteps.

It was subtle. Whenever they moved through a noisy patch of tall grass, an echo trailed behind them. A third pair of footfalls trying to blend in with theirs. Whoever was following them was at least more skilled than Acheron in muffling their movements. *But not skilled enough.*

Were they finally about to meet the mysterious hooded man?

"It's a jungle," Acheron muttered. His voice scraped across Brina's strained eardrums like a blunt saber. "Something's always mucking about."

"And I know exactly which is which," she hissed. "Keep walking. It'll be easier to ambush them if they think we're unaware. And watch your breathing. You sound like a three-legged erymanthian with lung rot."

They hugged the tree line up the final stretch of King's Barrow Hill, using the light of the chariots to navigate. It had been a good three hours since they'd set out from the distillery, and Acheron's poor physique was already slowing them down. If they wanted to reach Barrow's Perch and make it back under the cover of darkness, something needed to change.

"I don't see why you don't just burn something," Brina told him after a steep section left him doubled over with his hands on his knees. A snapping branch further down the hill confirmed they were still being followed. The good news was that she was now certain that their pursuer was alone.

"Can't," Acheron gasped. "I've relied on sigils for years. I'm barely more than a frame of twigs with strings attached. Somehow I doubt God's Maul's darkhelms will politely wait for me to catch my breath in between duels."

Brina shrugged, her ears still attuned to every crack and hoot around them. "If I could burn *Forte* for more than fifteen minutes at a time, I'd be dancing a jig atop the King's Barrow as we speak."

Acheron let out a sound halfway between a chuckle and a wheeze. "Which is exactly the problem."

They crested the hill just in time to watch Barrow's Perch and its countless grave hills disappear into the dark window. A sheet of black rolled in from over the ocean behind them, swallowed the overgrown hillside, then roved across the perch, erasing everything it touched. This was their chance.

"Hope you've been practicing, kid," Acheron said as his eyes lit up starburst with *Lux,* a new shape they'd been working on which rendered the user's eyesight so sensitive, a burning twig seemed like an inferno.

Brina stared into the darkness, willing the three spikes of *Lux* to appear there. To her astonishment, the shape flared into life immediately, clearer than it ever had before. A narrow black and gray version of Barrow's Perch appeared around her. It was blurry, and her eyesight didn't reach its usual distance, but it was more than enough to guide their path to Acheron's hideout.

"Stop grinning like an idiot." Acheron grunted. "You haven't mastered it yet. The trick is to keep it burning in the background while you go about your day."

Brina retrieved a torch from her pack and lit it with the touch of a finger and a quick burst of *Gnis*. It erupted into light with the ferocity of a star pulled down from the heavens itself. Brina, glad that she'd relinquished *Lux* to light the thing, looked away at once, blinking furiously.

"Ow," Acheron shouted, hands held up over his eyes, "Bone and marrow, what did you do that for?" He stumbled blindly, tripped over a protruding root and landed flat on his face in a thicket of barrow's knot.

"Put that out," he spat, wiping leaves and thorns off his robe. "This is our chance to lose the spy."

"I have no intention of losing them." Brina held the torch out in front of her and started the brief trek to the nearest barrow. "Which one of these was yours again?"

"One on the left," Acheron grumbled.

They stopped in front of a barrow whose metal doors stood ajar.

"You go in. I've got something to do first." Brina handed Acheron the torch and stole away into the night. She circled the barrow until the light of the torch was out of sight, then she slowly crept up, silent like a sheikan

## CHAPTER 34

waiting to pounce. She burned *Lux* when she made it to the top, giving her an overview of her surroundings.

Sure enough, there he was. Not fifty feet removed from them, grown brazen in the shroud afforded to him by the dark window, the man crept toward the barrow's open door. *A little closer, you bastard. That's it.*

Holding her breath, she watched as the man moved right up to the door and bent forward to peer inside. She struck.

Jumping down from the top of the barrow, she landed feet first on the spy's shoulders. There was a satisfying snap as his right clavicle shattered.

By the time he realized what had happened, Brina was sitting on top of him, pinning his arms with her knees, her dagger digging into the skin underneath his jawbone.

"Don't move," she hissed at him.

The man shook his head, lips quivering. "I won't. I swear it."

"Good," she told him, wiggling the point of the dagger to make sure he understood just how precarious his situation was. "Who are you, and who do you work for?"

"I don't work for anyone," he said. "I was lost, saw a light, figured someone out here might be able to help."

"Lies." Brina slapped him across the face with her free hand. "You were in The Wistful Chimera inn last week, watching me."

"Okay fine." He flinched as Brina raised her hand once more. "I was at the inn. I heard those bruisers talking about you when you left. They said you must make a fortune as a roamer. You know, all those contracts and all. So I wanted to ambush you, take your purse for myself."

"Unbelievable," Brina said, disgusted. "I gave you a chance to stop lying, and here you are, doing it again."

"I'm not," the man balked, his eyes rolling with panic. "I swear I'm not. Why would I tell you I wanted to rob you? That's madness. People get killed over less."

*Who's got their Heildamned claws into you?* Whoever they were, they must scare the living hell out of this poor babbling fool for him to prefer to die lying than live and tell her the truth.

"Look," she told the man, "I'll ask you nicely one more time. Who do you work for?"

"I can't," the man wailed. "They'll kill me."

Brina sighed. A heavy weight dropped into her stomach when she realized what she had to do. For the millionth time, Versa's face with those terrible glowing eyes appeared in front of her. She pushed it away. There would be time for more guilt later. *Add it to the list.*

She dug deep, forcing herself to sift through a haystack of useless thoughts and images to find *Consol*. She hadn't imprinted on it since that terrible night on the beach, but somehow she was certain that it was still there, somewhere in the depths of her mind, scorched into her brain for good.

It came to her, blackening curls of fire carved into the dark behind her eyelids.

"Who are you?" she asked the man, whose eyes had gone wide and blank.

"Murio Edmund Merovinger," he droned, his tone devoid of thought and emotion.

"Who do you work for?"

"I do not know her name. A Reynziel. Kept her face hidden."

"What does she want you to do?" Brina asked. She founded herself leaning closer and closer to the man's face, trying to assure herself that it wasn't Versa cowering beneath the force of her will. She hated Merovinger for what he was making her do.

Grief, guilt, and anger surged through her body in equal measures as she shook him.

"What is your mission?"

"She said dangerous irregulars might enter the camp of the outwalled soon. Described a man with white scars across his face and arms who escaped his cage on the night of the 13th of the 11th cycle. Said his accomplices were dangerous heretics and one of them had slain a bargheist. One hundred shards for each irregular caught.

"They lumped me in with the outwalled as a cover. I heard about a roamer who'd gone missing. Figured it was worth checking out."

The man was heaving now, exhausted from the strain of trying to resist the sigil and the continuous pressure Brina was exerting on his mind.

"Are you the only one hired?"

There was a flash of cognizance in the man's eyes. He forced his mouth shut when the answer began to flow. He shivered with the effort, but succeeded in locking his jaws.

Brina closed her eye, putting every ounce of strength she had left into the shape. She repeated the question.

"Can't. Say. Will kill. Me," he groaned through clenched teeth. His eyes, wide and red, found Brina's. "Please."

## CHAPTER 34

Brina could feel her power fade. The shape would soon wane, its store depleted. *No,* she thought desperately, *he's hiding something crucial.*

"Stop it," Acheron's voice called out. He looked utterly aghast. "He's dying. You're killing him."

Brina looked down to see Merovinger's pale face twisted into an impossible grimace. His whole body convulsed.

"Who else?" she barked at him, abandoning all reservations. "Who else is after us?"

"...black ships..." Merovinger gurgled, "...skullbeards..."

With one final shudder, Merovinger's body went limp.

The sigil faded.

It was like waking up from a trance. Brina jumped up, unwilling to touch Merovinger for one more second. She staggered backward into the barrow's metal door, staring down at what she had done. Merovinger's impassive mask of a face turned into Versa before her eyes.

"No," she whispered, "no, no, no..."

Acheron swept to his knees beside Merovinger and poked two fingers into his neck.

"There's a pulse," he grumbled. "It's faint, but it's there."

Brina sank down onto the ground, heaving. There was no relief. That Merovinger had survived meant nothing. *I was willing to kill a man in cold blood.* She closed her eyes to stave off an incoming wave of nausea. *Seven above, who am I becoming?*

A hand fell on her shoulder.

"It's okay, kid. You were putting the cause first. We'll all have to cross boundaries we'd rather steer clear of before the end." Acheron gave her a squeeze, then grabbed her arm and pulled her to her feet. "And it wasn't for nothing. We know more of them are after us now."

"I was willing to kill him, Ach. In the moment, it meant nothing to me. I just wanted to..."

"I know," Acheron said, "Believe me, kid, I know what war does to the soul." His eyes lingered on something in the darkness, as though he could see something she could not. "And make no mistake, this is war we're in."

"I did it to Versa too," Brina said, struggling to control her breath. "They refused to tell me anything. I got desperate."

A tear rolled down her cheek as it all came to a head. It was out in the open now.

"I tried to use the shape. I wanted to force them to tell me everything, but..." The lump in her throat blocked any further words from escaping.

Acheron looked at her with an odd expression, somewhere between pity and sadness.

"We've all given into the temptation the power of the sigils brings with it," he said. "Especially so when those powers are new and alien to us."

"I won't say you didn't mess up, kid, but you had the cause in mind. Never forget that. We do what we do for the cause, and we live with that weight so others won't have to."

Merovinger gave a full-body shudder, then began muttering to himself frantically as though he were trapped in a fever dream. Every fiber in his body seemed to jangle.

Brina reached out to grab him, but Acheron held her back.

"Don't wake him. It'll only make it worse. He'll be fine once the effects of the shape wear off."

"Then what do we do?" Brina asked. Merovinger had followed them all the way here. He'd seen the barrow and both of their faces. As soon as he had the chance, he'd run straight back to his mistress. If not out of loyalty, then certainly out of fear. Her heart clenched.

"We leave him here," Acheron said. "When he wakes, we'll be long gone, and everything of value will be back at headquarters. Let them dig up the entire barrow field, if they feel so inclined. It'll only distract them."

Brina nodded, trying to hide just how relieved she was that Acheron hadn't insisted they silence the man for good. She followed him back into the barrow and gasped.

It looked nothing like the poorly organized but functional space she remembered from her visit prior visit. Shards of pottery crunched under her feet with every step. Fragments of parchment fluttered around. Hundreds of them. Bones lay scattered everywhere, as though a small tornado had razed the place. Brina let out a low whistle. How could one man wreak this much havoc?

"Yeah, yeah," Acheron muttered as he saw her face. "I know. Are you going to help me put this back together or not?"

# CHAPTER 35

*24th day of the 12th cycle, 569KR*
**King's Barrow Hill**

The tension in Brina's shoulders evaporated as she exhaled the first lungful of fresh air. Not even the humidity and the cloying heat of the jungle simmering under the afternoon sun could dampen her spirits. Not after an entire week inside. She had been waiting for this moment for days now. After the encounter with the spy in Barrow's Perch, Saf and the others had agreed that it would be best if they kept a low profile for a while.

However, that had meant an entire week spent in the vaulted basement of the distillery, staring idly at the same scripts for hours on end. The only patch of light had been two new scripts they had retrieved from the piles of in Acheron's barrow.

Both of them controlled the user's weight. Acheron, in an uncharacteristic moment of thoughtfulness, had allowed Brina to name them. In keeping with the pre-Heilinist naming traditions of the other sigils in their possession, she had decided on "*Leve*" for "light" in pre-Heilinist speech, and "*Grave*" for "heavy" in pre-Heilinist speech. They weren't the most creative names, but at least they were easy to remember.

"So," Acheron called from behind her, "I hope you got some good practice in this week, kid. Because soon we're going to need everyone to pull their weight."

"What's that supposed to mean?" Brina asked, her eyebrows raising.

"It means that your little roamer tricks are fine in a fair fight, but against the sheer numbers the darkhelms have enlisted, we'll need to make the fight as unfair as possible."

"Well then, you'll be happy to hear that I've mastered almost half a dozen scripts. This week alone, I imprinted *Gnis*; its inverse, *Pruine*; *Forte*; and those two new scripts we found."

She omitted *Consol*, the tablet which Saf had slipped her on that fateful day on the beach with Versa. Twice now, the sigil had driven her to actions she'd regretted immediately. Its power frightened Brina. She wasn't to be trusted with it. The very thought of the sigil made her stomach recoil in shame. Shooting someone with a windup may not be pretty, but it was honest. There was no pretense in physical violence, no insidious manipulation of the target's free will. It was simple and out in the open.

Psychosigils were an entirely different cup of tea. A good psychosigilist could coerce a target into complying with their demands without ever realizing anything untoward had happened.

Acheron laughed.

"What's so funny?" Brina asked.

"Not lacking in confidence today, are we?" Acheron shook his head. "I'd say you're very far from mastering any sigil. Let alone half a dozen. When it comes to being a sparkgazer, you have only scratched the surface of what is possible." He let out another chuckle.

"Scratched the surface?" Brina scowled. She would call the eight to ten hours of training she'd put in every day for the past few weeks, anything but scratching the surface. Just when she was feeling pretty good about herself, of course, the old cynic had to ruin it.

"You can either burn the damn thing or you can't. That's it. I've learned how to." To emphasize her point, she touched *Forte* and kicked a loose branch on the trail. It shot off like a quarrel, narrowly missing Acheron's shoulder before arcing out of sight behind a fallen tree. To Brina's horror, an emerald glass-shielded beetle landed on the tip of her boot. She shook it off before the beetle's venomous stinger could pierce the leather tip of her boot. A shiver rolled down her back.

"Burning shapes is a decent start," Acheron said, "but what I've got lined up for you today is a whole new level. Frankly, I'd be surprised if you could complete even one of the exercises I have planned."

They entered a clearing in the jungle. Half a dozen fallen tree trunks lay rotting in the late afternoon sun. Enormous boulders hid much of the forest floor from sight.

"So," Acheron said, "today we are studying combinations. It's one thing to burn a single sigil consistently and to gain a single advantage, but if

## CHAPTER 35

you want to become a true sparkgazer, you'll need to learn how to combine shapes."

"Combine how?" Brina said. "You can only burn one at a time."

"True," Acheron said, "but nobody ever said how long you needed to hold a sigil, did they? Watch this."

He stepped onto one of the nearby tree trunks, feet slipping and skidding on the mossy surface. Then he bent his legs and shot into the air with the force of a catapult shot. He arced across the clearing, gliding forty feet through the air, before landing on top of a boulder with the silent grace of an owl touching down.

Brina's mouth fell open. It was as though the man had simply decided that physics didn't apply to him anymore. On the night they had met, Sneak had similarly catapulted both himself and Brina off the stoneward and into the city. But that had been a downward trajectory. Acheron was flying.

"Well, master," Acheron called, a smile playing on his lips, "why don't you join me?"

Brina shook her head in amusement. She clambered up onto the fallen tree, eyes trained on the boulder ahead of her. It seemed an impossible distance away.

"Aren't you going to tell me what to do?" she called out to Acheron.

He shrugged. "Why would I do that? I thought I was in the presence of a full-fledged sparkgazer. You'll figure it out."

Brina resisted the urge to fling a rock at his smug face. *Okay, you've got this,* she told herself. *It can't be that hard if he can do it.* Her first thought was to go for the shiny new objects in her arsenal. The *Leve* and *Grave* scripts. Yes, she thought, making herself lighter would obviously allow her to jump farther. She took a deep breath and searched for the stored power in her memories.

A sense of vindication overcame her as the sigil's upside-down teardrop appeared in her mind's eye. She had done the work. After endless repetition, she could call upon her stores with a smoothness she hadn't thought possible mere weeks ago. She flared the shape to the maximum and kicked off against the tree trunk.

It was like gravity abruptly grew tired. As her feet left the trunk, she rose a good six feet into the air before landing in a thicket of wakeroot bushes, painfully short of the distant boulder. Acheron might as well have been standing atop the moon.

Thorns pierced Brina's trousers, tearing her skin. She cursed, causing Acheron to laugh.

"Fine," he said. "Fine. I'll give you a hint. We are studying combinations. You've already made yourself lighter, making it easier to cover greater distance with a leap. What you lacked was power. See?"

He flared *Forte*, allowing Brina to notice the blue glare in his eyes. Again, he bent his knees in a slow and exaggerated motion, then whipped upward with explosive force. At the apex of the jump, his eyes switched to venom green, meaning that he was burning *Leve*. The force with which he launched himself made the giant boulder wobble as he shot off into the air. This time he soared straight upward, landing on a thick tree branch twenty feet above Brina. He took a bow and allowed his feet to slip off the branch.

Brina gasped as Acheron plummeted to the ground, legs outstretched. A second before impact, Acheron's eyes flashed blue, and he landed with a thump.

"Oh yes," he said, "you want to fortify your ankles and knees when doing this type of stuff. Better sparkgazers than you and I have shattered legs when they forgot that landing from great heights generates tremendous forces."

"I know I shouldn't add fuel to your already oversized ego," Brina said, "but that was amazing."

Acheron gave another exaggerated theater bow. "You'll get there soon enough if you keep up the practice."

Brina got back up on the fallen tree, dug through her mind for *Forte*, and jumped. After she kicked off, she tried the switch into *Leve*, but the shape had disappeared back into the rest of her stores. She rifled through them mentally, trying to dig out to the right one.

Her feet hit the mossy log at a bad angle, and she slid backward, hitting her tailbone hard against the wood. To add insult to injury, she toppled backward, landing on the soggy undergrowth with a thud. Even before she clambered back up, she could hear Acheron howling with laughter. When she got back up on the tree, she saw him doubled over, heaving.

Thick tears streamed across his cheeks, and every time he looked at Brina, a new fit of uproarious laughter escaped him. It was the most emotion Brina had ever seen him display. She tried to open her mouth to tell him to go violate himself, but every time she tried to speak, he held up a hand.

"No more," he begged, "please, no more. I can't take it."

## CHAPTER 35

Brina slapped him on the forehead. That seemed to sober him up somewhat.

It took her two dozen attempts before she switched into *Leve* right after burning *Forte*. When she managed it, she was so surprised to find herself soaring through the air that she forgot to burn *Forte* when she landed near a tree stump, causing her to tumble head over heels. Though the wind was knocked out of her, she couldn't help but smile. Rubbing her ribs, she clambered back up.

"That may be enough for today," Acheron said. "To be honest, I didn't even think you would get this far. Two out of three switches isn't half bad. Just try not to cripple yourself before you learn how to stick the landing."

Brina nodded, teeth clenched. She waved her arms, trying to shake off the jabs of pain radiating from her elbow through her entire arm. She was usually good about these things. As a roamer, cuts, bruises, and bites were unavoidable. Injury was a common part of life. But that didn't mean that she was immune to pain, and the slams she'd taken today would haunt her for a while. She shook herself, gritting her teeth.

There was a metallic clink above her, and when Brina looked at the tree behind her, a glimmering blade was lodged deep into its bark. She whirled around to see where it had come from, ready to dodge a better aimed projectile, but then she saw Acheron holding a handful of them up to her and grinning.

"I thought I'd bring something to cheer you up. I know how much you like sharpened steel."

Brina's mood lifted immediately. "Where did you get these?" She'd never seen anything like them. They resembled throwing daggers, but were star-shaped, with razor-sharp edges on all sides. It was made of good metal, too. The steel had been polished to a mirrorlike state, perfectly smooth to the touch. It was the sort of craftsmanship you just didn't get in Doorstep's Ditch.

Acheron shrugged. "I reached out to a few of my old contacts to have these specially made."

He handed the rest of them to Brina, and she immediately flung one at a nearby tree. It was lighter than she'd expected. It sailed through the air in a wide arc before striking the tree trunk dead center, making it extremely hard to parry with either a shield or blade. She was going to have fun with this.

When Brina went to throw a second one, Acheron blocked her arm.

"Wait. There's more to it than just blindly flinging them at stuff like a cave woman. There's finesse involved. These are traditional sigilist throwing stars. Sparkgazers have used them for centuries. Supposedly, everyone used to carry a pouch of these back in the days when scripts were everywhere. They were a highly common weapon, because they play together nicely with many sigils. For example…"

He whirled around, and a heartbeat later, three stars thwacked into the tree one after the other like the *rat-tat-tat* of a war drum.

This time, Brina was paying attention.

"You used *Veloce* for speed, then touched *Forte* for added power, right?"

"Good eye," Acheron said. "Glad you're catching on to the possibilities. Supposedly there used to be sigils which allowed gazers to enhance their accuracy when throwing these over long distances, too. But I've never seen one. I just use the stars in a rapid-fire way. Never heard any complaints." He shrugged.

It took him a while to get the stars back out of the tree. Most of them had embedded themselves over halfway into the trunk, and the slick steel made them hard to grip. When Brina's turn finally came, her hands trembled with excitement.

Once she'd mastered this, many of her contracts would become significantly easier. Most creatures she habitually hunted would never see it coming. A bubble of sadness rose in her chest at this thought. Her hand strayed to the clump of ruined flesh around her blind eye. Between her injury and the order's constant battle to stay out of sight, she doubted she would be fulfilling many contracts soon.

Taking a steadying breath, Brina burned Veloce, taking care to keep Forte present in the back of her mind. She let go of her thoughts, sinking into complete focus. It felt like one fluid motion. One after the other, the stars flew from her fingers like trapped birds set free.

The first four stars slammed into the hard bark, one after the other. A neat line of glinting metal formed. A rush of excitement filled Brina. *I've still got it.* With a throwing weapon, she already used to close one eye to improve, anyway. This was something she'd be able to do, something she might even get better at now that she was stuck with one eye.

In her enthusiasm, she threw the last star so hard that it sliced cleanly through the side of the tree, and flew out the other end. She heard it rustle in a thicket just behind the trees. As she ran off to retrieve it, Brina felt better than she had in weeks. She was home, rushing through the jungles,

## CHAPTER 35

refreshing and expanding her skills. For the first time in a long time, Brina felt like herself again.

Kneeling behind the tree, she began digging through the underbrush in search of the star. Her fingers brushed something metal deep in the thicket, and she instinctively pulled on it. There was enough to squelching sound, and Brina fell backward as the metallic thing came loose. When she looked at her hand, it was covered in a sticky black substance. A bloody windup quarrel lay in her hand. She flung it aside as though it were hot, unable to contain a yelp of disgust.

When she heard Acheron's footsteps approaching behind her, Brina began digging through the underbrush, snapping branches and uprooting the thicket, her heart beating wildly. Then her hands closed around a cloth tunic, Brina pulled on it, and the body slid out into the open. It took one agonizing second before Brina realized where she had seen that sharp nose and stubbly chin before. Those staring brown eyes had haunted her dreams for a week.

"That's..." Acheron began.

"Yes," Brina said, a heavy ball of lead forming in her stomach. "The spy I interrogated at Barrow's Perch."

A small hole between the man's eyes oozed a mixture of rank blood and decaying brains, like a foul well.

"They shot him," Brina said. "The bastards shot him."

Acheron remained silent. He knelt beside Brina and began running through the man's pockets, digging through his overcoat and trousers. If touching a decaying corpse disgusted him in any way, he gave no sign of it.

"This can only mean one thing," Acheron said. "They know he talked."

"Which means that he either told them he had talked to us, which would've been suicidal, or they had another spy following the spy." Brina shuddered.

Acheron nodded. He jerked back the sleeves of the man's tunic and examined the skin on his arms, legs, and torso. "No signs of torture." Acheron said. He groaned. "We're in trouble."

"How is that bad?"

"Because this means they had another way of forcing him to tell the truth."

Brina's thoughts flashed back to what she herself had done to this man. "You think the scepter has a sparkgazer?"

"Not exactly. There used to be rumors. But after what Sneak told us about the Reynziel he fought at the Scale, maybe they were more than rumors."

Then, as though he had just realized that he had left a candle burning at home, he jumped to his feet. "We need to go. Now."

# CHAPTER 36

*25th day of the 12th cycle, 569KR*
**Mallion's Bay**

The barrelman's horn tore through the quiet of Solana's cabin like a blade through flesh. Her jaw tensed. It was time. She snapped her prayerbook shut and stored it in her inside pocket. Her steel gauntlets rattled as she pulled them on and flexed her fingers to get every plate in the right place.

Finally, she snatched her helmet off the table and forced it over her head. As soon as the cool weight covered her head, an emotionless calm came over her. There were two versions of her. There was who she had been before Everberg, and then there was who she'd been forced to become. Tonight she would need to disappear completely into the latter. Thinking and feeling were fatal hindrances.

She reached for the scroll of parchment containing her orders from the Cardinal's office, clenched it in her fist, and tucked it away carefully in a pocket underneath her armor. She felt its coarse edges dig into her chest, like the burrowing of a parasite.

With one final breath, she kicked open the door of her cabin and strode out onto the deck. Dozens of shadowy figures scurried out of her way. Though she couldn't make out faces, she could smell the fear rise over the stink of their unwashed bodies. The mercenaries skittered across the deck like roaches, handing out weapons and armor, while the sailors tweaked the sails to facilitate their approach.

Even at a distance, Solana could smell the cooking fires, drying fish, and open latrines from the village carried on the wind. It took everything in her power not to retch. Sometimes she wished the Stigmata would have taken her nose as well. The whole world stank these days.

"You," she demanded, pointing an iron finger at a mercenary who tried to back away as she approached. "Are the other ships keeping up?"

"Aye, mistress. They're gearing up." The man's voice quaked with a mixture of terror and disgust.

"Signal them to approach us as close as possible. I want everyone to hear me."

"But, mistress," the man began, "wouldn't that be—"

"Now." She attuned to the prayer of compulsion. The command swelled in the air like the thrum of a thousand spears battering shields.

The man swallowed. "Of course, mistress. At once, mistress."

Solana stepped onto the quarterdeck, where the mercenary captain stood at the helm.

"It's time. Assemble your soldiers for briefing."

"The lads are still getting ready, miss. Give us a moment," the woman said. There was an unpleasant, cocky undertone to her voice. "Besides, we're still plenty far from shore."

Solana stared the woman down. On some level, she sympathized with the captain. She was undoubtedly accustomed to being the highest seat of authority aboard the ship. Taking orders from a client wasn't usually the skullbeards' way, but tonight was different. There couldn't be one inch of imprecision, not one second of hesitation.

"Did I stutter, freak?" the captain barked, clearly unnerved by Solana's presence continuing to loom over her. "We need more time."

Heads turned. The bustle on the deck stalled. The crew had heard.

Unfortunate.

Unacceptable.

"You forget yourself," Solana whispered, so only the captain would hear. "Apologize." She was being too soft, and she knew it.

"Apologize?" The captain barked a mirthless laugh. "This is my Heildamned crew, freak. You may fill our purses, but I decide how the job is done."

Solana attuned to the prayer of force. Infinite strength flooded her system. She could feel every fiber of her muscles swelling with the Keeper's light.

A handful of the mercenaries laughed at their captain's bravado. Solana clasped the captain's head in both of her steel hands and headbutted the woman squarely in the forehead.

Iron filled the air. The woman's skull shattered as the steel spikes on Solana's helmet sank into flesh and bone alike. She let out a squelching

## CHAPTER 36

rasp, spraying blood everywhere. Solana shoved the woman backward. She toppled over the quarterdeck's railing and crashed onto the main deck.

Silence fell. Two of the mercenaries inched toward the captain's twitching body.

"Leave her," Solana shouted. "Let her stinking corpse be a reminder to you all."

No one resisted.

"I'm glad we have sorted out this little confusion about who you obey tonight."

She whistled, attuning to the prayer of compulsion, and the mercenary legion assembled before her. To either side of the ship, large black shadows approached. The other ships had arrived just in time to witness the spectacle. *How efficient.*

"Behind us lies the city of light. The seat of all that is holy. The center of the known universe. Mallion's Depth."

She pointed at the city with a bloody gauntlet.

"On its very doorstep, a canker is growing. A ravenous tumor that swells in size every day. A hive of wretchedness, depravity, and heresy. Sedition has been brewing in the hearts and minds of those we have so benevolently granted a second chance at life."

The prayer of compulsion crescendoed in her mind. Her fingers curled into its shape as Solana yielded to it completely.

"You will stamp it out. You will burn and slash and pillage everything and everyone you find outside the stoneward. I want it erased. Come dawn, I want the world to have forgotten that Doorstep's Ditch ever existed."

The echo of her own words hit Solana like a punch to the temple, dazing her. As the mercenaries erupted into a deafening roar, she sank deep into a cocoon of rage, determination, and grief.

Grief for what she was about to do.

Grief for all who would cross her path.

Grief for everything she had once believed in.

# CHAPTER 37

*25th day of the 12th cycle, 569KR*
**Doorstep's Ditch**

Acheron sighed as the last piece slid into place. He stood back to observe the effect and smiled. Two completed scrolls lay spread out on the round table in the bell jar. It wasn't much. Not compared to the dozens of them he'd completed before the Signum had evaporated right before his eyes. Not even when compared to the armful he'd saved and stashed in his barrow afterward. But it was a start. Undeniable, tangible evidence that he hadn't always been a coward hiding in a dark hole.

*Look at Achie's little art project,* a voice cooed from across the table. *He thinks those doodles of his will make it all right.*

Acheron refused to look up at his mother, or the remnant of her that still rattled around his brain somewhere. *You're not here. None of you are.*

Ever since his confrontation with Saf, they had dogged his every step relentlessly. Azaria, Lagrima, his mother... the lot of them. Everyone he'd ever disappointed, harmed, or betrayed, watching over his shoulder and tormenting him.

His mouth went dry as he watched them lingering around the bell jar's walls, glaring at him from every angle. If only he could make them vanish, just for a moment. One brief, glorious moment of numbness was all he needed. He'd probably find one of Zot's minions within fifteen minutes if he wanted to.

*Not here, are we, Spider?* A broad-shouldered man with a majestic beard not unlike Bron's sat in an armchair in front of the dying embers in the hearth. *Just like you weren't there when we needed you?*

Acheron shook his head like a wet dog. He needed to focus on the present, on the work in front of him. The others had retreated into their

## CHAPTER 37

bunks hours ago. All except for the kid, who lay slumped in the chair beside him, her head lolling to one side. Had he ever been able to just fall asleep like that? If so, he couldn't remember what it was like. It looked peaceful.

*You know what would make you sleep like that, don't you?* This time, the voice was his own, but he dismissed it just the same. *Not today.* One more night without floating. Tomorrow he might cave, but not tonight.

Aside from the two scripts they'd managed to salvage, there must have been at least ten or fifteen more of them. Each had been torn and crumpled beyond all hope. They'd need an actual scrive to restore them and fill missing or damaged pieces. Since there may not be one of those left in the known world, they were out of luck.

Acheron leaned forward to study a shaky hand-drawn map of a tiny circular island.

"Metten." His chest constricted as he read the single word he'd scrawled above it.

Metten, the second part of Abrasax's grand plan. They'd stumbled onto the island after being carried off course by an unseasonably vehement storm. Its potential had become clear as soon as they'd spotted the first wall rising from the vines. The abandoned fortress had been consumed by centuries of the jungle's swarming and was more desirable for it.

It was supposed to become a rallying point for the rebellion after Estav's death, a central stronghold that not even the scepter's troops would easily wrest from the grasp of a determined defending force.

That could still be the future, he thought with a sideways glance at Brina and the shifting curtains that hid the sleeping quarters from sight. A new rebellion was blossoming right here under his nose, and he would make certain Abrasax would be there to fan the flames, no matter the cost.

They needed somewhere to go after God's Maul, somewhere Cardinal De Leliard wouldn't know to look. Metten could be that place.

"There's hope." Acheron stood up and smiled at the pale crowd surrounding him. A strange sensation overcame him as he heard the words come out of his own mouth, as though something else was speaking through him.

A hurricane of noise erupted on the floor above. There was the clanging of panicked wings beating against hollow pipes. The fleders' screeches blended in with shouting that was unmistakably human.

Brina snapped up in her seat. "Wha'z happening?" she asked, rubbing her eyes. "Who's there?"

Acheron shushed her. "Intruders," he hissed.

There was a loud thunk of metal impacting something solid. The yelling stopped. The silence that followed made the hairs on the back of his neck stand up.

"Seven phantoms, it's still twitching," a deep male voice grunted. "Damnable creatures."

"Shut it," a second voice said, which Acheron recognized at once as Dimimzy Zot's. "You've caused enough of a racket. Even a deaf monkey with a bag over its head could point the darkhelms in our direction."

Acheron swallowed. His debts had finally caught up with him. The last time he'd negotiated with Doorstep's Ditch's biggest cloud merchant, he'd swindled the man out of a brick of the stuff. Better people than him had been found floating in the bay for a lot less.

"Tear this place inside out," Zot said. "I know they're in here somewhere."

***

Brina woke up to find a dagger in her hand and a stinging pain where her left knee had slammed into the stone floor as she'd rolled off her chair.

The chandelier above the table rattled as heavy objects scraped against the floor above.

"It's Zot," Acheron whispered. "Wake the others."

Brina had made it halfway across the room before an axe head thundered through the trapdoor. Splinters rained down around Acheron, who just stood there like a sentenced man waiting for his turn on the rope.

The axe's second blow shattered the lock.

Dimimzy Zot's sharp features came into view at the top of the ladder. Over his shoulder, the tip of a windup bolt was aimed down at them. Zot looked straight at Acheron, and his face drooped into a distasteful scowl.

"There's no time for your games, sorcerer," he said. "I'm coming down, and you're going to let me. Understand?"

Brina couldn't help but admire Zot's confidence as the man descended the ladder, his back fully turned toward them. The curtain to the sleeping quarter rustled, and Sneak, Bron, and Saf appeared, all looking disheveled but ready for trouble.

"Ah," Zot said as he turned around to face five extremely tense sparkgazers. Two of his own cronies followed behind him, loaded windups held at their side. "I see the entire club is present. How convenient."

"Leave them out of it, Zot," Acheron growled. "It's me who owes you and me alone."

## CHAPTER 37

The corners of Zot's mouth turned into a malevolent grin. "What's this? You've suddenly come to care about the impact your actions have on others?"

"You know full well I wouldn't point the darkhelms to a bucket of piss if they were on fire. I don't know how they got you, but it wasn't me."

"As amusing as your excuses may be, they will have to wait. I'm not here on your account. And we have little time."

Zot turned to Brina, whose fingers tightened on the hilt of her dagger.

"Doorstep's Ditch is under attack. Half a dozen skullbeard mercenary ships arrived about an hour ago. They torched the beach district and are moving inward toward Wicket Row as we speak."

Brina's legs turned to jelly. She cast a sideways glance at Bron, who looked thunderstruck. The metal skulls in his beards jangled as he disappeared into his sleeping quarters.

"But why?" was the only thing Brina could think to say. "That makes no sense. What do we have except for mud and rum?"

"Use your head, girl," Zot snapped. He stepped up to the table and looked down at the torn-up map they had spent all night piecing together. Behind him, Acheron looked like he wanted nothing more than to slap Zot away from it. "This is no mistake. It's a Galleons move, and a damn brilliant one at that."

"Someone hired them," Brina said, more to herself than Zot. She remembered the spy Merovinger's words. He had known this was coming. Which could only mean one thing...

"De Leliard is getting rid of us," Zot said, his voice icy with anger. "We've been an eyesore for too long, and recent events have opened his eyes to the dangers of leaving weeds to bloom on their own accord for too long.

"He's amassing a fleet in Mallion's Depth's harbor, the likes of which haven't been seen in these parts for centuries. He can't risk the brats making a mess while daddy's off playing conqueror, can he?"

"Why are you telling us this?" Sneak asked. He walked forward until he was shoulder-to-shoulder with Brina. "Why risk coming all the way down here?"

"Your friend here saved my life," Zot said simply. He held out a hand toward Brina. "It may not have been out of the kindness of your heart, but without you, I would have starved. Allow me to settle that debt."

Brina took the short man's hand and pulled him closer so only he would hear.

"How did you know where to find us?" she whispered, squeezing Zot's fingers.

"I had eyes on the lookout for you ever since your little snake friend freed me from my unfortunate lodgings above Mallion's gate. I wanted to offer you a position in my organization, but the way things are looking right now, there may not be much left of it come dawn."

"This better not be your idea of a clever trap," Brina hissed at him.

"And if it was," Zot asked, cocking his head in amusement, "then what would you do?"

He took a step back, waved an arm at his men, and made for the ladder. "We're getting out of town, and I suggest you join us before it's too late."

"Where do we go?" Saf asked. She looked wide-eyed and frazzled. The news that the entire Ditch was under attack seemed to have dented her usual composure.

Brina put a hand on Acheron's shoulder.

"There's a ruined fortress on a small hill three miles north of King's Barrow. Do you know it?"

Acheron nodded.

"Take the group there, Zot included, if he wishes. Tell the baron I sent you. And for the love of the Seven, make sure the idiot locks his doors."

"And you?"

"I've got a debt of my own to settle."

# CHAPTER 38

*25th day of the 12th cycle, 569KR*
**Doorstep's Ditch**

urtains of thick smoke clogged the alleys of Doorstep's Ditch. Shadowy figures thundered past Brina left and right. Distant screams blended in with the sobs and howls from those who lay dying, like a discordant choir.

Brina jumped over a body. Man, woman, or child she could not tell. There was something profoundly unnatural about charging in the opposite direction from a fleeing mass, some animal instinct telling Brina that there was safety in following the herd.

She skidded across a corner and found herself in the middle of Wicket Row. The houses here were still intact, the street dividing them eerily empty. Here and there, people dashed out of their front doors, bundles of clothes and blankets clutched in their hands as they made for the town's edge.

There was only one figure standing still as a statue a good fifty feet away. A tall, thin frame that could only belong to one person.

Brina found Versa, an axe in each hand, standing in front of The Wistful Chimera's open door. A gleaming steel mask shielded the innkeeper's face from view. As Brina approached, they twisted toward her, weapons raised.

"Oh," Versa rumbled, "it's you."

"You sound disappointed to see me instead of a band of mercenaries storming down your front door."

It was a feeble attempt at humor, meant mostly to cover up Brina's acute embarrassment at facing them after what she had done. At least Versa hadn't attacked her on sight.

When no reply came, she added, "I've come to apologize."

"You have an interesting sense of timing, Brina Springtide," Versa said, barely audible over the din of clattering steel and shouts rising in the beach district on the other side of the street. "By sunrise, our petty regrets and futile ambitions will have faded into irrelevance. Better to wish for a cup of rum than forgiveness right now."

"Does that mean my apology is accepted?" Brina tried awkwardly.

"It means that it doesn't matter anymore. We had our time to do with as we saw fit, and now it is coming to a close." There was a resigned defiance in their voice that Brina didn't like one bit.

Her eyes and nostrils burned as the smoke thickened around them. It wouldn't be long before resistance near the beach gave out, and the raiders flooded onto Wicket Row.

"We've got to go, Verse," Brina yelled. "there's only two of us. What can we do?"

"No," Versa said, looking away, "there's one of me. I have heard your apology. Now it is time for you to go."

A lump swelled in Brina's throat, and a tear that had nothing to do with smoke or heat welled in the corner of her eye.

"No," she replied. "I'm not going anywhere without you. I lost sight of what was important once. I can't let that happen again."

"All of us have made mistakes in the pursuit of what we thought was right. The difference is that your journey lies ahead, while mine has chased me down for the last time tonight. I will make my stand right here, defending what is mine.

"I am tired of running, tired of hiding and cowering and hoping to be finally left alone. I won't watch as they burn what little I have built up with my own ruined hands."

The thrumming of heavy footfalls made both of them look up. A group of six skullbeards, clad in black and gold armor, stomped onto Wicket Row. The bronze, silver, and gold skulls woven into their beards and hair clattered ominously against their breastplates. The last two of them carried torches instead of the spears their compatriots wielded. Brina unslung her windup from her shoulder.

One of the torchbearers raised his arm to fling his torch into a thatched roof on the opposite end of the street. In doing so, the man exposed an open spot in his armor. He went down with a silent groan as Brina's quarrel struck home in his armpit.

"What are you doing?" Versa hissed.

## CHAPTER 38

"Making a stand," Brina said, her heart racing as the five remaining mercenaries charged toward them with a roar.

"So be it," Versa said, righting themselves into a stiff fighting stance.

Brina swung her windup over her shoulder and drew a dagger from each of her boots. Compared to the Biori's spears, her reach would be laughably short.

The first of the skullbeards lashed out three times in quick succession, his spear darting back and forth with the speed of a viper defending its nest.

Brina dodged the first blow, narrowly parried the second with her dagger, then felt a searing swipe slash her right cheek as she ducked sideways a fraction of a second too late. Hot blood dribbled down her neck.

She swore, cursing her dead eye. Her depth perception still wasn't what it had once been, and in combat, every inch might as well be a foot. *Time to level the playing field, bastard.*

She burned *Forte* as her overconfident adversary closed the gap between them with a lazy thrust of his spear. *Too slow.*

Her fingers closed around the spear's shaft, and she jerked it as hard as she could. The skullbeard was pulled off balance and stumbled. Her dagger plunged into his neck before he hit the ground.

Brina jerked the shield from under his body. *That's better.* With her first foe dead at her feet, her fear flipped into the adrenaline-fueled numbness she knew so well from her days as a roamer. Human or not, right now, she was simply dodging and disabling threats.

Ten feet to her left, Versa's axe sank through the helmet of one of their opponents with a wet crunch. Two others leapt forward to pin them against the wall of the inn. Brina flung her dagger at the nearest of the two, hitting the woman in the shoulder. Aided by *Forte*, the dagger plunged through the steel armor as though it were a slab of meat. The woman's spear fell into the mud below as she hobbled backward to avoid Versa's axe. Her companion wasn't so lucky. A head went flying. Its body slumped against the inn's wall.

The remaining skullbeards did the math and found themselves no longer outnumbering their opponents two to one. The woman who had Brina's dagger still poking out of her arm raised a small golden horn. A melancholy high-pitched howl rang out through the night.

"Drop it," Brina shouted at her. She held up her second dagger, ready for a second attempt at the neck. The woman didn't need to be told twice. She threw the horn at Brina's feet and, along with her companion, scurried back toward the alley they had come from. But the damage was done. The signal had been given.

"You're injured," Versa said. They lowered their axe and gestured at Brina's face.

"Just a cut," Brina said, waving them off. She dabbed at the wound with her sleeve and was unpleasantly surprised when it came back soaked. "Not like I could get more mangled, anyway."

"Oh, believe me, it could be much, much worse," Versa said grimly. "Do you have that script with you, the pyramid?"

Brina froze.

"Yes," Versa said impatiently, "I knew what it was the moment I saw it. I'd close that cut if I were you."

Before Brina could reach for the pyramid, two groups of skullbeards piled into the street. Within moments, Brina and Versa found themselves in the middle of a half circle of lowered spears. With their backs against The Wistful Chimera's facade, there was nowhere to run.

Brina bent down and picked up a discarded spear. It was too long and heavy for her taste, nothing like any weapon she'd ever wielded. But faced with a dozen spears closing in on them, her dagger felt tiny and inconsequential.

"Get closer to me," Versa hissed, not taking their eyes off the advancing spear tips. Brina sidestepped, her shield held out in front of her. With one swooping motion, Versa glided into the space between Brina and the oncoming skullbeards.

"I guess this is it, Springtide," they muttered. "On the count of three, I charge. Run through the Chimera and out the back door. It's unlocked. You know the alleys as well as anyone. You can still lose them."

The skullbeards surrounding them hesitated, casting sideways glances at each other. Though they had the upper hand, enough of their comrades lay dead in the surrounding mud to give them pause. This moment of reprieve wouldn't last long, however. More of them already poured out of alleys on both sides of Wicket Row.

"Don't be stupid," Brina snapped. "Either both of us escape, or neither of us do."

Versa let out a mirthless laugh. "Ever Abrasax's daughter, aren't you?"

Brina bit her lip. There was something about the way they spoke her father's name that tugged at her nerves. There was a familiarity there.

"It's ironic, really," Versa went on. "After all I've cost that man, it's my

## CHAPTER 38

attempt to make things right and to keep you safe that will end up costing him dearest of all."

"What's that supposed to mean?"

Before Versa could reply, a collective shudder rippled across the skullbeards surrounding them. Brina braced herself, expecting a charge.

"Dismissed." A harsh female voice cut through the air like a razor through skin. The sea of skullbeards split down the middle as a robed figure, a good head taller than any of them, shambled forward. Brina didn't need the expressions of quiet unrest on the mercenaries' faces to realize they were in the presence of something far more powerful than any of them. Brina's heart hammered in her throat. *She's just another minion,* she told herself, *just another target to dispatch.*

"Disperse. Light it all. I will handle this." The robed woman's orders were followed with the swift discipline only sheer terror could inspire. Torches went up all around them like shooting stars.

"That voice..." Versa stumbled backward, eyes wide. "It can't be."

The woman lowered her hood, revealing a tightly fitted helmet that covered her entire face. Its surface was covered in spikes that flickered orange in the light of the buildings catching fire all around them. Even though the helmet ought to blind the woman completely, her head flicked back and forth between Brina and Versa like a hawk's.

Making use of her partial cover behind Versa, Brina dropped her shield and spear. They landed in the mud with a squelch as Brina reached for her windup bow. She began cranking back the string as quickly as she could. The woman might hear well enough to gauge where they were, but that wouldn't help her dodge a bolt she couldn't see coming.

To Brina's surprise, Versa put a shaking hand on the bow, forcing it down.

"No, don't," they murmured. "Don't hurt her." Brina gave them an incredulous look. If they allowed this woman to close the gap between them, their window of opportunity would close.

"You are outmatched, heretics," the woman rasped. "Surrender, and your lives shall be spared. For now."

"I'm afraid we'll have to decline that very enticing offer," Brina called back. "I've already made dinner plans I'd hate to miss out on."

"Then you shall die." The priestess raised her hands, revealing heavy steel gauntlets dripping with fresh blood.

Brina shoved Versa's arm aside and raised the windup. Her sight had landed on an unguarded spot in the crook of the woman's neck when Versa rushed forward, hands outstretched toward the priestess as if to grab them.

"What have they done to you?" Versa croaked. "They told me you would be spared. They told me they would leave you out of it."

The priestess halted.

"Luna, sister, please." Versa's fingers were almost close enough to touch the priestess now. "This isn't who you are. End this madness."

"I don't know you." The priestess's right fist lashed out and crashed into Versa's wrist with a sickening crunch. The force of the blow sent them spinning into the mud.

Brina pulled the trigger. There was a whir in the air before the bolt impacted just below the priestess's shoulder.

"No!" Versa screamed. Their shattered arm hung forgotten by their side as they threw out the other in front of the priest. "She's all I have left."

"For the love of the Seven, get away from there." Brina darted forward to pull Versa out of harm's way and rushed headlong into a wall of cold, the like of which she had never experienced. It was like slipping underneath the ice atop a frozen lake. Versa's movements stalled, their fingers locked in place like a claw. Beneath them, the mud turned icy white.

"I gave you a chance," the priestess barked. She held up one hand, fingers twisted into a triangular sign. With the other, she jerked the bloody quarrel out of her chest and cast it aside. "The Keeper will not rue your destruction, but first you will tell me where to find the others."

The cold intensified, spreading outward like a cloud. Brina flung herself sideways to avoid the brunt of its impact. She had never been so relieved to land in a puddle of good old disgusting Ditch water. Versa wasn't so fortunate. Hoarfrost crept up from the ground, crawling over their clothes until it covered every inch of cloth and skin.

"How many are there?" The priestess leaned over Versa's petrified form, a heavy boot hovering over the innkeeper's neck.

"I. Don't. Know." Versa's voice was a hollow moan, their lips all but frozen shut.

The boot flashed upward.

"No," Brina shouted.

The priestess looked up.

"They don't know anything." Brina stooped to reload the windup. *Come on, idiot, focus on me.*

## CHAPTER 38

"You have five seconds to tell me what I want to know." The priestess rested her foot on Versa's head in an unspoken threat.

Each breath seemed to pulse through Brina like a shot of kelp rum, steadying her nerves. Should she risk the shot? The last one had hit the woman squarely in the chest, to no avail. If that happened again, Versa was dead. And now she had to keep talking, making the tough shot all but impossible.

"There's one more," Brina lied, taking care to sound desperate. "You know of whom I speak. He was recently apprehended by the darkh—I mean, the city watch."

"So it *is* you," the priest hissed. "That little stunt of yours cost me everything. Everything."

"Now, if it were me whose friend's life hung in the balance," she whispered, "I wouldn't. Lie."

She stomped down. The boot sank into Versa's chest with inhuman force. Brina could hear ribs breaking and skin tearing. A gurgling sound emanated from Versa's body as streams of blood poured from the wound and froze on the innkeeper's cloak.

"I know there are more of you," the priestess screamed. "I was there. I saw."

All bets were off. Brina watched her friend's lifeless form spread out across the unnatural sheet of ice and something snapped. She squeezed the trigger. The quarrel hissed through the air.

With a flick of her wrist, the priestess slapped it off course with a steel gauntlet. There was a thud as the projectile thudded into a clay wall on the opposite side of the street.

A sudden wave of scorching heat consumed the area as the unnatural cold lifted. All around them, flames leapt from one thatched roof to the next like a ravenous cluster of wampyr.

The priestess's fist swung at Brina's head with lightning speed. Brina burned *Veloce* just in time to lean backward, dodging the blow as if in slow motion. Air brushed her chin as unforgiving steel missed it by an inch. A second attack put a hole through the inn's wall.

Carried forward by the momentum, the priestess overbalanced ever so slightly. Brina lashed out with a low kick to the woman's shin, bringing her down on one knee.

There was a roar from the gap in the inn's wall as the sudden flow of oxygen caused flames inside to swell. The street side windows exploded, raining shards everywhere.

"Enough."

A silence fell. No more shouts, no more cries, no more creaks and groans of wooden structures on the verge of collapse. Only perfect, peaceful silence. Time slowed to a comfortable meandering pace, and Brina struggled to hold on to the adrenaline-fueled urgency that had controlled her since she'd exited the distillery. Everything was fine. Great. Wonderful.

The priestess rose. She was so close that their hands could have touched if she reached out. Her hands were folded in a complicated symbol in front of her chest.

"See, that wasn't so hard." The priestess's voice drifted across a vast cave before it reached Brina's ears. It was a song from another world, a lifeline in a vast sea of indifference. "Now tell me, who are you and what do you want?"

"Brina Springtide." A vague alarm signal irked at the corners of Brina's empty mind, akin to the distant concern that one might have forgotten to extinguish a lantern before leaving home. "What I want is a family, somewhere to call home and be safe."

The words slipped out without conscious thought, and yet Brina knew they were the truth. It was like her brain had sunk into her mouth, its contents spilling out without resistance.

"Who else was with you on the night you freed the bald fire-eyes?"

"There were five of us in total." The alarm intensified. The desires to acquiesce to the question and to shut her damn mouth clashed like fire and ice, jolting part of her back to reality.

"Me, Acheron..." she began. Panic spread in her chest like internal bleeding, but her mouth refused to stop. "... Sneak, Bron, and Saf."

"Good, very good," the priestess purred. "Where are they now?"

The image of Baron De Malheur's ruined fortress atop Barrow's Perch forced its way into Brina's mind. She couldn't, mustn't, say. It would be a death sentence, not just for the Order, but for the Baron, for Harrod Wane. It would be a death sentence for her father.

"They're. Gone." The words broke from Brina's mouth as though her lips were being forced apart by a crowbar. *No,* she told herself, *shut up.*

The priest put two ironclad hands on either side of Brina's face. Cool spikes dug into Brina's forehead. Brina could feel the priestess's grasp on her psyche intensify, a surge of power against which there could be no resistance.

Deep inside, guilt reared its ugly head. *This is what I did to my friend.*

## CHAPTER 38

"You're doing well. Just relax. Everything will be fine. Now tell me, where are the—"

There was a dull crunch, and the priestess was hurled sideways into a rain barrel, where she lay dazed. Blood seeped from underneath the monstrous helmet.

Behind her, Versa stood on wobbly feet, holding a spear, blunt end first, their eyes glowing blue with *Forte* against the sunset orange of the inferno that had once been the Ditch's main street. A bustling hive of activity turned to ashes.

"Help me," they croaked. "We've got to get inside the Chimera before all is lost."

Brina rushed to their side, draping their staggering form over her shoulder.

One look at The Wistful Chimera told her Versa's request was madness. Flames shot out of the inn's roof, dancing against the night sky like demons. On the other side of the shattered windows, the common room was veiled in thick smoke that even now threatened to close Brina's throat.

"Damn it, Springtide, trust me," Versa snapped.

The priestess stirred, clawing at a nearby wall to stand up.

Against better judgment and every instinct in her body, Brina hauled the innkeeper toward the crooked front door. A billowing cloud of smoke rushed out to meet them as Brina kicked it open.

"The basement." Versa coughed as the smoke entered both their lungs. "Behind the counter."

Brina tried to flare *Lux*, but it was no use. If anything, the sigil made her eye sting worse. Leveraging years of habitual drinking at the Chimera, Brina navigated a path around the bar.

She had seen Versa disappear down the trapdoor that led to the basement a thousand times, but now that every moment mattered, the iron ring eluded her. Brina's hands skittered across the scorching hot floor like panicked spiders.

"Here," Versa called somewhere to her left. "I got it."

The first lungful of breathable air went down like water after a long drought. *Lux* revealed a cobwebbed basement stacked to the brim with rum casks, bottles, and a dozen sacks of dried seaweed.

"Down there, behind the row of casks."

Versa slumped against a support beam while Brina flung heavy casks full of perfectly good rum aside to reveal a narrow earthen tunnel.

"What the..." Brina stared at in disbelief, then turned toward Versa, who shrugged.

"You don't come back from an extended vacation at God's Maul without a healthy amount of trust issues."

"May the Seven bless your paranoia for decades to come, my friend."

Together, they disappeared into the dark as the inn collapsed overhead.

# CHAPTER 39

*25th day of the 12th cycle, 569KR*
**Mallion's Depth**

Solana stumbled through the streets of Mallion's Depth, ears ringing with the screams of mothers put to the spear and the roar of shanties turned torches. Hot rivulets of blood streamed down her forehead and into her mouth as she gasped for breath underneath her vise of a helmet.

The grand cathedral of Heil couldn't be far now. She could feel the first weak tendrils of ocean breeze licking at her bare hands and the hum of the hundreds of jelly lanterns that lined Keeper's Square.

She imagined the twinkling lights swaying in the breeze. It was a view she'd loved ever since she'd been a child, like walking amongst the stars. She would never see it again. Her world was one of darkness now. An endless murk of gray shadows and those damnable headaches that battered the walls of her skull.

"Your Purity," watchman Elphias Genstrom whispered to her left, "I must insist you rest. You are losing blood rapidly." He sounded terrified. They all did when they addressed her.

"The Keeper shall keep me on my feet," she said, rubbing her hands together to prevent the numbness from spreading. There could be no delays. His Eminence had been quite clear on that point.

"Your Purity…" Genstrom began again, his voice drooping into a whine.

"Do you doubt Her?"

"No," the man conceded hastily. "Of course not."

"Then you shall guide me onward."

When they reached the threshold of the grand temple, Solana's weak hold on consciousness slipped further, and her echolocation failed. The gray shadows that made up her world faded into black. She was a rudderless vessel, adrift in a vast abyss. *None of them must know I am vulnerable.* His Eminence would find a way to use it against her.

"Lead me to His Eminence," she directed Genstrom. Using the pattering of his clumsy steps as a guide, she trod up the winding staircase of the temple's main spire, leaning against the outer wall for support. When they reached the top, Genstrom led her out of the spire and onto a narrow balcony overlooking the whole of Mallion's Depth and the bay. It must have been quite the sight. She pictured the long, grasping arms of the docks as they extended into the Sundered Sea. The bustle of sailors scuttling across decks. Hundreds of lights bobbing up and down on the waves. She would never see any of it again.

"Reynziel Solana." De Leliard's rank, wine-soaked breath engulfed her. It was all she could do to keep the contents of her stomach out of her helmet. "What news of your mission?"

She held out a demonstrative hand, feeling the twinge of distant fires on the wind.

"The pigsty has been purified, as per your orders."

"So it seems," De Leliard mused. Solana suppressed a shudder as she felt the man's greasy bulk brush her side. "Tragic business. All those homes and lives destroyed. It wounds the soul, does it not?"

Solana's hand closed into a fist in her pocket, crumpling the scroll that contained De Leliard's own orders, stating that no dwelling or person was to be spared.

*What do you know about wounded souls?* She could still smell the blood and piss clinging to her boots, could still hear the pleading and the subsequent squelch when steel meets flesh. And here *His Eminence* was, acting the troubled housefather.

"Was this not His Eminence's wish?" She fought to keep the accusation out of her voice.

"This isn't about what I wish, it's about what the empire needs." His fingers drummed out an irregular pattern against the balcony's marble railing. "It is about correcting old, flawed procedures. No great monuments can be erected upon a crooked foundation, can they?"

"I suppose not." What remained of Solana's strength was rapidly depleting. With each drop of blood rolling down her chin, she could feel it ebb further. *Heil almighty, keeper of souls and intentions, grant me strength to walk the given path you have laid out before me.* She silently mouthed

## CHAPTER 39

the prayer, drawing fortitude from every word. "Was there anything else His Eminence wished to discuss? It has been a long and trying night."

"There is." De Leliard's tone turned hungry, the way a crow might whisper to a soldier bleeding out on the battlefield. "What of Saphara Al Noor and her band of undesirables? Have your troops finally detained them?"

Solana gritted her teeth. The wound on the back of her head throbbed painfully as she remembered how the girl and her accomplice had bested her. *Luna, sister, please.* The echo of those words had been rattling around in the back of her mind for hours now. Could it be? Could her mother have lied all these years? Her jaws worked furiously. This wasn't the time to reopen old wounds. All that mattered was that the fire-eyes had gotten away yet again.

To admit to the truth was to sign her own death warrant. To lie to De Leliard was tantamount to lying to Heil herself. She could deceive the former, but the latter would know, and she would pay. Maybe not today, but somewhere down the line, she would pay.

"There was no trace of them, Your Eminence. Every house was searched, every potential informant questioned." The lies flooded from her mouth as naturally as water from a gargoyle. "There is reason to believe they may have left the island altogether after their first narrow escape."

"False," a second voice rang out. Solana's guts turned to ice as she recognized Medina, her former apprentice. "I just spoke to Captain Grung Bahr-Il-Te of the skullbeards, Your Eminence. He demanded we up their pay for tonight's work. According to him, their crew sustained multiple casualties doing battle with a duo of what he called 'glow-faces.' The remaining skullbeards are angry. They feel that our officer in the field failed to prepare them for what they would face."

"Preposterous." Solana had spoken too quickly, too defensively, and De Leliard had noticed. Solana heard it in the stutter of his breath. "Bahr-Il-Te isn't captain. He's barely even an officer. That walking louse-colony was just bluffing to shake an extra handful or two of gems out of the scepter's treasury."

"Oh, but he is captain, Reynziel." It was impossible to miss Medina's refusal to use the more deferential title "Your Purity." She fancied herself on even footing with Solana. *How quickly loyalties shift behind this wall.* "The previous captain fell during the raid. The skullbeards elected Bahr-Il-Te as his successor no more than an hour ago."

"Which begs the question," De Leliard said, wriggling back into the discussion like a spider poised to strike, "why you are unaware of such crucial details?"

He sighed, sending a cloud of sour wine-breath into Solana's face. "It almost sounds as though you are unmotivated to tell me the full truth."

"Inconceivable, Your Eminence." Solana bowed, feeling the steady trickle of fresh blood run down the back of her neck. "My devotion to the church is complete. I would die before I forsake my oaths."

Not so long ago, that would have been the truth, but now the words were vinegar on her tongue.

"Good. Because it might soon come to that." A series of squelching gulps was followed by the sound of a goblet clattering off the temple's shingled roof. Solana tensed. *He treats the grand cathedral like a third-rate brothel.* It was an indignity to the Keeper which would have cost anyone but De Leliard their title.

"If only you could see it, Solana," De Leliard slurred. His voice lingered on the word "see" with undisguised glee. "Mallion's bay is littered with the empire's greatest warships, basking in the beacon of war which you have lit. With one torch, we have started a fire that will spread throughout the whole of the Sundered Isles.

"Within seven dawns, legions of the empire's bravest will depart for Morassia, Onderheem, and Barangia, where they will reinforce our existing presence. After that, the stage will be set for the greatest campaign these lands have ever seen. Estav's meek push at the bay of bones will pale compared to the glory I shall heap upon the Keeper's name. Heil's name will spread across the world like blood staining parchment."

"I can sense them, Your Eminence," Solana lied. "The Keeper is surely smiling upon such a grand undertaking."

"Undoubtedly." De Leliard dismissed the attempt at flattery. "Which is why I cannot have my efforts undermined by your repeated incompetence and dishonesty."

Solana swallowed. Fury such as she had never known welled up like viscera flooding from an opened belly. He was so close. One push, and his arrogant, dishonorable body would shatter on the paved square below. Her fingers twitched, longing for the soft flesh under the Cardinal's many chins. She would gladly plummet alongside him, just to watch the impact up close.

*Heil almighty, keeper of souls and intentions, grant me strength to walk the given path you have laid out before me.*

## CHAPTER 39

"I have served the church faithfully for years," she muttered, trying with all her might not to scream. "Only two hours ago I stood up to my ankles in the blood of strangers who had done me no wrong, for you."

Before she knew it, she had lifted her helmet, exposing her maimed, bloody face.

De Leliard stumbled backward. Medina gasped.

"I allowed myself to be tied down and blinded for you."

"Reynziel, put that helmet back on at once. You are among your betters." The tremor in De Leliard's voice made Solana smile.

*Not so keen to see me unmasked now, are we?*

"You created this visage, *Your Eminence*. Does it not please you?"

"You will put that helmet on, or I swear upon all the stars in heaven that I will have you outwalled." De Leliard's tone had gone from distaste to outright terror.

"I told you she was unhinged," Medina chimed in. "Your Eminence has been far too permitting with her, if I may say so."

*Even now it's politics first.*

"Look at me," Solana screamed. "What more can I give?"

Her heart raced, pumping around the dangerously low quantity of blood in her veins. She felt her knees buckle, shins colliding with the unforgiving limestone floor. With her last ounce of willpower, she reached overhead and replaced the helmet on her head.

It was one thing for De Leliard and Medina to see her face, both of them having seen it on prior occasions. But if she was going to die here, she would be damned if some common watchman was going to look upon her naked face. As her strength ran out, anger turned to a deep shame. She had thrown it all away. Years of faithful service, wiped out with a single tantrum.

"Forgive me." She hated herself for every word. "I have lost so much blood. I didn't know what I was saying."

De Leliard stood over her, cackling.

"You have just simplified matters a great deal," he said. "I have a job that needs doing, which all of your brothers and sisters from Everberg have refused. *You* will do this, successfully this time. Or I will have you outwalled. Your choice."

Solana nodded.

"It will be done."

# CHAPTER 40

*26th day of the 12th cycle, 569KR*
**Mallion's Depth**

They arrived at De Malheur's fortress an hour or two after the dark window. The faint glow of dawn lingered on the ocean, just beyond the horizon. Brina panted with the effort of dragging an increasingly heavy Versa with her.

Both of their stores had run out during their rush to exit the town, leaving them to trudge through the dark jungle the old-fashioned, painful way. Without the sigil's artificial strength, the full extent of Versa's injuries had all but incapacitated them. Each breath came with a whistling noise that betrayed the kind of internal damage Brina couldn't allow herself to think about as she hauled the innkeeper toward their destination.

It only took a single knock to summon Baron Don Lonzo De Malheur. The man almost stumbled over himself as he stepped aside, holding open his poorly painted white gate.

"Please, enter my good folks, enter," he boomed. "From what I've gathered, it's a poor night to be standing around on doorsteps. Very poor indeed." He did a double-take when he saw Versa's limp form draped over Brina's shoulders, his eyes wide. Brina cursed. Versa's mask had slipped halfway off, revealing raw, gray scar tissue and features like those of a wax doll held to a flame.

"What in the world happened to them?" De Malheur asked, openly gaping now.

"Cardinal De Leliard happened." Brina shoved the mask back over Versa's face.

The door clicked shut behind them, and De Malheur set about sealing three deadbolts, two locks with tiny keyholes, and a wooden crossbar.

## CHAPTER 39

He seemed jittery, maybe a little scared, but most of all, the self-proclaimed baron was brimming with poorly hidden excitement.

"What a sight," he declared, gesturing for them to follow him down a stone corridor. "What a sight. I was watching the smoke rise over the trees from my balcony when your friends arrived. I nearly keeled over backward when they told me what had happened, if you can believe me. 'Of course,' I said at once, 'I will harbor any friend of Miss Springtide for as long as necessary.'"

"Thanks," Brina said. "That's very generous of you."

De Malheur held aside a moth-eaten, red-velvet curtain and led them into a small bedchamber that held a somewhat moldy goose-feather bed. Brina gently lowered Versa onto it. They groaned once, then passed out. Had it not been for the staccato rise and fall of their chest, Brina would have feared them dead.

"We have to get Acheron in here at once," Brina said. "If there's anyone who can help, it's him."

"Is he the erm... rather *direct fellow*?" De Malheur asked. His cheeks turned scarlet.

"That would be the one." Despite everything, Brina couldn't help smirking.

"I see." De Malheur tapped the tips of his fingers together nervously. "I will ask, though I'm unsure how cooperative I will find him."

"He'll cooperate," Brina replied. *Or else.*

She followed De Malheur up a flight of uneven stone steps onto the second floor.

"The sitting room is just at the end of the hallway. I have provided a small meal, feel free to—" De Malheur broke off as heated voices drifted into the hallway.

"It's not a riot we need, it's sigils, a ship, and enough men to create a diversion," Acheron's deep voice boomed. "Once De Leliard sees any kind of resistance forming under his nose, Abrasax's is the first head he'll come for. He'll make an example out of him. You know this."

"I am well aware," Zot shot back in his raspy, high-pitched voice. "But I still don't see why we should load all our cloud onto one wagon. De Leliard must die, that is the priority. Everything else follows from there. As far as I'm concerned, the Cardinal slayer is already lost. You couldn't even break into an apothecary without getting us both locked up. Now you want me to bankroll your suicide mission into God's Maul?" Zot let out a laugh like nails on a chalkboard.

"You don't know what I'm capable of, Zot." Acheron snarled. "And let me make one thing very clear. If Abrasax dies, I don't give one nib about your 'bigger picture.' The Viper walks free or I walk."

"I cannot reason with this man," Zot said in exasperation. "You will forgive me for being wary of gambling what little of my fortune remains after tonight on a man who stole a rock of cloud the size of my head from my dealer just last month. I've been selling that stuff since I was eleven. I know what it does to people's brains."

A third voice Brina recognized as Saf intervened. "We have discussed this earlier tonight, Dimimzy. Acheron offered to pay you back, and you were gracious enough to decline his coin. It's in the past."

"It's not his coin that concerns me, it's his wits."

A chair scraped against the stone floor, and more shouting followed. The hollow echoes made it impossible to make out who was saying what, though it sounded to Brina like more people had joined in.

They walked into the sitting room to find Bron standing over Zot. Their eyebrows all but touched.

"Leave my tribe out of this," Bron roared. "Those cowards that exchange their honor for gem dust aren't fit to carry broken spears soaked in shark piss."

"The point stands," Zot said. "Clearly, not everyone under the scepter's boot is opposed to remaining their lapdogs."

"The tribes of Bior have been waiting for a chance at freedom for decades." The metal skulls in Bron's beard tinkled menacingly as he spoke. "Once they see that we have put a crack in the empire's shield, they will come."

"Ahem." De Malheur cleared his throat with excessive force. He pointed at Brina, who felt herself grow red in the face as every eye in the sitting room turned toward her.

"You made it." The next thing Brina saw was a cloud of curly black hair as Saf swept her into a tight hug. "We feared the worst."

"I told you she was fine, didn't I?" Acheron said, though he too smiled faintly, which to his standards might as well be jumping up and down with joy. Bron and Sneak simply winked at her, as though they hadn't worried for a moment.

"It was closer than I'd like to admit." Brina wrestled herself free from

## CHAPTER 40

Saf's embrace, cheeks burning for entirely different reasons, and plopped down into a vacant armchair. Her entire body felt like jelly. Bruises and cuts she hadn't even noticed yet clamored for attention. They'd have to wait.

"Speaking of close calls," De Malheur said with the air of a man approaching a beehive with a stick, "I could use your assistance with Miss Springtide's wounded companion. I'm afraid it's urgent."

As Acheron disappeared down the stairs in a whirl of robes and muttered curses, Brina reached for the half-empty bottle of rum. Too worn down to fiddle around with cups, she took a long draught straight from the bottle. It burned just enough on the way down to jolt her into speech.

"I ran into another eyeless Reynziel. A woman this time." She nodded at Sneak, who sat on a red-velvet cushion on the floor with his legs folded. "Except this was different."

"Different how?" Saf asked.

"It was like she was burning sigils, extremely efficient ones. She held out her hands and froze the air around her. It locked Versa in place immediately, and I avoided the same by inches. Transmitting that kind of energy outside of the body should have incapacitated any sparkgazer, no matter how strong they are, but she didn't even stumble." Brina shook her head. "To make matters worse, she should have been blinded by that wicked spiked helmet, and yet she moved with the precise grace of a Hawqallian serpent warrior. It was like trying to stab at a wisp of smoke."

The others stared at her for what felt like hours before Zot broke the silence.

"This isn't the first I've heard of such things. One of my smuggling crews had a run in with a scepter patrol led by an eyeless priest last year. There were three survivors out of two dozen quality bruisers." He shook his head. "And that was only because they jumped overboard when the eyeless beast began its rampage."

"This is troubling," Saf said. She tapped her tongue against her teeth nervously. "The Heilinists have spent generations weeding out every last sparkgazer. They've destroyed scripts by the hundreds, all in the name of the war against blasphemy.

"What if that was all just a front? If they've discovered some other way of accessing the locked consciousness, things could get very grim quickly. They could have an entire army of trained priests while we're stuck digging up ruins and grave hills, struggling to find scripts to fuel ourselves."

"Yes, it's all rather brilliant," Zot sneered. "Just a shame we're on the arse end of the donkey here."

"Which is exactly why we'll need to band together, whether we'd like to or not." Saf gave Zot a stern look. "If we continue to butt heads, the empire will have us all at the end of a noose before long."

Zot sighed.

"Fine, fine. I'll see what I can do to aid your little jailbreak plan. If only because I recently had a taste of the cage myself." He spat onto De Malheur's moth-eaten rug. "But I will have no one nosing in my business, understood?"

"Believe me, the less I know, the easier it will be to tolerate your presence," Saf said.

Zot bared a row of sharp teeth.

"Now if you'll excuse me, I have some sleep to catch up on."

# CHAPTER 41

*2nd day of the 1st cycle, 570KR*
**Fortress De Malheur**

Over the following days, De Malheur's usually empty home turned into a fortress preparing for a siege. A round-the-clock watch system was instated to ensure that someone had eyes on the surrounding hills at all hours. Bron had fortified De Malheur's rickety old front door with multiple fist-wide tree branches, and the once cozy sitting room now looked like something a library might spew into a gutter after a night of heavy drinking. What scrolls and books the order had salvaged before their flight lay strewn on every surface, and the room's single desk had turned into a mess of ink stains and torn scraps of parchment with discarded ideas.

Even amongst all that uninvited chaos, De Malheur's mood was stuck at an almost annoying high. He could be found strutting the castle's corridors at all times of the day, a huge grin plastered on his boyish face. "This is just like Goldhorn's *Woes of Count Demis,*" he'd say with unbridled enthusiasm each time the subject of the empire's tightening grasp came up. Brina was unsure whether the baron had secretly been lonely all these years or if his grasp on reality had finally slipped completely. At Year's End he'd insisted on organizing a rather extravagant feast, complete with a huge smoked ham from his own pantry and a one-man play that had become significantly more entertaining as Brina had glugged her way through most of De Malheur's wine reserves.

On the opposite end of the spectrum, Versa sank further away from them with every passing day.

"I don't get it," Acheron said. They stood in front of the closed door to Versa's improvised hospice chamber, where Brina had been waiting for an update to the innkeeper's condition. "I've done everything there is to be done. They should have stabilized by now." Beads of sweat clustered on his forehead.

"What do you mean *should have*?"

"Physically speaking, they are past the most dangerous stage. The swelling is going down, and I've successfully kept the wounds rot-free." There was an uncharacteristic note of worry in Acheron's voice. "I expected them to wake up days ago."

Brina chewed on her bottom lip. *Physically speaking.* What if there was something else keeping Versa suspended in this borderland between life and death? Wounds that ran deeper than blood and bone.

"Can I go in?"

"I guess." Acheron shrugged. He held open the door and stood aside. "Gotta warn you though, kid. It's like conversing with a mural."

They lay in the middle of the dim room, their lanky, pale form obscured to the shoulders by a mottled white sheet. There was a chill to the room that had nothing to do with temperature. The air was frigid with silence, and even the small bundle of daylight that streamed in through a circular slot high on the wall felt like a thin replica of the real thing. This was a place where things came to die.

Brina's guts twisted as she gazed upon Versa's masked face. Even in their present condition, Brina had made Acheron swear he would leave the metal mask on the innkeeper's face. It was the least she could do.

"We've received news from the Ditch," she began, "or what's left of it, anyway." The words came gingerly, as though she was afraid to choke on them. "Wicket Row burned down completely. I'm afraid the Chimera is lost. Sneak said there was nothing left to salvage…"

She trailed off. Versa's face remained still. Acheron had been right. It was like talking to a mural. Brina shuffled awkwardly, increasingly unsure of where to look.

"We'll make them pay for this, Verse. I promise.

"We've got Zot on our side now. He's already made contact with what's left of his organization on the island. Just imagine what we could do with an army like that on our side."

She tried a smile. It felt like grease paint slathered across her face.

"Anyway." She placed two fingers on the innkeeper's shoulder. It was burning to the touch, the only outward sign that life was still raging somewhere deep inside that shrunken body. "I'd better run. Big meeting coming up."

## CHAPTER 41

When the door creaked shut behind Brina, she was embarrassed to find the seed of a tear blooming in the corner of her eye.

***

Dimimzy Zot leaned back in one of the deranged baron's moderately comfortable chairs. Under any other circumstances, he wouldn't have touched the emerald velvet monstrosity with its holes and dust-riddled feather stuffing, but for now it would have to do. He'd have to make do without many of the comforts he was accustomed to in the coming months.

Maybe that was for the better. His empire hadn't been built by soft hands and pampered behinds, but by the sort of ruthless ambition that could only be fueled by hunger and rage. Now that all of it balanced on a knife's edge, he'd have to tap into that old well once more.

Outside of the reading room's vaulted window, the cerulean sea bucked and heaved under a dark sky. Foam topped the rolling waves as they hurtled toward the beach below at breakneck speed. Half a dozen red sails were scattered throughout the bay, crimson patches sewn into a blanket of blue. *One of those is mine. Mine.*

Zot pursed his lips, his mouth sour with the taste of un-screamed curses. Decades. It had cost him decades to procure two perfect galleons and turn them into his very own floating palace. A worthy abode in the style of the villas of old. *Andrassa* and *Yugon,* the sword and the scale of his empire. Now all he had left was the sword.

Zot sprang up from the seat as he imagined some green-behind-the-ears scepter brat lounging in the *Yugon*'s cabin, sampling his wine collection, and riffling through his precious books. Not to mention what they had undoubtedly done to his precious pets. Mahrovia, his trusted righthand woman, was likely dead. *She better be.* Death before surrender, that had been the order, and Dimimzy Zot expected nothing short of complete follow-through.

*There's still Andrassa,* he told himself as he paced back and forth. As soon as balance had returned to his business dealings, he'd get behind *Andrassa*'s wheel himself to chase down what was his. He would be the first to board the *Yugon,* and he would make examples of every darkhelm who stood in his way. All he had to do was wait for his faithful lieutenant to send word of where the galleon lay moored.

"I thought I heard war drums. Turns out it was you dusting the carpet." It was Springtide. She stood in the sitting room's open door with a smirk that ought to have annoyed him. They were even now. More even than she could ever know. He had almost deserted the island on the *Yugon* himself, only to find the strings of his conscience tugging at him. Who'd known that he even possessed such a thing anymore?

The roamer wore an eyepatch of black leather that matched the color of her braided hair. Her gray traveling cloak still carried the unmistakable stains of dried blood.

"If only your dagger were half as sharp as your tongue," Zot said, "we'd be feasting in the Cardinal's dining hall by nightfall."

"And miss the sixth round of kelp stew the baron's cooking up? Not a chance."

She plopped down in a chair beside the window with a sigh.

"You should get rid of that cloak," Zot said. He held a perfumed sleeve to his nose, filling it with the fading echoes of cinnamon and sandalwood. "It's beginning to stink."

"Beginning to?" Springtide raised an eyebrow. "This thing smelled long before I found it. It's like a cloak of invisibility to wildlife. Not even an erymanthian could smell the human underneath all the filth."

"I can, and I don't care for it." Zot wafted the sleeve back and forth to ward off the overpowering stench.

Springtide let out a barking laugh.

"Who'd have thought? Dimimzy Zot, the man whose name inspires fear and awe in anyone this side of the wall, is too delicate to handle a little musk."

"You better remember who you're talking to, Springtide," he grumbled automatically. It had been a long time since anyone had spoken to him with such relaxed irreverence. He was used to straightened backs, downcast eyes, and rehearsed words. It hadn't even been a week, and standards were already slipping.

"Oh, I know who I'm talking to," Springtide said. Her demeanor grew serious. "Which is why I came up here before the others arrive."

"Is that so?" He ran an absent hand through his beard. It was getting much too coarse without the application of his daily oils. Soon he'd be just another vagrant.

"Stay away from Acheron."

"Excuse me?"

"You heard me. Stay away from him." She glared at him like he was

## CHAPTER 41

something slimy found at the bottom of a fishing net. Zot was embarrassed to feel a twinge of unease. His gaze flicked toward the closed door.

"What makes you think I want anything to do with that wreck?"

"You've seen what he looks like." She mimed the sorcerer's trembling hands. "He's going through cloud sickness. Where do you think he'll turn when it becomes too much to bear?"

Zot smiled. He'd noticed it too, of course. Over the past decade, the sorcerer had appeared on his doorstep dozens of times, looking a lot worse. Most of those occasions had proved very lucrative opportunities. Until it had all gone so very wrong that last time. Zot had let his curiosity get the better of him, that was all. The final tally of their little collaborations was still firmly in the black.

He may have need of the sorcerer's services in the near future. It would be foolish to give that up by helping him kick the habit.

"Just because I trade in white gems, you assume some will rain out of my pockets if I turn my jacket inside out? My warehouses burned to very expensive ashes."

Springtide leaned forward in her chair.

"I don't care. If I see you hand Acheron so much as a bag of wampyr dung, you'll have me to deal with."

"Is that supposed to scare me?" He knew better than to approach her. His stature would stack up unfavorably against the lanky roamer. "Here's a word of advice. Don't make threats you can't follow through on."

"You know what?" Springtide's fingers drummed against her knees. "I used to think you were some kind of genius, the way you turned a bunch of crooks into a disciplined organization.

"I assumed you must be different. A man with vision where others simply chased the next handful of shards. Now I see you're just a crow like the rest of them."

"You have no idea what I am." Zot could feel the blood drain from his face. Watching his life's work be destroyed was one thing, but this disrespect was too much.

"I have been turning mud into bricks since before you were born, Springtide. Doorstep's Ditch may be a plague-ridden dump, but by the Seven, at least I've tried to make something of it instead of hiding in the jungle all my life."

Springtide's eyes narrowed. She opened her mouth to speak, but fell silent when an unexpected voice rang out.

"What are you ladies prattling on about?"

Both of their heads spun round as the old sorcerer hobbled into the sitting room. In the heat of their argument, neither of them had heard the door open. How much had the sorcerer overheard?

"Zot here was just telling me about some of his charity work," Springtide said, her brown eye fixed on Zot's own.

The sorcerer sighed, then shook his head. "Fine, keep your secrets. I came here to tell you the others are waiting in the dining hall downstairs."

"Why the dining hall?" Springtide asked, jumping to her feet. "I thought the meeting was supposed to take place here?"

"Saf says we need a bigger table or something." The sorcerer shrugged. "I wasn't really listening."

\*\*\*

None of them said a word as they made their way down the stairs. Brina watched the back of Zot's head disappear around the corner into the dining room, wondering what was going on inside that bald head. It struck her that they knew little, too little, about the crime lord's intentions. He'd appeared in the nick of time with a warning, and just like that, he'd wormed his way into their midst. *And I was the one who let him in.*

It would be foolish to believe his pretenses about wanting to repay Brina. He had to be working an angle. On Hammerstroke, there was always an angle. From now on, she'd keep an eye on the man at all times.

All of them were ready and waiting by the time she sat down on the last remaining chair between Wane and Bron. The entire length of De Malheur's mahogany dining table was covered by a scroll of parchment covered in black lines and squiggles.

"Now that all of us are finally present," Saf said, her tone steeped in annoyance, "I suggest we get to work. There's plenty to discuss before I leave."

"You're leaving?" Brina gaped at the woman. "*Now?*"

There was a conspicuous lack of reaction from the others.

"You knew about this?" She glared up and down the table, meeting a series of averted gazes. The only one who seemed taken aback by the news was Zot, whose eyes narrowed to black pinpricks.

"It'll only be for a few weeks," Saf said, "a month at the most."

Brina didn't know which was worse, Saf's departure or the fact that almost everyone else had known before her. Something ugly stirred in her guts as she looked at Saf's detached smile, though she had a hard time putting her finger on the feeling.

## CHAPTER 41

"Why now, of all times?" Brina asked, unable to keep her voice from rising.

"There are things I must do. Things I had hoped to put off a little while longer, but if last week's disaster has told us anything, it's that the situation is evolving much quicker than any of us had anticipated."

"Why be vague about it?" *Betrayal, that's what I feel.*

"Because this concerns me alone. It would be unfair to involve anyone else."

Brina's jaw worked. There was a lot more she would've liked to say, but Acheron gingerly put up a hand to interrupt her.

"It's for the better, kid." His dark eye fixed on Brina's. "Trust me on this one."

Brina sighed, then waved a hand for Saf to continue speaking.

"I will be back before anyone has noticed I'm missing," Saf said, her usual businesslike tone firmly back in place. "As I was saying, there's a lot to get to. Bron, what's the status in the bay?"

The Biori cleared his throat and stood up.

"The bay is busy. Busier than usual. Since Thursday, we have counted six dozen redsails. They arrive at Mallion's Harbor individually and sail out in groups of five or ten."

Saf pointed at the roll of parchment, indicating an intricate drawing of Mallion's Harbor in the bottom left corner. She bent down and marked six dozen lines.

"Do we know what direction they are headed?"

"Aye. About half seemed to make for the Mist Strait." Bron pointed a stubby finger at the strait on the map. "The other half were spread out here, here and here." He pointed out three different channels between the islets surrounding Hammerstroke. "We lost sight after that."

"Why now, though?" Sneak asked. "What are we missing?"

"Isn't it obvious?" Zot bared his pointy teeth in a sardonic grin. "De Leliard is tightening the net. The waters around Merkede and Onderheem have been ideal smuggling routes for two decades. Technically, the scepter holds sway over Merkedian waters, but foreign goods and ideas have been slipping through the cracks. Now the darkhelms want to show everyone that they're still on top before it's too late."

"I agree," Saf said. "The burning of Doorstep's Ditch was just the first step in a larger plan."

"Excellent." Everyone looked at Acheron, who was rubbing at red eyes. "They've finally shown their hand."

"How is *any* of this excellent, you demented ghoul?" Zot snapped. "The entire town lies in ruins. My supply lines are being cut off as we speak. Do you have any idea what kind of dark age we are about to enter here?"

"The Cardinal fears us," Acheron said with a grin that tugged at his scars. "He didn't dare send his troops to the provinces before he was convinced that the morale of the outwalled was shattered."

"Which. It. Is," Zot said through clenched teeth.

A rush of excitement came over Brina as the full implications of this hit her.

"They don't have the numbers to stop an uprising on two fronts," she said.

"Exactly," Acheron said. "They can suppress unrest here or in the provinces, but not both at the same time."

Saf nodded and began furiously scribbling something in the map's margin.

"That would've been great to know two months ago," Zot said, "but as you've so keenly observed, morale amongst the outwalled is rightfully at an all-time low."

"Morale shmorale," Acheron said, waving a hand over his shoulder. "There is an opening. A definitive chance to break the cycle."

"Then go out there," Zot said. "Go walk amongst the smoldering ruins of Wicket Row and tell those sleeping under the bare sky that now is a great time to charge into a volley of windup bolts."

"We don't need to tell them anything." Acheron jabbed his finger into a blank spot on the map labeled *God's Maul*. "We'll show them."

"Hear hear," Bron called out. "All this talk is tiring. It's time for doing."

Zot rubbed his fingers against his temples as though he were fighting off a leviathan-sized hangover.

"Fine. What do we need?" He looked at Saf, who nodded.

"Our first concern is crossing the water unseen. That will be challenging, as the bay is infested with redsails."

"Then we'll hide in plain sight," Sneak said. "How hard can it be to stitch together some red cloth?"

"If we set sail at dusk, it should be close enough," Brina agreed.

"We won't get through the gate." Bron drummed his fingers against the tabletop. "It only opens once a week for provisions. They'll realize something's wrong."

"Unless we figure out when the next shipment is due," Saf said.

## CHAPTER 41

"We could intercept it," Zot said, his eyes glittering. "We approach them, disguised as one of them. Then we board their ship and send every last one of them to the bottom of the bay."

"There will be no unnecessary bloodshed." Saf glared at Zot.

"That won't work." Everyone turned to face Harrod Wane, who went wide-eyed under the sudden attention of the entire order. Brina chuckled. She'd almost forgotten the kid was there. By the looks of it, so had the others.

"Why not?" Zot glowered at the kid as though he'd just insulted his mother.

"A galleon like the ones the enlightened watch—I mean, the darkhelms—use aren't easy to navigate. We need a full crew with experience, or we could end up drifting in circles until the other redsails snatch us up."

"I know some good lads," Zot said, "but they don't come cheap. Especially not for an undertaking like this."

"One should think money would be the least of your worries?" Acheron raised his eyebrows at Zot. "I have it on good authority that you've got a pile of gemstones that most dragons would envy."

"I did." Zot's jaw clenched and unclenched. "I mean, I do, but what's left of it is currently halfway across the sundered islands, and I..." He thumped his fist against the table in an outburst of fury. "I don't know where it is, damn it all."

"How much do we need?" Brina asked, thinking of the pouch of shards she'd so carefully saved up through years of hard work.

"For a job like this? Not a nib under two hundred and fifty shards. These are lives we're buying, not services."

Brina's heart sank. It would take months to get a sum of that magnitude together.

"Oh, that reminds me." Wane's hand dipped into his vest, and he pulled out a crumpled wad of parchment.

Smoothing it out on the table, he read:

*Wanted: Griffin slayer.*

*Whosoever can free us from the menace of the griffin that hunts the South - North passage through Undercling's Reach will be paid handsomely for their efforts. Further employment opportunities may be offered.*

*Reward: One hundred and fifty emerald shards paid upon delivery of proof*

*Carthage, Orner, and Wells*
*South - North Trading Confederation*

"I found this a while back, thought it might come in handy," the kid said, beaming.

Brina felt a dozen eyes turn toward her.

"Absolutely not."

"But you're a roamer," Sneak said. "You must've killed a dozen monsters thrice as dangerous as a griffin."

"That's not the problem." Brina could feel anger bubbling in the pit of her stomach. She'd never liked being the center of attention, and she outright hated it when others meddled in her business. "There are only two or three breeding pairs left on the island. If I take out this one, I'd be directly responsible if they go extinct."

"So?" Zot shrugged. "Nobody will miss them. Without that pile of gems, this plan is going nowhere."

"Brina has the right of it," Bron grunted. "The forests birthed us, and it's up to us to keep them in balance."

"Enough of that primitive nonsense." Zot waved a dismissive hand. "These are actual problems we're discussing."

"Watch who you call primitive." Sneak stood up, leaning over the table toward the crime lord.

"Stay out of it, schoolboy." Zot jabbed a finger at Sneak as though it were a sword.

Bron slammed a throwing axe on the table. His long mustache quivered with rage. Somewhere in the background, Acheron giggled madly. For a moment, it looked like Zot might get to his feet, but he seemed to think better of it at the last moment.

"Enough." It was Saf who cut through the chaos without raising her voice. When Brina looked at her, she thought she could see the fading

## CHAPTER 41

remnants of a purple glow leaving her eyes. "We will find a way to pay your crew, Dimimzy, but you will respect my people." She needed no sigils to put weight behind the words. It was perfectly clear to all that the topic was closed.

"So, let's say we pass through the outer gate," Acheron said, continuing as though nothing had happened. "Then what do we do?"

All eyes fell on the blank spot on the map that signified the inside of God's Maul. The great unknown. For the first time since they had sat down, silence reigned.

# CHAPTER 42

*10th day of the 1st cycle, 570KR*
**Fortress De Malheur**

Saf's departure from the fortress was like a thumb lifting from a scale. The fragile balance that was only maintained by her careful navigation of the mounting tensions between De Malheur's guests was lost. Ever since they had all but come to blows, Bron and Sneak avoided Zot, treating any room he was in as empty. From his side, Zot's mind seemed occupied by worries that extended far beyond the confines of De Malheur's castle. He spent most of his days in the sitting room, poring over the baron's antique maps and gazing out of the slanted windows at the ships traversing the bay.

The only one who seemed unperturbed by recent events was Wane, who had taken it upon himself to steal anything that even remotely resembled red cloth wherever he could get it. So far, the growing pile in the corner of the dining room contained handkerchiefs, torn tunics, socks full of holes, and a selection of women's undergarments. At the rate he was going, the kid would have enough materials to sew red sails for an entire fleet by the beginning of the next cycle.

Then there was Brina, who spent increasingly prolonged stretches of time sitting at Versa's bedside, watching for the slightest twitch or gurgle that would signal any kind of improvement in the innkeeper's condition. So far, she'd been sorely disappointed. Instead, the hours spent in that dim and depressing room became moments of reflection where she'd pore over all the details of the plan until her brain threatened to flow out of her ears in a pulp.

It was on one of these long nights spent sitting and waiting that a knock on the door pulled her out of a deep imprintation trance. The *Leve*

## CHAPTER 42

script she was holding jolted in her hands as she jumped up, disrupting the process.

"Miss Sabrina," De Malheur whispered through a crack in the door, "I hope I am not interrupting?"

She was on the verge of unleashing a week's worth of pent-up frustrations on him when the anxious look on his face stopped her. Here was a man who'd opened his home to a group of complete strangers, whose collection of fine liquors was being drained at an alarming rate, and whose precious books were thumbed through by more hands than they'd seen in the last two centuries. De Malheur hadn't complained once. Maybe the round-faced buffoon had some noble blood in him after all.

"Not interrupting at all, baron." She put on as friendly a tone as she could muster. "What's the trouble?"

"It concerns the pantry, Miss Sabrina," he said. "I was just taking inventory, and I'm afraid we've been burning through the stored goods much quicker than I had anticipated. My stores were designed to last many comfortable months, but of course, that was assuming I would be by myself. Since there are eight of us now, I'm afraid we'll run out sometime this week." He fidgeted with his crude iron crown, his lips working as though he was chewing on something unpleasant.

"Now, I'm the last man to allow my guests to pay for anything they are offered under my roof, but..." He waved a hand as if to wave away whatever he was going to say next. "Never mind, never mind."

He made to close the door.

"Wait." Brina got up and put a foot between the closing door. "I understand. You weren't expecting to feed and house a gang of eight."

De Malheur bit his lip. "I was planning another trip into the village to sell a cartload of mirrors and perfumes from the north settlement, but given the circumstances, I doubt people will have use nor gems for them."

"We'll contribute. It's only fair. What do we need?"

They sat down together at the long dining hall table to make up a list. Brina was mortified to learn that in just three weeks, the company had chewed its way through almost one hundred shards' worth of smoked hams, aged cheeses, potted olives, and so on. And that was excluding the bottles of wine and rum De Malheur had provided from his own collection in the cellar. To replenish the stores with more modest fare for the month to come, they'd need to scrounge up at least fifty more from amongst themselves.

A quick tour of everyone's pockets yielded a grand total of twenty-three sapphire shards among them, most of which were donated by a grumbling Zot who muttered something about "boatloads" and "thieving darkhelms." Brina threw in every shard she possessed, excluding the small pouch of savings she kept tied to her stomach at all times.

She wasn't ready to part with the nest egg she had spent so many years building up. In her mind, that money had always been meant for grander things than bread and butter. Besides, every shard she took out of the floorboard fund took them further away from being able to hire a ship and crew to take them across the bay.

"I suppose we could cut down to rations of grain and water," De Malheur said doubtfully as he counted the meager pile of shards for the fifth time. He pursed his lips. "We could try fishing. Though I have the skill nor the musculature for it."

Brina sighed, watching the baron stir the shards around the table with his stubby fingers.

"I know!" He beamed with sudden enthusiasm. "I will ride out on a hunt. That's a noble pursuit if ever there was one. I think there's still a spear in the cellar somewhere. I'll go out and chase down the largest wild boar this castle's kitchen has ever had the delight to prepare."

"There are no wild boar on Hammerstroke," Brina said. She suppressed a giggle at the image of the rotund man riding around the jungle with a rusty spear in search of a creature that only existed in tales from the far reaches of the north. "The closest thing are the erymanthian in Bior, but I doubt you'll have enough spears to take one down."

"Perhaps a mighty stag, then?"

Brina shook her head, causing De Malheur to deflate like a punctured fish bladder.

"Then I suppose there will be no hunt."

Something clicked in Brina's head as the last word rolled from De Malheur's tongue. *Maybe there will be a hunt after all.*

She retrieved a folded scrap of parchment from a pocket in her gray traveler's cloak. "Wanted: Griffin Slayer."

*We do what we do for the cause.* Acheron's words came back to her. It had been his way of making her feel better after she'd all but killed the spy in Barrow's Perch. Back then, it had seemed hollow. An easy excuse to pawn off responsibility for your actions. Now she understood. It was about knowingly and willingly crossing the line, about sacrificing not only life

## CHAPTER 42

and limb, but your conscience alongside it. For the first time, she thought she understood how Acheron had become what he was, a half man living forever in the shadow of the things he had done in the pursuit of a future that had never come to be.

Then something hit her like a battering ram to the guts.

*"After all I've cost that man. It's my attempt to make things right that will end up costing him dearest of all."*

Why didn't I see it sooner?

"Where are you going?" De Malheur called after her.

She slammed the door behind her, sprinted down the hallway and entered Versa's sleeping chamber.

"I know what you did."

The words clattered against the brick-and-mortar walls like armored bodies tumbling from a fortification to the cobbles below. Brina's composure shattered. She leaned forward, grabbing a fistful of the clean gown she herself had put on Versa's lifeless form that morning.

"That woman, the priest, you called her 'sister'. You tried to protect her, didn't you?"

A tremor ran through the innkeeper's body as Brina shook them. Heavy tears tumbled from Brina's cheeks, leaving dark stains on the innkeeper's gray gown.

"You betrayed my father in exchange for your sister's life. That's what happened, isn't it? Him for her. That's why you made it out of God's Maul."

"But they still took her. They turned her into one of them."

Versa remained still, their eyes closed behind the simple wooden mask. Brina let out a roar of despair.

"It's not your fault." She was yelling now, not caring who heard. "It's what they do. They lie, they lie, and they torture, and they destroy. Anyone would have done what you had to."

She placed a hand below the innkeeper's head and, cradling their neck, bent down to clutch Versa into an awkward embrace.

"We can make them pay. Together. For what they did to your sister, for what they did to you." A wave of dizzying pent-up grief washed over her. "For what they did to all of us."

Brina let go of the lifeless body, a steel gauntlet squeezing her heart. Maybe whatever was left of Versa was buried too deep now. For a moment, she had been so sure she knew what had broken Versa's spirit. *Maybe all of it was wrong.*

Looking down on the thin, mangled shape of her oldest friend, she wiped what remained of her tears away on her sleeve. This would be the last time she came here, she told herself. It was time to accept that they were gone.

"I forgive you. Goodbye."

As she made to leave, a single tear streaked down the masked face, followed by a hoarse croak.

"I'm sorry."

# CHAPTER 43

*11th day of the 1st cycle, 570KR*
**Barrow's Perch**

After two weeks spent within the stuffy, dark confines of De Malheur's castle, Brina felt a weight lift from her shoulders as she exited the castle's front door and hiked down the trail toward Barrow's Perch. She was back where she belonged, surrounded by green under a roof of blue.

She kept to the tree line, never exposing herself to the open plains of Barrow's Perch. If she was to encounter anyone this far from Doorstep's Ditch, she'd be the one to spot them first. The precaution slowed her down, but not as much as being detained by the darkhelms would.

The rations of bread and cheese De Malheur had prepared for her dangled awkwardly from her shoulder as she hopped over fallen trees and maneuvered her way through dense thickets of bramble. Her provisions ought to last for four days, but Brina hoped to get the job done in two. Winter had begun its steady forward march, and two nights under the stars would be more than enough shivering for one trip.

By the time she made it to the old mill, the sun had reached its zenith. She slipped inside and was pleased to find that everything was still in its rightful place.

With the automatic comfort of familiarity, she dipped underneath the staircase where she plucked her leather-bound copy of *Carralnar's Cracking Compendium of Critters* from her book chest. She riffled to the letter G until a crude illustration of a graybeak griffin stared back at her from the faded page.

# Graybeak Griffin

*Most commonly found on craggy hillsides, where it builds its nest by toppling boulders off cliffs to break them down into building blocks. The graybeak is said to lay a single egg every thirteen years, upon which it broods for thirteen weeks. During this time, and only during this time, the graybeak sings in a low hum that carries on the wind for miles. Like other griffin subspecies, the graybeak's diet consists chiefly of pronghorn, horses, and other similar sized mammals. However, it is worth noting that reports from across the Miststrait have claimed to see griffins hunt prey as large as erymanthian. It is known to swallow stones rich in ore to restore its metallic beak and claws. An intelligent creature, the griffin uses bait to lure its prey, then dives to snatch it.*

*In the Hammerstroke region, adult Graybeak have been observed to reach wingspans exceeding twenty feet.*

Brina sighed as she snapped the book shut. They were magnificent creatures. She had always considered spotting one a rare treat, and after hand-feeding the chick she'd found all those years ago, her love had only grown. Now she was going to wipe out one of the last remaining bloodlines on the island. *Keep it together, Springtide. One moment of doubt when the time comes, and it'll be fatal.*

The time for thinking was done. She'd made a decision. Now she needed to act. The book said griffins placed bait. That would be her ticket to luring it out into the open.

She opened a small trapdoor under her favorite armchair, unlocking a small compartment underneath the floorboards. The sack of equipment she'd stashed down there stank of dust and mold as she pulled it out and poured the contents onto the seat of her chair. A small windup bow fell out and toppled onto the floor with a thunk. Brina raised it, peering down the sight. It felt light and flimsy compared to her full-sized model. The spyglass she'd mounted on it was rusty and would probably need adjusting, but it would have to do, since she'd left her best bow in the mud in front

## CHAPTER 43

of The Wistful Chimera. A small leather quiver held a little over a dozen quarrels. That was plenty.

The herb cabinet tinkled cheerily as Brina riffled through labeled glass vials. She ground up a handful of dried stoneflower buds together with her last leaf of cripple's clover. Then she blended the mixture with weepingbark resin.

Careful not to touch the stuff with her bare hands, she coated the tip of each quarrel with the paralyzing agent. With any luck, the beast would die on impact when it fell out of the sky. At least that way it wouldn't have to suffer.

When she left the mill, her backpack stuffed to the brim with as many of her worldly possessions as it could hold, she didn't dare look back. Who knew how long it would be before she'd step foot across its threshold again?

\*\*\*

Brina reached Splitcrack Gorge as the first chariot crested the horizon. Its two granite spires rose from the earth like twin giants. It was the edge of dusk, where the starburst hues of late afternoon clash with the rising pallor of night.

Brina sat down on a fallen tree surrounded by thickets of brambles to dip into De Malheur's rations for the first time. Ahead of her, the path snaked out of the trees and up a steep, mountainous slope.

Another hour's march would take her to Undercling's Reach, where the troublesome bird was supposedly wreaking havoc. That would have to wait until morning. Aside from a lone griffin, the mountains also housed a dwindling population of sheikan, who would be all too grateful for a defenseless morsel to walk into their territory at night.

Brina was three bites deep into a loaf of rye when the sharp smell of fire hit her nostrils. She instinctively took a knee, the sappy undergrowth of the forest soaking through the fabric of her trousers. As she crept closer to the edge of the forest, loud voices drifted toward her, suspended on the wind like a church bell. There were two of them. Male. Though Brina couldn't make out the words, they didn't seem the least bit worried about keeping their presence hidden. *Idiots.* If that was how the South-North Trading Company operated, it was a miracle there were still enough of them around to put out a contract on the griffin.

Even so, she would need to be extra careful not to reveal her presence. Not until she knew for certain the party wasn't a threat. What if the contract had been a ruse to draw her out of hiding? Unease spread in her stomach like poison in a well. It was a good thing she was at least two steps ahead of whoever was up there.

As the night deepened, Brina wrapped herself in her traveling cloak underneath a bush. A small part of her was jealous of the morons up on the mountainside, whose fire was now visible for miles around. At least they were warm.

To distract herself from the moist underground and the creeping frost, she went over some of the shapes she'd been practicing.

*Forte.* The blue square appeared in her mind's eye at once. Brina's fingers closed around a nearby tree root. It groaned as she jerked almost a foot of it from the soil before relinquishing the shape. She switched over into *Lux* and watched as the night came alive around her. The fire above her turned into a white flare, obscuring most of its surroundings in a blaze of light. She enjoyed the view regardless. A landscape she had only known through sound now came alive before her. She watched as a three-foot-long millipede traipsed its way across a branch above her head. There was a rustling of vines as a family of skullhelmed chimps swung past. One of them looked down, Brina's single yellow eye reflected in its own.

A sense of peace filled Brina as she watched life in the jungle unfold around her. She was home. Away from the noises and smells of having people around at all times. Before she knew it, *Lux* faded away, and she sank into a deep sleep.

# CHAPTER 44

*8th day of the 1st cycle, 570KR*
**North Settlement, Hammerstroke**

Saf raised her hood as she entered The Radiant Reynziel, the North Settlement's only inn. As far as watering holes for sailors went, the Reynziel was clean and quiet to the point of dullness, but a strange face around these parts still drew eyes. The less they could describe to the scepter spies that were doubtlessly trailing her every move, the better.

She sat down at a square table meant for two in a shadowy corner of the common room. The goosebumps on her back clamored to be nearer to the roaring fire in the hearth. They would need to wait.

The North Settlement was Mallion's Depth's rowdier little brother. Because of its isolated location surrounded by jungle to the south and shallow stretches of ocean littered with sandbanks and tiny islets to the north, the settlers here had never bothered to create a formally outwalled class. Nor were Heil's tenets adhered to all that strictly. Strangers who irritated the locals simply ended up vanishing without a trace, and that was that. Not that many risked traveling up the long and treacherous road to begin with.

Twice a year, the northerners sent casks of tax collections to Mallion's Depth by sea. In exchange, they appointed their own watchmen, educated their own Reynziels, and elected their own archbishop once every three years.

Nipping at a mug of lukewarm, clumpy beer, Saf sat back and observed. The success or failure of using psychosigils to attain one's goals started long before the actual burning of the shape. Phoclesia Al-Soph, her sigilist mentor, had been a master at selecting her targets, and Saf had only improved on the method since.

Three weatherworn fisherwomen sat huddled around a game of Galleons, quietly shoving around handfuls of polished sapphire nibs and sipping crystal-clear flower water. *Too wealthy.*

The meager dozen shards in Saf's purse would do little to impress a woman who could spend her nights gambling and drinking away a manual laborer's weekly wage. *If you offer water to a fish, don't be surprised to see it swim away,* as Phoclesia had put it.

Then there was the lone man, reading a thick leather-bound tome in an armchair besides the hearth. The flaking gilded lettering on the cover read *Beastes Der Wathre*. A roamer. One who could read pre-Heilinist script, no less. A professional in every sense of the word. Though she couldn't see his face, the clean trim of his fingernails and the polished state of his boots told Saf all she needed to know. He was here to do a job. A well-paid, likely prestigious one. Even if the man owned a ship of his own, which she doubted, he would be hard to distract from his mission. It would take every ounce of her *Consol* and *Rhetoris* stores to keep him in the right headspace throughout their journey to Snake Island. A delicate undertaking, painfully prone to disastrous errors.

The door opened, allowing a gust of icy wind to sneak in. Saf shivered. Her momentary annoyance with the newcomer was quickly assuaged when she saw the state of the man's boots. No sailor with a single shard to his name would set out to sea with gaping seams like that. Poor man probably spent most of his days with numb, sopping wet feet. His shoulder length gray hair had thinned on top, leaving only a half circle of wispy, matted locks.

Her suspicions were confirmed when he placed a clay pot full of clams on the counter. The inn-keep threw a small drawstring pouch at the man, who tucked it into his pocket. With the decisive movements of a man fighting the urge to buy a drink he can't afford, the destitute fisherman turned on his heel and exited.

Saf counted to five before getting up after him. The inn-keep grunted an absentminded *g'night* before the door fell shut behind her. She spotted the sailor in a narrow alley between two slanting wooden houses. Two steps later, he'd vanished into the gloom.

As she trailed the man, following his footsteps in the mud, she planned her approach. Money was one incentive, of course, but it always served to have two or three combined. Using one's stores economically was a subtle, but surefire mark of a great sigilist.

## CHAPTER 44

She halted as the man leaned against a palm tree at the seafront. He just stood there, staring at the moonlit waves. *Sentimental, check.* A cover story began forming in the back of her mind.

They trudged onward along an exposed stretch of beach. Saf touched *Leve*, muffling the sound of her steps. She was out in the open now. If the man looked back, she needed to be ready to strike.

He didn't. Instead, he sauntered onto a rickety pontoon, beside which a handful of tiny fishing vessels were moored. All of them were decades past their prime, but none more so than the flaky green and white bundle of driftwood that the fisherman hopped onto.

As she approached, the man reached for a piece of parchment that had been nailed to the ship's mast. Without reading, he snatched it, crumpled it up, and cast it aside. He spat angrily into the sea, muttering curses more colorful than any Acheron could come up with on his worst days.

"Excuse me."

The man's head jerked around as Saf approached, waving. She added a little rigidity to her step, as though she were nervous.

"What do you want?" he barked, brown eyes narrowing with suspicion. His eyes scanned the beach, like he was expecting an ambush.

"My apologies. I didn't mean to startle you." She put on a smile. "There's something I wanted to ask you."

"It couldn't wait until daylight?" Though he spoke curtly, his shoulders relaxed. The hard, porous skin on his brow betrayed many years of braving the elements.

"I'm afraid it can't, sir."

"No one's called me sir in decades." The sailor waved a dismissive hand. A smile twisted the corners of his mouth. "Call me Smet."

Saf nodded eagerly.

"Now," Smet added, "what d'you need at this Heilforsaken hour?"

A fork in the road. Smet seemed like the type of man to get annoyed when people beat around the bush. At the same time, Saf wanted to pace him through her demands. Unloading them all at once would shock him into refusing them outright. As a rule, she tried to avoid direct coercion wherever possible. It was always preferable to grant people the illusion of self-determination.

"I need to charter a ship for an urgent journey." She maintained eye contact, touching *Consol* just enough to make him want to help her, while producing only a glimmer in her eye that Smet could explain away as a trick of the moonlight.

"That so?"

"It's my hus—" She made a last-minute tweak as she noticed Smet's barren ring finger. It couldn't hurt to keep her options open. "My brother. He's stationed overseas. We haven't seen him for ages, and our father has fallen gravely ill. We need him at home, but none of our letters seem to reach him."

"Sorry to hear about that." Smet swallowed, switching his weight from one foot to the next. "But I don't know if I'm the man to be asking, young miss. My *Deandra* has her best days behind her. One halfway decent storm could be the end of her."

*And everyone on board,* Saf thought, suppressing a shudder. She'd never liked seafaring, and the soft groans of the *Deandra*'s mast swaying in the breeze made her meager dinner swirl around in her stomach.

On the deck, just behind Smet, lay the piece of parchment he'd so furiously discarded before he noticed Saf was there. The wrinkled heading read "Notice of Disownment," below which Saf could vaguely make out a stamp of two crossed scepters. *Looks like our friend Smet is feeling the weight of the scepter's boot. Interesting.*

"I'm sorry," she said, covering her eyes to wipe at feigned tears. She flared *Rhetoris* to add urgency to her voice. "It's just that I need to speak with him personally." She pretended to hesitate.

"I don't trust these Reynziels anymore. They keep saying they'll deliver my letters, but it's been months. Months. It'd be an inconvenience to the watch if my brother had to return home. I bet that's why they keep him in the dark."

Smet rubbed his calloused hands together. "That's dangerous talk, miss... What did you say your name was again?"

"Rubine." Saf curtsied halfheartedly. "Rubine Grichard."

"Grichard, eh?" Smet's eyes narrowed.

Saf nodded. The Grichards were one of a dozen titled families who tilled the harsh lands in the center of Hammerstroke. If Smet had by some chance heard of them, it would take months, if not years, before he realized the deceit.

"Your *da* once lent me three dozen shards after a cyclone tore all my nets to shreds. Decent man." To Saf's horror, the old captain's mouth twitched as though he were suppressing tears. "Don't surprise me nothing to hear

## CHAPTER 44

the scepter's playing a trick on one of their own again. A man can break his back paying taxes his whole life, and then when he needs a little wind in the sails, those greedy bastards go and send the sharks after 'im."

He stomped on the ball of parchment, grinding the heel of his boot into it.

"Aye," he said, "I'll help. One good turn deserves another. And it sure as Heil won't be coming from those tin-headed automatons in Mallion's Depth. Enlightened Watch, my arse. Where'd you need to go?"

"Snake Island." Saf swallowed. This was where things got tricky.

Smet's eyes widened. He took a step back and leaned against the deck railing, shaking his head. Behind him, the second chariot arose from the ocean, ready for its nightly race against its brighter companion. Saf couldn't help but smile as a familiar sense of peace overcame her at the sight.

"What in the Keeper's name is that boy doing up there?" Smet spat. "An ugly place if ever I've seen one."

"You know it?" Saf pried innocently.

"Not by choice, believe you me. Many years ago, I passed it when I still fished for diamond scale crabs in those waters." He plucked a wad of tobacco out of his inner pocket and began chewing it vigorously. "I don't care what those poor bastards did. Nobody deserves *that*. Sweating under the boiling sun, acres on acres of herz to maintain, all by hand."

Saf's fingers instinctively found the raised brand on her forearm. She rubbed at it, feeling the old rage boil deep inside like magma struggling to reach the surface.

"That sounds terrible."

"That's because it is." Smet spat the glob of tobacco overboard.

"When they shipped Matheo there, he did not know where he was going," Saf improvised. "You have to help me get him away from there."

Smet sighed.

Before he could open his mouth to speak, Saf produced the pouch containing fifteen shards from her belt loop. She held it out to Smet. "Our family would be most grateful."

Smet took the pouch and tucked it away without looking inside. A roguish grin appeared on his withered face.

"Eh, Heil be damned, what's the worst that could happen?"

# CHAPTER 45

*12th day of the 1st cycle, 570KR*
**Splitcrack Gorge**

A deep screech, like a sword slicing across an empty suit of plate, woke Brina from the state of half-sleep she'd dozed off to. She twisted onto her stomach, fingers wrapped around her dagger. A peremptory glance showed her immediate surroundings to be deserted. *I am safe.* She took a deep breath, trying to shake off the jittery rush of adrenaline that rattled in her bones.

Then she heard it again, up on the hillside. It was loud like a war horn, piercing like a quarrel to the gut. In between the griffin's cries, there was a second, high-pitched sound. *Screaming.*

Brina took off at a run, her windup clutched tightly against her chest. She leapt across a fallen tree and found herself back on the trail. As the dense forest fell away around her, her legs locked up with hesitation. It was right there, hanging between the twin spires.

A black outline against the rising dawn. The griffin's massive wings beat slowly, keeping it high in the air. Trapped in its steel claws, a small humanoid figure writhed and kicked. If the voice hadn't been that of an adult man, Brina would have mistaken him for a child.

Near the top of the hill, a column of dark smoke rose where the fire had been hours prior. Shaking her head at the sheer idiocy, Brina forced herself up the steep incline to get closer to the griffin and its prey.

As she crested the hill, a second man came into view. He stood beside the remains of the fire, aiming a gilded windup into the sky. The sapphire studs on his black leather armor glimmered in the rising sun. *Mattheus.*

Brina flung herself behind a boulder just as her pounding footsteps made him glance backward. Fortunately, renewed yelling from his compatriot

## CHAPTER 45

drew Mattheus's attention away. Brina cursed herself. *Might as well have impaled myself on his quarrel.*

She edged sideways behind a lone thicket of brambles to ensure she was completely out of Mattheus's view before peering through the spyglass mounted to her bow. She recognized the unfortunate soul clutched in the griffin's claws as the man with the bristly beard whose shoulder she had broken on the night of the Scarlet Nocturne. *Serves him right,* she thought bitterly. *Let's hope the beast has room for seconds.*

"Don't shoot," Bristlebeard howled, waving a weak arm. "It'll drop me."

"What else can I do?" Mattheus called out. "It won't come closer." Brina was pleased to hear the panic in Mattheus's voice. *Sounds like you finally met your match.*

"I don't bloody know, do I?" There was a scream as the griffin's claws pierced Bristlebeard's belly, followed by the *thwack* of a bowstring being released. There was the susurrus of the quarrel, then a rush of wind as the griffin dove toward Mattheus. Its vast bulk plummeted in a vertical descent.

For a moment, it looked like the creature might have miscalculated. Brina winced, anticipating the crunch of shattering bone. It pulled out of the dive at the very last second, relinquishing Bristlebeard as it did so.

The man's body shot through the air like a projectile. Mattheus's eyes widened in shock as his compatriot's dumb weight struck his chest. There was a dull thud, and both men crumpled without a sound, their bodies broken. Brina's heart raced, her mind struggling to catch up with what she'd just witnessed. Mattheus was dead.

She had fantasized about this moment for nights on end after she'd woken up mangled and bruised in Acheron's tomb. She'd imagined it happening a hundred different ways, each time anticipating the relief and satisfaction that would come alongside the prick's demise. But now that it had happened right in front of her, it felt just like any other untimely death she'd witnessed over the years. Pointless and wasteful. Nothing had changed. No slights were set right. It was just over.

A gust wafted over her as the griffin touched down beside its prey. It flapped its wings once, then dug its beak into Bristlebeard's back, tearing at the flesh with animal indifference. *Now is my chance.*

She raised the windup, aiming right between the beast's eyes. Her hand strayed toward the trigger, then lingered there. A single squeeze, and it would all be over.

The griffin, unaware of the imminent danger that awaited it, flapped its wings lazily. A shower of gold and obsidian sparkled against the sun like a waterfall of molten metals. Brina hesitated.

It had done nothing wrong. Defending its territory was in its nature.

Brina's jaw tensed, bile rising in the back of her throat. It cost all of her self-control not to scream in frustration. *Just do it. Pull. The. Damned. Trigger.* The windup homed in on its target once more.

There was a spluttering sound from the camp ahead.

"No... get away... shoo..."

*He's alive.* Brina's windup drooped to her side, forgotten. The griffin's head cocked sideways as it considered the figure that had stirred underneath its claws. The steel beak slammed down right where Mattheus's head had been a fraction of a second prior. Mattheus jerked a single arm free from underneath Bristlebeard's dead weight. He pulled and pushed at the corpse on top of him with panicked fervor. It wouldn't budge. The griffin's beak struck at him a second time, missing by inches.

Brina jumped to her feet and charged.

"Back off," she yelled at the beast, acutely aware of how catastrophically stupid this was. "Go on. Take off."

She waved the windup in the air.

"Springtide?" Mattheus muttered. "What are you...?"

"I don't bloody know."

The griffin reared back on its hind legs, screeching and bucking. Its beak snapped at Brina, who sidestepped the attack with ease.

"No." She raised a hand. "You will not harm him." Acting on instinct and fueled by sheer terror, she flared *Consol* so intensely that the shape momentarily blinded her as it appeared in her mind's eye. Then it shifted. Instead of the usual chaotic overlap between sigil and vision, she could see both at once, neither taking away clarity from the other. The partial blackness left behind by the absence of sight in her dead eye burst into life with the bends and curls of *Consol*. A power unlike any she'd ever felt flowed through her.

The griffin fell silent, observing her every movement.

"Good," Brina heard herself saying, "let's calm down, shall we? No one needs to get hurt."

To her astonishment, the beast relaxed.

With a confidence that was alien to her, Brina approached the creature, her hands stretched out toward its golden head.

"Steady," she murmured as her hand contacted its silky plumage.

## CHAPTER 45

The griffin nudged its beak against her hand as though encouraging her to continue.

For a moment, they were one. The griffin's crimson eye and Brina's purple one linked in an understanding that couldn't be trapped in the mold of words. Then she looked down and spotted its front left claw. It was missing half of its middle toe.

"Razorwing. I can't believe it." She stared into the creature's face and saw a spark of recognition. "You wait here, okay?"

She backed away from Razorwing, keeping her eye on him for as long as she could, worried that their moment of peace would be over as soon as she broke eye contact.

"Can you stand?" she asked Mattheus out of the corner of her mouth, not daring to look down at him.

"Not a chance," he groaned. "I think I'm dying, Springtide. I can't feel a thing."

She dragged Bristlebeard's bloody corpse aside, hoping it would give the blond roamer room to breathe. "Better?"

"It's no use." Mattheus coughed up a spray of blood. "I'm sorry. About everything."

"Don't—"

"No," he urged. "I mean it. Some Heilinist, a woman named Medina, cornered me while I was drinking at the Squiggly Squid. She knew about our"—he coughed—"disagreement at the Chimera. Asked me all kinds of questions. Paid for the answers, too."

Brina's eyes flicked down at the Mattheus's pale face involuntarily. Razorwing stayed where he was.

"What?"

"It was strange," Mattheus rambled, a trickle of blood drooping from the corner of his mouth. "She wanted to know what that trinket I tried to steal looked like. Whether I knew where you had gotten it, and so on.

"I told her what I knew. I was angry and embarrassed, so I figured I could at least make some money off the whole thing. She kept buying me drinks."

"Then what?" Brina knelt down, resisting the urge to grab Mattheus by the collar.

"When we were done, she said she'd pay me five thousand shards if I could bring her proof of your death..." He trailed off, staring through Brina with wide eyes.

"So you weren't lying that day at the Chimera," Brina said. "Someone *did* pay you."

Mattheus nodded with great effort. "It was stupid. You bruised my ego, that was all. I acted like a coward."

He spat a glob of blood onto the ground beside him. His whole body shivered as the last ounce of color drained from his face.

There was a scratching noise as Razorwing approached. The griffin nudged its beak against Brina's elbow, demanding attention. She scratched at its pointy ear absentmindedly, her mind whirring with everything she had just learned.

"Guess you were right after all, eh? I mean, who does that?" Mattheus let out a gurgling chuckle. "Who in their right mind pets a griffin like it's a parrot?"

"Someone who sees them as beings rather than walking gem dust," she said, tracing a finger down the black stripe between Razorwing's eyes.

"Are you going to let that thing eat me once I croak?" Mattheus eyed Razorwing with a mixture of apprehension and delirious mirth.

Brina sighed. *I'm going to kick myself for this one.* She got down on one knee and removed the pyramid's chain from around her neck.

"Look at this," she said. "Focus on the patterns like they're the last thing you'll ever see, or they *will* be the last thing you ever see. Understood?"

Mattheus's eyes widened as he took in the twists and curves of the pyramid.

"So it was demonic after all," he said, smiling faintly as his eyes turned red and the healing began. "The Reynziels are wrong about this. It's not half bad." As soon as the tiniest bit of color returned to his face, Mattheus's features contorted in shock.

"I almost forgot. There's something in my chest pocket you need to see. Now."

He raised an arm, which shook, then collapsed into the dust. Brina bent forward and reached into Mattheus's armor. Her chest tightened as she pulled out a folded piece of scarlet parchment.

"They moved it up," Mattheus muttered. "They want your father dead the day after next."

# CHAPTER 46

*12th day of the 1st cycle, 570KR*
**Hammerstroke**

Terror and exhilaration warred inside Brina as she soared above the dense jungle, her fingers wrapped tightly around the feathers in Razorwing's neck. To her left, the stoneward traced a white ring through the landscape, enclosing thousands of red-tiled roofs.

Ahead, the trees opened into the rolling hills of Barrow's Perch, behind which the waters of Mallion's Bay shimmered in the rising dawn.

De Malheur's fortress wasn't far now.

"How are we going to land this thing?" Mattheus groaned. His grip on Brina's shoulder was weak, and she could feel his whole body shiver.

"Razorwing has been doing this all his life," she shouted back. "He'll manage." *I hope.*

Flying the griffin was like paddling a raft down white water rapids. You could fight the current all you wanted, but in the end, it was up to the river to decide the journey's destination.

She almost missed the fortress as it flooded past underneath them, hidden amongst the trees. Brina yanked a handful of feathers in the griffin's neck to get the bird to lower its course, but all she got in response was a reproachful squawk. The fortress disappeared behind them. *Uh oh.*

"Do that voice thing again," Mattheus croaked. "It listens to you."

"Oh. Right." Brina cleared her throat, digging deep to find what little remained of her *Consol* store. "Razorwing, turn. Head for the top of that square tower."

At once, the griffin fell into a steep descent. Brina ducked as treetops whirred by dangerously close on either side of them. The jagged stone facade of the fortress loomed up ahead of them.

"We're too low." Mattheus let out a howl as the masonry rushed forward to meet them.

At the last second, Razorwing folded his wings and hopped onto the battlements of the tower with the light grace of a butterfly touching down on a flower petal.

"Never again." Mattheus slumped sideways, kept on Razorwing's back only by a swift reaction on Brina's part. There was a bluish hue to his lips, and pearls of sweat clustered on his pale forehead.

Brina slid off the griffin's back and half pulled, half carried Mattheus down after her. He staggered but stayed on his feet.

"You did great," Brina told Razorwing, stroking the creature's smooth obsidian beak. "I'll get you something to eat later, but first there's urgent business." She felt foolish talking to the beast, but it seemed to take her general meaning all the same.

Razorwing clicked its beak twice, then curled up against the battlements and laid its head down.

Getting Mattheus down the spiraling wooden staircase proved to be an epic struggle worthy of song. He kept stumbling and slipping, leaning more heavily on Brina's shoulder with every step.

"Come on, you sack of rocks," Brina panted. "You're not even trying."

"Oh," Mattheus spat, "I forgot I was supposed to *try*. Silly me, let me just fix my broken ribs by *trying*."

A door opened on the landing below.

"Kid, is that you?" Acheron called.

Before she could call back, Acheron came up on the stairs below them. There were dark stains underneath his eyes, and his black robe looked like an army had used it as a doormat. From the looks of it, he hadn't slept a wink all night.

"What is *that* doing here?" He glared from Mattheus to Brina and back several times, incredulity and disgust trading places on his face.

"*You.*" Mattheus muttered, eyes wide with terror. He gave a shudder and promptly fainted.

"Happy reunions can wait." Brina waved a hand. "There are more pressing matters to discuss. Help me get him down."

Together, they dragged Mattheus down the stairs. The back of the roamer's head kept banging against the steps, but Acheron seemed not to notice.

"So what's this great emergency?" Acheron asked as they dropped Mattheus on a sofa in De Malheur's library.

## CHAPTER 46

Brina swallowed. Rather than forcing herself to say the words out loud, she pressed the scarlet pamphlet into Acheron's hands.

"This is a disaster." The muscles in Acheron's jaw clenched. What felt like an era of silence slipped by. The unspoken knowledge that they were far from ready to go through with the plan hung between them like the buzz of static before a thunderstorm. "We should call a meeting. Right now."

Brina nodded. "Saf will know..." she trailed off, remembering that Saf, the rallying force of the group, was gone. Brina shook her head as her worry turned to despair. How could it all have gone so catastrophically wrong?

"I'll rouse the others," Acheron said, placing a hand on her shoulder. "Eat something. Have a drink. There must be a way around this, and believe me, we'll find it."

\*\*\*

*10th day of the 1st cycle, 570KR*
**Northern Sea**

'My, my. Hey, miss, why don't you come have a look at this?'

Saf tucked her notebook away in her inside pocket and joined Smet at the edge of the *Deandra*'s deck. The northern edges of the Sundered Isles were as beautiful as they were treacherous. Craggy spires of basalt rock rose from the water like the pillars framing the temples of old.

One lapse of attention and even experienced sailors could run their ships aground in these parts. Countless tiny islands and sandbanks were scattered throughout the region, though most comprised nothing but white beaches and a few clumps of overgrown palm trees.

Ancient historians had deemed the area to be of great historical value. Hundreds of wrecked ships and their passengers littered the seabed, while ruins of former habitation could in some places be seen below the surface. The very seeds of human civilization lay buried here. Many intellectuals of the late royal period had predicted great technological advances would be made once the area had given up its secrets.

What they couldn't have foreseen, however, was the crushing rise of the Church of Heil. No excavations had been allowed here for five centuries, and that wasn't about to change. *Wouldn't want to remind people that there was a time where the Sundered Isles were as diverse as they were free,* Saf thought bitterly.

"Heil almighty, lass," Smet said, tapping her on the shoulder, "I thought you would at least be somewhat interested. It's not every day you get to see one up close."

"I'm sorry," Saf said, shaking the onslaught of thoughts out of her head. "What were you trying to show me?"

"This." Smet pointed.

A massive tree trunk floated just underneath the surface, bobbing up and down in the current. It was at least twice as long as the *Deandra*, and a good three feet thick. Black and white barnacles encrusted its smooth outer bark in massive clumps.

Then the tree trunk moved. It rippled. The *Deandra* swayed violently as the trunk breached the surface. It glistened in the sunlight, rising a good five feet out of the water before slamming down again. *That's not a tree.*

Saf gripped the splintery railing as two long rows of suckers opened and closed, making horrible squelching noises.

"Smet," she said, failing to keep her voice level. "Tell me that's not what I think it is."

"A leviathan, yep," Smet said, grinning from ear to ear. He reached with a gnarled hand and petted the enormous tentacle, rubbing its outer skin in smooth circular motions. "This one must have been terribly disturbed for it to come this close to the surface."

Saf watched him with apprehension. She imagined her guide disappearing into the depths in a whirl of tentacles and countless oversized teeth. Smet, on the other hand, merely grinned at the beast as though he petted one every day.

"Shame," he muttered, as much to himself as to Saf. "It's all those damn redsails prancing up and down the coast these days. It riles these poor creatures up to no end. All the noise, the disturbance of the water."

He shook his head.

"Gone are the days when one could come out here to get away from all the nattering and the posturing."

Saf watched the man's expression intently. If he suspected that he'd been lied to, he might very well be baiting Saf into making incriminating statements regarding the church. She settled for playing dumb.

"What do you mean?"

Smet let go of the tentacle, and it slid back underneath the surface.

"A storm's brewing," he snapped suddenly. "That's what I mean. Sure, there's always been a few patrols here and there, but never like this.

"Cardinal De Leliard is no longer content merely maintaining our borders, it seems. The ports at Barangia and Onderheem have filled to

# CHAPTER 46

the brim with watchers double- and triple-checking every signature on a man's papers like they suspect their own citizens of treason.

"Mark my words." Smet spat into the ocean. "Once a cardinal's pride swells too much, war is sure to follow."

An unexpected wave of sympathy for the old sailor overcame Saf. It was easy—too easy—to forget that not all titled citizens were the enemy. It hadn't been Smet holding the whip in the slave colony, nor had he been the one who had ordered Doorstep's Ditch burned to the ground.

"You don't want the old borders restored?"

"What do I care about borders?" The sailor shrugged. "In my years as a deckhand, I've worked with Heemians, Hawqallians, Biori, the lot. Never mattered nothing to me what man called himself their ruler."

"No," he grunted, shaking his head, "if you ask me, things can only get worse from here."

"It always does before something really changes," Saf replied, staring out at the distant speck of green she knew to be Snake Island. "The pot needs to boil before the stew is made."

Smet gave her a sideways glare.

"You seem to know a great deal about these things, for a farm girl."

"Just something someone told me once." *Before they pressed the brand into my skin.*

# CHAPTER 47

*10th day of the 1st cycle, 570KR*
**Snake Island**

he first thing Saf heard was the clinking. The ceaseless battering of a hundred hammers on a hundred anvils, like the rattling cogs of a ravenous automaton.

Next came the smoke. Thick plumes of black snaking their way through a perfect azure morning sky. Even from her hideout in a clump of dense reeds, she could feel it prickle in her nostrils and seep into the fabric of her robe.

The Snake Island slave colony had changed. Gone were the endless rows of golden herz stalks and the muddy irrigation ditches that ran through them like the lines in a hand palm. Gone were the sickles, and the baskets, and the rhythmic humming of slaves going about their labor. Song had been the one luxury the darkhelms had allowed in Saf's years on the field. Now even that had been stripped away.

She crept along a muddy creek that ran straight to the back of a giant barn that served as a bunkhouse for the slaves. Men, woman, and children, all squished between the same narrow walls. As she neared the island's center, the vegetation thinned for a span, and Saf's mouth fell open.

Three furnaces, each large enough to fit two fully grown oxen, stood side by side. On either side of them, two mountains of coal and iron ore were piled up underneath half-open wooden shelters. Each of them must have been over twenty feet high.

Soot-stained workers trudged up and down with wheelbarrows loaded to the breaking point. Three streams of molten steel flooded through stone gutters into separate containers, where darkhelms wearing thick leather gloves and aprons filled one mold after another.

Further down the line, dozens of prisoners were hammering away at

## CHAPTER 47

wonky anvils, forging swords, daggers, and steel studs for leather armor by the crate.

*They're preparing for war.* Saf gulped down a mouthful of acrid air. Her eyes teared up as it burned in her lungs.

Crate after crate of weaponry was hauled away on ox-drawn carts and stashed in a warehouse further up on the hill, where a fortified castle presided over Snake Island like a king on a towering throne.

Saf huddled between two overgrown blackberry bushes, heart racing. De Leliard was moving rashly, and faster than anyone could have predicted. Depending on how long this operation had been running, he could already have enough sharpened steel to arm a dozen legions of darkhelms.

The raid on Doorstep's Ditch had only been the beginning, a sinister prelude to a devastating symphony of violence that was about to sweep over the sundered lands with the force of a rogue wave.

Bior's troops had been bleeding numbers for decades. Archdruidess Evana of Morrassia had slowly but surely been driven back to the very core of her fortifications in the densest parts of the Morassian swamps. And Hawqal? They would sell the territories on their eastern shores to the highest bidder and keep their oil-smoothened hands out of the fire. None of them were prepared for a large-scale assault, and while De Leliard shifted his pawns into strategic positions, they risked being caught unawares.

*We have to warn them.* But what did that mean for her plans here? She had already sent Smet on his way, insisting that she'd find her own way home. She had come all this way to take revenge on the institution that had trapped and exploited her for years, to help those who were in the same situation now.

However, if she got herself captured or killed, there would be no one to warn the other nations of the impending threat of De Leliard's armies. The Sundered Isles would be swept under the scepter's rule in one fell stroke. Thousands would perish, and even more would be forced into slavery.

But who else would care about the fate of those being worked to death in a remote slave colony?

Acheron hadn't been doing the math that night he and the Signum had freed her all those years ago. He'd done it because he knew nobody else would. He hadn't turned a blind eye to her suffering. She wouldn't do so now. *I'll just have to aim for two birds with one stone.*

Saf knelt down, unfastened a leather pouch from the inside of her robe, and retrieved the handful of scripts she'd brought with her.

She placed them in a circle around her and began her preparations.

***

### 12th day of the 1st cycle, 570KR
### Fortress De Malheur

"We won't get in," Sneak said, scratching at his forehead. "All we know is that the prison receives provisions roughly once a week, but so far it's never been the same day, nor the same ship. There's nothing to go on."

Brina sighed. They sat around the long table in De Malheur's dining hall, leaning over their woefully incomplete map of God's Maul. Their brainstorming session was rapidly descending into a brain freeze as they came to terms with the impossibility of the task at hand.

"The best laid plans shatter at the tip of an enemy spear." Bron waved his hands dismissively. "I say we sharpen our own and get to work."

Brina gave the Biori an approving nod, grateful that at least one of them still possessed an ounce of courage.

"I've got an idea, but it'll need some work." Brina turned toward Zot, who reclined in his seat at the far end of the table with the air of a man observing a rather uneventful play. "In your long, illustrious career as king of the no-goods, have you ever resorted to setting a fire?"

Zot shrugged. "Once or twice."

"Do you think you can get me in touch with an expert?"

"I could," he began slowly, "but they're a somewhat volatile type. It could end poorly."

"Oh, I'm counting on it." Brina grinned.

"Suit yourself," he said, getting to his feet. He bent forward and wrote something down on a corner of the parchment map, then tore it off and flung it at Brina. "Here. That's everything you need to know. Tell her I sent you. There's a fifty-fifty chance that'll convince her not to incinerate you on sight."

"Where do you think you're going?" Acheron snapped as Zot started walking toward the dining hall's door.

"To get us a ship." Zot raised his eyebrows. "Or are you planning on swimming?"

"How much money do you need?" Brina asked, her hand straying toward the pouch on her hip.

## CHAPTER 47

"Money?" Zot cackled. "The hour has grown too late for that. I'm going to need to cut some corners and burn a couple of bridges."

He jabbed a finger at Harrod Wane, who sat beside Sneak, fiddling with a pocketknife. "You're with me, wallboy."

"Me?" Wane stammered, eyes growing to a size that could make the pale chariots insecure.

"Don't make me repeat myself." Zot strode toward the dining hall door. He turned towards the others. "Meet us in the cove near Turncoat's Pike at sunset."

With Wane in tow, Zot vanished down the hallway. Moments later, the front door slammed.

"So." Acheron cleared his throat. "Back to the matter at hand.

"Versa has been trying to remember some of what we can expect of God's Maul once we pass through the front gate." He pointed at a few shaky lines on a previously blank section of the map. "That's the good news. The bad news is that everything they've remembered so far bodes ill for us.

"Once we pass underneath the metal grate *here*"—he illustrated with his index finger—"we'll be stuck amongst nothing but smooth rock until the guards open a passage *here*, from within."

"So if they smell trouble," Sneak said, rubbing his temples, "we—"

"Will be trapped like firejellies in a lamp." Acheron supplied. "So you better dust off that wallborn accent of yours and sell it like a merchant with a gambling problem."

"Divine, Murio Acheron," Sneak replied in a haughty, and thoroughly over-the-top wallfolk accent. "Last time I employed such conversational tonalities, I merely proceeded to get the whole of Mallion's Depth locked down. I would be hard pressed to attain an even less favorable outcome this time."

"Blood of my mothers, we are dead men walking." Bron shook his head tragically, drawing a chuckle from Brina.

"Not to worry," Acheron boomed on. "After that there's only the minor issue of a hundred identical corridors leading nowhere. According to the innkeeper, only a select subclass of guards known as navigators are aware of the intricacies of the system."

"If only Saf were here," Sneak said. "She'd have a dozen of them singing songs as they brought us wherever we wanted to go. I've never quite gotten the hang of psychosigils."

"Nor has anyone else. Not like Saphara Al Noor has mastered them,"

Acheron said. "We will have to resort to such crude measures as hostage taking."

"There might be another way."

All of them whipped round in their chairs to stare at the newcomer. Versa clutched the doorframe, swaying on their feet. The simple wooden mask Brina had carved for them was visible deep inside the black hood of their cloak. They looked thinner than Brina had ever seen them, but they were up. She rushed toward her old friend to offer an arm.

"The warden keeps a ledger of all the prisoners' details, including the number of their cell and, possibly, the path that leads to it."

"How do you know?" Bron asked.

"The guards brought me into his office on multiple occasions to sign my confessions. On one of them, he had my file open on his desk."

Brina tensed as she noticed Acheron's narrowing eyes. If he were to find out, or even suspect, what Versa had told the church, there was no telling what he might do. That confession was the rolling pebble that had triggered the avalanche that had swept away everything and everyone Acheron had cared about.

"The cell blocks themselves are divided over five towers, each of which is guarded by a dedicated regiment of guards. I was in Locktower A, and as far as I could tell, none of the captured Signum-members were assigned to my block. Of course, Abrasax might have been reassigned in the years since."

"Interesting," Acheron said. He motioned for Versa to take a seat. "Very interesting. What else can you tell us about the guards' daily routine?"

As Versa recounted every detail about daily life in the prison as they remembered it, Brina slipped out of the dining hall and back up the main tower.

A sigh of relief escaped her when she found Razorwing still lying against the ramparts. "Good griffin," Brina said. She touched *Consol* as she knelt beside the bird and offered it the last of De Malheur's smoked hams. "We might need your help again soon. Do you think you're up to it?"

The griffin clicked its beak, then blinked.

# CHAPTER 48

*12th day of the 1st cycle, 570KR*
**The Enclave - Doorstep's Ditch**

"Act natural, wallboy," Zot said out of the corner of his mouth. "There are more darkhelms on these walls than skeletons in a Reynziel's closet."

Zot feigned a sudden interest in the laces of his leather boots as he and the boy passed through the gilded Enclave gates. It would only take one glance, a spark of recognition, to ruin his day.

Though a handful of stores were open, the paved square was deserted. There probably wasn't a single outwalled left who had gem dust to spare for anything other than bread and cheap kelp. Not with half the town in ashes and the other half besieged by an army of newly homeless sods begging, borrowing, and stealing to survive.

Crimson pamphlets were plastered across store windows, doors, and the reinforced wall itself.

"Where are we going?" Wane asked. The boy stared wide-eyed at the dozens of darkhelms in gleaming steel armor patrolling above their heads.

"What did I say about asking questions?" Zot hissed.

The boy fell silent, though undoubtedly not for long.

Light flickered beyond the window of Huygen's Herbs and Tinctures. Of course, it was open. Old Huygen probably hadn't even noticed all the death and destruction just outside his door.

A bell tinkled as Zot opened the door, ushering in the boy ahead of him. The sharp scent of ginger pricked in his nostrils as the door closed behind them. What a man would give for a vial of sandalwood perfume.

Huygen was nowhere to be seen.

Zot marched between shelves stacked with all sorts of unsavory body parts and foul-smelling plants. He sauntered up to the desk with the boy in tow, then dipped behind the counter.

"I don't think we're supposed to go back there," Wane piped up.

Zot smiled to hide his growing annoyance with the boy's uninvited opinions. "I think Mr. Huygen will forgive us an indiscretion or two."

They found him sitting on a stool, slumped forward onto his workbench, a monstrous dead spider floating in a glass bowl beside him. Clutched in Huygen's hand was a ticking timepiece.

"Sick." Wane grimaced as he took in the scene.

"For once, we are in agreement," Zot said. Even in his better years, Huygen had been a distasteful creature, but recently the onset of senility had unleashed a vileness within him that even Zot found hard to stomach. That Huygen paid him a generous monthly dividend did little to assuage his disdain.

He grabbed the old man by the shoulder and shook him.

"Wake up, Karoling," he cooed in singsong tones. "Time to go to work, you malignant old coot."

Huygen started. He gazed at the drowned spider with ill-disguised hunger ravaging his face. "Forty-seven minutes," he chortled. "A new record." Then he noticed he was not alone.

"What—who?" He looked up into Zot's eyes with just the right dose of fear visible in the lines of his face.

"The time has come," Zot said. "I need passage."

"Now?" Huygen looked from Zot to Wane, his greedy eyes shrinking.

"Now." Zot pulled the stool from under Huygen's useless bones, forcing him to his feet. "Get to it."

"And what's in it for me?"

Zot's mouth fell open. The codger's mind really must be on its way out. "Because I own this place, Karoling. And I own you. Now get to it, before I decide my interests would be better served under new management."

Huygen grumbled something, but at least he had the decency to do it under his breath. He hobbled toward an old wardrobe. Shoving aside a stack of moth-eaten doublets that hadn't been in fashion since the sundering, he uncovered a fist-sized hole in the wardrobe's back wall.

"Two coming through, Borsavo," Huygen yelled into the hole. Then he bent down, his joints clicking and snapping, and removed the wooden bottom.

"There you go, master Zot," he said with the tone of a man who'd just

## CHAPTER 48

been forced to eat his own excrement. "Borsavo will let you out on the other side."

Zot shoved the Wane boy toward the hole and gestured for him to go ahead. As soon as the boy was out of earshot, Zot grabbed Huygen by the front of his robes.

"By the Seven, man. This is a store, not a torture chamber," he hissed, forcing Huygen to look at the dead spider in the bowl. "I'm going to be sending people to check up on you, and they better not find you doing any more of these *experiments*."

Huygen gave him an insolent look that didn't much please him.

He backhanded the old man across the face. "Do I make myself clear?"

"Yes," Huygen muttered. He spat a mouthful of blood onto the tiled floor.

"Good."

Zot lowered himself into the passage, where he found the kid waiting.

"Go on." He gave the kid a push in the right direction. "What are you waiting for?"

"How do you know he won't report us to the darkhelms?"

Zot considered this for a moment, then grinned. The kid was quick on the uptake. "Now that you mention it, he's definitely stupid enough to try that. We better hurry along."

As he watched the kid crawl out through a gap on the other side of the passageway, he smiled. The boy was sharp. Just like Zot himself had been at that age. He had a bright future ahead of him, that one. Provided he was surrounded by the right people. Zot wasn't sure whether he qualified under that category. He didn't have the best track record when it came to child rearing.

They clambered out of the tunnel and into a seedy pub on the outskirts of Mallion's Depth. The owner, a heavyset, bearded man named Borsavo, glared after them as they left without pausing for a drink.

Wane looked at the sandstone houses with their clay shingle roofs with something akin to wonder. Multiple times, Zot caught the boy staring down alleys, a longing look on his face.

"You miss it," Zot said.

Wane nodded, then shook his head. "I don't miss the fear," he said. "Everyone's so uptight in the city. Everything needs to be perfect all the time, *or else.*" He mimed a disapproving finger.

"I know what you mean," Zot said. "The other side of the wall is brutal and filthy, but it feels more honest, doesn't it?"

"Exactly." Wane laughed, then his face fell. "I miss Madame Arturia's home, though. I miss my family."

Zot dug deep, feigning a callousness he didn't feel.

"That will have to wait, boy. We have business to attend to. Business that could end up shaping the way all our families live."

The kid wiped away a stray tear with the back of his hand. "Yes," he said. "They will understand how important this is."

"That's right," Zot said, placing a hand on the boy's shoulder. He was pleased when Wane didn't shake it off immediately.

Before they knew it, the tightly wound streets opened up into the largest industrial port on this side of Hawqal. Four long stone docks extended a quarter mile each into the open sea. Vessels from all over the known world moored here every week. Many of which had done so on Zot's orders, carrying everything one could sell for a profit. Not least among them, blocks of cloud straight from the deserts.

He began walking down the first dock, inspecting each of the ships they passed. First, they'd need to find a suitable target on the far side of the docks, then... well, then the improvisation would begin. A shiver of anticipation ran down Zot's spine. It'd been years since he had pulled a job in person. *It's like swimming,* he told himself. *Once you throw yourself into the deep end, you'll find a way to keep your head above water.*

They were strolling down the rightmost pier, when the sun reflected off a gilded figurehead in the distance. Zot's pulse quickened. *It can't be.* Trying desperately not to let his eagerness get the better of him, he picked up the pace, leaving the kid struggling to keep up.

As he approached, the leviathan-shaped figurehead came into focus. Its golden tentacles ran down the ship's bow, as though it was attempting to pull the ship into the abyss. Its single, monstrous eye was made of polished marble, with a solid ruby for a pupil.

The *Yugon.*

Right when he had thought the vessel was lost forever, it fell back into his lap. A dozen sailors scurried back and forth across its deck, loading a cartload of crates and barrels into the hull. Two darkhelms guarded the gangplank, watching.

*Arrogant bastards.* Had they really thought they could steal his ship and then keep it right under his nose? Disrespect, that's what it was. They un-

## CHAPTER 48

derestimated him. Treated him like some teenage hoodlum, too dumb to scratch his own arse with a sapphire shard. Zot's jaw clenched. The sheer gall of it all made him want to stab something.

"It's too big."

Zot whirled round to find Wane shaking his head.

"Not this one," the boy said. "It's the largest ship here. We'll draw too much attention. Besides, we'd need a full crew to even get that beast in motion."

"I'll figure it out."

"But—"

"Who do you think you're talking to, boy?" Zot's jaws clenched. He shouldn't direct his anger at the kid, but damn, was the whiny brat making it difficult. "I'm Dimimzy Zot. I've wriggled my way out of much tighter corners, believe me."

The boy scowled at him. "Fine. Then what's the plan?"

Zot fell silent. What *was* the plan?

\*\*\*

*12th day of the 1st cycle, 570KR*
**Hammerstroke**

Brina strode down the last stretch of the King's Barrow path, pressed forward by the ticking away of what precious little time she had left. With every passing hour, her father's execution rushed forward to meet her.

At the end of the path, Wicket Row ran through Doorstep's Ditch like a black serpent of ash and soot. The lingering stench of smoke made her nostrils burn as she moved through a maze of blackened ruins. The narrow streets were filled with debris and possessions left behind, never to be reclaimed.

Brina drew her hood lower over her face as she passed a group of emaciated men and women huddled around the burning remains of a kitchen cabinet. Their camp was little more than a sopping wet blanket hung over two sections of crumbling wall.

A twist of guilt struck her as her hand brushed the full pouch of savings hidden away under her cloak. *They can't eat gems,* she told herself sternly.

She meandered through the wreckage until she reached the stubby ruin of a tower on the outskirts of the eastern district, which had mostly been spared from the flames, as it was farthest away from the beach.

She glanced up and down the street to ensure it was deserted, then slammed the metal handle of her dagger against the tower's iron door. Three times fast, two times slow. When no one answered, she repeated the pattern. It was only on the fifth time that the sharp smells of lead and mercury escaped through a crack in the door.

"Go away," a gruff female voice barked.

"Dimimzy Zot sent me. I'm sure you know who—"

"I don't care if you were sent by the Cardinal himself."

The door closed. With a flash of *Forte*, Brina jammed her boot into the gap.

"Wait. It's important."

"Not to me." There was a renewed effort from inside to force the door shut, squashing Brina's foot.

"I've got money. Quite a bit of it."

The pulling stopped.

"How much are we talking?"

"That depends on whether you can help me." Brina jangled the purse under her cloak.

"Fine. Get in." A beefy forearm reached out through the crack and yanked Brina inside. The door clicked shut at once. "These aren't times for showing up on people's doorsteps, much less for lingering on them."

The laboratory was lit with two dozen jelly lamps stacked precariously on top of books, boxes, and crooked shelves.

The woman who stood before Brina was built like a dray horse and looked like she could consume one whole without breaking a sweat. She wore a brass device that looked like two spyglasses strapped together, which made her eyes look huge and insect-like. Her tan overalls were covered in soot and riddled with singe marks.

"You must be Miss Haymer," Brina said, recalling the name Zot had written down for her.

"Call me Oppen. I don't care for formalities," the woman snapped. She wiped her sweaty brow, leaving behind a smudge of soot. "What do you want?"

"I'm looking for a device that can be thrown and ignites on impact."

"I see." There was a keen undertone to her voice now. "What are we incinerating, thatch, paneled wood, solid wood, painted, unpainted..."

## CHAPTER 48

When Brina didn't reply, she kept going, her eyebrows traveling further up her forehead with every suggestion.

"... wattle and daub, stone, steel?"

"What I plan to light is my business," Brina said. "Let's just say I need a good deal of zest."

"Zesty it is. When do you need them?"

"This afternoon."

Oppen sighed. She looked wistfully over her shoulder at a beaker half full of a blue liquid that bubbled of its own accord, letting out tiny rings of smoke.

"I was sort of busy," Oppen said with a shrug. "I'm not a big fan of changing plans once I've made them."

"Believe me, Miss Haymer, what I've got planned is a work of art. The kind of sparks that will be spoken of on this island for years to come. You might even get to see part of the show for yourself. Now, can you help me or not?"

Oppen's jowls quivered. "Fine. How many do you need?"

"As many as these will buy me."

Brina untied the heavy pouch that contained every single shard she'd saved up over the past decade and lobbed it at Oppen, who caught it with both hands. Oppen felt the weight of it. For the first time, a grin spread across her face.

"For this kind of compensation, I can do *extra zesty.*"

***

*12th day of the 1st cycle, 570KR*
**Mallion's Depth**

"How's it going, lads?" Zot put a hand on his back, massaging an imaginary hernia. "Rough one out here today, isn't it? That wind cuts like a shark fin through blood-streaked waters."

Both darkhelms turned. Zot could swear he heard one of them sigh underneath that obnoxious, shiny helmet.

"It's not that bad," the left one replied in a baritone that wouldn't have been out of place in an opera hall.

"Ah," Zot breathed, "I see you are men of marble, as my old man used to say. Cheers to that!" He produced a half-empty flask of kelp he'd completely forgotten in his inside pocket and took a feigned swig.

"Can I interest you gentlemen in a little liquid warmth?"

"Won't say no to that," the other darkhelm muttered. He took the flask and made to take a drink.

His colleague stopped him with a hand on the wrist.

"Hang on, Wilhelm." The darkhelm bent down to look at Zot more closely. "How do we know you didn't poison that flask?" Zot imagined a trollish face behind the closed visor, screwed up in an effort to think.

"I just drank from it in front of you, didn't I?" Zot said with mock outrage. "But fine, I'll have it back then. It's bleeding good stuff."

Both of them looked at each other in silent debate.

Over their shoulders, Zot could see Wane clamber onto the *Yugon*'s deck. It took everything in his power not to laugh out loud.

Wilhelm shrugged and tipped the flask in his mouth. He gulped down two mouthfuls of the stuff and smacked his lips.

"Now what'd I say?" Zot laughed. He clapped the man on the shoulder, causing his armor to rattle.

"Hits the spot," Wilhelm agreed, holding out the flask to his partner. "Don't be such a killjoy, Guyard. We've been out here all week. Have a little fun."

Guyard let out another sigh before accepting the flask.

"Don't mind him," Wilhelm said. "He's a little paranoid after that nasty business at the Scale."

He leaned closer and whispered to Zot. "He was stationed there when it happened. Those barbarians nearly slaughtered him on the way out."

"Scary business," Zot agreed with a nod. Guyard handed him the flask back, and Zot took another fake draught. On the *Yugon*'s quarterdeck, Wane was now whispering to a man wearing a captain's hat. A trickle of kelp ran down Zot's chin as he recognized the man as Patricion Horbaz, a smuggler who had been running Zot's cargo for almost a decade. *Still going wherever the money takes you, eh, Horbaz?* Zot spat onto the cobbles, hands trembling with anger. Was everyone around him a damn coward?

Both darkhelms looked over their shoulders, but all they saw was a captain talking to a junior crew member. "Everything alright, sailor? You look like you've seen a ghost."

*Oh, he will be. He will be.* Zot took an actual gulp from the flask to stop his jangling nerves.

## CHAPTER 48

"All those heretics running around in the city recently give me the creeps, that's all," he said. He did his best to refocus his attention on the guards. All he could do now was keep them occupied for as long as possible. The cards were on the table.

Wilhelm nodded. "It's a nasty situation, alright. Good thing those skullbeards cleaned up the mess on our front step. Should keep the vermin away for a good while, I reckon."

There was a scream, followed by a splash.

The two darkhelms whirled round, drawing their weapons in a flash. Zot reacted instinctively. He reached out with both hands and gave them a shove in the back. Caught off guard, the darkhelms wobbled on the edge of the dock for a split second before cascading into the water below. The weight of their metal armor dragged them to the bottom of the sea like anchors.

"Over here!" Wane stood behind the wheel of the *Yugon*, waving his hands.

Zot didn't need to be told twice. He stormed across the gangplank, kicking it into the water behind him as soon as he reached the ship's deck.

A roar went up all around him.

"It's the boss! He's back!"

Zot looked up to find at least a dozen of the *Yugon*'s original crew bowing their heads as he passed them. A handful of strangers stood frozen near the open trapdoor leading to the hold, looking thunderstruck.

"What are you waiting for?" Zot yelled at his crew. "Either get to work or go for a swim. You have ten seconds to decide."

With a lazy flick of his hand, he directed two of his nearby sailors to cast one of the strangers overboard. He didn't like the look on the man's face. The man's scream as he went flying over the banister was enough to jolt the others into action.

Smiling more broadly than he had in weeks, Zot charged up the stairs to the quarterdeck and took his rightful place behind the Yugon's wheel.

The galleon lurched sideways as the mainsail dropped and caught a favorable breeze. It was enough to take them away from the quay, where a platoon of darkhelms approached in the distance, but they needed more speed, fast.

"Oars!" he bellowed. At once, a dozen sailors descended onto the oar deck. With slow, jerky movements, the *Yugon* picked up speed.

The darkhelms on the dockside sent a volley of windup quarrels their way, but most of the projectiles splashed into the water. The Seven be praised, they were out of reach.

"I'm sorry," a small voice behind Zot murmured. Wane stood at the banister, looking back at the shrinking figurines on the distant dock. "I tried to convince him, but he claimed he didn't know you. He was going to call the darkhelms."

"So you pushed him overboard?" Zot asked, grinning.

"I didn't have a choice," the kid said. He swallowed. "I hope he didn't drown."

"Don't worry about Horbaz, boy. Rats aren't drowned so easily."

"You said we wouldn't have to hurt anyone," Wane said. Those reproachful eyes pricked at Zot's sentimental side.

Zot patted him on the shoulder. "You did good, kid. Better than I could have expected."

When they reached the harbor's edge, their sails caught the wind, and the Yugon sped off into the afternoon sun like a loosed arrow.

# CHAPTER 49

*27th day of the 8th cycle, 553KR*
**Merkede**

riple castle." Acheron smirked. He slapped his cards down onto the table, then downed the dregs of kelp from his mug. "Pay up, ladies."

He held out his hand to each of his unfortunate opponents in turn. Three of them flung glittering ruby shards his way, contenting themselves with curses muttered under their breath. The fourth, a young woman by the name of Elstaka Mahrovia, remained still as a statue, her cards clamped in calloused hands.

"Why so confident?" she demanded, a wry smile playing on her lips. "There are multiple combinations that beat yours."

*And you are holding none of them.* She was holding a jester, a sword, and a tower, but Acheron guessed that naming her cards outright wouldn't do him many favors in a town where his reputation had been steadily deteriorating. Instead, he shot the woman an apologetic smile.

"Of course. My mistake." He stacked the rubies he'd collected in the middle of the table. *"Can* you beat me?"

Her jaw worked.

"No." She flipped her cards and threw another ruby his way, her eyes trained on him like a bloodhound watching a hare.

Acheron nodded and swept the rubies into his purse. A good actor knows when to exit stage left. His time in Merkede had come.

"My friends, I thank you for the pleasant diversion, but I'm afraid I have urgent business in the morning, for which I'll need at least a moderately clear head."

He made to get up, but Mahrovia's hand closed around his wrist.

"You're cheating," she hissed, just loud enough only he would hear over the din of weary sailors drowning their brains in whatever poison they fancied.

"Excuse me?" Curses he could accept. Insults too. By the Seven, he doubted even the most hardened sailors could come up with anything his mother hadn't flung at him threefold. All of that was just the price of admission if you were as good at gambling as he was.

The one thing he couldn't let slide was the C-word. Being labeled a cheater was as good as a death sentence. He leaned forward, both hands on the table, his face so close to the woman's that they almost kissed.

"You heard me." Mahrovia's eyes narrowed. "You're a filthy card addler. I don't know how you're doing it, but once I find out, I'll have you drug around the bay behind a schooner, mark my words."

"Take that back." His blood was up, pumping around the copious helping of kelp he'd downed to bridge the gap until his next smoke.

"Not a chance."

Silence fell over the inn with the abruptness of a hammer striking an anvil. Dozens of eyes and pricked-up ears pointed their way. Acheron sighed. *Not this again.*

"This tattered beggar is cheating," Mahrovia shouted, springing to her feet. Acheron had never liked it much when people pointed at him.

"Sore losers would do best to stay away from card games," he said, as much to the throng of red-faced drunks around them as to Mahrovia. "Maybe try knitting."

"That's it." Mahrovia's dagger slammed down point first into the table. It sank into the wood, standing upright like a way-point. Acheron's heart sank. *Swerdreht. The right of the blade.*

A collective gasp of excitement rippled through the onlookers, followed by scattered laughter. Wood scraped against wood as people began clearing away the tables and stools from the center of the room. Acheron swallowed.

The right of the blade stated that any conflict might be resolved by a public duel, carried out without armor and a single dagger each. Death was optional, but much preferred. The challenged party was allowed to decline, but doing so was considered an admission of guilt and acceptance of whatever punishment was customary for the transgression in question.

The penalty for manipulating the cards was drowning.

Death or a fight to the death.

Acheron sighed. He'd known it would come to this eventually. Truth be told, he was surprised he'd even made it this far. He'd been emptying purses

## CHAPTER 49

at the Galleons table ever since he was six. His luck was bound to run out. His only regret was that he wouldn't get to smoke the crystal-clear nugget of cloud he'd been saving for a special occasion. Maybe he could still…

Someone shoved him forward, and he stumbled into a circle of jeering sailors holding up stools to protect themselves from stray slashes.

"Oi," he shouted at Mahrovia, who stood on the opposite end of the circle, blade drawn, looking relaxed as a bee in a hive. "Let's agree to disagree, eh? No need for steel. Or blood."

She darted forward, dagger slicing the air. There was a whoosh in Acheron's ears as he flung himself aside, tumbling to the sticky floor. Stale beer and secondhand smoke cluttered his nostrils. He rolled, barely avoiding Mahrovia's boot as it thundered down.

"Last chance," he tried, jumping up like a puppet in a box.

"I'll risk it."

So be it.

"A blade!" he yelled, holding up his hand. "Will no one give me a blade?"

Half a dozen of them rained down, thumping into the wooden floor like hailstones. He dipped into a crouch as Mahrovia's dagger sliced the air where his neck had been a heartbeat earlier, fingers grasping for the first piece of steel he could find. A sharp edge bit into his palm, drawing blood.

He fumbled with the weapon, its haft slippery against a stream of burning blood.

"Gotcha," Mahrovia breathed, slicing downward.

Acheron held his arm in front of his face instinctively. White-hot pain seared its way down his forearm. Blood spattered from a deep gash just below his elbow.

He countered with a desperate lunge, but his opponent blocked it with her free forearm.

"Stop! Enough!"

Time seemed to freeze. Mahrovia halted mid-strike, her dagger perched above Acheron's undefended neck like a viper caught in a sudden frost. The sailors at the edge of the circle, who had been chanting for blood mere moments prior, fell silent, their voices carried off by the wind that entered through the inn's open door. Even Acheron felt his burning desire to run clash with an unseen barrier that held him in place.

He stood in the doorway, a black hood drawn deep over his face. A pair of fiery magenta eyes stared back at Acheron.

The stranger strode forward. The crowd parted before him like chaff in a storm.

"Is this it?" He demanded. Acheron swallowed. The stranger was unmistakably addressing him. "Is this how you want to die? Bleeding out like a sacrificial goat on a crooked kelp-stained floor amongst strangers?"

Acheron's jaw worked. He would have loved to shoot back something witty, something that the folk heroes in the tales of old would have spat at a doubting critic, but nothing came to mind except the truth.

"Help me," he whimpered, his eyes fixed on Mahrovia's quivering dagger and its clear path to his jugular. "I'm not ready for this. I'm not ready for any of it."

Mahrovia's eyes darted from the stranger, to Acheron, to her own arm, which trembled with the effort of keeping it outstretched at an awkward angle.

"What is this?" she growled, her voice constricted between fear and fury. "What are you doing to me?"

"My bad," the stranger said. There was a pleasant twinkle in his voice. "You can lower that now. If you promise to behave."

The woman's arm drooped to her side as though a string had been cut. Mahrovia flexed the fingers, staring at them as though they were new appendages she'd grown overnight.

"I am going to take this man with me now." The stranger didn't have to raise his voice for it to carry to every nook and cranny of *The Tone Deaf Siren*—it was like mist drifting on the air. "None of you will stop us. None of you will follow us. When this door closes behind us, you will forget what happened here tonight."

There was a lot of blinking and shuffling from the Siren's patrons, including its owner, Bartolomew Crookridge, but no one interrupted.

Acheron unglued himself from the beer-stained floor, snatched up his gem pouch and—still expecting to be knifed at any second—scampered toward the open doorframe where the stranger stood waiting for him. He had one foot on the threshold when the gnawing dissatisfaction in his guts got the better of him.

"Here." He tossed Mahrovia's ruby shard toward her. She caught it mechanically, a scowl creasing her brow.

"And for the record," he addressed the circle of onlookers now. "I didn't cheat. I'm just that good."

With that, he slammed the Siren's door shut behind him and hob-

## CHAPTER 49

bled off, following the cloaked stranger through the narrow alleyways of Merkede.

"That was genius," he said, grinning ear to ear. His hands shook uncontrollably as the adrenaline and tension exited his body through the path of least resistance. "I thought I was a goner."

"And what a waste that would have been." The stranger's tone betrayed no glee nor excitement at what had just transpired. "You have a gift, my friend. A highly rare one at that. One of a kind, maybe."

"Beg your pardon?" It all made sense now. The stranger had mistaken him for someone else.

"How long have you been able to do it?"

"Do what?"

A faint smile curled the stranger's lips under the black hood. "Back in the Siren just now, a man sat on the staircase with a mug of ale. What was he wearing?"

"What man? I was a little distracted by all the knives and the threat of rapidly approaching death and all that."

"What was he wearing?" the stranger repeated simply.

Acheron came to a stop, two inches of mud sucking at his boots. He closed his eyes and at once the scene flooded back to surround him. He stood in the circle. Mahrovia, suspended in memory, was frozen in a hunched fighting stance. Acheron looked around and located a staircase in the far corner of the room. There he was. A bald man, built like a sack of potatoes, wearing a torn blue tunic, leather trousers, and dirty fur loafers.

Acheron described the man to the stranger, who nodded. It clicked.

"Who are you? How do you know about my memories?" Nobody knew. Nobody had ever known. Not even his mother had fully understood what he could do.

"The latter is a long tale with many tangents. As for the former,"—he lowered his hood, revealing a sharp face framed by a mane of long black hair—"my name is Abrasax. Abrasax Springtide."

\*\*\*

*12th day of the 1st cycle, 570KR*
**De Malheur's Fortress**

Acheron woke to find his face stuck to a scrap of parchment. A puddle of drool had caused the ink on his carefully scratched notes to run. Sticky black coated his cheek and temple, turning him to a human stamp. It was a good thing he'd allowed his standards of hygiene to slip over the years. He couldn't get much more filthy than he already was.

He sighed, peeling the parchment off his face. The whole thing was a mess. When he held it against the light, not even he could read what remained of the inscriptions. Judging by the sun outside his bedroom window, it was already late afternoon. Just like him to fall asleep and waste precious hours right before their assault on God's Maul. It didn't matter. Not now. Not when what little time they had left had suddenly been cut short. They would just have to roll the dice, and hope they came up sixes. It wasn't ideal. Abrasax himself would never have allowed the old Signum to storm into danger so heedlessly. But times had changed, and recklessness was born out of necessity.

As he gathered the scripts he'd set out around himself, he found his eyes drifting to the two maps of Metten on his desk. He'd spent the better part of the day copying the original he'd sketched all those years ago. It was one thing to improvise a plan, but it would mean that the job wouldn't be clean. They needed a backup plan. He carefully folded the map and tucked it into an inside pocket of his robe. He'd figure out where to hide the second one later.

When he sat down on the splintery floor to imprint, Acheron's hackles rose. It was in these dead moments, with nothing but his own mind to keep him company, that the ghosts of his past crept up on him. It was painfully clear to him now, just how deep he had allowed himself to sink. When Abrasax had taught him how to burn his first sigil, he'd felt like all his prayers had been answered.

All his life he'd been unwanted, a roach on the wall of decent society. Then, for the very first time, he had felt like he had something to offer. Like he was special. His perfect memory had predisposed him to become an exceptional sparkgazer. Once in a generation, Abrasax had claimed. Back then, Acheron didn't even need to imprint. Once a sigil was lodged in his mind, it stayed seared into his memory indefinitely. He had taken all that for granted.

A decade of drowning his mind in whatever he could get his hands on had slowly eroded that ability. He could still take in massive stores of most sigils, but it was no longer effortless. To the contrary. The harder he tried to force what remained of his brain cells into focus, the further away the shapes seemed to shift, as though the circular tower room was expanding.

## CHAPTER 49

It was like trying to catch water in crippled hands. Acheron let out a groan as the first of the phantoms appeared. His mother, hanging upside down in front of his tiny window, leered at him.

"Morning, Mother," Acheron said. He couldn't contain a chuckle. *Great, talking to myself now, a certain mark of a healthy and stable mind.* He ignored her as she began breaking every bone in her shoulders, trying to wriggle inside, her eyes rolling in her translucent skull.

*Back to the task at hand. Focus on the task at hand.* He repeated the mantra over and over until he finally locked on to *Forte*.

He always started and ended his sessions with it these days. His body was giving up on him. In the absence of a copious store of the sigil, he found his joints aching, and painful stabs emanating from the lower regions of his guts. He didn't need to be a surgeon to know that his organs were deteriorating rapidly. *Finally. It's about time.* For years, smoking himself to death had been his only goal. Now that he was close to achieving it, he couldn't help but feel the burn of regret. They were going to need him.

The kid was learning quickly, and though she would one day outgrow even his capabilities, she needed a firm hand to keep her on track. There were still too many techniques and secrets that no one else could teach her. Not to mention the implications her partial blindness would have on her future training. Once she was ready, and with the right guidance, the kid would transcend all of them. Had to transcend all of them. Saphara Al Noor was a capable sigilist in her own right, but leaving Brina's education in her hands didn't sit right with Acheron. Something about that woman gnawed at Acheron's soul. She was too similar to himself, and that put him on edge. Her hatred for the church and its teachings could in the long run prove an obstacle once Brina was ready to embrace her full power.

Acheron jumped to his feet, knocking over the *Forte* script. It was no use trying to imprint. Not with this many thoughts swirling in his mind like turds in a latrine. His bare feet slipped on the icy stone steps as he descended to the main floor. It took him a good fifteen minutes to locate the bumbling baron in the fortress's library.

Though somewhat cramped, the place must have held close to a thousand manuscripts. They were stashed on impeccably maintained shelves that rose all the way to the vaulted ceiling. In addition to the usual dust-and-mold smell associated with stashed parchment, the baron's library had a distinct odor of sandalwood and cinnamon. De Malheur's considerable bulk shrank as he saw Acheron approach.

"Master Acheron," De Malheur said. His jowls jiggled as he gave a curt nod.

"De Malheur." Acheron gestured toward a nearby reading table surrounded by two leather armchairs. He pulled one out for De Malheur to sit on and plopped down into the other one. "Have you determined yet what your role will be in tonight's undertaking?"

"I, I," the baron sputtered. "Am I supposed to...?"

"No," Acheron said. "You are not. Here is what you are going to do. You will come down with me to Turncoat's Pike at sunset. You will pluck Harrod Wane off whatever ship he and Zot have acquired. Wane is to stay here and help you take care of Fortuyn's and Versa's injuries. Understood?"

De Malheur dabbed at his forehead with a silk handkerchief. "The boy seemed rather adamant on joining you... What if he resists?"

Acheron let out an exasperated sigh and stared De Malheur down.

"Fine. Fine."

"Good. Then, should we fail to return by sunrise, you are to assume that we have failed and are either dead or captured. You are to erase every trace of our presence here and keep yourself, Wane, and the wounded from falling into the enemy's hands at all costs."

"Is it likely someone will come looking?" De Malheur gulped. "Here?"

"Yes." Acheron suppressed a chuckle as the skin underneath the baron's chin grew bright red. "Once Abrasax is free, the church will search every nook and cranny on the island. Luckily, we have the advantage."

"We do?"

"I have warned you in advance." Acheron smiled. "I'd say you've got about twenty-four hours to prepare."

# CHAPTER 50

*10th day of the 1st cycle, 570KR*
**Snake Island**

Eight guards. Two in front of the bunkhouse, and another three duos patrolling the dark work yard and the path leading to the fortress on the hill. A laughably understaffed security detail for an institution that incarcerated a hundred men and women whose muscles had been steeled through continuous hard labor.

Then again, that had always been the darkhelms' mistake. They saw Snake Island's slaves as barely more than tools. Hammers, pliers, and shovels to be locked away in storerooms when they were done with them. The thought that they might rebel was as alien to them as the suggestion that one's cooking pots would run away at night. Tonight, they would learn the hard way.

The problem would be to avoid raising the alarm. The fortress on top of the hill and its warehouses would undoubtedly be much better guarded. If reinforcements arrived, a bloodbath would be inevitable.

Saf skirted the edge of the bunkhouse, her hearing amplified by *Auris*. The gentle crackling of twigs and dried leaves crushed under her boot was interspersed with the violent thumping of her heart. For years she'd dreamed of tonight, had imagined how it would feel to trudge through that yellow mud again. A free woman this time. Unfettered and stronger than she'd ever dared dream while the quartermaster's whip loomed over her. The roles had been reversed. The Cardinal's lapdogs just didn't know it yet.

"Cold one, eh?" A man's voice drifted around the bunkhouse's corner up ahead. His low voice had the coarse edge of a man who'd been drinking more than his share for decades.

"I've been telling you, Hannes," a woman replied with a hint of exasperation, "go to the captain and demand he order you one of those woolen undershirts. They're supposed to issue them to all of us."

Hannes made a dismissive noise. "You know how he gets. Productivity this, frugality that."

"Evening, colleagues," Saf said, strolling around the corner as though she did so every night. "Care for some tea?" A low burn of *Consol* added a convincing cheery edge to her words.

Hannes and his female companion stiffened. They sat with their backs against the barn's wooden door. Their raven helmets lay off to the side, forgotten.

"Who..." Hannes squinted to get a better look at her.

"Frea," Saf responded, giving the woman a familiar wink as though they were lifelong friends, "Frea Demall, the captain's new logistics assistant."

Saf held out two half-full mugs she'd heated with *Gnis* moments prior.

"Logiwhat?" Hannes scratched at his crooked nose.

"Logistics," the woman beside him muttered, shaking her head. "It means someone who takes care of all the practical stuff the squadron needs." She took the mug with an annoyed glance at Hannes. "Isn't that right, Sister Demall?"

"Spot on." Saf beamed at the pair and poked at Hannes's shoulder with the remaining mug.

"Hang on," he drawled. Saf tensed, ready to pounce as soon as the man gave any sign of calling her out as an impostor. "Would that mean you can get me a pair of them woolen umber shirts?"

"*Undershirts,*" his colleague hissed. She took a large gulp of her steaming mug.

"I definitely could," Saf said quickly. "Here, grab your tea, and I'll return to the captain's office to put the order in tonight."

*Come on, you fool, take it.* It was paramount that he drink soon.

"That would be terrific." Hannes stretched his arms above his head and yawned. "I get awfully sleepy when I'm cold."

"Nothing like some hot tea to remedy that, I reckon." Saf looked over her shoulder to hide her eyes as she flared *Rhetoris*. As the sigil's star-shaped rune burst to life in her mind's eye, the suggestion turned to a command.

"Right you are." Hannes's eyes gained the familiar dull tint as the shape's influence took hold. He took the mug, a sheepish grin pasted across his round face.

*Drink. Drink. Drink.*

## CHAPTER 50

Hannes raised the cup to his lips, then lowered it again.

"I don't suppose there are colors to choose from?"

"What?" Saf snapped.

"The underthingies. What color did you say they came in again?"

"Anything you like." She had a hard time keeping her growing frustration out of her voice.

"Good," Hannes said pensively. "I think I might go with lilac. That an option?"

The female guard swayed on the spot, then dropped like a sack of rocks.

Hannes took a step back, mouth open in horror. His eyes darted from the unconscious woman at his feet to the mug still clutched in his hands, finally coming to a rest on Saf. "You," he muttered. "You did something."

Saf's patience broke.

"And you're going to drink." She seized *Rhetoris* fully, putting all of her mental force behind it. There was no more time for mild encouragement and gentle nudges. She would just have to treat him like a puppet on a string.

She grabbed both sides of the man's helmet, forcing him to look straight into her burning eyes.

"You're going to drink every drop in that mug, or I will make you wish you were never born."

Hannes's eyes rolled back in their sockets, his entire being shivered with supernatural terror.

"I - I - I don't want to," he stammered. Urine ran down his leg, pattering on the sand below.

"You. Will." Saf pressed her forehead into his. He wouldn't be able to resist the shape much longer before the effort caused him to pass out. If he hadn't drunk the sleeping serum by then, she would need to ensure his silence through cruder means.

*Might as well inform the man of the options.*

"Drink this, and you will wake up tomorrow with a slight headache and a fuzzy memory," she snarled at him, opening the sigil to its fullest potential. "If you don't, I will drive this dagger"—she tapped it lightly on top of his helmet—"straight through your left eyeball. Do I make myself clear?"

Hannes nodded slowly, like a scolded child. He slopped most of the serum down his chin in his terrified haste to get it down, but it would suffice.

"Good boy." Saf shoved him in the chest, and he keeled over like a toppled statue.

***

The bunkhouse was exactly as Saf remembered it. Four rows of identical wooden cots stacked three high. The cloying stink of soiled straw filled her lungs at once, lingering in the back of her throat as though it had never left. A handful of lanterns hung from a central roofing beam, casting a dreary light over the bunkhouse's interior.

As Saf dragged in the unconscious guards, dozens of faces stared back at her from their bunks. Some were terrified, others curious. All of them were filthy. Stained with soot and dirt from slogging around the foundry all day. There were close to a hundred of them.

"Who are you?" A towering Hawqallian woman with matted black hair jumped down from her cot. She looked down at the two bodies at Saf's feet as though she were worried they might explode at any second.

"My name is Saphara Al Noor. I am here to give you a choice." All around her, captives were waking up and sliding out of their own beds, crowding in around Saf and the tall Hawqallian.

"You are going to get us all whipped, Saphara Al Noor," the woman said. She poked one of her bare feet into Hannes's cheek. The man snorted, then went silent again.

"Nobody in this room will be whipped ever again," Saf said, touching *Rhetoris* for effect. She looked around, making sure all of them saw her burning eyes. "By dawn, all of you will be free to live your own lives the way you see fit."

Mutters echoed throughout the bunkhouse. Uncertain faces turned to the large Hawqallian woman.

"How do we know this isn't just another trick to test us?"

Saf held out her arm and pulled back the sleeve of her robe. The brand glistened in the lantern light. A three-inch long scepter, seared into her skin forever. It was just as bright as it had been on that very first night aboard the slave galley.

A renewed round of murmuring echoed off the wooden walls, drawing a shush from the large Hawqallian woman.

"Looks like our prayers have been answered." She grinned, baring two rows of long, white teeth. "Well met, sister. My name is Ak-Zul."

Saf nodded at Ak-Zul and beckoned for the other captives to come closer. Before she could speak further, however, Ak-Zul held out a large hand.

## CHAPTER 50

"Do me a favor and lend me that shiny dagger on your hip, Saphara. I've been waiting to get back at one of these pigs for years." Ak-Zul put a foot on Hannes's slowly heaving chest and pressed down.

The surrounding prisoners drew closer. Eager expressions rose on their faces. There was hunger there. A hunger no amount of bread and meat and butter would ever assuage. It was the same hunger that shoved Saf out of bed each morning and kept her out of it at night.

"No." She looked Ak-Zul in the eye. "No one needs to die tonight."

"It is our just deserts," Ak-Zul spat. She lifted her filthy tunic, revealing a chest and back covered in striped scars. Saf knew them well. Her hands searched for the thick strips of destroyed flesh on her own ribs. "We have bled by their hands. All of us. Now you want to deprive us of our chance to get even?"

"We will get even," Saf said. "But not like this. Killing someone in cold blood won't heal your wounds. Believe me, I've tried."

"Those pricks need to know we won't take it anymore." Ak-Zul's nose twitched as she stared at the guard at her feet. Her voice quivered, as though she were on the verge of screaming. "We need to hurt them. We need to send a message."

Saf put a hand on the woman's shoulder and looked into her eyes. For a moment, it looked like she might shake it off, but she allowed it.

"Listen to me. The scepter's armies are on the move as we speak. The Cardinal has ordered a campaign the likes of which hasn't been seen in generations. Soon they will need steel by the boatload to replenish lost weapons and armor. I say we cut off their supply at the source."

A rustle of excitement passed through the bunkhouse.

"Is that acceptable?" Saf asked. She looked at Ak-Zul, but the question was meant for all of them.

The Hawqallian woman nodded reluctantly. "It is the better choice."

"I was here when the grain was burned and we built the foundry in its place," a razor thin Biori behind Ak-Zul said, pushing his way through the crowd. His skin was saggy with age and malnourishment, but his eyes were bright blue and sharp. "Shoddy work, it was. Built all in a rush. Most of it was improvised right here. With a little pressure in the right spots, a lot of damage could be done."

Saf grinned. "That's what I'm counting on. What's your name, friend?"

"They called me Bahov once, back when I was a warrior. Though I have fought nothing but my own empty stomach for many cycles."

The name rattled something in Saf's memory. "Hang on. Did you once mentor a young man by the name of Bron Brokenspear?"

"We didn't call him Brokenspear back then," Bahov said, though a roguish grin appeared on his face at the name. "But aye, I taught the lad. You know him?"

"You could say that," Saf said. "Let's get to work, shall we?"

\*\*\*

Saf crept along the outside of buildings, snuck through the underbrush, and at certain points, crawled on her belly as the column of escapees made its way from the bunkhouse to the foundry. Led by Bahov and Ak-Zul, they proceeded quickly and quietly, though were forced multiple times to jump behind hedgerows to avoid the lantern beams of an incoming patrol.

When they reached the foundry itself, they found it dark and abandoned. The three ovens and their chimneys loomed over them, casting long shadows in the moonlight.

At once, Bahov sprang into action, directing his fellow prisoners on how to stack the ovens with wood and coal to ensure maximum pressure could be generated. A handful of brave and agile escapees scaled the chimneys to clog them with large stones.

The work progressed slower than Saf had hoped. With all tools stashed away in sheds near the castle on top of the hill, they had to use their bare hands, the fronts of their tunics, and stray buckets to carry the loose coals to the ovens.

As they worked, Saf burned *Lux* and acted as a lookout. She circled the foundry, alert for any sign of incoming danger. Her heart was beating faster than it usually did in these situations.

Something about being back here seemed to erase most of the calluses she had built up over the past few years. The person she had been back then would've been nervous, terrified even, to stand in the church's way. And though she had committed many more grievous crimes since, she couldn't help but feel a fragment of that old fear and helplessness rise to the top of her consciousness.

It said a great deal about the torture they had been through, that she had found most of the island's prisoners willing to help her destroy the foundry. Instead of running straight for the nearest boat, they had marched to the center of the island, determined to leave their captors with the largest pos-

## CHAPTER 50

sible mess. They worked efficiently. Forming three teams divided between each of the ovens, they glided past each other with ease and formed chains to get the ovens filled up as quickly as possible. Their muscles, hardened by months or years of forced labor, gleamed in the moonlight as they pushed themselves to the limit.

"What the?" Saf gasped as she tripped over the outstretched leg of a darkhelm leaning against the back of a wooden shed. Beside him, a second guard lay slumped in the mud. Empty bottles of rum littered the ground beside them. The man whose leg she had stepped on looked up at her with bleary eyes, as though trying to determine whether he was in trouble.

"Good evening, gentlemen," Saf snapped. She put on a stern tone, as though she'd been the man's supervisor for a decade. "I thought I might find you two knuckleheads out here."

The second man opened his eyes, staring her up and down, drunken confusion on his face. Both of them were so far gone, they didn't even seem to know where they were. In their eagerness to hide the fact that they were piss drunk during patrol duty, they jumped to their feet at once. One of them almost fell straight back down, but his buddy caught him under the arm just in time.

"What have I told you guys about drinking during working hours?" Saf said. "How many damn times does this have to happen before I send you two nitwits down to sleep with the captives?"

The men looked from each other to Saf. A seed of suspicion was sprouting in the corners of their eyes. They took in her plain black robes, slowly putting two and two together. Saf shook her head and put her hand over her eyes, as though she couldn't believe how dumb these two were.

She burned *Consol.* "You know what, I'll give you two one last chance. We're having the prisoners load up the ovens, so they're ready to go in the morning. New procedure. March on over there and give them a hand, will you? You make sure I get in bed sooner tonight. I just might refrain from sending your asses to the Scale at Mallion's Depth."

The two nodded. The effect of the sigil combined with the alcohol made them look like puppets on strings as they slouched unsteadily toward the ovens. Saf motioned over to Ak-Zul, to signal that the two darkhelms were under her control and no cause for concern. Even so, the rest of the workers gave them a wide berth as the guards began scooping up coal with their bare hands and helping them load the ovens.

A few minutes later, Bahov jogged over. "We've got them ready. All we need to do now is to get a solid fire going. That will take time, though. It would be better if you go ahead. I'll stay here and tend to the ovens. By the time they realize people are missing, I should be ready to surprise them with a sizable distraction."

Saf smiled down at the man. Even now, old, emaciated and scarred, Bahov would put his life on the line to make sure that his fellows could escape. "No," she said, "I admire your courage, but that won't be necessary. I have a few tricks of my own up my sleeve. You and Ak-Zul should lead your brothers and sisters to the docks right now. Don't worry about me. I won't be far behind." Bahov gave her a skeptical look, but when he saw the glare of *Lux* in her eyes, he seemed to gain more confidence.

"Very well." With a small bow, he vanished.

As the workers disappeared into the darkness in single file, Saf leaned into the first oven, burying her arms up to the crook of the elbow in coal and stacked wood. She burned *Gnis*. Immediately, the triangular rune appeared in her mind's eye. It flared into an almost blinding scorch as she threw her full weight behind it. She closed her eyes, focusing on feeling the heat of her blood gather on her skin. Smoke stung in her eyes and nose as the oven ignited.

Saf jerked her arms back as flames rose. She swung the heavy steel door shut, trapping the heat. She flared *Gnis* again, clutching the metal handle and hinges with her hands. The metal melted away under her touch, ensuring that even if a patrol noticed what was happening, they wouldn't be able to get the door open until it was too late.

She repeated the procedure with the second and third ovens, feeling increasingly anxious about the pressure building up in the first one. She had no idea how long it would take before the pressure reached a critical point, and she wasn't sticking around to find out.

As soon as she had melted the hinges off the last door, she dismissed the two drunk guards, who stood swaying beside the stack of coal, looking befuddled and lost. As they lumbered off into the dark, Saf broke into a dead sprint.

\*\*\*

Saf reached Snake Island's dock as the second chariot touched the horizon, illuminating jagged stone pillars sticking out of the sea in the distance. In a handful of minutes, the dark window would be upon them. It was

## CHAPTER 50

essential that they be well out on the water when that happened. Here, they would be sitting ducks. Excitement and anxiety mingled in her chest.

They were so close to success, Saf could almost taste it, but the foundry had remained deathly silent. If those ovens refused to blow up, there would be no diversion to cover their escape. The scepter would simply send another shipment of unfortunates to fuel their machine of war.

Dense clusters of reeds obscured the dock from view. A handful of galleys lay moored to the wobbly old pier. Just enough to get the darkhelms stationed there to safety in case of emergency, Saf presumed.

A smile played on her lips as she drew her dagger. Before they left, she would cut the ropes tethering all the leftover ships to the dock. With any luck, they would drift out far enough to be lost. Leaving the entire Snake Island garrison marooned was just about the best bonus she could have asked for.

"Psst, over here." It was Ak-Zul. She waved a long arm over the edge of the nearest galley, beckoning. When Saf approached, she could see a handful of darkhelms laying hogtied on the ship's deck. Saf was pleased to see that the escapees hadn't killed them. They would make a clean escape.

About half of the ex-slaves sat huddled together to keep out of sight. As soon as they noticed Saf's arrival, multiple dozens of faces peered over the edges of the other galleys, as though waiting for further guidance.

"Freedom lies ahead," Saf said, sweeping an arm at the galleys that lay moored in between the high patches of reeds. "Take your pick. From now on, you choose your own path."

"And where will you go?" Ak-Zul asked.

"This isn't over," Saf replied. "At this very moment, thousands risk suffering the same torture we were forced to endure at the Cardinal's hands. I intend to do whatever it takes to keep that from happening."

"Then I will go with you." Ak-Zul's fiery eyes found Saf's. "I'd dive down a leviathan's throat if I thought it might annoy the church."

Saf smiled and nodded her acceptance. As Ak-Zul began throwing the bound darkhelms back onto the dock, Bahov called out from a galley to Saf's left.

"Count me in. I wonder how young Brokenspear is faring these days."

Soon, dozens of voices were shouting out similar declarations of loyalty, and Saf accepted each of their pledges gratefully. They divided those who wanted to join the cause over two galleys, while the other half of the ex-slaves sailed off in small groups, hoping to return to their homelands.

Once each of the galleys had either set sail or been cut loose from their mooring posts, Saf nodded at Ak-Zul to unmoor their own galley.

They had made it a few hundred feet onto open water when an earth-shattering shock wave rattled the reeds surrounding the island, followed by three thunderous roars as each of the foundry's ovens exploded. Towers of flame shot skyward over the island like distress beacons.

"Blood of my mothers," Bahov breathed, "if that isn't the most beautiful thing I have ever seen."

# CHAPTER 51

*12th day of the 1st cycle, 570KR*
**God's Maul**

Solana's head was pounding. It hardly ever stopped these days. She would wake up to a dull thrum in the back of her eye sockets which built as the day wore on. Most nights she passed out rather than fell asleep.

It was just one of the many side effects that came with seeing the world as she did, a shadowy approximation mapped out in her mind's eye through unnaturally sensitive hearing, touch, and smell.

The latter was torture as she strode around the outer edge of Locktower C. A ceaseless assault of every foul smell imaginable battered against the gates of her self-restraint.

Excrement, sweat, urine, and the moldy undertone of stale air traded places on the foreground, never dulling through habituation, forever as fresh as when she'd stepped into this Heilforsaken place two days ago.

"This is new," a sandpaper voice to her left said. "An actual sense-surger come to guard my old bones. I'm flattered."

Solana remained silent, not breaking her stride around the compound. So far, Locktower C's only prisoner hadn't bothered to acknowledge her presence, content to watch her from the dark recesses of his cell. He had been surprised, even a twinge frightened, when she had dismissed the block's regular guard detail. She had heard as much in the stutter of his breath.

There was a hum of skin on metal as the man's hands curled around the bars of his cell. His hot breath, rank with tooth decay, wafted across the exposed skin on her hand, making it crawl.

"Of course." Abrasax Springtide gave a hoarse chuckle. "You are under strict orders not to bandy a single mirthless word with a venomous specimen, such as myself." There was a deranged quality to his laughter. It was misery pushed over the edge into perverse humor. "They wouldn't want me to fill your head with dangerous nonsense, would they?"

Solana ignored him. De Leliard had ordered her not to trade a word with the Cardinal slayer. Under no circumstances was he to know just how close he was to death. *"It could provoke him into trying something desperate,"* De Leliard had written. Solana wrinkled her nose underneath her heavy, spiked helmet. She could almost smell the memory. Once she would have killed to receive her orders directly from the scepter-wielder himself; now she didn't want to spend a single moment longer in his presence than she had to.

That didn't matter. An order was an order, and she would obey it. De Leliard had made the consequences of not doing so clear.

"Oh, come on." Abrasax tapped the bars. "I haven't talked to a soul in ten years. All I get is a nervous shuffle here and a cough there." He sighed. "What harm could I possibly do? I'll be dead in a few days, anyway."

Solana halted in front of the cell. Springtide smelled like wet dog. Though she couldn't see him, she imagined long hair matted with years' worth of grime.

"Ahh," he said. "So it's true. The day has finally come."

There was a rustle as he slid down the slick stone wall and sat on the hard floor. "Probably for the best. It's not like I'm any use to anyone in here."

"It must seem pointless now. What you did." Solana could have kicked herself. One explicit guideline. How hard was it to stick to one guideline? Still, the Cardinal slayer's treason had intrigued her for years. She remembered the shock wave it had sent rippling through the city when the people awoke to a new Cardinal. It had been a stark reminder of just how fragile the empire's peace was.

Now she stood a handful of feet from the man who had orchestrated all of it, and soon he would be dead. This was her—anyone's—last chance to peer into the heretic's soul. To find out what made a terrorist tick. What could be the harm?

"Pointless?" Abrasax asked, mildly interested. "Oh, no. I can't say that it does."

"You will hang like a common criminal on the orders of the very institution you tried to destroy," Solana said. "You made no difference."

"The fact remains that a decade later, the church feels the need to make an example out of us. De Leliard is so terrified of my words alone that he

## CHAPTER 51

forbids his thralls from conversing with me. He understands the weight of ideas as I do."

"He understands that he, like all tyrants, is a sheep amongst collared wolves and that all it takes is for one to chew through its leash." He tapped a fingernail against the steel bars. "We proved that to everyone who lives under the empire's thumb. That cannot be erased, and I'll gladly die for it."

An icy shiver ran down Solana's back. *He's a madman. An utter lunatic.* The distant calm with which he accepted his incoming doom unnerved her.

"You proved nothing," she snapped. "Estav was replaced before the sun went up. The empire didn't spend a single leaderless day."

"I'll admit De Leliard was one step ahead of me on that count." Abrasax let out a laugh which turned into a howl as it went on.

"What do you mean?"

"I suppose the enlightened council has put in a great deal of effort to bury what happened. After it had been suitably rearranged, of course." There was the crackling of fingers trailing through a filthy beard. "Tell me, how long did it take Methusal to oust Evarion from the top seat?"

"Reynziel Evarion stepped down on account of his health," Solana snapped. She had heard just about enough of the murderer's ramblings. Engaging him had been a mistake. Maybe Heil did abandon some hopeless cases.

"Probably true." Abrasax chuckled. The noise rankled Solana like fingers on a chalkboard. "The old sod's health might have taken a serious dive if he refused De Leliard. That bastard had it all planned out, you know.

"He knew we were coming for Estav that night. He waited to intervene until he was sure the job was done. Then he swooped in, acted the hero, and placed himself on the throne. All in a day's work. It was the perfect coup." Abrasax spit on the wall of his cell. "It would have been brilliant had it not been so damn frustrating. I never much liked the feeling of being used. Do you know what I mean?"

"That's enough." Solana held up a hand. In her anger, a brief surge of heat escaped from her fingertips. There was a hissing sound, and the murderer yanked his burnt hand back from the bars. A deep-seated uneasiness was brewing in her stomach. Springtide had been locked in here since the night of Estav's death. He shouldn't have known that Reynziel Methusal had replaced Evarion as the Keeper Chosen.

Then there were the slanderous accusations regarding Cardinal De Leliard, a man widely regarded as the church's guiding beacon in these troubling times. Still, there was a ruthless streak to the man. One she had experienced firsthand on multiple occasions now. *And he wears Estav's crown.*

"Impressive." Abrasax blew on his singed fingers. "For a cult that condemns sparkgazers, you sense-surgers sure aren't shy around a sigil."

"Our power is granted by Heil herself, heretic. We make sacrifices, and in return she provides us with the tools to stamp out those who defy her will."

"Was it worth it, the eye thing? I don't think I could ever willingly give that up." He lingered for a touch of a second on the word *willingly.*

Solana's jaw worked. This man couldn't die soon enough. He knew far too much, had a way of putting his grubby fingers on sore spots he had no business knowing were there. Unbidden images and sensations flooded back to her. She watched in her mind's eye as a dozen arms held her down while the knife ripped and tore. Her piercing headache spiked. Somewhere in the recesses of her mind, De Leliard's voice echoed. *"Your mother will be notified of your failings."*

Her mother. Solana hadn't seen her in months. Not since that fateful night. De Leliard had guaranteed the church would care for her in Solana's absence. There had been no choice but to believe him.

"Make peace with whatever you believe in, Springtide. This conversation is over."

"Don't worry, I know what I'm dying for. I would do it a thousand times over if I had to.

"But you, Your Purity, what will you die for?"

# CHAPTER 52

*12th day of the 1st cycle, 570KR*
**Mallion's Bay**

s soon as Razorwing's huge wings lifted her above the treeline, Brina's anxiety turned to determination. She had made the leap. Now it was time to focus on sticking the landing.

The air turned icy as Mallion's Depth shrank below her, the lights of the city turning into stars in an upside-down firmament. Brina twisted the reins of Razorwing's improvised bridle around her wrists and gave them a gentle tug to stop the griffin's ascent.

She watched as a toy version of the *Yugon* cleaved its way through the bay below. *Thank the Seven for a clear night.*

As Razorwing swooped toward God's Maul's distant towers, Brina spotted at least half a dozen redsails, noting the location and course of each. This high up, it was impossible to tell the difference between the *Yugon* and any other ship of similar size. Mixing them up would be catastrophic.

Brina swallowed as the giant black fortress passed by underneath her. She had never fully appreciated the sheer size and bulk of the structure until now. Dozens of jelly lanterns floated above the prison's tower and battlements. If any of the prison's guards were to look up, all they would see would be a massive bird drifting along on the breeze.

"Alright, Razorwing," she bellowed over the rushing wind, "it's showtime."

The griffin slowed, then plummeted into a smooth dive. As they hurtled toward the billowing red sail of a schooner below, Brina reached into the pouch slung across her shoulder and grabbed one of the two dozen ceramic balls Oppen had given her in return for a life's worth of savings.

It felt entirely too light to pack much of a punch. Brina shook the ball. For all she knew, it was full of air. *You better not have ripped me off, wom-*

*an*. With a quick prayer to all that was holy, she took aim and hurled it at the rapidly nearing ship.

"*Up,*" she urged Razorwing, digging her heels into the griffin's shoulder blades. As soon as the bomb impacted, they'd become the prime target of every windup on that ship.

Razorwing soared toward a veil of low-hanging clouds. Right before they vanished, there was a roar that reverberated in Brina's throat. A flash withdrew the ship from sight. Then it was engulfed in blue flames. They gnawed their way up the ship's mast, feeding on the rigging before the mainsail went up like a pyre. All along the deck, tiny figures scuttled to lower boats and filled up buckets of saltwater.

Brina whooped. It had worked. There was a smoke signal that would be visible to every single guard atop God's Maul. *And this is just the beginning.*

When Brina was certain they'd passed the prison, she dipped below the clouds once more, prowling for her next target. She found it in the form of a red-sailed galleon that had changed course to investigate its burning compatriot. The first bomb caught its front mast. The second shattered against the topsails on the mainmast, definitively hamstringing its movements.

\*\*\*

"By the Seven, it's like a Biori wedding." Sneak laughed, pointing out the burning ships as they went up one after another. "We won't even have to pretend there's an emergency. It's chaos out here."

"Stop shouting," Acheron snapped, though he had trouble keeping a smile off his own face. "It'll be a real laugh if the darkhelms hear you before we've even tried to sell the story."

He stood on the *Yugon*'s bow, taking in the spectacle, the silty wind and the icy spatter of the waves cool on his weary face. There was beauty to it, he thought as he watched the writhing sapphire flames carve through the black of night. They looked like ghosts escaping their tombs after centuries of imprisonment, fleeing into the skies.

"He doesn't want to see you," a nasty voice rasped in his ear. "He is in there because of you. We were all in there because of you."

Acheron sighed, refusing to look at Azaria, or the part of his own mind that took her form. The visions had grown more intense as the day wore on. Somewhere in the deep crevices of his brain, something dark and twist-

## CHAPTER 52

ed lived. Something that fed on all the images he could not forget, and now that his chance at redemption was drawing near, it feared for its life.

"Abrasax doesn't have a choice," Acheron muttered, his eyes firmly fixed on the growing shadow ahead. "Whether he likes it or not, I'm on my way."

\*\*\*

"That's the last of them, Razorwing, let's get out of here."

Beneath them, the dark water of the bay was strewn with close to a dozen pillars of blue flame. A spectacle that would be visible to even the rats in the sewers of Mallion's Depth, let alone the watchtowers of God's Maul.

Brina grinned wickedly as she imagined Cardinal De Leliard being informed that his mighty war fleet was going up in flames. At that very moment, the darkhelms would be stumbling all over themselves to send out reinforcements. By the time they found out that the real target was the prison, her father would be long gone.

The only survivor of the calamity, the *Yugon*, approached God's Maul's gate. Brina circled high above, waiting for her cue.

\*\*\*

"Help," Sneak bellowed, summoning his best approximation of a wall-born accent. "We are under attack. Let us in."

Shadows stirred on the battlements of the towers above. Sneak swallowed, fearing a volley of quarrels in reply.

"Do you carry the beacon?" a woman called back from beneath an eerie helmet shaped like an owl's head.

"Damn the beacon," Sneak growled, hoping to the Seven and beyond that he wasn't overplaying his hand. "Do you not see the carnage in our wake? They could come for us at any moment. For Heil's sake, open the gate."

"If you do not carry the beacon, I cannot allow you entry, as I'm sure you'll understand."

"You better hope the Cardinal understands why you let his last galleon in the bay get torched like the rest of those poor souls out there. I'm sure he'll be thrilled to hear you refused to help us salvage his property."

There was a good deal of shuffling and muttering atop the tower. Sneak's heart pounded in his neck like a drum in the stretching silence. Then the air was filled with the most wonderful sound he'd ever heard, the slow clink of steel chains coming taut. In slow, jerky movements, the thick metal grate rose from the water, bringing with it the stench of wet seaweed. A thick layer of barnacles covered every inch of the rusty iron.

"A thousand blessings to you and your families," Sneak boomed, gesturing at his fake crew to proceed through the monstrous arch before the darkhelm officer could change her mind.

As the ship creaked into motion, Sneak marched down the deck to find Acheron.

"You're up," Sneak said. He placed a hand on Acheron's shoulder. The old man shook it off and wandered unsteadily toward the ship's bow. A gnawing twitch of doubt pulled at Sneak's guts.

"I really wish Saf was here," he told Bron, who was lowering the mainsail, while Zot barked commands from the top deck. The dozen crew members Zot had convinced or bribed to join their cause disappeared below the deck to man the oars.

"You speak true," the Biori replied, narrowing his eyes at Acheron's receding back. "But there's something about that one that none of us have yet seen."

"Then let him dig it up right now," Sneak said. He swallowed painfully against a lump in his throat as the grate rattled down behind them.

# CHAPTER 53

*12th day of the 1st cycle, 570KR*
**God's Maul**

cheron took a deep breath. There was a tingling in his gut that he hadn't felt in a lifetime. The thrill of a rapidly approaching battle.

Out of the corners of his eyes, he could see all of them lining the rails of the deck. Azaria, Ghar-Ul, the other members of the Signum, and worst of all, his mother. The only family he'd ever known.

She leered at him, baring unnaturally sharp teeth. A crimson scarf covered most of her short black hair, as it had on the day it happened.

*Achie's heart is filled with murder,* she crooned. *Always filled with murder.* Her eyes widened as she spat out the last word. Acheron's mouth worked. The memory was there. Eternal. Lurking just below the surface of his thoughts like an anchor, waiting for a tug on its chain to rise from the muddy seafloor. Images crawled their way into his head. Her hand raised in a fist. His own, held up to shield his face. Then the shove.

*Not now,* he told himself, his fingers digging into the scarred flesh of his forearms. *Abrasax needs me, the kid needs me.*

A sharp grinding noise pulled him out of the nauseating guilt that threatened to overwhelm him. On the far wall of the prison's watery courtyard, an entrance appeared in the solid black rock. A lone, hooded figure stood waiting for them, motionless.

"Are you up to this?" Sneak asked as the two of them rowed a hastily lowered sloop to meet the unsuspecting prison warden. "You look jittery."

"Just stay out of my way," he replied through clenched teeth. An army of ghosts glided across the water beside them, silent spectators of what was to come.

Sneak moored the boat to a rusty iron peg in the wall and they clambered into the entrance with less than professional grace. Their hooded host beckoned with a spindly hand, a glimmer of obsidian reflecting where a face ought to have been.

"What do you want?" a raspy voice demanded.

Acheron fought the urge to cringe as Sneak stepped forward, his hand outstretched. Every fiber in his body screamed that something was wrong.

"We thank you kindly for offering us refuge, our fleet is under—" He broke off as the hooded figure drew in a long, rattling breath.

"You are not members of the enlightened watch."

"I assure you—"

"You are not members of the enlightened watch." The cloaked woman took a step forward. "Who are you?"

"I told you," Sneak stammered, "my name is officer Bennet Tangrivsky, captain of the *Yugon*."

Acheron saw the surge coming a splinter of a second before it would have smashed Sneak's face like an overripe avocado. He flared *Veloce* and jerked Sneak aside.

"Mother of..." Sneak cursed as his back struck the stone wall.

The sense-surger stepped back into a stable stance to absorb the recoil of the missed surge. Acheron flared *Gnis,* his entire being focused on the triangular rune as he advanced on the eyeless priestess. She lunged for him, swinging an iron-clad fist. Acheron ducked under her outstretched arm and shoved a burning hand into the woman's face. The metal helmet deformed under his grasping fingers as it melted.

There was the sizzle of searing flesh, before the priestess blew out a rattling breath colder than the most vicious winter storm. The ice-surge enveloped Acheron's hand. It was all he could do to jump aside. *Gnis* vanished as his body temperature plummeted. Somewhere in the distance, a horn resounded.

"Clever trick," Acheron shouted, circling the priestess. "Shame it cost you your eyes and soul to learn."

"Your arrogance will cost you a far greater price, heretic," she snarled. "I know why you are here, and it is futile."

"We'll decide what's futile," a high-pitched voice called out from the mouth of the entrance.

Zot strode forward, flanked by Sneak and Bron, whose eyes were ablaze with light. Zot looked over his shoulder, then back at Acheron and the priestess.

## CHAPTER 53

"Don't mind me," he said, waving an impatient hand, "you sorcerers go about your sorcerers' business. I've got somewhere else to be."

\*\*\*

A short blast of a Biori war horn cracked through the night like a whip, followed by a second blast, and finally a third, longer blast. *Three. Locktower C.*

This was it. The diversion was under way. The others were fighting to buy her time, drawing away the attention of the darkhelms. It was a window of opportunity that had begun closing as soon as it had opened. Brina rubbed her clammy hands together. The fortress seemed like a sandcastle below them.

"That's our cue, buddy." She stroked Razorwing's soft neck, then jerked the reins, pulling him into the dive. With the wind rushing in her ears, Brina let out a whoop of exhilaration. The unforgiving stone of the prison's outer walls neared at a breakneck pace. At the very last moment, the griffin broke the dive and aimed for the top of the highest tower.

Razorwing soared across the top of the tower. Shouts of surprise rang out as its claws closed around two unsuspecting guards, followed by drawn-out screams when the griffin dropped them a good hundred feet above sea level.

A third guard fired a quarrel which missed Brina's shoulder by inches. She pulled the reins, guiding the griffin into a wide arc.

*C, which one's C?*

Brina closed her eyes, trying to conjure up the image of the floor plan Versa had drawn up.

It was right ahead of them. A single quarrel flew from between the tower's battlements, forcing Razorwing into a sharp dodge.

As they soared past the tower, Brina let go of Razorwing's feathers and threw herself sideways over the battlements, where she collided with a bewildered guard who was trying desperately to reload her windup. The woman toppled backward. The weapon went skidding across the stone floor.

"I'm sorry about this," Brina said, picking up the windup. The guard struggled to get up, but Brina swept her legs out from under her. A flash of *Forte*, one swooping motion, and a thunk as the windup's stock collided with the guard's helmet. The woman slumped backward against the battlements. She'd have a headache in the morning, but she'd live.

Brina dumped the windup over the edge and heard it explode on the rocks below. Razorwing had already disappeared into the clouds above. Brina swallowed, praying to everything good in this world that the bird had understood what it was supposed to do.

With fingers numb from the cold and a healthy dose of terror, Brina removed the unconscious guard's armor and helmet. The steel owl's head of the God's Maul guards was heavier than she'd expected. For all the times she'd seen darkhelms strut around in their raven helmets, she'd never actually held one in her hands. When she put it on, she found that it severely impaired her vision. It was like trying to use a spyglass indoors. Everything was narrow and framed in darkness. It would be very easy to get disoriented in this thing.

The stone staircase leading into the tower had tiny, uneven steps, worn smooth through centuries of use. Brina shuffled slowly downward, testing each step with her foot before committing her weight to it.

"Paschendael, is that you?" a man shouted from somewhere below. "What in the Keeper's name is going on?"

"It's me," Brina called back, flaring *Rhetoris* to make herself sound convincing. "There seems to be trouble near the warden's office. I thought I'd check it out. We're no use to anyone stuck up here."

She rounded a final winding turn and entered a round room. Sections of bars lined the edges, behind which dark recesses gaped. They were about the size of two wardrobes glued together. Anxiety trickled through the veins in Brina's forearms like beads of boiling lead. Was this it? Was she about to come face to face with what remained of the man who had raised her?

To her disappointment, the cells were shrouded in shadow, making it impossible to see who was inside. She didn't dare move closer for fear of looking suspicious. Paschendael would be expected to know who was in which cell.

"So that's why the eyeless freak abandoned her post." The man who had called out to her stood in the middle of the circular room, shaking his head. His owl-helmet was encrusted with gilded feathers, and the trim of his armor made it clear he was a station above the regular guards. "I just went to check on our special prisoner, but when I knocked at the wing's entrance, I found it locked, but unguarded."

"I'll take over while she's gone," Brina said, a little too eagerly. "I'll make sure Springtide is secure."

The officer raised an eyebrow. Brina winced.

## CHAPTER 53

"I don't know, Paschendael," he said. "The warden was quite clear that only the Reynziel was to guard the Cardinal slayer."

"Obviously," Brina said, "but I'm sure he didn't expect her to be drawn away by a security crisis, did he?" She looked down at her shoes, hoping to disguise the low gray glow of *Rhetoris* in her eyes.

"I suppose," the officer conceded. "I guess we'd better both go. Check on each other, so to speak. That way, no one can imply anything untoward occurred."

"What about this lot?" Brina waved at the bars. "Can't leave them unsupervised, can we?"

The officer chuckled. "Good one. But come on, let's get going. I've got a funny feeling about this."

Brina suppressed a roar of frustration as the officer preceded her down the stairs. *One more obstacle to get rid of.*

"Funny feeling?" She tried to sound casual, but landed on nervously giggly.

"There's nothing funny about this," the officer snapped. "The warden might be in real danger. We all might be."

"I mean you just said—"

"I know what I said."

They carried on in tense silence, their booted footfalls thumping against the stone stairs like muted drums. When they reached a second landing, the officer marched toward a heavy steel door with three keyholes. He pulled out a key ring that held over a dozen seemingly identical steel keys. He carefully picked one, made to insert it into the lock, then cursed.

"See?" he demanded, jabbing a finger at the crack between door and wall. "It's not properly locked. This is the sort of sloppy work you get when you bring in De Leliard's favorites. I've kept the Cardinal slayer contained for eleven years. You'd think they'd grant me the honor of letting me finish the damn job. But no..." He went on, rambling about protocol this and nepotism that, his hand resting on the black door handle.

Brina nodded vigorously, trying not to let her mounting excitement overrule her judgment. Every fiber in her body was tense, ready to pounce. *Not yet. Wait it out.* But how much longer would she have? She remembered how the air had frozen around the eyeless priestess the night Doorstep's Ditch had burned. If a sense-surger was here, things could go horribly wrong, fast.

"Anyway," the officer said, holding open the door and beckoning for Brina to enter, "let's pick up the slack where others have dropped it, shall we?"

The room beyond was pitch black. In the watery light of the firejelly jars hanging in the hallway, Brina could barely make out a series of barred cells like on the floor above. There were no chairs or tables for guards to sit. The room was completely empty.

"Right," Brina said, nodding as she passed the officer. She grinned widely under her helmet. They were here. She couldn't believe the plan had gone this smoothly. All she had to do now was...

*Slam.* The door crashed shut behind her. Immediately, a series of rattles, pops, and clicks cemented it into place.

"Hey," she called, "what are you doing?"

"You're not Paschendael," the officer shouted back, a maniacal triumph in his voice. "How stupid do you think I am? I've worked with the woman for two decades."

Brina swore. *Springtide, you sevenfold damned moron.* She flung the heavy owl's helmet into the dark. It clattered away into oblivion. She was so close.

"And don't bother trying your filthy heretic signs," the officer gloated. "We've been containing your kind since before you were born. Ask the Cardinal slayer in there. He knows all about it." There was a laugh at the other side of the door, followed by footsteps receding down the stairs.

Brina burned *Lux*, and its starburst hues spread out through the empty room.

"Now this *is* interesting," a gravelly voice intoned.

# CHAPTER 54

*12th day of the 1st cycle, 570KR*
**God's Maul**

Zot pressed his dagger into the kneeling warden's exposed neck, drawing a string of red beads across the pale flesh. He was utterly, undeniably surrounded.

"Step back," he told the growing crowd of guards streaming into Bibber's office. "One false move, and you'll watch your boss leak like an old barrel."

They hesitated. Though they outnumbered him a dozen to one, they wouldn't risk the loss of the man who lined their pockets every week. It was all simple mathematics. The time it would take them to disarm him, minus the second it would take for his dagger to plunge into the warden's neck. For now, they seemed to think that number unfavorable.

*This had better end up being worth it,* he thought bitterly, stealing a glance at the open seas outside. The bald sorcerer had been the only one whose capabilities he had an unquestioning faith in, and that one had skittered up the stairs after the hooded priestess, disappearing from sight. For all Zot knew, Acheron was already dead.

To make matters worse, the other two had left him here as a distraction while they took care of the final step of the plan. Though he had agreed to the plan, it now seemed ludicrous, bordering on the suicidal, to leave the only one of them without access to the supernatural in the most precarious position.

"You." He pointed at one of the smaller darkhelms in the doorway. "Collect everyone's weapons and pile them in front of the carpet right there." He wriggled the fingers on the hand holding the dagger. "I don't need to tell you how urgent this is, do I?"

The darkhelm sighed, then turned around to mutter something to the group crowding the doorway behind him. A series of reluctant clinks followed as daggers and maces fell to the warden's rug. There was a suspicious lack of windups or other bows. Zot sighed, imagining half a dozen sharpshooters ready to turn him into a human hedgehog as soon as he stepped within sight of the door.

"Your troops are skirting the edge, warden," he hissed in Bibber's ear, pointing his free hand at the lackluster pile of weaponry. "Could you kindly remind them that I shall also need their bows?"

"Who are you?" Bibber muttered, his voice trembled like rope stretched to the breaking point.

"The man who writes your dialog from now on." Zot flicked a finger against the man's forehead. "Tell them to bring me their windups."

Before Bibber could call out, there was a commotion on the landing beyond the door.

"I've got one," a man panted between heaving breaths. "She's locked up on the Cardinal slayer's floor. They're not going anywhere."

Zot swore. If that was true, the attempt had failed. His leverage was diminishing rapidly. He cursed himself for having been suckered into this moronic business. He'd let his anger toward the church get the better of him, and now he would pay the ultimate price. There was a yelp from the warden. Zot looked down and realized he'd been squeezing the knife tighter against the man's throat, drawing a trickle of blood.

"Get up," he snapped at Bibber. "We're going for a walk."

He marched the man toward the doorway, using him as a shield against any incoming quarrels. The darkhelms parted before him like ants before a flame.

Under his barrage of threats, the darkhelms marched back up the staircase, leaving him a path to reach the ground floor unhindered.

"Good," he called out to the army that was following behind, careful to stay out of his field of vision. "Nobody needs to get hurt. You let me go. I let the warden go."

He marched backward down the entrance leading to the waterlogged courtyard, where he hoped the sloop would still be moored at the entrance.

\*\*\*

"Unless my life before these bars was a fever dream, I know who that voice belongs to."

He was thin. Emaciated might be a better term. His hair was clumped

## CHAPTER 54

with grime and hung down to his waist. It was impossible to tell where it ended and his scraggy black beard began. He was a wreck, even more so than Brina had ever dare imagine. Then there were his eyes. The same beads of polished amber that stared back at her when she looked into a mirror. A torrent of memories that didn't quite take form flooded past her. It was him, and yet he felt like a stranger, as though there were two men fused into one body.

"Father," she said, approaching the bars of his cell. It was about four feet wide and seven deep, a tiny rectangle of stone with some loose straw on the floor and a filthy bucket in the corner. "You're coming home."

She didn't know precisely where that was. Going back to the mill was out of the question after tonight. De Malheur's fortress would only keep them safe for a short while. They would have to figure that out as they went.

There was a sad quality to Abrasax's smile. "You shouldn't have come here, Sabrina. Not on my account. They won't let us get away."

Brina waved his comment away as she took a few steps back, Lux-enhanced eyes focused on the cell door's heavy, but slightly rusty lock.

"Stand back."

She rushed forward and stomped on the cell's lock. The faint blue light of *Forte* illuminated the bars just enough to aim.

Her foot struck the lock with a resounding clank, and the bars rattled and creaked but refused to budge. Breathing heavily, she moved back and landed another kick. There was a snapping sound, and Brina hoped to the Seven that it had come from the lock, rather than the leg she'd been abusing as a battering ram.

She jerked the door back and forth, flaring the sigil with all her might. The hinges groaned like an old horse galloping uphill, but still the lock would not yield.

As she went in for a third kick, her *Forte* store winked out, completely drained. Her foot impacted hard against the solid metal door. Without the support of the sigil, a spike of pain shot up her ankle as it bent almost double under the force of the kick.

She let out a cry of pain that turned into a scream of frustration midway. So close. So excruciatingly close.

"I'm sorry it had to go like this." Abrasax put a hand on her shoulder through the bars. "You tried, kid. Just like I did. I suppose it just wasn't in our blood, eh?"

"Shut your mouth, you coward." Brina froze as she heard the words come out of her own mouth. Something inside her had dislodged right alongside her ankle.

"How dare you?" she demanded. "*It's not in our blood?* I spent the last decade being shunned and cursed for what's in my blood. Now you're going to tell me it was all a lie?"

She shook her head repeatedly, like a horse engulfed in a swarm of flies. "No," she spat. "That's unacceptable. I don't try. I do."

She flung her shoulder against the door with all her might. Then again, and again, and again. Never in her life had she felt this angry, scared, and frustrated all at once. Her shoulder exploded with white-hot pain, but she was beyond caring.

"Stop," Abrasax shouted. "You're going to kill yourself."

"Better to do it myself than to wait for the hangman." She charged at the door, kicked off with her good foot, and flew headlong into the rattling door.

When she burst through, she stumbled right into her father's arms.

"I'm sorry," he said, holding up her weight, "about everything."

"That'll have to wait," she snapped, though there was no real bite to her voice. "You can tell me all about it when we get out of here."

Supported by Abrasax, she limped toward the heavy black door carved into the opposite wall.

She grinned at it. Then reached into her pocket and pulled out the two remaining balls of Oppen's concoction.

\*\*\*

Acheron was gaining ground. One step at a time, he forced the sense-surger backward up the spiraling staircase. Though she had some awareness of her surroundings, her lack of vision slowed her down on the tightly winding, uneven steps. All Acheron had to do now was keep her on the defensive so he could push her further and further out of her element.

He tried another blitz, burning *Veloce* into *Gnis*, hoping to strike a weak spot. Every time he got close, the sense-surger countered with another blast of icy breath. Glittering ice crystals covered the walls. Already drawing dangerous amounts of heat from his own blood, Acheron could feel the chill seep into his bones. If he kept this up, he'd sink into hypothermia quickly.

*Let's see if the lady can call a bluff.* With another tap of *Veloce,* he leapt

## CHAPTER 54

forward, dodged a blow of the priestess's heavy steel gauntlet, and reached toward her face.

Instead of going for contact, he burned *Pruine* at the last second, drawing on the cold that had settled in his blood. The priestess blew out another wave of frost. This time, *Pruine* kept her breath from escaping. The combined cold waves turned the moisture in the air solid, encrusting her spiked helmet with a thick layer of translucent ice. She drew a raspy breath, and stumbled.

Acheron grinned. It was dangerous business, playing with one's breath. If you couldn't get it all out, the remaining air settled in your lungs. She was effectively freezing herself from the inside out.

The sense-surger was forced to redirect her energy. Steam rose from the helmet as she tried to clear her windpipe. The momentary distraction was just what Acheron needed.

He reached for his sigilist's stars. Three silver stars glittered in the red glow of the jelly lanterns built into the wall. Two high, one low. The first struck the top of the priestess's helmet, where it stuck. *So close.* Acheron cursed.

She saw the second one coming and attempted to dodge by sinking into a crouch. The third, lowest, one sliced clean through the leather armor on her shoulder. A deep gash opened. Rivers of red cascaded down her black cloak.

With a roar, the sense-surger launched herself at him. She swung wildly with the steel gauntlets, aiming to shatter his skull.

Acheron ducked, causing the gauntlet to slam into the wall, where it left a shallow crater. A second blow passed so close in front of his cheek that he could feel the displaced air brush his skin.

Punch after punch sailed his way, accentuated with screams of rage from the sense-surger. A twinge of fear stirred in Acheron's chest. The force behind those reckless strikes was awe-inspiring. All it would take was for one to connect with his head, and it would all be over. His movements were severely limited by the cramped staircase. It was like being trapped in a cage with a wounded bargheist.

*Keep it together, Spider,* he told himself. *Keep buying time.* With every passing second, the kid and the others were getting closer to Abrasax. That was all that mattered.

Forced to keep burning *Veloce,* Acheron was rapidly getting out of breath. His decrepit body was giving up on him. If they kept this up, there was only one outcome. A decidedly unpleasant one.

He bent over, hands on his knees, panting. The sense-surger's fist lashed out at once. Acheron side-stepped. The momentum of her own strike pulled the priestess forward, off balance. Acheron planted a foot between her exposed shoulder blades and kicked her down the stairs.

She rolled over, helmet clanking against the smooth stone. Before she could regain balance, Acheron sprinted up the staircase. Heavy footsteps raced up the stairs behind him.

At the top of the tower, a heavy steel door blocked his path. He flared *Forte* and kicked it straight off its hinges. Three guards clutching windups spun around from their positions at the battlements as he came barreling toward them. Bowstrings twanged. A flash of *Veloce*. Acheron leapt behind one of the darkhelms. The man gurgled piteously as his colleagues' quarrels struck him squarely in the chest.

He picked up the fallen darkhelm's windup. There was no time to reload, so he just chucked it at the nearest guard's head. The bow's stock thumped into her helmet, and she stumbled.

With a roar, the sense-surger leapt out of the staircase. The third darkhelm fired his reloaded bow. The priestess drew a rattling breath as the bolt whizzed over her shoulder.

She exhaled a tornado. Acheron's eyes went wide as a fierce wind swept over the top of the tower. Both darkhelms were lifted off their feet and hurled over the battlements. Acheron reflexively burned *Grave*. Wind rushed in his ears, but by the grace of the Seven, his feet remained planted. He gaped at the place where the darkhelms had vanished over the battlements. *Who needs enemies with allies like these.*

Any sigilist worth their scripts ought to have known how easily a cheap shot like that was countered. Though her power was immense, the priestess lacked experience, and it was costing her. An idea struck him.

"Why did they send you?" He held up his hands, suggesting a temporary truce.

No response came. The priestess lurched forward, swinging wildly with her gauntlets. Acheron easily dodged.

"You've never fought an experienced sigilist before, have you?"

Another blow. Another dodge. She was getting agitated. Now that he had room to move, he was rapidly regaining energy.

"What is he holding over your head?"

The priestess's third strike was slow, with no real vigor behind it. She stepped back.

## CHAPTER 54

"You don't know what you're talking about," she growled.

"That so?" Acheron asked, raising his eyebrows. "De Leliard sacrificed Estav, knowing he would be in prime position to take over the top seat. When he was inquisitor, he had his own people tortured by the score if they didn't bend to his every whim. Why would you be different?'

"Lies." Her iron fingers twitched.

"Then tell me you chose to give up your vision out of your own free will, knowing up front what would be expected."

Silence. Acheron smiled sadly.

"It was you." The priestess's voice had sunk to a whisper. There was a volcanic anger in her tone, threatening to erupt. "You did this to me."

Acheron frowned, confused.

"You weren't supposed to escape that cage. You were bait. It almost worked."

"Almost," Acheron agreed, unable to keep a grin off his face. "Through no fault of my own, I seem to be a rather slippery fellow to hold on to."

"I lost everything!" she screamed. In a flash, she was upon him. Acheron dodged the first blow, but the second one hit him in the shoulder. He spun round, hit the back of his head on the ramparts. He rolled just in time to watch a third swing of the gauntlet shatter multiple bricks. Stone rained down on him.

Acheron flared *Forte* and swept her feet out from underneath her. He backed away, holding up his hands.

"It wasn't us holding that knife, though, was it?" He poked a finger at his own eyes. "It wasn't us who ordered you to murder all those families in cold blood in Doorstep's Ditch."

It was a guess that the surger Brina had met that night was the same woman, but an educated one. A more experienced surger would have finished the job right then. "I bet that one eats at you at night, doesn't it?"

"It was a necessary evil. You heretics were whipping up a frenzy. Do you have any idea of the bloodshed an empire-wide rebellion would have caused? I murdered a thousand to save a hundred thousand. I maintained balance."

"Then I'm sure De Leliard rewarded you handsomely?"

She shook her head like a wet dog, fists clenching and unclenching.

"He has my mother. She's sick. Her medicine for my service, that was the agreement. I can't renege on that now. I've sacrificed too much."

Acheron nodded. They had finally reached the truth.

"It's not too late to change." It wasn't a gambit, or a ruse. It was an earnest offer. "I'm good with alchemy. We could get her out of there, treat her illness."

"And dishonor the Keeper? Never." She advanced on him. "His Eminence may have my mortal body, but Heil has my undying soul. A man is just a man, but I've got the divine on my side. When our time comes, I will watch you burn as I bask in her eternal light."

"Priests." Acheron rolled his eyes.

A wave of cold rolled over him. He blocked it with a cold front of his own. Just like that, the duel was back on, his offer rejected. The fight took on a performative feeling. Like two automatons programmed to put on a show, but not to destroy. Strike. Parry. Counter.

Strike. Parry. Counter.

Acheron could feel his stores slowly diminishing. He was stuck in a war of attrition with no idea whose powers would give out first.

A roar like an earthquake broke their rhythm. The tower vibrated beneath Acheron's feet. The eyeless priestess clamped pale hands to her ears as a second, louder explosion resounded.

Acheron made use of the moment to charge. He touched *Veloce*, then swapped into *Forte* at the last moment, delivering a devastating kick to his opponent's stomach. He knew it was a bad move the second he made contact. The priestess grabbed on to his foot and yanked it, pulling him off balance. Acheron saw the iron gauntlet soaring toward his face a moment too late. It struck his right temple, splintering his vision into a thousand shades of gray.

\*\*\*

Icy wind lashed Brina's face as she stumbled onto the top of Locktower C, supported by her father. Her ankle protested with every step, but she forced herself to keep going. Abrasax's bony arms pressed painfully into her armpit as he strained to keep her upright.

As they neared the parapet, his eyes widened. Brina could see stars reflecting in them.

"The chariots," he muttered. "The swirling mist above the Sundered Sea. I thought I'd never see any of it again."

"If we don't get out of here fast, it might very well be the last time." Brina rubbed her hands together nervously, scanning the night sky for the

## CHAPTER 54

circling shadow that would reveal Razorwing's presence. The damn bird was nowhere to be seen.

There was a rush of air, followed by the twang of steel on stone as a wind-up quarrel ricocheted off the parapet next to Brina's ear. She cursed and pulled Abrasax to the floor beside her, narrowly avoiding two more arrows.

"They're up there," a woman shouted. "Locktower C. Let the priest deal with the bald wizard. The cardinal slayer's our priority."

Brina swore. Acheron was in trouble. Soon they would be too. She pressed two fingers to her lips and blew with all her might, producing a piercing whistle. It dissipated in the wind like tears in a pond. *Come on, you stupid sack of feathers.*

"I'm sorry, child," Abrasax said, eying the trapdoor leading to the staircase. "I'm afraid I'll be worse than useless if it comes to a fight. What strength I once possessed has been meticulously shaved away over the years."

A scream echoed against the fortress's mighty walls.

"It's got me. Shoot it, for Heil's sake, shoot it."

Brina's heart leapt as Razorwing's vast shadow soared overhead, a wriggling guard clamped in the griffin's steel claws. The beast went into a sharp arc, dodging a volley of quarrels.

Razorwing screeched as one of the barbed tips pierced its left wing. The darkhelm went sailing through the night, let out a scream, then bounced off the lower fortifications and into the roiling sea.

Brina whooped, waving her arms overhead to draw the beast's attention.

"What on earth is that?" Abrasax dropped into a crouch as the griffin passed overhead.

"Our ride. Come on," she said. "Help me get up here."

For one glorious moment they stood on the edge of the tower, in plain view of any archer with quarrels left to shoot. Jelly lamps glittered below them like fallen stars. All around them, the moonlit Sundered Sea stretched to the ends of the world. From up there, it looked infinite. A vast canvas of boundless opportunity.

Brina grinned as quarrels whizzed past. They were so close now. All they had to do was stick the landing.

Brina stepped off the edge into nothingness, pulling Abrasax down with her. Razorwing swooped in beneath them and they landed right where the griffin's neck met its shoulder blades.

Brina pulled at Razorwing's feathers, urging the beast upward, out of arrow's range.

A drawn-out, inhuman scream pierced Brina's ears like a drill against her temples. The sense-surger stood atop Locktower A, arms outstretched. Acheron lay on the floor, motionless. Razorwing screeched and bucked as the priestess's voice rose in pitch.

"It's a vocal surge," Abrasax shouted in Brina's ear. "We need to get out of range now or it will knock us straight out of the air."

"Where the Heil did you think I was trying to go? I'm losing control." Razorwing's neck jerked, and Brina felt her grasp on the griffin's quills slip through her fingers. The beast's wings beat clumsily, almost lazily, as the ground began rushing up to meet them.

# CHAPTER 55

*12th day of the 1st cycle, 570KR*
**God's Maul**

he Spider of Rothmoor, bested by a single priest. Voices swirled around Acheron as he sank deeper and deeper into the void. His head felt like it was caving in on itself. *Did you really think that all those years of cloud wouldn't demand their toll?*

*You've squandered your only gift. You were put on this sphere to play one crucial part in history. To do one thing right after a lifetime of wrongs. This was it. You've missed it.*

"No," he muttered, struggling against his closing throat. "Leave me alone. I'm dying. You're not supposed to follow me here."

*Oh, but I am,* his mother whispered. *You made it so when your skinny little worm fingers closed around my neck. Remember?*

There was a jerk behind his navel, and he fell.

Acheron's back slammed into a dusty wooden floor. He kept his eyes shut, though he knew it wouldn't help him now. Not when he was back in the wardrobe. Not on that fateful day.

He shrank back against his mother's moth-eaten coats, folding child-sized arms in front of his face.

A crash resounded on the other side of the shoddy paneling. Acheron's heart squeezed painfully. It always began this way.

Before he knew it, daylight flooded the wardrobe and his mother's bony fingers pinched down on his ear. He tried to get up, but she jerked his ear downward, forcing him to the ground.

"Why are you still here?" She gave his ear another violent tug. "You've already missed a shipment of Biori sailors. D'you have any idea what kind of money those savages throw away at the card's table?"

Acheron cringed. He'd overslept. He'd been too tired and bruised from a beating he'd received at the Menacing Mermaid the night before. The older he got, the more he got accused of cheating and the more brutal the "punishments" became. Not to mention the hiding his mother gave him whenever he came home empty-handed.

Maybe soon some drunk would smash in his skull once and for all and it would finally all be over. He'd considered doing it himself, but some ancient, animal part of himself wouldn't allow itself to be destroyed.

"I can hardly stand," he protested, raising black and blue arms, partly to show her just how bad he'd gotten it, mostly to shield his swollen nose from the slap he knew was coming.

"Is that so?" She lifted the heel of her boot and stomped, aiming for his shin. He withdrew it at the last second. The heel thumped against the wood, causing the floorboards to rattle. "Your legs seem fine to me. So march your useless bones to the Mermaid."

Acheron hoisted himself up, holding on to the edge of the bed to pull himself into an unstable stance. His mother picked up her favorite soot-stained goblet from her bedside table, delicately dropped a pebble of cloud into the bowl, and fumbled with a match.

Moments later, white vapors rose from the goblet. Acheron's stomach lurched as he watched those delicious coils of relief vanish into his mother's lungs. He eyed the goblet hungrily, imagining how good it would feel to forget about the countless cuts and bruises on his limbs for a brief spell. His bony arms instinctively extended toward the cup.

"Don't even think about it, boy," his mother snapped, turning her back on him as though to shield a babe from a hungry sheikan. "You've got lost shards to make up for."

She waved a dismissive hand at the front door.

To his own surprise, Acheron's feet remained planted. He'd been dismissed. He ought to leave and get to work, as he had done countless times before. But he didn't, and he wouldn't.

"No." The word hummed nervously in his throat.

"What did you just say to me?" Mother whipped round, her misty eyes addled equally by cloud and rage.

"No."

She flung a nearby chair, but he was ready for it. He ducked, causing the chair to crash into the wall behind him, where it shattered.

Before he knew it, she was on top of him. The goblet of cloud swayed precariously in one fist while the other slammed into his already broken

## CHAPTER 55

nose. Acheron could feel the bone squash into fragments. He howled, trying to cover his face.

"You don't talk back to me, boy," Mother screeched, each word emphasized with a punch to his raised arms. "You have ruined my life, every dream I ever had." She drew a rattling breath, siphoning up every last wisp of the cloud sizzling in the goblet. "And now you dare tell me 'no'?"

Her free hand closed around Acheron's throat. "I should have strangled you the day you were born, you worthless brat. It would have saved me so much heartache." She squeezed; Acheron's eyes bulged. "Maybe it's not too late."

He struggled, prying at her locked fingers with both hands. Mother dropped the goblet and tried to pin his wrists with her second hand. The smoldering snow-colored nugget rolled out of the cup, coming to a stop right beside him. Sweet vapors traveled up his nose, numbing his terror and clouding his mind.

*Just give up,* they told him. *Let her finish the job. You'll be at peace. Forever.*

He couldn't. Every fiber of his being screamed for him to resist, to fight, to survive.

With the strength of a cornered animal, he heaved Mother off himself. She toppled. As he forced himself upward, he grabbed the front of her patched and stained tunic and slammed her backward into the floorboards. The back of her head collided with the wood with a sickening crack. Her face went slack as blood trickled down the grooves in the wood.

Panic and relief warred in Acheron's guts. He had killed her. The only family he had ever known, gone. He was safe. He was alone.

Mother drew a deep, rattling breath. The discovery that she was alive inspired far greater terror in Acheron than her death ever could have. When she woke up, he was as good as dead. He needed to leave, to go someplace where she couldn't find him.

*Or,* a small voice in the back of his mind suggested, *there is a permanent solution.*

"No," he said out loud, watching the blood pool under his mother's head. "I can't."

Acheron's hands trembled as they skittered across the floor, searching for the unfinished lump of cloud his mother had dropped during their struggle. He lit what remained in the tin goblet, drinking in every wisp of smoke as he stared at his mother's slowly heaving chest.

As the familiar lightness took hold, he crawled toward her. She had to die, or he would spend the rest of his life looking over his shoulder. She deserved it.

"This isn't real," he told himself. "This isn't how it happened. This isn't real."

It took every ounce of willpower he had to fight against the dream. He forced his hands away from her throat, felt the world tilt into a dizzy spin.

Acheron's eyes snapped open. He gasped like a drowning man cast suddenly onto shore. The blurry outline of jagged battlements surrounded him. His ears rang with the sense-surger's supernatural screech.

She stood atop the parapet, arms outstretched. A mere fifteen feet above her, the kid was fighting a losing battle against gravity as Razorwing bucked and twitched in midair, rendered to panic by the vocal surge.

On the surrounding towers, guards were hastily rewinding enough windups to turn the griffin into a pincushion. The attempt was failing. Between the eyeless priestess and the legions of guards streaming out onto the walls below, the net was closing around them rapidly.

It was happening again. Against his better judgment, he'd allowed himself to hope. He'd failed to keep a safe distance from his co-conspirators—no, he corrected himself, his friends—and now he would lose all of them again.

*There slips freedom's last hope,* Azaria's voice whispered in his ear, every syllable dripping with malice, *and once again you are just letting it happen.*

"No," he growled, voice burning in his throat. "Never again." He had to do something. Anything. He tried to get to his knees and bit down a scream as his shattered legs buckled beneath his weight. He reached for *Forte* to mask the pain, desperate for any remnant of strength left untapped in his spent body.

The shape wasn't there. Panic pierced his chest like a blade. He tried again, searching with all his might for the rune, one he'd drawn upon thousands of times over the years. The space behind his eyes remained deafeningly blank. He dug around for the other stores. Any other store. All he found was fog, a nauseating emptiness inside as from a missing organ. The shapes had deserted him.

*You've finally done it,* his mother croaked. *You've huffed and smoked away the only talent you ever had.*

"Screw you," Acheron whispered, refusing to look at the white shapes clambering over the tower's battlements around him. He pushed himself up, forcing his weight onto his legs. Fire engulfed his entire lower body.

## CHAPTER 55

He endured.

One excruciating step at a time, he staggered toward the eyeless priestess's turned back. Abrasax and the kid were almost level with her now. Soon, she would make the leap.

Acheron's jaw worked. There were no tricks left up his sleeve, no gods or martyrs to pray to, just the waning power of his will and the courage he'd lacked all those years ago.

When she finally spun around to face him, it was already too late. Acheron's shaking hands closed around the collar of her robes. He launched himself forward with one last burst of strength summoned out of thin air.

There was a moment. A fragment of a second when the pair of them tipped over the edge, where Brina's eyes met his own, her mouth open in a scream that never reached him.

Acheron smiled at her. She had given him so much. More than she could ever know.

"It's okay," he mouthed.

Wind rushed in his ears as they plummeted. The priestess struggled against his grip. They spun in midair.

Dozens of spectral white shapes launched themselves off the tower after them, determined to haunt him until the very end.

Acheron laughed out loud as they dissolved on their way down, blending in with the scattered stars of the night sky.

# CHAPTER 56

*12th day of the 1st cycle, 570KR*
**God's Maul**

It seemed to take hours.

Acheron, limbs entwined with the eyeless priestess, bounced off the lower ramparts and tumbled head over heels down the jagged cliff at the base of the fortress into the roiling sea.

Brina's scream was lost to the rush of the wind as Razorwing hurtled toward a veil of low-hanging clouds.

"No, you stupid bird," she screamed. "Turn back. Go down."

She tugged at the griffin's feathers, ground her heels into its side, but it was no use. Panicked and injured, the beast was completely beyond her control.

Abrasax shushed her. "Give the poor creature a moment. Let's be grateful it hasn't bucked us off yet."

"We have to go back. Now." Below them, the dark outline of God's Maul was ablaze with dozens of jelly lanterns running around on the towers and walls. From up here, it looked like a disturbed hive of fire ants. "We have to help him. We could still... It's not too..."

"Sabrina, he's gone." Abrasax gulped, looking back at the rapidly shrinking fortress.

"He'll have burned something. Anything."

"No sigil can save him now. Not after an impact like that."

Brina bit down on her bottom lip. He was right. A steady trickle of iron filled her mouth. The pain drew her back into the present.

"Was it just the two of you in there?" Abrasax asked, looking back at the swarming lights of God's Maul.

Brina's lungs shriveled. *The others.* She'd been so caught up in her own

## CHAPTER 56

deafening panic that she'd all but forgotten that Sneak, Bron, and Zot were still trapped in the prison's lower levels. *Not them too. I won't allow it.*

She put her hands on the sides of Razorwing's neck and gently stroked the frantic bird's feathers.

"One more trip," she whispered in the bird's ear. "One more, and we'll be safe."

*Consol*'s warm gleam reflected off the griffin's plumage like a blossoming flower.

"Looks like you've been busy," Abrasax said. It was hard to tell whether he was impressed or disturbed by Brina's mastery of the sigil.

"Busier than you know," she replied, eyes fixed on the prison's waterlogged courtyard far below them.

\*\*\*

"No good deed goes unpunished," Zot grumbled to himself as yet another quarrel thudded into the *Yugon*'s rear mast, inches from his ear. "If I live to see another dawn, with the Seven as my witness, I'll be done with all this savior complex shit."

Sloops, filled with a dozen darkhelms apiece, glided through the courtyard's inky waters, surrounding the ship. Zot let go of the boat's wheel as the first barbed boarding hook crashed onto the ship's deck, drawing deep gouges in the pristine wood before lodging itself tightly behind the railing.

"Oi," he screamed, "that's Morassian hardwood. Fifteen Heildamned shards per square foot."

When Zot reached the hook, a lone guard had already shimmied up the rope. As the man struggled to vault onto the ship's deck, Zot kicked him in the jaw, sending him toppling backward onto his comrades.

With a mighty heave, Zot dislodged the hook and flung it into a second sloop. There was a lot of shouting and cursing as the two commanders tried to get their sloops and soldiers untangled from the mess.

"Hey, Zot," Sneak's voice called from the gatehouse directly ahead of the ship's bow, "get a move on. This thing's heavier than Bron's dad after the yearly erymanthian roast."

In slow, jerky motions, the barnacled iron grate that separated the *Yugon* from open water rose from the depths, spraying water and seaweed everywhere.

As though the guards only now realized just how close they were to the embarrassment of the century, three more boarding hooks clattered onto the deck.

"Duck, idiot!"

"Brina?"

Zot dropped to the deck moments before two enormous claws snatched up the nearest hook. Two darkhelms went flying into the water as the rope they were holding onto was jerked up into the night. The heavy hook came tumbling back down amidst an incoming boatload of guards. All of them abandoned the sloop, only to disappear below the surface as their heavy armor dragged them to the depths.

Zot whooped, using the momentary chaos to slice the ropes attached to the other hooks with his dagger. There was much shouting and pointing amongst the darkhelms as the griffin dove a second time, this time landing smoothly on the *Yugon*'s quarterdeck.

Brina slid off the beast's back with a grimace and helped a frail stranger down.

"So you found him, then?" Zot eyed the stranger. He'd met many assassins in his day, but none as decrepit as Abrasax Springtide. He looked like one shot of good kelp could finish him off.

"No," Brina spat, "he's the Cardinal's favorite jester."

Zot shrugged, then craned his neck to look over the pair of them. "Where's my favorite cloudhound?"

"He's..." The choke in her voice told him all he needed to know.

"Too bad," Zot said, wincing as a quarrel ricocheted off the ship's railing a mere foot away. "We could've used the manpower."

"Leave that to me," Brina said. "You get us out of here."

Zot ground his teeth. He'd never responded well to orders. A man of his refined qualities was much better suited to handing them out. Leaving the bloody work to someone else, however, that he could live with.

"You," he barked at the disappointing remains of the Cardinal slayer, "what do you know about sailing ships?"

"That you're not going to get anywhere by yourself," Abrasax replied, the hint of a smile rustling his filthy mustache.

"Good enough. We need all the hands we can get at the oars."

\*\*\*

## CHAPTER 56

"Go!"

Brina waved her arms, trying to get Razorwing to take off, but the griffin refused to budge. Its bright yellow eyes locked on to hers in what could only be interpreted as staunch defiance.

"Fine," she snapped. She ran her fingers up and down Razorwing's side to convey the gratitude she couldn't voice. "But it's your feathery behind on the line."

There was a jerk, and the *Yugon* crept into motion.

"Miss Springtide, behind you," a crewman shouted. Only his head was visible from the hatch leading to the lower deck, but he looked terrified.

She turned just in time to see an armored shape flop over the ship's railing and onto the deck. The man raised a mace with one trembling hand. With the other, he flung a throwing knife straight at Brina's chest.

Brina touched *Veloce*. The world slowed down around her, as though everything had suddenly been drowned in molasses. She sidestepped the knife with lazy precision. As it passed her, she plucked it out of the air and threw it back, adding a touch of *Forte* at the last moment, a trick Acheron had taught her. The knife struck home in the exposed flesh between the man's helmet and chest plate.

He hacked, and a spray of crimson spattered down his glittering black armor.

Brina closed the distance and landed a fortified kick on the man's chest. There was a chorus of shouts and splashes as the corpse landed on its living brothers-in-arms.

"We're not moving fast enough," Zot shouted from the helm. His fists pummeled the wooden wheel. "There's no Heildamned wind in here because of the bleeding walls."

"It was designed that way," Abrasax said, emerging from the oar deck looking as though he might pass out at any moment. "The crew are pulling as hard as they can, but with no assistance from the wind, we'll need some time to build momentum."

"Time is the one thing we don't have." Zot punched the wheel, face screwed up with rage.

Brina loosened yet another boarding hook. She had almost chucked it down into the water when an idea struck her.

"How much extra power do we need?" She shouted at Zot.

"Do I look like a mathematician?" Zot threw up his hands. "I'll take whatever I can get. The *Yugon* is an absolute workhorse. All she needs is a little nudge."

"That I can help with."

Brina hauled up the rope attached to the boarding hook and sprinted along the length of the ship toward the bow. When she'd properly fastened the rope around the front mast, she whistled, burning *Consol*.

It took a single flap of Razorwing's massive wings to reach her.

"That way." Brina pointed at the open gate ahead.

The griffin clicked its beak, showing it had understood. Brina held out the steel hook, and one of Razorwing's claws closed around it.

The rope uncoiled with a whisper, then went taut. Razorwing screeched and fought, beating its wings. The water below rippled and danced under the force of the rising wings. Brina whooped with adrenaline-fueled excitement as the ship, slowly but surely, sped up.

The griffin immediately became a target.

The grinding noise of windups being reloaded echoed all around her.

Brina saw red.

She leapt across the ship's railing into the open air, screaming like an entire platoon of skullbeards. The stabs of agony in her sprained ankle were little more than mosquitoes buzzing in her ear. A distraction, but nothing more.

She touched *Leve* at the apex of her jump, boosting her range drastically. Right before she landed, she flared the shape to smooth her landing.

Half of the darkhelms in the sloop abandoned ship as soon as they saw her coming. The other four tried to take ill-advised swings at her, but only succeeded in hindering each other's movements.

Brina caught a clumsily swung mace in her hand and pulled the weapon from its owner's grip. One furious swipe of it was enough to knock the remaining soldiers over the sloop's sides. Brina flared *Veloce* to catch one of them by the collar of their armor right before they disappeared into the black.

"Your bow," she snarled at the woman.

"Wha—?" The woman cowered, raising her hands in front of her face. Not in the mood to repeat herself, Brina tore the strap attaching the windup to the woman's shoulder and jabbed the weapon's pointy end into the darkhelm's belly.

"Ammo."

## CHAPTER 56

This time, the woman understood, throwing a bandolier containing two dozen quarrels at Brina's feet.

"Excellent." Brina looked over the sloop's side, where fading clouds of bubbles marked the places where the armored darkhelms had been dragged to the bottom. "Take off your plate and your helmet."

The woman's eyes narrowed into a contemptuous glare, but she did as she was told, handing over first her helmet, then her leather cuirass. "Happy?"

"Not particularly." Brina smiled sourly. "But you're going to be."

She shoved the woman into the water. For a moment, it looked like she would drown anyway as she was sucked beneath the surface. Then she re-emerged twenty feet away near the side of another sloop.

Aided by *Veloce,* Brina reloaded the windup in a fraction of the usual time. *Let the hunter become the hunted.* She smiled grimly as her first shot skewered an archer who was homing in on Razorwing. The woman raised a feeble hand to the feather sticking out of her neck, then toppled sideways into the water.

Brina's next target, realizing the sudden danger, flung himself to the sloop's floor, narrowly avoiding certain death.

"Sabrina," her father's voice echoed across the courtyard, "get back here."

With a final tug of Razorwing's mighty wings, the *Yugon*'s bow slid underneath the prison's open gate.

Brina swore. In the commotion, she'd allowed herself to drift farther and farther away from the ship in her efforts to protect its escape. Now she was at risk of being left behind.

The sloop's oars had vanished over the sides alongside its crew, leaving her rudderless and adrift. *Think, Springtide, think.*

As boiling panic snaked its way down her throat and into her chest, Acheron's voice bubbled up from some place deep inside to meet it. *Imprinting on sigils is one thing, given enough time and bananas, a monkey could do it. What distinguishes a sparkgazer is our ability to see the path when others cannot.*

Brina took a deep breath. As she surveyed the sloops bobbing up and down all around her, it became obvious what needed to be done. She sighed, rubbing at her destroyed eye. Of course, her entire future hinged on the one technique she'd never mastered.

As she stood frozen, staring at the unsteady platforms she'd need to hit with perfect precision, the *Yugon*'s front mast slid underneath the gate.

It was now or never. She dug deep, hoping against hope that there was some scrap of *Forte* buried deep inside that could reignite her empty store.

*She who hides too long in a tree, waiting for the perfect opportunity, risks getting struck by lightning first.*

Brina found it. A tiny sparkle of *Forte*, flickering like a candle in a gale. The sloop shifted underfoot as she launched herself, causing her to spin. Her feet kicked at nothing as she arced over the water. At the apex of the jump, she successfully switched into *Leve*.

Her lightened body was carried forward an impossible distance by the momentum of the jump. She almost overshot the empty sloop she was aiming for. It wobbled precariously as she landed with both feet on one of its sides. If her weight hadn't been reduced by *Leve*, it would certainly have tipped.

She steadied herself and launched herself a second time. This time she hit her target full on, landing among a group of surprised darkhelms. By the time they realized what had happened, Brina was already soaring onward.

She let out a howl of excitement as the black water slipped by under her feet. A sense of complete control flooded her. She was whole again. No injury could stop her. This was what Razorwing must feel like. Graceful, light, and free.

As she descended on the final sloop between her and the *Yugon*, she jumped from one helmed head to another, laughing as the guards cursed and shouted.

She launched herself one last time, eyes trained on the gilded galleon ahead.

"Bloody wizards." Zot shook his head wearily as Brina flew over the ship's helm, aiming for a smooth landing on the ship's main deck.

Something hissed in Brina's ear, and the world turned upside down. Her left shoulder went numb as a windup quarrel punched through her armor just below her clavicle.

She spiraled through the air and hit the ship's deck at speed. The impact sent her rolling until her back slammed into the ship's central mast. A jolt of lightning shot up her spine, causing her limbs to flail involuntarily. Then she lay still, not daring to move. Sticky blood leaked from the hole in her armor like sap from a cut tree.

Abrasax's gaunt face appeared above her. He looked terrified. He extended a hand toward the quarrel stuck in Brina's shoulder, then retracted it as though stung by a wasp. His fingertips were coated in dark blood.

## CHAPTER 56

"What do I do?" he muttered, eyes wild with panic. "What do I do?"

"My talisman," Brina croaked. "Around my neck."

Abrasax nodded, then gingerly felt the skin on the back of her neck until he found the pyramid's silver chain. He removed the trinket and held it out to Brina.

"What now?" he asked.

"Just. Hold. It." Brina took a shallow breath, wincing as a torrent of fire flooded her lungs. She eyed the pyramid's complex pattern of twirls and curls with distrust. It had been betraying her for months now. There was every chance it would let her bleed out.

She peered into her father's pale face, saw the tremor in his hands as he raised the pyramid in front of her. *He's not ready. God's Maul has broken him.*

If she died, who would be there to guide him back toward the right path? For all they knew, Saf had died on whatever mission had drawn her away from Hammerstroke. The group would dissolve.

She imagined Abrasax wandering the hills of Barrow's Perch, a second Acheron, strung out on life and cloud.

She ground her teeth and forced herself to drown out the surrounding chaos. Her eye burned, but she refused to blink. Every detail mattered.

Then it was there. Like dawn born from darkness, a droplet of crimson formed in the pyramid's center. It rolled through the metal grooves, forming the sigil. It burned in her mind's eye, as complex and perfectly smooth as a snowflake. A tear welled in the corner of Brina's eye.

"Do it," she told Abrasax. "Pull it out. Now."

Abrasax let out a stuttering breath as his fist closed around the quarrel. "Are you..."

"Now," she screamed. The shape would slip any moment now, closing her window of opportunity.

With a horrendous squelching rip, the quarrel came free. At once, blood spurted from the wound. Brina's body convulsed as what little strength she had left ebbed away.

She clung to the sigil like a drunk to the bottle.

The flow stopped. The edges of the wound tingled as her body began knitting her torn flesh.

A metallic roar jolted Brina back to the present, and the shape slipped. God's Maul's gate thundered shut behind the *Yugon*, trapping their pursuers' sloops behind the mossy grates. Brina smiled to herself. They had done it. They had escaped. As the galleon picked up speed, Sneak and

Bron dove from the top of the gatehouse, turning in midair to land beside Zot on the top deck.

"How are you feeling?" Abrasax asked, still clutching the pyramid. He looked thrice his age, wrinkled with worry and fear.

"Better than the Cardinal will be when he hears about this," Brina said, grinning.

# CHAPTER 57

*13th day of the 1st cycle, 570KR*
**Mallion's Bay**

Brina sat with her back against an empty barrel, watching Zot bark orders at anyone who would listen. Behind them, God's Maul was slowly receding, its monstrous shadows looming over the water in patches of black.

The crime lord's long, gnarled fingers battered the boat's wheel.

"We're not making speed," he muttered. "Not enough to outrun the redsails."

"Relax, we turned most of the fleet into ashes, remember?" Brina chuckled and immediately regretted it as a stab of agony shot through her shoulder.

"I'm serious, Springtide," Zot snapped. "The wind's against us. By the time we reach Hammerstroke, the entire Mallion's Depth garrison will be swarming the shoreline to greet us."

"What are you saying?"

"I'm saying that we can't go back." Zot's eyes wandered to the shimmering lights of Mallion's Depth to their right. "We've poked the bear one too many times."

"But where would we go?" Brina tried to sit up, but found her legs hesitant to obey her.

Zot shrugged. "If I had a clue, I'd be changing course right now."

"Acheron would have known." Brina swallowed. The name caught in her throat, swelling to painful proportions.

"Bastard always had something up his sleeve," Zot agreed. "What happened to him, anyway?"

Brina gritted her teeth as the scene on top of the tower replayed in her mind for the hundredth time, each moment seared into her memory for good.

"He was fighting that eyeless priestess," Brina began. Each word felt like navigating a thicket of sleepthorn, like she was one false move away from collapse. "She was trying to prevent us from escaping."

She tilted her head back and looked up at the countless stars spread out above them like celestial writing.

"And?" Zot urged.

"He grabbed her and pulled her off the tower. They both fell."

Zot let out a low whistle.

"I've always known that man was crazy," he said, though there was undeniable awe in his voice. Zot shook his head. "Flung himself off a tower. What an end."

Brina couldn't think of anything to say to this, so she nodded.

"Shame that he took everything in that massive brain of his with him, though," Zot said as he rotated the wheel with labored movements.

"Wait a minute," Brina said, excitement momentarily blocking out the pain. "Razorwing's saddlebag. I almost forgot."

"What about it?"

"He said it contained emergency supplies." Brina waved an impatient hand. "Get someone to bring it."

Moments later, Sneak trudged up the stairs, carrying the leather saddlebag.

"It's not heavy, Cap'n," he said doubtfully, weighing the bag in his hand. "Doesn't feel like there's anything valuable in there."

"There's a great many valuable things in this world that weigh next to nothing. Give it here."

Brina rummaged through the pack, casting aside a few rolls of bandaging, a handful of stoppered vials containing brightly colored liquids, and finally, a chunk of cloud the size of a chicken's egg, wrapped in stained parchment. Brina shrank back against the barrel, defeated.

"This is it?" she demanded, glaring at Sneak as though this was all his fault. "Acheron dies, and he leaves us with *this?*" She waved the milky white ball in Sneak's face, then threw it at Zot's head.

"Here. It was probably yours to being with."

"Ow, you lunatic," he shouted, rubbing his head. He kicked the chunk aside. It bounced across the deck, then rolled off the side of the ship, lost to the waves.

# CHAPTER 57

Brina made to fling away the parchment it had come in, but Sneak's hand closed around her own.

"Wait," he gasped, tugging at it. "It's been folded double. Look, there's something on the inside."

He unfurled the parchment and held it out to Brina. Though they were hard to make out in the gloom, black lines were etched across the wrinkled page.

"What does it say?" Sneak asked, bending his neck to look over the top.

"It's not writing," Brina said, screwing up her eyes. "Looks more like a drawing. It's hard to see in this light. Could you get me a lantern?"

"A lantern?" Sneak shook his head. "Are you a sparkgazer or not?"

"Right."

She burned *Lux*. At once, the faint smudges turned into crisp lines of black ink, weaving interconnected paths across the parchment. At the top, a single word in Acheron's brisk angled handwriting read "Metten."

"It's a map." Brina's pulse quickened. She sat upright to get a better look. "An island called Metten, somewhere between Morrassia and Bior to the east."

"Are there coordinates?" Zot let go of the wheel, staring at Brina.

She scanned the page, then shook her head.

"Give me that," Zot snapped. He pulled the map out of Sneak's hands and glared at it as though it owed him money. "Why would the old floater leave us this? Did he ever mention this place to you?"

Brina shook her head. "He didn't like to talk about what he did before."

"And with good reason." All eyes turned to Abrasax, who had quietly ascended the stairs to the upper deck.

"Sure," Zot began. Red tinges bloomed on his cheeks. "His secrecy does us a great service now while we're stuck in no-man's-land, waiting for the scepter to come and wrap us up into a neat little bundle."

"The power of Metten is its location," Abrasax said. He took a few steps toward Zot, whose face fell as the larger man towered over him. "It's borderline impossible to find for anyone who doesn't already know it's there. This map holds just enough information for a dedicated crew to find it through trial-and-error."

"There's no bleeding time for trial-and-error," Zot burst out, waving his hands wildly at God's Maul behind them. "I hope you were comfortable in there, Viper, because we're moments away from becoming bunkmates."

"That sounds exceedingly unpleasant," Abrasax said, smiling mildly. "Good thing I know exactly how to reach Metten."

*\*\**

Zot didn't know whether to cuff the crooked old assassin around the ears for wasting so much time or if he wanted to kiss him.

Before he had time to decide, however, a deafening roar caused the sea to roil beneath the Yugon.

As the crew watched in horror, an entire section of God's Maul impenetrable walls shifted sideways. A flood of warbling firelight escaped the fortress as a subterranean dock opened.

"What in the name of Bron's gristly third nipple is that?" Sneak shouted. He pointed and waved, quite unnecessarily, as a short and stocky vessel exited the cavern, heading straight toward them.

It was unlike any seacraft Zot had ever seen. His first thought was of a huge metal turtle floating atop the waves. Spiked steel plates covered the incoming ship's hull and deck. Three huge black cylinders protruded from this airtight shell, two at the bow and one near the stern.

Zot grabbed on to Abrasax's tattered prison robes and shook him.

"Where in the Seven do we go, Viper?"

Abrasax stood transfixed, staring at the steel turtle with petrified horror.

"The wyvern..." he muttered. "It's real. God and martyrs above, it's real."

"We can all bloody see that." Zot felt his own legs tremble. "Let's go."

Abrasax didn't respond. He seemed lost somehow. As though the connection between his body and soul had been severed, leaving only a rudderless husk.

"Dad?" Brina's voice was softer and gentler than Zot had ever heard it. He was surprised the woman was even capable of anything other than biting sarcasm.

The word seemed to jerk Abrasax back to the present. He shuddered, dug his nails into his own forearm, then nodded vigorously to himself.

"Right," he said. "Right. I'll lead us there."

Sailing the *Yugon* with a skeleton crew was one thing if you were going on a leisurely tour of the bay, but under the pressure of being pursued, the lacking efficiency with which the ship was catching wind became painfully obvious. The handful of trusted men and women he'd brought

## CHAPTER 57

along for tonight's journey executed his every instruction at the mere beckon of a hand.

All of them had accepted the risk that came with the generous payment he'd promised them. And yet, Zot felt a pang of guilt at having brought them into this mess. All of them would disappear into God's Maul right alongside him. They had been the last faithful remaining of his old crew, and this was how he repaid their loyalty.

He abandoned the wheel, shoving Abrasax into his position at the helm.

He ran crisscross across the deck, shouting orders at Bron and Sneak while he himself hauled in rope and adjusted sails. All the while, he could see the moonlight glittering off the steel wyvern's armor as it gained speed on them.

"You, son of Bior." He jabbed a thumb at Bron. "Open the storage hatch and throw everything you find overboard. I don't care what it is. If it's not screwed down, it's going."

With every barrel of trading goods the Biori chucked over the railing, a piece of Zot's soul died. Only the Seven knew how many thousands of shards of merchandise were now drifting aimlessly into the darkness. It was the type of money that would have allowed him to pay his mercenaries for months to come. He could've gotten back every inch of ground those scepter bastards had gained on him when they'd put Doorstep's Ditch to the torch.

Now all he could hope for was that the flotsam would hinder the wyvern's pursuit while lightening the *Yugon* enough to gain the advantage.

"It's working," Sneak shouted from atop the front mast. "They're falling behind."

Zot sprinted up to the rear deck, nearly bumping into Springtide's pet griffin on the way up.

"Look at that," he shouted, hardly daring to believe his own eyes. "They're giving up."

A hundred yards away, the wyvern had come to a full stop, surrounded by bobbing barrels.

Abrasax turned around, both hands clasped tightly to the massive boat's wheel.

"That doesn't make any sense," he said, voice trembling. "Rumors about the iron wyvern as a war-changing siege engine have been rife for almost two decades now. It shouldn't be outrun by a fat prize operated by a minimal crew."

"Watch your mouth about my *Yugon*," Zot grumbled. He stroked the ship's railing ostentatiously. "She was built on my specific orders by the best shipwrights in all of Merkede. Cost me three fortunes and a half. Worth every—"

The rest of his sentence was drowned out by a booming explosion that sent shock waves rippling across the surface.

A flash of fire rolled over the iron wyvern's exterior as a small sun was catapulted in Zot's direction.

Abrasax spun the wheel. The force of the turn knocked Zot off his feet.

A blast of scorching heat washed over the deck as the projectile narrowly missed the Yugon. As it made contact with the water, the sphere exploded, spitting shards of fire everywhere.

A handful of them landed in the front sail. Greedy flames spread across the red canvas like a plague in a shantytown, gnawing at everything it touched.

"Don't just stand there, you idiots," Zot howled, bounding across the deck. "Put it out."

It was no use.

Before he'd so much as dropped a roped bucket into the icy saltwater, the entire front mast looked like the witch pyres of old.

The iron wyvern let out a second bark.

The world dissolved in a haze of splintering wood and all-consuming flames.

# CHAPTER 58

*13th day of the 1st cycle, 570KR*
**Mallion's Bay**

 hick, black smoke surrounded Brina, burning in her nose and lungs. Her forearms, which she had used to shield her face from the hail of splintered wood, resembled pin cushions.

A bony hand reached out through the murk, and Brina grabbed it. It was her father.

He looked at her with wide, shocked eyes.

"I—I'm," he stuttered. "I'm sorry. So very sorry. For all of it."

The *Yugon* tilted sideways.

"We're taking water," Sneak's voice called out from what sounded like miles away.

Brina grabbed on to the boat's wheel as she began sliding across the deck. "Sabrina!"

Abrasax's outstretched arms disappeared into the smoke as he slid away from her.

"Razorwing, help him," Brina screeched. A moment later, her weakened body gave up. The ship's wheel slipped from her grasp, and she tumbled down the almost vertical deck.

As she rushed toward the railing, Bron's tattooed form came rushing forward to grab her, eyes burning blue with the effort of holding on.

"Sneak's trying to untangle a sloop." Bron jabbed a finger over his shoulder. "Get over there. I'll look for the viper."

Brina gritted her teeth, wanted to protest, but was forced to accept she was about to collapse like a poorly mixed loaf of bread.

She grabbed both sides of Bron's head and bumped her forehead against his in the traditional Bioran gesture of brotherhood.

"Thanks."

"We all get out or no one does," Bron said simply. Two bounding leaps later, he vanished out of sight.

Brina crept across the deck, using the railing as a walkway, until she spotted two beams of blue light fifteen feet above her.

"Watch out," Sneak called through the murk. "It's coming down any second now."

"Where's Zot?" she shouted back. "Have you seen him?"

The beams of light shook no. "He was right where the blast hit."

Brina cursed. Zot might not share many of her views on life and the revolution, but he had still risked it all to rescue her father from God's Maul. If he'd followed his own selfish advice, he would be back at De Malheur's castle sipping on whatever fermented drink the baron had scrounged up from his cellar. *He's dead,* a rational part of her brain droned. *Don't do anything stupid on account of a dead man.*

She sat down on the ship's railing, feet dangling above the steadily nearing surface of the water.

Ropes creaked as Sneak lowered one of the *Yugon*'s sloops past the railing and into the water. Brina lowered herself into it and held on to the railing to prevent the boat from floating away.

She scoured the debris floating in the water, hoping to spot any trace of Zot, but the smoke billowing from inside the ship's burning hull limited her already impaired vision severely. Anxiety brewed in her stomach as she waited. Had the iron wyvern reloaded yet? A third explosion would wipe out what remained of the *Yugon* like a sponge on wet ink.

Wings rustled overhead. Between two plumes of smoke, Razorwing's outline was briefly visible as the griffin took to the skies. Alone.

*It's a wild animal,* Brina told herself. *Fleeing is in its nature.* And yet she couldn't help but feel abandoned. She thought of the day she'd found Razorwing, remembering how she'd cradled the baby bird in her arms while feeding it first grubs, then increasingly large rodents, until finally she'd had to accept that Razorwing was better off learning to fend for himself. She had walked away from him that day, leaving him to his own devices. He was doing the same to her now.

Moments later, Bron hopped into the sloop, supporting Abrasax, who was sopping wet and shivering like a twig in a storm.

"That's all of us, I reckon," Sneak said, casting one last glance at the *Yugon*'s burning deck. He handed one set of oars to Bron and grabbed

## CHAPTER 58

hold of the second pair himself. "Let's get out of here before they decide we're not dead enough yet."

"We can't leave without Zot," Brina said, suddenly making up her mind.

"Cap, he's gone." Sneak shook his head, giving a half shrug. "There's nothing we can do."

Brina squeezed the last of her *Lux*-store, trying to penetrate the dark, willing to see some trace of the drug lord or what had become of him. Her hands clenched against the sloop's bench as she saw it.

An enormous shadow loomed up through the smoke, gliding toward them with at a glacial, but unrelenting pace.

"They're here." Brina gulped. It was over. After everything they had been through, after all the blood that had been spilled tonight, the wyvern had caught up with them.

"You did good, kid," Abrasax croaked. "I'm sorry about everything." He stared up as the ship's bow drew closer. His face was drawn and awestruck, as though the skies had just cracked open to reveal Heil's face glowering at them.

Sneak cast aside his oars in frustration and slumped in his seat.

"Come on, you cowards," Bron roared. His hand searched for the spear on his back. When he realized that it alone was no match for the ship looming up before them, he let out a hoarse barking laugh that sounded worse than any cry ever could have. He snapped one of his oars on his knee, fashioning two makeshift clubs. "Let them come down here to get us," he breathed. "I dare them."

Someone whistled from aboard the ship as it drew level with them.

"Hey idiots, grab this."

A rope fell into the sloop with a thud.

Brina looked up to see Zot sneering down at them. Right beside him stood Saf.

"Come on," she shouted. "We haven't got much time. The next volley can come in at any time."

It took every ounce of what little strength remained in Brina's broken body to scale the rope and topple onto the galley's deck.

She felt the rough wood underneath her back and just lay there, trying to keep the exhaustion and the aftereffects of an entire evening of borrowing energy she didn't possess through *Forte*. All around her, tattered but strong looking people of all corners of the Sundered Isles scurried across the deck, haphazardly making adjustments to sail the ship back into safer water.

Saf's face appeared above her.

"I thought you'd abandoned me," Brina muttered. She had meant to say "us."

Saf bent down and grabbed her hands, smiling. "Not just yet."

# CHAPTER 59

*20th day of the 1st cycle, 570KR*
**Metten**

**S**and crept in between Brina's bare toes as she strolled along Metten's jagged shoreline. Not even the pleasant tingle of the afternoon sun could stop the full-body shivers that had wracked her since she'd woken up at dawn. Not today, not until it was done.

"He was the one who found this place, you know," Abrasax said. He wandered beside her, hands stuffed deep in the pockets of a pair of loose gray trousers Sneak had lent him. His shaggy black beard was tied in three simple braids. A handful of solid meals had turned his gaunt face into something resembling a living human being.

"Until Spider—I'm sorry, Acheron—washed up here after a raid gone wrong. The fortress of Metten had been completely forgotten by history. None of our charts even mentioned the isle, let alone the ruined keep that lay ripe for the taking."

"I wonder why he never told me about it," Brina muttered. There was so much Acheron had never explained, so many questions that would remain unanswered.

A crab skittered away between two boulders as she approached. The leaning palm trees in the jungle's edge cast crooked shadows on the white sand, like obsidian pillars on a marble floor.

"He never was the strongest communicator." Abrasax gave a sad chuckle. "But I've never met anyone more dedicated to the cause."

"If that cause was self-destruction and wanton belligerence, I agree." Brina's laugh died in her throat. It wasn't the same without him here to fire back some half-baked insult with that scar-torn grin of his.

They clambered over a section of mossy rock and descended into the narrow cove where the slave galley that had carried them here lay moored.

It was the perfect place, invisible from the open sea, yet close enough to make a quick escape should the need arise. The ship was deserted.

"We'd better hurry," Brina said, pointing out the empty deck. "Looks like we're going to be the last ones there."

"After a decade in a dark room, I find it hard to worry about half an hour more or less." Abrasax smiled. "Though I wish I'd gotten even half that time to talk to my old friend."

"He blamed himself," Brina said, unsure where she was going with this.

"What for?"

"For not being there when the rest of you were captured. It ate him alive. He couldn't forgive himself."

"The line between cowardice and wisdom is a thin one," Abrasax said, fiddling with the braids in his beard. "Almost as thin as that which separates trust and idiocy. If anyone is to blame for what transpired there that day, it was me and the rat who betrayed us."

His face hardened.

"How different history could have been…" He trailed off, his voice thick with emotion.

Brina's stomach squirmed as though she'd swallowed a live squid. At this very moment, Versa lay recovering in a cramped, dark room at De Malheur's fortress. If Brina told her father what she knew, would he seek to exact revenge? She kicked aside a loose branch.

Not telling him would be tantamount to a second betrayal. Versa's confession had directly led to the death of almost all members of the Signum. It was the sole reason Brina had grown up an orphan. Until now, everything had been such a blur of near misses and imminent disaster, that Brina had been able to push the issue from her mind, but as they strode along the empty beach, she realized she wouldn't be able to ignore what had happened forever.

Even though she knew Versa had only cooperated under severe duress, Brina felt an unwelcome stab of anger when she pictured the innkeeper's tall, scarecrow frame. *It wasn't their fault.* She knew that, but knowing and feeling were two very different things.

Ahead of them, a withered circular temple stood in a clearing. If it hadn't been marked on Acheron's map, it might have taken them weeks to stumble upon the site by accident.

Vines were wrapped around white marble pillars from top to bottom and heavy layers of moss and fungi covered the red-tiled roof. *Saved by*

## CHAPTER 59

*the bell,* Brina thought. For now, she'd sidestepped the dilemma, but she'd need to come to a decision, and quickly.

The others were already gathered inside, standing around a hole in the floor, three feet in diameter.

"That's the altar well," Abrasax said, noting Brina's confusion. She'd never seen a proper temple dedicated to the Seven before, only the makeshift backrooms dressed with hanging rugs that passed for houses of worship in Doorstep's Ditch. "It's where death sacrifices are sent straight to the below world."

Brina nodded. In the Ditch, minor sacrifices were common. A splash of rum on plowed soil to plead for a good harvest, a drop of blood in the sea to lure diamond crabs, and so on. But no outwalled in their right mind would discard so much as a moldy oat for a dead compatriot.

The others opened up the circle, making room for Brina and Abrasax. Before Brina could take her place, however, Bron waved her over.

"Here," he said, extending a closed fist toward her. "I want you to have this."

Confused, Brina stretched out her own hand. Bron took it in both of his. Something cool and smooth pressed into her palm.

"It was wrought by my grandfather. My father earned it by killing an erymanthian single-handedly. It was passed on to me after I defended our village from a darkhelm raid. Now, I want you to have it. It has been an honor to fight at your side."

Brina looked down and found an intricately crafted golden skull glittering in her palm. The highest honor a Biori warrior could achieve.

Bron beamed. "Normally, it's worn in the beard, but I think you will find a way."

"Thank you." Brina clapped him on the shoulder, looking at her shoes to hide the tears welling in her eyes. "It's beautiful."

She loosened one of her braids and threaded the loose lock through the skull's open mouth.

"Now that all of us are present," Saf said, beckoning for them to rejoin the circle, "let the ceremony commence. Dimimzy, would you do the honors?"

Zot nodded grimly. He opened a jute sack that stood at his feet and tipped it upside down above the dark depths of the well. Dozens of fist-sized chunks of cloud clattered as they bounced off the sides of the well, before landing on the bottom.

Brina gaped as she watched thousands of shards of product vanish into the darkness. She grinned as she imagined what Acheron would say if he could've seen all that cloud wasted.

"The very last of my supply," Zot growled. He looked down into the well as though he'd just watched his pet dog drown in it. "I'm done peddling poison. It's not worth it."

An echo of "hear, hear," rippled through the circle.

It was Abrasax who broke the silence next. Brina looked at him intently. It was still strange to see him among them, a free man breathing fresh air. Part of her couldn't believe that they had actually pulled it off. At this very moment, every darkhelm in the empire was on the lookout for them. The gallows in the Enclave would remain unused. *For now.*

"My old friend," Abrasax began. "A thrice cracked boulder rests on my shoulders this day. The lower part is a harsh one, filled with the knowledge that we shall never speak again. It chafes at my skin and bites my fingers. All those years, you shouldered a burden that wasn't rightfully yours to bear. I wish I could have made you see this before the end.

"The middle part is hollow, and therefore impossible to balance. It consists of the anger and resolve to fend off the enemy that your loss inspires in our hearts. We beg you for the strength to judge the church and not its pawns, and to always remember that there's a face behind every blackened visor.

"The final part lies on top and presses down with unmitigated brutality, eager to see me fold at the knees. It is the debt of knowing you traded your life for my own. I promise to see our work through until the end, and when it is done, every soul east of Hawqal will know your name."

"Hear, hear." The chorus rang out in the hollow temple.

Sneak, Bron, and Saf each said a few words after that, but Brina had a hard time focusing. Images of Acheron, clasping tight to the sense-surger's chest as the both of them tilted into oblivion played over and over in her mind's eye.

"*It's okay.*"

Had those really been his last words, or had she simply imagined it in the shock of the moment? She would never know for certain, though the anxious squeezes in her belly quietened at the thought.

"Cap'n?" Sneak asked.

She looked up to see all eyes turned toward her. They had made their

## CHAPTER 59

way around the circle, and now it was her turn to speak. Sneak held out a torch to her, and she took it with shaking hands.

*A single, well-placed spark can cause as much wreckage as a blaze*, Acheron had said during their very first lesson. At the time, those words had sounded hollow to her, but as she stood here, at the edge of the altar well, they finally clicked.

"We light this fire in your memory," she began, both hands clasped tightly around the torch. "And we will not rest until it has spread to every corner of the empire."

She touched *Gnis,* and the torch turned to a fireball in her hands. She flung it downward, every muscle jangling with a mixture of grief and rage.

There was a furious roar as the death sacrifice ignited. Brina drew her dagger and held it over the fire.

"This is war."

# EPILOGUE

### Parts Unknown, 570KR

olana's fingers dug into coarse, wet sand. Frigid water lapped at her ankles, coming and going alongside her shallow breaths. Fierce winds tugged at her uncovered hair for the first time in ages, her helmet having been washed away by the current. She felt naked without it. For the past decade, that piece of shiny metal had defined her. No matter how often the abbot told her that the church's helmets were only utilitarian tools, now that it was gone, she felt like part of her identity had washed away alongside it.

First, it had been shaped like the raven of the watch, then the griffin had marked her as a Reynziel until finally, she had adopted the spiked cage of the sense-surger. Now, like before her adoption into the church, she was just a woman cast adrift.

Shivering, Solana crawled farther up the beach, terrified that at any moment a larger wave would sweep her back out into open sea.

*Heil almighty, keeper of souls and intentions, grant me strength.*

Only fragments remained of what had occurred at the fortress of the cardinals. She had been dueling one of the sigilists, when suddenly the earth had given way beneath her feet.

Bitter tears sprouted from her damaged sockets as she remembered how grateful she had been that her suffering was finally drawing to a close, how she had longed for an honorable death in defense of the virtues of Heil, who she had dedicated her entire life to. Heil had rejected her offering.

Her given path was not at an end just yet.

It took a while for her hearing to regain enough of its unnatural sensitivity to form a picture of her immediate surroundings.

To her back, a gray stain that could only be the sea drowned out the more delicate sounds of a patch of jungle ahead of her. She wasn't on

# EPILOGUE

Hammerstroke. Judging by the stretch of shoreline she could discern using echolocation, this isle was no larger than a handful of acres.

She called out into that gray void, waving her arms above her head.

No response came. No help would come.

She muttered a mantra of gratitude as her hand found her prayerbook, still safely contained within its fortified pocket on the inside of her robes. There were no coincidences, only divine intervention. Heil had washed away her helmet, but kept the fearsome power of her light within Solana's reach. That meant something, even if her mind was too slow right now to figure it out.

Her fingers automatically found the prayer of flames. With each repetition, more warmth spread to her numb extremities.

She wandered the shoreline until she could feel the rising sun on her skin. Though she would never again see the golden hues of dawn crest the azure waters of the Sundered sea, she couldn't help but feel a rare seed of joy unfurling in her chest at the mental image.

A newfound sense of freedom overwhelmed her. De Leliard would think her dead. Knowing him, he would make no attempt to locate her body before writing her off as a casualty. The church would canonize her as a martyr, as was the law when a Reynziel of Solana's rank perished in the line of duty.

Her status as a martyr would ensure that her mother would be well cared for by the church. Even the Cardinal wouldn't be able to circumvent that much. It would make him look cruel in the eyes of the entire clergy.

If Solana were to return to Mallion's Depth, however, all of that would change. Her actions at God's Maul would become subject to scrutiny, De Leliard would see to that. If he managed to convince the enlightened council that her disappearance during the battle was an act of desertion, both she and her mother would lose it all. It was a non-option.

She sat down on a mossy boulder, hands shaking.

For the first time in her life, her future was her own to shape.

# STOP!

Okay, you're right. That was a little bit dramatic. My bad. I just wanted to keep you from closing this book before I had a chance to thank you. You made it all the way to the end. They said it couldn't be done, yet here you are.

That fact, in itself, means the world to me. THANK YOU for spending your precious time with my book. There's a gazillion books out there, and you chose this one. I don't take that for granted. May your lineage prosper and your coffers overflow.

You've already given me so much, and yet here I am, about to ask you for ONE LAST THING. And it's the big one.

If you enjoyed this book, leaving a review would help me a lot. As a new author, reviews help me get my foot into more readers' doors. I want to keep telling stories, and I want to get them in the hands of people who might love them. You can help me do that.

On the next page you will find links to my various listings. Leaving a review on one (or more) of these websites would go a long way towards helping me along on my author journey.

If you are busy, even leaving just a star rating would make a world of difference.

To be notified of my upcoming releases, join my newsletter at www.danfswinnen.com.

Scan this code to review on Goodreads.

Scan this code to review on all major retailers.

**Scan this code to review on Amazon.**

If you want to dive further into
the life of Brina Springtide:
Get the FREE novella Springtide at
www.danfswinnen.com

# THE SPARKGAZER SAGA BOOK 2:

# THE SPARKS OF DISSENT

**AVAILABLE FROM THE 5TH OF JUNE 2025**

www.ingramcontent.com/pod-product-compliance
Lightning Source LLC
LaVergne TN
LVHW091658070526
838199LV00050B/2198